the
american

NADIA DALBUONO

SCRIBE

Melbourne • London

For my family

Scribe Publications
18–20 Edward St, Brunswick, Victoria 3056, Australia
2 John St, Clerkenwell, London, WC1N 2ES, United Kingdom

First published by Scribe 2015
This edition published in 2016
Copyright © Nadia Dalbuono 2015

Typeset in 12.75 / 16.5 pt Dante MT by the publishers
Printed and bound in the UK by CPI Group (UK) Ltd, Croydon CR0 4YY

9781925106749 (Australian paperback)
9781925228199 (UK paperback)
9781925307023 (e-book)

CIP records for this title are available from the British Library and
the National Library of Australia

scribepublications.com.au
scribepublications.co.uk

THE AMERICAN

Nadia Dalbuono was educated at Queen's College, Oxford, where she read history and German. For the last sixteen years she has worked as a documentary director and consultant for Channel 4, ITV, Discovery, and *National Geographic*. *The American* is the sequel to her first novel, *The Few*.

Reader praise for *The Few* (Leone Scamarcio #1)

'Nicely sitting alongside the ranks of Donna Leon, Michael Dibdin and Tobias Jones, Nadia Dalbuono has crafted an engaging thriller with a fascinating and likeable police protagonist.' — *Crime Fiction Lover*

'I loved this book. A real page turner that keeps you hooked all the way through.' — Tanya, Goodreads.com

'A brilliant debut thriller from a very promising writer ... I was reminded of Donna Leon and other authors mining the same vein. *The Few* can certainly stand shoulder to shoulder with the best.' — vagabond, Amazon.co.uk

'Powerful, tightly plotted and with chilling echoes of real life events, *The Few* is an emotive and exhilarating read, and Scamarcio a character who could quickly become another cult detective.' — *We Love This Book*

'This ranks up with the best of Camilleri, Dibdin and Leon ... Clever and stimulating.' — Harry B., Amazon.co.uk

'A fantastic first novel which paints an uncompromising picture of the rot and corruption at the top of Italian politics ... A gripping read.' — Charlotte, Goodreads.com

'This debut novel really struck a chord with me ... Focusing on the less salubrious activities of a group of Italian politicians, and the disappearance of a young American girl on holiday in Italy with her parents, Dalbuono has constructed a compelling plot, that will keep you guessing until the end ... A thoroughly accomplished debut crime novel that will leave you itching for another in the series ... Perfect for fans of top notch Euro crime thrillers.' — *Raven Crime Reads* 'Book of the Month'

'A terrific book that is very well written, develops really interesting characters, and tells us a lot about contemporary Italy in an engaging way.' — Brian Stoddart, Goodreads.com

'Absolutely gripping ... Scamarcio's magnetism develops through the conflict between his police career and Mafia parentage; determined and brave, yet vulnerable and flawed – the reader is compelled to follow his progress ... Great storytelling and skilful characterisation.' — Bookish, Amazon.co.uk

'Nadia Dalbuono is writing this with both the detachment of an outsider and the understanding of a resident. As with Donna Leon, Dalbuono clearly sees the terrible stagnation and immorality of the system. But Scamarcio is much more affected and frustrated than Leon's Brunetti. Brunetti's career and family carry on; Scamarcio's way of life and existence is threatened by what he sees ... *The Few* is an exciting and compelling read, with the additional flavour of an insider's view of the civilisation that is Italy and comes highly recommended.' — *Crime Squad*

Part I

He felt a sadness; a deep, deep sadness. He felt lonely: my
Son in His humanity felt a deeper sadness than anyone could
ever feel because He was pure of heart.

From *Mysteries of the Rosary: Agony in the Garden*

1

It was a bright, clear morning the day they bribed the truck driver. It wasn't yet 9.00 am, but the fierce sun was already baking the cracked earth, and the humidity clung heavy to Carter's skin. The fresh shirt he'd put on just an hour before was now pressed tightly against his spine, and the hair at the back of his neck was wet. It was impossible to stay clean in this hole.

The truck pulled into the stop outside the roadside café, just as they knew it would. Several seconds passed, and then the driver manoeuvred himself out onto the ledge and locked the door of the cabin before springing to the ground, adjusting the belt on his trousers, and running a quick hand through his greasy hair. He turned towards the café — no doubt anticipating the eggs and croquetas, the freshly brewed coffee, and the weekly flirt with the pretty young waitress — but Carter was already waiting for him, barring his path. He stepped right up to the driver's face, so close that he could smell his nicotine breath, and shoved a hard hand against his chest. They stood like that for many seconds, frozen, staring each other out; the drivers' eyes alive with fear, Carter's dancing with excitement. Then, eventually, he looked away and used his other hand to retrieve the wad of cash from his pocket.

'We just need to borrow your truck for ten minutes.'

'Why?' asked the driver, his eyes still bright with fear.

'Here's one thousand US dollars. No more questions.'

The driver looked down at the cash, wide eyed.

Carter knew that he was holding more money than this man could hope to make in ten years hauling milk around this godforsaken island.

'Deal?'

The driver nodded, and took the money in a movement so fluid that Carter wondered if it had actually happened.

'Open the back.'

They walked towards the rear of the truck, and the driver stepped up onto the platform, where he used a key on his belt to release a huge padlock. The doors groaned apart, and Carter was hit by a blast of refrigerated air. It was a relief.

'Ten minutes,' he repeated.

The driver nodded and jumped down, hastily turning back towards the café.

Once the driver had entered through the swing doors, Carter hurried to his car and unloaded a sack of cement from the boot. He hauled it onto his shoulder and walked back to the lorry, sweating under the load. He heaved it onto the platform, clambered up alongside it, and stepped into the refrigerated cool, dragging the sack behind him. Ahead of him was the huge silver silo of milk. He laid down the sack and then headed towards the silo. He climbed onto the rack beneath it, took the seven steps to the top, and tried to unscrew the thick black plug. It took several attempts, but when he had finally managed it, he scrambled back down and returned to the doors of the truck to retrieve the sack.

Pouring the cement into the hole was an effort, but after a minute or so he had succeeded in emptying the bag. He took a few breaths, and then replaced the plug and descended the steps, making for the sunlight and the warmth beyond the truck. He walked out onto the platform and swung the doors shut behind him — grateful for the heat now — and then hopped down and headed back to his car, where he stowed the empty sack and the scissors in the boot. Once this was done, he climbed behind the wheel and waited for the driver to return. The goldfinches were chirping noisily in the trees now, and the morning traffic was building steadily on the highway. He turned on the radio: Fidel was giving a speech, claiming that Kennedy was trying to sabotage the economy and discredit the revolution. He killed the noise and just sat listening to the birdsong, observing the to and fro of tired customers and the listless sweeping of the street cleaners. Then the driver was back, his eyes tightly focussed on the ground, his hands balled into fists by his side, as if he knew he was being watched but didn't want to acknowledge it. He headed quickly for the rear of the truck and jumped up onto the platform to relock the doors before springing straight back down again. He jogged back around to his cabin and hoisted himself nimbly onto the ledge, unlocking the driver's door, his eyes still fixed firmly ahead. He climbed in quickly, and after several seconds the old engine hummed and spluttered to life.

Just a few moments later, the truck and its driver had disappeared from view, and the only sound was the anxious chatter of the birds in the palms.

Carter leant back slowly against the headrest, closed his eyes, and exhaled.

Since when did we declare war on schoolchildren? *he asked himself.*

A PLANE HUNG LOW in the sky on its approach into Fiumincino, its pale trace blending with the few fragile clouds still clinging to the hills after the night storm. There was a freshness to the streets this morning, a sober cleanliness, that lifted Scamarcio's mood and made him feel that this day could prove significant; that it might offer some kind of compensation. Even the starlings in the plane trees of Via Fratte sounded newly energised, plumped up, and primed for their impending exodus.

Along the Ponte Sant'Angelo, the early-morning sunlight was setting the faces of the angels aglow. Kaleidoscopic teardrops of rainwater fell from the Angel with the Cross, dripping softly onto the stonework below, pooling and then breaking, as if quietly mourning the corpse awaiting Scamarcio beneath the Angel with the Whips.

To his left, the Tiber was bright and pulsing — an infinity of crystals dancing and splintering far out into the horizon, and from under the bridge beneath him, knots of autumn branches sped by, their russet and gold tendrils marking time. A new salty tang replaced the usual mossy musk, and he breathed it in, trying to draw it deep into his lungs, hoping that it might clear his mind.

After he'd stood for many seconds with his eyes shut, he returned his gaze to the scene some twenty metres up ahead: strewn across the bridge were the metal cases of the CSIs, glinting in the sun like discarded chocolate wrappers at a late-summer picnic. Manetti, stooped and balding, was down on both knees, his gloved hand searching for something below the balustrade. As Scamarcio drew closer to the blue tickertape of police ribbon, he saw that the chief CSI was reaching for the noose; he was trying to stop the blond head from swinging like a pendulum.

Scamarcio flashed his badge at the uniform guarding the scene, and then lifted the tape, making for the edge of the bridge. Manetti was to his right now, and Scamarcio joined him on his hands and knees, head bent low so he could survey the tableau below.

A man with light, greying hair was hanging from the lower railing, a fat noose of rope tied around his neck. He wore an expensive-looking grey suit and a white shirt, the top four buttons wide open. A blue silk tie was pushed off to one side, the front panel snaking across his shoulder. His feet were spinning above the water in grey silk socks. There was no sign of any shoes. The stranger's eyes had rolled back in his head, as was customary with the victims of hanging, but it was his thick hair standing up in strange tufts that was disquieting, that gave the sense that this was a man who would normally be combed down and salesman prepped, who would never allow himself to be seen in public like this. *What an invasion of privacy death is*, thought Scamarcio, not for the first time.

Manetti called over to the police photographer, standing a few metres away: 'You done here?'

The guy nodded. 'Yeah, he's all yours.'

Manetti motioned to two of his assistants. The more muscular of the two stepped onto the thin platform above the water and began slowly hoisting the body onto the ledge. It took a considerable effort, despite the CSI's strength. Once he'd cut the rope free from the ironwork, Manetti and the other assistant leant over the balustrade, and the three men carefully manoeuvred the body up over the railing. When they'd got it clear, they laid the corpse out on the pavement.

Manetti began patting down the arms and legs. He stopped at the trouser pockets, and felt them again on both sides before reaching into a pocket with his gloved right hand and pulling out a fistful of something bulky. When Manetti opened his hand, Scamarcio saw that he was holding cracked and broken chunks of brick — masonry rubble.

'What do you make of that?' asked the chief CSI, who had sensed his colleague's silent approach but had been too absorbed in his work to acknowledge it.

'Reminds me of something.'

'In the sixteenth century, this bridge was used to expose the bodies of the executed.'

'No, that's not it.'

With his left hand, Manetti pulled a plastic evidence-bag from his pocket and poured in the rubble from his right. He then extracted the debris from the man's other pocket and repeated the process.

'Probably another poor sod who couldn't make it to the end of the month. There seems to be a suicide a day at the moment. You hear about that guy who set fire to himself in front of the tax office?'

Scamarcio ignored the question — he was sick of the constant talk of 'the crisis'. Just because some parasite bankers had placed a bad bet on Italy, why should they all be castrating themselves to settle their casino tab? The German chancellor and her cronies had the country in a stranglehold, and people were starting to pay with their lives. At a dinner party the other day, someone had said that it was the new nazism for the twenty-first century. He had smiled at the time, but had gone home and quietly wondered about that.

'You find any ID?' he asked.

'Nothing as yet. We're getting the frogmen out, but there's quite a current after the storm.'

'He doesn't look Italian to me.'

'Hmm, now you say it ...' Manetti gently patted the corpse again before lifting the collar of the man's suit. 'Saks, 5th Avenue.'

'Yeah, that's what I thought.'

'Enlighten me then — what does it remind you of?'

Scamarcio took a cigarette from his pocket and lit up, breathing out into the cool air and then sucking it back in. After a few seconds, he said: 'God's Banker.'

Manetti inclined his head slowly to one side, thinking it over. 'God's Banker,' he repeated, trying it for size.

They both looked out across the river to their right, where the dome of St Peter's Basilica rose up, resplendent in the early-morning sunlight.

'Yeah, now you say it ...' said the chief CSI eventually. 'And I thought it would be a home-by-six day.'

2

SCAMARCIO REMEMBERED VERY LITTLE about the case at the time it first broke. His memories were more of his late father's reaction, his certainty that Roberto Calvi had been 'done in', that he'd been stupid enough to embezzle funds from Cosa Nostra. Now, as he googled the story, the basic facts came back to him: Calvi, dubbed 'God's Banker' by the press, had been chairman of the ill-fated Banco Ambrosiano, of which the Vatican Bank was the main shareholder. In connivance with Paul Marcinkus, the American prelate who ran the bank, he had been laundering billions of lire for the mafia and Italy's corrupt elites. When, in June 1982, Calvi had been found hanging under Blackfriars Bridge in London, his pockets filled with masonry rubble, many had claimed that his shadowy clients had finally come for him. Money had gone missing, and they wanted answers he was unable to provide. Later, when it emerged that Calvi had been a member of the right-wing P2 Masonic lodge, suspicion fell on the lodge's grand master and his mafioso chums, but the judges threw out the case, citing lack of evidence.

Now, more than thirty years on, it seemed that a foreigner, possibly an American, had died in similar circumstances. *Why?* thought Scamarcio. *And, more importantly, why now?* The Ponte Sant'Angelo was an interesting touch, being so close to Vatican City. He rubbed his eyes and looked up from the computer screen. He reminded himself that there was a compelling argument for listening to Manetti. Despite the rubble in the pocket, it was possible that this was simply another suicide, another small businessman caving in to financial pressures, another anguished father unable to carry the guilt of having been fired. There was no confirmation yet that their guy was a foreigner. The smart suit might just attest to a successful executive fallen on hard times. And the masonry rubble might just be coincidence — the nearest thing he could find to weigh himself down with. But Scamarcio knew the banks of the Tiber, and masonry rubble was not that easy to come by. General garbage, used condoms, and needles, yes, but masonry? Had the guy simply brought it with him from somewhere else?

Scamarcio picked up a small green paper clip, unwound it, and straightened it before doing the same with another one — white this time. Then he got up from his desk and headed for the coffee machine. Was the rubble there as a message, and did the Ponte Sant'Angelo hold some significance? Those were the key questions. He fed in his 50 for an espresso, and when it popped into the tray he loaded it with extra sugar from a grimy bag on the shelf before returning to his desk, from where he could call up the latest national and Interpol alerts.

He scanned in the fingerprint data that Manetti had provided; the computer buzzed through the thousands of entries in the system, but, after several minutes, no matches appeared. Even a general trawl failed to retrieve anything promising. He searched his contacts for the telephone number and email address of their police liaison at the US embassy; when he'd found them, he sent them a photo of the corpse and a brief explanation of where and when the body had been found. For the moment, that was the best he could come up with.

He glanced up from his screen and saw that Garramone was standing in his office doorway, waving him in. 'Can you give me five minutes?' asked the chief.

Scamarcio wasn't really in the mood, but he wasn't in a position to refuse. They were both still testing the waters

with each other after the disturbing events of the summer —
Garramone keen to shift things onto more orthodox ground, and
Scamarcio still unsure quite how he felt about the whole matter,
where it left him. Whether or not he had been compromised by
his involvement, chosen or not, was still unclear. Whether the
powerful figures implicated in his investigation now had him in
their sights remained to be seen.

Garramone was wearing a dark-grey pullover with leather
patches on the elbows. It fitted him well across the shoulders, and
Scamarcio felt sure his wife had chosen it for him, having tired of
his total absence of interest in all things sartorial — almost a crime
in itself in Italy.

As Scamarcio entered his office, the chief rubbed at the grey
rings beneath his right eye, and eased back into his swivel chair.
Scamarcio noted that the plastic was peeling from the back: he
could see yellow sponge beneath.

'That stiff under the bridge this morning ...' Garramone began
rolling a biro up and down a small patch of desk in front of him,
taking turns with either hand.

'Yep.'

'Murder or suicide?'

'Jury's out for the moment, but instinct says suicide might not
be the whole story,' said Scamarcio, pulling out a seat.

'Go on.'

'Might be a murder made to look like a suicide. Might be a
forced suicide.'

'Forced?'

'They might've made him do it, helped him up there, and given
him a hand with the noose. It wouldn't be the first time.'

'Are there any signs of that?'

'Not yet. But Manetti tells me it was an expert noose. We've
not found any ID on the victim. Most interesting thing so far
is masonry rubble in the pockets.' Scamarcio knew that the

connection to Calvi would not be lost on the chief.

'That so?' Garramone looked up at the ceiling for a moment. Scamarcio followed his gaze, and saw damp patches, maybe mildew.

'Ponte Sant'Angelo, right?'

'Right.'

'Hmm,' said the chief. 'That's interesting.'

'Why?'

'There's a hubbub at the Vatican this morning.'

'Hubbub?'

'Obviously they're not going to let us anywhere near it, but the scanner chat suggests a corpse. Nothing official out yet, of course; we'll probably have to wait a few days for that.'

'Any idea who?'

'A big cheese — if the general hysteria is anything to go by.'

Scamarcio paused for a moment. 'You think it could be connected?'

'I'm not sure, but right now it seems like a bit of a coincidence.'

Garramone's battered old telephone rang, and he reached across the desk to take the call. Before he lifted the receiver he said, 'Anyway, keep me posted. Let me know if an ID comes through.'

'Will do,' said Scamarcio, getting up from his seat. This case was beginning to seem more complex than the early-morning call had first suggested. Manetti was right; it probably wouldn't be a home-by-six day.

When Scamarcio left the boss's office, he found the desk sergeant waiting for him in the entrance to the squad room. 'You've got visitors,' he said.

He was holding open the swing doors for two tall strangers in dark suits. They both wore silver Aviator sunglasses, and their hair was cropped militarily short. Scamarcio's instinctive assessment was that they were secret service, and probably the Anglo-Saxon variety — English or American.

He walked over to shake their hands, and motioned them to his desk. There was only one spare chair, so he pulled out another from a neighbouring table. The strangers' arrival was stirring interest among his colleagues, who also knew a spook when they saw one.

He had expected the two men to remove their sunglasses when they sat down, but for some reason they chose to keep them on.

'English OK?' said the one on the left, who had blond hair and deeply pitted skin. The accent was American, but Scamarcio couldn't pin it to a region.

'Sure,' he said, wondering if they already knew that he had spent time in the States.

The one on his right crossed his legs, and Scamarcio spotted a gun strapped to an ankle holster. It looked like a Beretta 92 — maybe their standard issue, if they had one.

'The body you found under the bridge this morning ...' continued the man on the left.

'What about it?'

'He's one of ours.'

'A colleague?'

'No — a suspect.'

'You're fast workers. I only sent the photo to our liaison a few minutes ago.'

The stranger didn't offer an explanation, so Scamarcio asked, 'What agency are you from? Do you have cards?'

'We're US authorities.'

'That doesn't tell me much.'

'That's all you need to know.'

That settled it. He would give them the bare minimum, nothing more. They were about to piss all over the place — to mark out their territory, as usual.

Pitted skin continued. 'The guy you pulled out from under

that bridge was a fraudster, responsible for manufacturing millions in counterfeit dollars. It was a major op. We'd been on his tail for some time, but it was only recently that he came to realise it. When he sensed that his time was up, he decided to end his life.'

'Why come all the way to Rome?'

'He had family here. We think he wanted to say his goodbyes.'

'This fraudster have a name?'

'It's need-to-know.'

'*I* need to know.'

'We don't share that assessment.'

Scamarcio took a breath, and bit down on a pencil. He tasted lead in his mouth, and wished he could wash it away, but he didn't want to get up.

'Listen, Detective, we're just trying to do you a favour. We know you flying squad guys have your hands full, so we wanted to spare you the legwork and take this one off your slate. We'll supply you with all the relevant paperwork so you can dot your I's, cross your Italian T's. No point breaking a sweat when someone is happy to clean up for you.'

Scamarcio said nothing for a few moments. 'You know it's not that simple. This happened on Italian soil, so I'm obliged to investigate.'

'You're not listening, Detective,' said the guy on the right, whose southern lilt was deep and smooth like a Louisiana whisky. Although his eyes weren't visible, his terracotta tan and perfect white smile seemed to suggest that he was much better looking than his colleague. 'All we're saying is that we can help you sew up your case nice and tight in time for you to head out to the coast for the weekend. You guys still go to the beach in October? — seems warm enough to me.'

Scamarcio said nothing. He wasn't going to be their foreign stooge they could squeeze any which way they wanted. 'What paperwork do you have?' he asked eventually.

'It will be on your desk by close of play tomorrow, and then you can head down to Amalfi for a nice bit of R and R. That's what I'd do in your position. Really I would.'

The southerner's words sounded less like a suggestion and more like a threat this time.

3

'I fear that the old tactics of 1948 won't work,' said the cardinal, his voice barely a whisper.

Van Brulen knew the date was significant, but he couldn't quite remember why.

'You look confused, Director. I understand — you're so very young to hold the position you do.' There seemed to be no resentment there, just quiet admiration. 'Your people assisted us then with funding for our little pressure group, Catholic Action. Just weeks before the general election, you helped us form more than 18,000 civic committees to get out the anti-communist vote. It had seemed a certainty that the communists would prevail, but thanks to the superb propaganda machine we created, the Christian Democrats scored a decisive victory. We turned the tables — with your invaluable help, of course.'

Van Brulen nodded, the story slowly coming back to him. 'Yeah, but like you say, propaganda won't cut it now. We're concerned by the recent turn of events — Italy is one of our most valuable allies in the region after all. The summer of '68 has made a lot of people nervous, including President Johnson himself.'

'What do you suggest?'

'There's an approach that is starting to yield results in other places.'

The cardinal inclined his head, his face a question.

'We're finding that if you have instability in a country, if you have the beginnings of chaos, the electorate is more inclined to vote for a safe pair of hands. In a climate of fear and uncertainty, it is extremely difficult for the communists to prevail.'

'But such things are beyond your control.'

'Not always — it's just a question of nurturing certain interests.'

'Nurturing them?'

'Fermenting them.'

The cardinal looked bewildered.

'If extremists were to be blowing up railway stations or banks or post offices, people would inevitably look to their government for reassurance and stability.'

'Of course …' The cardinal still seemed to be struggling.

'So we find these extremists, and we set them to work.'

The cardinal paled. 'Extremists on the left or the right?' he asked eventually.

'It doesn't really matter. But often it is useful to blame the left.'

'But how do you persuade these people to do this? How do you convince them?'

Van Brulen smiled. 'There's no need for persuasion. You simply take a situation that is playing out naturally and hitch a ride, being careful though to steer the cart in the right direction.'

'How do you find these people?'

'Ah, that is where we thought you might come in.'

The cardinal frowned, as if he had tasted something bitter. 'I don't follow.'

'You have powerful friends, who in turn have powerful friends. We know that some of them share our point of view — we know, for example, that Gelli has come close to organising a coup on more than one occasion.'

The cardinal blinked and looked down, studying a tip of polished shoe poking out from beneath his robes.

'Gelli has connections; he has a network. We need to tap into that — it will help us find the people we need,' said Van Brulen.

The cardinal's brow was damp now. 'The terrorists,' he said eventually.

'Is that a problem?'

The cardinal shook his head slowly. 'So I'm to be a conduit?'

Van Brulen had expected to read a weary hesitation, a reluctance; but when the cardinal looked up, he was surprised to see a flinty-eyed conviction there.

'That's exactly how we see you,' he replied.

AT HOME IN HIS FLAT that night, Scamarcio spooled back through the day's strange events. The story spun by his American visitors didn't ring true. They needed him to step aside, but for what? Why were they so keen to keep this case to themselves? And why the heavy-handed approach — barging into the squad room like that? It didn't seem CIA or FBI style, if that was who they were.

He had the sinking feeling that he really didn't know where to start with this case, especially if he didn't yet have an identity for the corpse. He padded into the kitchen and poured himself a large glass of Nero d'Avola before returning to his spot on the settee. He mulled over the problem. After several minutes, it occurred to him that there was, in fact, one person who might be able to shed some light on the dead man's identity. One of his roommates from his post-grad years in Los Angeles had gone on to become a journalist, now reporting for the *Washington Post*. Last time they'd spoken, John Blakemore had told him he was dealing with intelligence stories — CIA, NCIS, all the acronyms. If a bunch of spooks were interested in the dead man under the Ponte Sant'Angelo, there was a small chance that someone among Blakemore's contacts might know why. It was a long shot, but Scamarcio decided it was worth a try. It would be 4.00 pm in Washington, and he hoped the reporter wouldn't be in a meeting and could pick up. He didn't want to spend days playing phone tag.

It rang just three times.

'Blakemore.' He sounded upbeat, high on life. It disappointed Scamarcio somehow.

'John, it's Leone. Is now a good time?'

'Leo, how great to hear from you! How's life? Still keeping

the filth off the streets?'

Even after having lived in the States for so long, Scamarcio was still thrown by the effusiveness of the people. He knew it was genuine, but it didn't quite gel with him; it was in a different key from the one he was used to.

'Doing my best — you?'

'Things are good — I just got promoted to News Editor!'

Scamarcio's heart sank. He hoped he had hung onto his sources in the Intel world.

He congratulated him, and then paused for a moment to change tack. 'Listen, I'm sorry to bother you with this, but I had some unusual visitors today.' Scamarcio filled him in on the two Americans and his early-morning call to the Ponte Sant'Angelo.

When he was finished, the reporter said, 'Send me a photo of your dead guy. I'll pass it around my sources — see if it rings any bells.'

'I owe you one.'

'You should pay me a visit.'

'I've been meaning to come out for a while, actually, to see if life is still better on the other side.'

'Yeah,' said Blakemore. 'From what I hear, things are a bit of a mess over there.'

'That's an understatement.' As he said this, something on the muted TV in the corner caught Scamarcio's eye. The evening news was on, and they were playing images of Vatican City, followed by stock footage of a priest giving communion in what looked like Milan Cathedral. The tracker along the bottom of the screen read *Cardinal Abbiati found murdered*.

'Listen, something's come up. Can I ring you back?'

'Let's leave it that I'll call you if I have any leads on that picture.'

'Sure.'

Scamarcio replaced the receiver and reached for the remote. When the audio returned, the newsreader was explaining that

Abbiati had been found stabbed that morning in his apartments overlooking the Nicholas V Tower, home to the Vatican Bank. Abbiati was a prominent figure in Opus Dei, added a commentator in a live link from St Peter's Square.

Scamarcio switched channels, and came across one of the hundreds of nightly studio-discussion programmes that featured the usual mutton-dressed-as-lamb cabinet ministers, Northern League foamers at the mouth, and clinically obese newspaper editors.

'Abbiati was clearly the victim of a power struggle between the Freemasons and Opus Dei, a struggle that has been raging inside the Vatican for decades,' said his least favourite editor, who had thankfully just retired. 'The same power struggle that forced the last pope to step down.' Scamarcio felt sure that the speculation would go on for weeks, if not months — with, as usual, no clarity whatsoever provided by the Vatican.

It was curious that Abbiati's death had come so close to that of the unknown man on the bridge, that the ghost of Roberto Calvi seemed to be hovering somewhere in the background. Did Abbiati have any connection to the Vatican Bank, besides the location of his apartments, Scamarcio wondered.

He sank back into the sofa. This new death piqued his curiosity; but, as his chief had said, they wouldn't be able to get anywhere near it. For them, the Vatican was another country, a foreign land where they held no jurisdiction. Abbiati might as well have died in Ulan Bator. Scamarcio sighed. *Actually, that would probably have been easier.* He took a sip of his wine and turned his attention to his neighbours in the apartment opposite. They were arguing again — the third time this week. He sensed that they had money worries and that the stress of it was unravelling their marriage. He felt sorry for their little kid witnessing it all, night after night. An old anxiety stirred, and he took another sip.

He told himself that the possibility remained that there was nothing linking Abbiati and the stranger on the bridge — that it might just prove to be coincidence. The man in the noose could indeed have killed himself; the post-mortem results tomorrow would settle that. He took another sip. In his line of work, you very rarely came across coincidences. Nine times out of ten, there was a deeper, far more difficult, explanation.

His mobile rang. He checked the caller ID, and saw that it was Aurelia. Once again, he experienced the same unsettling mix of pleasure and fear that had been plaguing him for the past month whenever her name appeared on his phone.

'Leo, you OK?' was her opener.

'Yes, why?'

'You've been quiet — haven't heard from you for a while.'

He wished he could tell her not to say things like this, that it didn't help him stay on track, that it made him want to make a break for it, come up for air.

Instead he said, 'I had a case come in; it's been pretty full on.'

'I heard you got the guy under the bridge.'

'Yep.' He didn't want to go into details.

'Not a straight suicide then?'

'I'm not sure. I'm going down to Giangrande in the morning. I'll get the word from him.'

'I don't think he's got around to it. We've had our hands full.'

'Sure.'

The conversation was stilted, and that was probably his fault, but he didn't know how to right it. He felt too tired, and he couldn't get his brain to tick over.

'So I guess I'll see you at the morgue.'

'Yes. I should be in in the morning.'

'Yeah, you said that.'

He paused, trying to focus. 'Look, sorry. It's been a difficult day …' He had been going to say that he would take her for lunch, but she'd already hung up.

4

The chief accountant studied the ledger for the fifth time. The money had come out of a corporate account held at the Vatican, passed to the Banco Ambrosiano in Milan, gone through Nassau, entered and exited the Continental Illinois Bank in Chicago, and then found its way back to Italy and a youth group in Lombardy. From the name, he felt sure that it was a right-wing group; he remembered hearing about them in the papers. They were supposed to have links to Ordine Nuovo.

'Why are we sending money to a fascist youth club?' he asked the cardinal when he arrived at the office later that morning.

'You must be mistaken.'

'I'm not. And the money has come out of one of Gelli's accounts.'

'I think you're losing yourself,' said the cardinal.

'No. It's not me who's lost my way,' he whispered before leaving the office and slamming the door behind him.

GIANGRANDE WAS WEIGHING a liver when Scamarcio walked in, his red-rimmed half moons perched at the end of his elegant roman nose.

'That mine?'

'If it was, you'd be in serious trouble.'

Giangrande was quite the joker. Scamarcio forced a reluctant smile. 'Is that my guy?'

'No. This belongs to a loan shark who was shot in the face five times.'

You always had to do the dance with Giangrande. Scamarcio found it tiresome.

'Nice. You got around to mine then?'

'He was my first of the day.'

'Good. Are you writing it up as suicide?'

'Well, I was about to.'

'What stopped you?'

The chief pathologist put down the liver, wiped his hands on a paper towel, and then tossed it in the trash. His skin was smooth and tanned, and his light-blue eyes were bright and alive. Scamarcio remembered hearing that he owned a yacht that he took out most weekends — inherited money.

'Follow me.'

Giangrande headed for the metal refrigerator unit at the back of the autopsy room. He raised his arm and rested a hand on the drawer marked number 125, but didn't open it.

'I hear you're seeing Aurelia.'

Scamarcio was taken aback for a moment. 'Is that a problem?'

'Just be good to her. She's a rare find, and deserves to be treated as such.'

Scamarcio knew that Giangrande, twenty years her senior, had been something of a mentor to her.

'Duly noted.' He paused for a moment to allow them to return to the matter in hand. 'So, no suicide then?'

'It had all the makings: no defence wounds, noose tied in just the right way, measurements from the bridge all tickety-boo ...' he trailed off.

'But ...'

'But I wasn't counting on a liver and kidney all turned to mush.'

'Mush?'

'When I took them out, they practically fell apart in my hands.'

'And that means what?'

'Severe dehydration.'

Scamarcio wasn't sure he quite grasped the significance.

21

'Maybe he took a long time to die, became dehydrated out there on the bridge, hanging there like that. Or maybe he was dehydrated before he fixed the noose.'

'No, Detective, that's not it. This level of dehydration cannot occur naturally. I found elevated levels of sodium and urea nitrates.'

'Which means?'

'Poisoning: either someone poisoned your guy before he strung himself up to die, or he decided on a double whammy and did it himself before he stepped into the noose.'

Scamarcio felt suddenly tired. 'Any idea which poison?'

'No. I need to test the liver tissue against different samples, and get back to you.' His hand was still on the drawer to 125. 'Want to take a look now?'

Scamarcio didn't really. He wanted to hurry back to the office, given the new turn of events, but he sensed he ought to appear willing. 'OK. Wheel him out.'

Giangrande turned the handle, and slowly pulled out the long tray with its custom-white sheet. From where Scamarcio was standing, the platform looked strangely empty.

'That's weird,' said the chief pathologist, throwing back the sheet. 'He was here earlier this morning. One of the lab technicians must have moved him, and not bothered to tell me. Cretins. Give me a second while I throttle them.'

He shuffled off towards the back room where the files were kept and, through the dividing glass, Scamarcio saw him gesticulating wildly, reading his underlings the riot act. Giangrande was known for having quite a temper. But his staff did not seem to be intimidated by the big man, and were shaking their heads in denial; despite the bullyboy tactics, it seemed that they would not be swayed. Within seconds, the three of them were back in the room, crowded around the empty tray to 125.

'This is most odd,' Giangrande was saying, wiping the

condensation from his glasses. 'They insist they haven't moved him.'

'We didn't, Sir, we promise. We would have told you, we know the system,' said the taller of the two youths, while the other nodded furiously. Scamarcio had never seen two people look more worried. No doubt they saw their comfortable government positions going up in smoke.

Giangrande sighed and asked, 'You know what this means?'

'A shitload of trouble,' replied Scamarcio.

5

They retreated to the bushes, waiting. Dobbs held the detonator in his hand, his fingers poised, like a grotesque statue. The sweat was soaking through the back of his Doors T-shirt, and the ink had started to run.

'They're on their way,' Carter told him, adjusting the binoculars. They'd become slippery in his grip, and the lenses were starting to steam. It was already 38 degrees in this hole, and the shade offered little comfort.

'How many?' asked Dobbs.

'At least fifty.'

This was market day, and they knew that the women and children would be crossing the bridge about this time.

Dobbs started humming a tune. It sounded like 'Paint it Black' by the Stones. The noise irritated Carter.

The humming suddenly ceased, and Dobbs asked, 'Are they there yet?'

'Almost.'

They both fell silent for a few seconds, neither of them breathing, and then Carter whispered, 'Now!'

Dobbs pushed the button, and they both fell to the ground, the pressure wave breaking out across the dried earth, the flattened air around them pushing up against their skin, stinging their eyes, making their ears pop. It was the most intense silence Carter had ever known; but then a baby started to cry, and the unmistakeable screams of the injured began.

'Let's get out of here,' said Dobbs.

Carter tried to stand, but his legs wouldn't hold him. He thought he was going to throw up.

'Come on, get a grip,' Dobbs hissed.

Carter tried to get his legs to move, but they wouldn't. He forced *himself to take a breath, and then another. 'How can you do this?' he asked him. 'How can you sleep?'*

'It's the fortunes of war.'

'But we're not at war here.'

Dobbs didn't seem to have heard, and was already running into the jungle.

'YOU THINK THOSE AMERICAN wise guys made off with our stiff?' asked Garramone as he used a biro to swirl the sugar into his espresso. He was using the writing end, rather than the top, and Scamarcio wondered if he realised.

'Right now, it's the most likely explanation. They were all over my case yesterday, throwing their weight around. It was clear they didn't want us anywhere near it.'

'And Giangrande smelt foul play?'

'He said the liver was all turned to mush, that there were clear signs of poisoning.'

'Hmm,' said Garramone, gazing out his tiny window at the building opposite. Someone was cleaning the windows high up on the sixth floor of an American bank. 'No one ever cleans our windows anymore,' he said. 'Next thing, they'll make us do it as part of the contract'.

'What do we do now?' asked Scamarcio. 'Is there some kind of protocol we should follow?'

'I need to get onto someone at US Liaison, and also probably the Farnesina. They need to be aware.'

'How can the Foreign Office help?' asked Scamarcio.

'I'm not sure they can, but it's the most appropriate channel. I have to send it up their way, or I'll get my wrists slapped.' Garramone crushed the plastic espresso cup in his right hand and tossed it into the bin beneath his window. His aim was good. 'You think the Americans tied him to that bridge?' he asked.

'I'm not sure yet. Obviously, it's a possibility we need to consider.'

'But why the clumsy approach — all the weird symbolism? We all know Calvi, we all know the case. Are they trying to send us some kind of message?'

'It just doesn't seem their style. Usually, those agency hits are subtle and under the radar. And anyway, if a message *is* being sent, I doubt it was intended for us.'

Garramone sighed and crushed a piece of paper this time, throwing that into the trash as well. Perfect aim again. 'Let's see what your college friend has. I'm interested in this not just because of our American vermin, but the Abbiati thing is intriguing, coming when it has. You know his apartments were opposite the Vatican Bank?'

'Is that significant?'

'I've put some feelers out, and I get the sense it might be. I need you to pin that down.'

'You think he worked at the bank — that he was involved in the clean-up operation the last pope was trying to implement?'

'I don't know — that's what we need to find out. If he was, he would have been on the other side; he would have been part of the group resisting the change.'

The previous pope had been intent on rendering the practices of the Vatican Bank more transparent following recent allegations of money laundering, but had met considerable resistance from factions inside the Church. Many claimed that Opus Dei was heading up this resistance, that they had the most to lose.

'Because he was Opus Dei?' asked Scamarcio.

'They *say* he was Opus Dei,' corrected Garramone. 'But nothing's for sure when you're dealing with that lot. It's always smoke and mirrors.'

'So I've got to get inside all that.'

Garramone nodded, saying nothing.

'That's no easy task.'

'If it was, I would have put someone else onto it.'

Scamarcio was unsettled by the flattery. That wasn't Garramone's usual approach. And, anyway, it didn't ring true. No one knew it wasn't a simple suicide when they allocated him the early-morning call. What was the chief's agenda?

'Do you have any contacts inside the Vatican?' asked Scamarcio.

'A few,' replied Garramone, his tone noncommittal.

Scamarcio wondered why he wasn't proposing to use them, but instead he chose to remain silent, and just studied the spider-web cracks in the greying linoleum.

The chief leant back in his swivel chair, easing out a crick in his neck. 'I'd say don't let those American fuckers push you around, but I know you won't.'

Scamarcio felt a growing sense of unease. He studied the boss: the hooded lids, the deep, grey bags beneath his eyes, the slightest of tremors in his mottled hands. He had a sudden instinct that Garramone was scared of something or someone. He was no longer quite himself; he was pretending to be himself, but he wasn't quite succeeding.

Scamarcio was too caught up in this thought to respond, but when he finally came to, he said, 'Sure. I won't let them bulldoze me.' As he rose from his chair, he tried to meet the boss's eye, to seek out the old Garramone, but he was already looking down, and had seemingly turned his attention to some suddenly urgent paperwork.

6

The brief had been to target the enemy, to kill or capture. But he quickly realised that they were just shooting fish in a barrel — that most of the villagers supported the other side. The way they saw it, they were simply fighting for liberation from foreign domination.

He'd sent in his reports, he'd told them straight that the Communist Party was much more effective than they'd estimated. There was glowing praise for the thoroughness of his work, and then came that strange call from Washington just a few days later, telling him he'd been shut down.

'Carter, you've done a great job, but we're winding up the program.'

It had come as a shock; but now, when he thought it through, it all made sense. Of course they were closing him down. The policy had to dictate the intelligence, and not the other way around. They couldn't let it be known that hundreds of thousands of Thai villagers supported the party, because then they would have had to say the same about Vietnam, and it would have meant shutting down that war, too.

He remembered the screams of the children, and he reached for his whisky once more.

IT WAS DARK outside the window, but Scamarcio could see the argument of the couple in the apartment opposite all lit up like a Verdi opera at la Scala. He had a bowl of something in his hand, and was shaking it in her face. She was crying. He didn't want to see any more — he didn't want to find the little boy in the scene, hunched up somewhere in a corner. He pulled down the blind, feeling newly depressed.

The nightly news on Rai 2 was leading with the Abbiati story.

'It is believed he was stabbed repeatedly in a frenzied killing, but, for now, the Vatican is still refusing to release details. However, they *are* promising a press conference to follow in a few days' time,' said the announcer. *Yeah, like that's going to happen,* thought Scamarcio.

His mobile rang, and he saw the US prefix and thought of Blakemore.

'Leo,' said the reporter. 'Is now good?'

'Sure.'

'I got a hit on that picture.'

'I'd figured it was a long shot.'

'One of my contacts reckons he knows him. He's ex Agency.'

'Who — your contact or my guy?'

'Both.'

'CIA?'

'Yep, those guys. Your dead man used to go by the names of Simeon Carter or Shaun Bartlett. He gained his stripes in Latin America and Eastern Europe during the Cold War, and then, when they had to start looking for new enemies, they shoved him behind a desk in Washington. He was just a couple of months off a very comfortable retirement.'

'Then what?'

'He suddenly went AWOL. None of his colleagues knew why, or they profess not to know.'

'What did his bosses do?'

'They went after him, because in that line of work you don't just disappear. They ease you out of it very gently, very thoroughly, with a serious debriefing.'

'Did they find him?'

'They kept it all under the radar. No one knew how it had gone down until you showed up with your photo.'

'What does your contact make of the suicide story?'

'He says it might not be that way out there. Word was that

Carter had been depressed of late, that he'd been hitting the bottle; there might have been trouble at home.'

'What was he doing out in Eastern Europe and Latin America?'

'My source wouldn't say.'

'Did he say in which countries Carter was active?'

'No.'

'Is that because he didn't want to or because he didn't know?'

'No idea.'

'Could he be persuaded to go into greater detail?'

'Is there a story in it?'

Scamarcio paused for a moment before replying. 'Perhaps, if you can be patient.'

'It's my middle name.' said Blakemore. He fell silent for a moment and then said cheerily. 'And, Leo, my source said to watch your back.'

Scamarcio felt the earlier anxiety return. He thanked Blakemore, and went to put down the phone, but it rang again before he had even set it on the table. Maybe the reporter had remembered something else.

But he saw that it was Aurelia, and he felt newly on edge.

'I heard about your missing body,' she said. He sensed that she was trying to sound upbeat, but he knew that she really wanted to ask why he hadn't sought her out after his visit to Giangrande. The truth was that he simply hadn't had the time. But he didn't feel like apologising; he shouldn't have to justify the use of his working hours. So, instead, he said, 'Yes, that's a first. For both me and Giangrande, I think.'

'We lost a body once. But just for five minutes. Someone had left it in the admin suite while he answered a call of nature.'

It sounded a bit forced, and Scamarcio couldn't muster an amusing response. His silence hung heavily on the line, and he tried to unscramble his brain so that he could push the conversation on. Eventually, he said, 'You want to get a bite to eat tomorrow night?' It came out false, as if he didn't really want to. He didn't; he needed time to think. But how do you ask someone for that without it sounding like the end?

'OK.' The response was tentative, as if she sensed that there was bad news coming.

'We can go to that Japanese place you like.'

'That would be good.' She sounded a bit more convinced now, as if she figured that he wouldn't ask her to her favourite restaurant if he was planning on ending things.

Was he planning on ending things? He didn't know. He couldn't now, anyway. If he had wanted to, he shouldn't have mentioned the Japanese place.

'Anyway, I had better go,' she said. 'This weird American has just come around again — no idea what he wants.' She put down the phone before he had a chance to reply.

He stopped, still holding the mobile in his hand. He took in the darkness outside, and vaguely registered the sound of an old Vespa putt-putting down his street.

What weird American? *His Americans?* He tried calling her back, but she didn't answer. He waited ten seconds and then tried again, but still there was no response. He grabbed his jacket and house keys, and headed out, not bothering to switch off the TV.

7

The trade unionists and the students were out in force, fired up by the socialist dream that was sweeping south through the continent. Their numbers were growing stronger by the day, and he'd had to work fast to falsify the documents and push the lecturer off his podium and into jail.

Carter remembered that, while seated across from him at the prison, the chief of the secret police had smelt of garlic. It had unsettled his stomach and had made him want to run. Then, when the moans had started coming through the walls, followed later by the gurgling screams, he had looked across at him, searching for an explanation.

'I've put my specialist onto him,' said the chief. 'He's in good hands now.'

Carter had fabricated the whole Soviet angle; he'd given the chief the lecturer's name, wrapped him up with a ribbon and bow, and delivered him straight to his door.

A car had passed, and 'Dreams' by Fleetwood Mac had pounded into the prison walls.

That first thrill of being on the inside, of knowing things the government wanted to hide, was absent now. All that remained was the memory of those screams and the cries of the children on the bridge.

IT WAS ALMOST PITCH-BLACK in the gardens outside the morgue. Three of the lights lining the walkway had failed, and it seemed that nobody had bothered to replace them. Maybe the city council reckoned that, given so many of the people who entered here were already dead, there was little chance of them slipping on the path, breaking a leg, and suing them.

The flickering sodium lamp of the hallway was spilling out across the top step, and Scamarcio made towards it, trying to orientate himself. There was no one manning the entry desk tonight, and he wondered about that. Security seemed lax. He made for Aurelia's office, and heard fragmented voices coming towards him down the hall. *Hers and someone else's*, he thought. There was laughter, so he figured things had to be OK; but when he reached her office, the door was open and the room was empty. He peered deeper down the corridor to his left, seeking the source of the voices, and saw two distant figures in white coats slowly wheeling a gurney towards him. But as they drew closer he realised that neither of them was Aurelia. His chest grew tight, and he felt moisture at the back of his neck. As they passed him, he asked the two strangers if they'd seen her, but they just shook their heads.

Light was coming from one of the three offices at the back, but when he opened the door there was nobody inside. He retraced his steps back up the hallway, and entered the anteroom to the autopsy suites. Each suite had a viewing window that connected with the anteroom; it was usually covered by a roller blind to avoid unfortunate incidents with relatives. But the blinds were up. The two technicians he had met in the corridor were now in the room directly ahead of him, unloading the body from its gurney, and adjusting the lights above the autopsy table.

He pulled his mobile from his pocket and dialled Aurelia for the fifth time since she had ended their call, and for the fifth time she failed to pick up. He wondered whether he should ring Chief Garramone and tell him what he was thinking, before figuring it would look off. Then he decided that doing nothing was worse, so he called the squad room, hoping someone decent would pick up.

Sartori answered. He was an OK guy, Sartori, originally from Rimini — jovial, a bit overweight, prematurely balding.

'You on a night shift?' asked Scamarcio.

'Not exactly — you know I've got four kids?'

'Right …' Scamarcio wasn't sure where this was heading, and he didn't have the time.

'Well, sometimes it's easier to be in the office than home.'

Scamarcio pondered this for a moment; he figured that things at home must be pretty dire. The squad room was not what you would call a pleasant environment. Blue paint was peeling from the walls, there weren't enough windows, and the usual smells of decades-old sweat and stale nicotine hung all about the place.

'What are you doing right now?'

'I've got my feet up watching *The Inheritance*.'

'Nothing going down?'

'Just a drive-by. There's a team out on that, so I've almost got the place to myself — just how I like it.'

'Can you do me a favour?'

'Name it.' Sartori sounded distracted, his mind clearly still on the game show.

'Can you call up the mobile-phone people and get me a triangulation?'

'Could take a while — you know what they're like.'

'Tell them it's a matter of life and death.'

'Is it?'

'Might be.'

Sartori moved in his chair, and the sound from the TV died. 'Why the fuck have you been chit-chatting with me then?'

'Got a pen?'

'Hang on.' He heard something roll off the desk and hit the floor. Sartori swore again. 'OK, standing by.'

Scamarcio reeled off Aurelia's mobile-phone number, and then said, 'Put the pressure on, try to get it ASAP. Call me as soon as it comes in.'

'You bet.'

He cut the call, and leant up against the wall of the anteroom. The body laid out in the suite in front of him was severely overweight. There were bluey-grey patches on the arms and legs — probably decomposition — and a bright-red chain of blood around the neck. Strangely, there was blood on the soles of the feet, too, as if the man had strolled through his own crime scene. Scamarcio pulled out a cigarette from his jacket pocket, and tapped it against the packet. He decided the mortuary gardens would be preferable to this, so he headed back out into the corridor, the yellow sodium from the strip lights flickering a trail to the swing doors.

There was a bite to the air tonight, and it gave him a kick and stirred his deadened senses back to life. The cold breeze against his neck made him think of winters past and of those yet to come. What did they want with Aurelia, and was she in trouble? It depended on how desperate they were. Sure, they'd been a bit heavy-handed, but they hadn't struck him as desperate when they'd met. He pulled up his jacket against the cold, and drew the smoke down deep. He should have been kinder to Aurelia these past days. He needed to get it together. You couldn't screw with people's heads like this, not if you didn't want to end up permanently screwed yourself. One day soon, he needed to break the cycle. His past was wearing him down, and the older he got, the more he wanted rid of it. He was sick of carrying the shame around like a rock. Hell, it felt like *he* had masonry rubble in his pockets.

He finished the cigarette, and ground it out slowly on the path. When he looked up, a tall figure in a long woollen coat was striding towards him: Giangrande. But, strangely, he made no sign of noticing Scamarcio; perhaps it was too dark. *Why is he working so late?* he wondered. Giangrande carried on straight past him towards the swing doors; but before he entered the mortuary, the chief pathologist came to a stop, and Scamarcio felt sure he was about to turn and ask him what he was doing, lurking there in the shadows like that. But instead Giangrande checked to his right and then to his left, pausing several seconds before going in, as if he were the one who wasn't supposed to be there.

8

*It was a rainy day in Washington. Everything beyond the window
seemed tinged with grey: the slow columns of cars, the pedestrians, the
threadbare winter birds. Somewhere down the hallway, Madonna was
playing on the radio of the Latino cleaning crew.*

*'So I hear you don't like getting your hands dirty,' said the boss. 'Is it
because of your faith?'*

*Carter surveyed this squat, balding man with his missing arm, and
considered the enormous power he wielded. From his office on the fifth
floor, he could decide whether governments rose or fell, whether entire
populations starved or struggled by, whether wars became hot or stayed
cold.*

'Perhaps that has something to do with it.'

*'Then I have just the job for you.' The boss rose from his desk and
walked over to the window. He scratched beneath an eye and then just
stood there, watching the traffic. After a minute had passed, he said,
'We had a good guy out in Rome, but unfortunately he's had to move
on. Van Brulen laid us some solid groundwork, formed us some strong
friendships. How would you feel about stepping into his shoes and
nurturing all that?'*

SCAMARCIO HAD DECIDED to head to a wine bar he knew on
Vicolo del Cinque while he waited for Sartori to call with the
triangulation. He had passed by Aurelia's flat in Trastevere, not
really expecting to find her home; and indeed, her place was
locked up, probably exactly as she had left it that morning. He
would have liked to take a look inside, and assure himself that all

was well, but he'd remembered that he didn't have the keys she had cut for him. He'd consigned them to a kitchen drawer, not really liking the feel of them in his pocket. He'd called out her name a few times, but there had been no response — although when he'd placed his ear to the door, he'd felt sure he could hear her ancient tomcat meowing softly, hungry by now, no doubt.

Garramone's number appeared on his mobile, and as he couldn't hear the phone above the music, he was pretty tempted to ignore it. But then he figured he'd only have to call him later. He quickly drained his glass.

'Who is Sartori getting a triangulation for?' was Garramone's opener.

Scamarcio took a moment to map out a response. He didn't want him wading in just now, playing the boss card. He wasn't sure yet how to handle their American body-snatchers, but sensed that it was far too early to blow a bomb under the whole thing. So he just said, 'It's a hunch — nothing for you to worry about at this stage.'

Garramone had been about to reply, but Scamarcio's call waiting was kicking in, so he said, 'Can I ring you back? I have a source on hold.'

The boss sighed. 'I'll phone you tomorrow. Then you can fill me in properly.' It sounded like a threat.

Scamarcio switched callers, and saw that it was Sartori ringing from the squad room. He hoped that Garramone had been calling from home and couldn't hear what was being discussed.

'I've got your trace. They've put it in the vicinity of Via della Scala in Trastevere — they can't be exact, though.'

The location was just a few minutes away. Scamarcio knew the street — there was a bar somewhere near the end, where it joined Via della Pelliccia. They'd been a few times. He'd hazard a guess that was where she was now.

He thanked Sartori for the fast work, and hung up. Stepping

back out into the night, he felt the cold bite once more, and was glad of the wine to warm him. A raucous group of teenagers passed, high on a good night out, and he felt a stab of envy. He'd never been able to enjoy all that; it hadn't been available to him back then.

He came to the end of Vicolo del Cinque, and noticed that the pavement restaurants seemed emptier than usual. Maybe it was the onset of autumn; maybe it was the crisis. He passed the little osteria where people paid a small fortune to be insulted by the staff. It seemed like nobody wanted to be insulted tonight. When he got to Via Sacchi, two men were having a fight outside a locked-up bakery. He pondered briefly whether to intervene, but he walked on, keen to reach Aurelia as soon as possible.

When he arrived at the bar it was surprisingly full. A jazz band was playing, and the atmosphere was livelier than the place he'd been in before. There was an irritating, artsy-craftsy feel to the decor — strange knick-knacks were dotted all about, and abstract paintings covered the walls. Aurelia had always seemed to like it, but he found it pretentious. The wine was cheaper here: four euro a glass, as opposed to six, and it seemed that the owners were winning all the business.

He spied Aurelia and the American almost immediately — they were in a corner by a bookshelf overloaded with fake spines. She was laughing, tossing back her hair, while the good-looking American was refilling her glass from a bottle of red, leaning in, all smiles. Something about that flipped a switch, and the next thing Scamarcio knew he was by the table lunging for the man's throat. Then he was dragging him from his chair and hauling him up against the stupid bookcase, smashing him against the shelf, sending fake books and pointless trinkets tumbling. Somewhere, a woman started to scream. He felt hands on his arms trying to pull him off, so he pushed back an elbow and tried to butt them away. He smashed the American's head against the shelf once more.

'What are you doing? Have you lost your mind?' someone was shouting.

After a while, he realised it was Aurelia. He took a breath and looked about him. The American was on the floor, and there was blood oozing from his lip. Aurelia had slumped back into her chair, her head in her hands. She appeared to be crying.

Scamarcio grabbed her, pulling her up from the table, 'Come on,' he said.

She pushed him off her with a shove that was much stronger than he would have expected. 'I'm not going anywhere with you,' she hissed. He saw hatred in her eyes, and smelt alcohol. She and the American had clearly been enjoying themselves.

He gripped her wrist tighter. 'We need to go.'

She looked at him as if he were mad, and then yanked back his little finger, releasing his grip, before running out into the night, all the eyes of the bar upon her.

9

There was a strong smell of leather and sandalwood in the library. The president took a seat opposite his Holiness, and their respective advisors filed out through the wide mahogany doors. Carter was the only one allowed to remain.

'It seems that you and I have been saved for a special mission,' began the president. 'The forces of evil have been placed in our paths, but Providence has intervened on both occasions.'

Reagan still had that Hollywood magic. And he was still milking the Hinckley shooting for all it was worth. Hell, he'd been talking about little else for weeks.

His Holiness nodded solemnly. 'It is indeed a miracle. It seems that right must now prevail in this divine plan of His.'

The president smiled, and took a sip of the ginger beer that had been laid out for him.

'After the Second World War, a great mistake was made at Yalta, and now it is finally up to us to do something about it,' he said. 'The collapse is near; I can feel it. We must seize this opportunity to push for it hard. A free, non-communist state in the centre of their empire would be a dagger to their heart; if Poland becomes democratic, other states will soon follow, and the whole system will topple, like a house of cards. The movement is our weapon for bringing this about because it is an organisation of the workers. Nothing like it has ever existed in Eastern Europe before. It's completely contrary to anything the Soviets or the communists would ever want.'

His Holiness nodded slowly once more. He had such a soft face, thought Carter, the face of an aged cherub.

'We will give you all the help you need. The flame must not be extinguished; we must work hard to keep it burning underground.'

'I am so very glad we are in agreement on this,' said the president.

'I am communicating daily by radio with my cardinal in Warsaw. We have stressed to Walesa that on no account should they take the fight out onto the streets. We cannot risk a Warsaw Pact intervention or a civil war.'

'Exactly,' said Reagan. 'We must give them everything they need to grow and flourish out of sight. Money must not be a problem.'

The pope laid a hand on his arm. 'We have a system in place. Right now, I can think of no better cause.'

SCAMARCIO HAD FOLLOWED AURELIA to her flat, but she wouldn't let him in, so he ended up explaining it all through the front door, unsure whether she was listening. He asked her to call him in the morning, knowing that he'd be heading over to the morgue first thing anyway.

Now it was 8.00 am, and Giangrande was giving him the once-over. 'What's wrong with Aurelia? You two had a fight?' If he'd seen him in the gardens last night, he was clearly going to make no mention of it now.

'No, why?'

'Her eyes are all red and puffy.'

Scamarcio shrugged, as if his guess was as good as Giangrande's. 'Where is she, anyway?'

'Why? She's not handling your case— I am.'

The man was an arsehole.

'Well, you lost my body, so right now I have fuck-all to work with, unless you've still got that liver-tissue sample. Tell me we have that, at least.'

'I hadn't got around to collecting it before they took the corpse.' There was nothing sheepish in his tone. The man was arrogance personified.

'As I said, "Fuck all."' Scamarcio stormed out, slamming the door behind him, infuriated by the absence of any tangible evidence. Something about Giangrande's attitude to the theft was not adding up.

When he entered her office, Aurelia was at her desk, slowly stirring a cup of coffee, absently gazing out into the middle distance. She spotted him, and immediately looked away as if ignoring him would make him disappear. He tried a smile, and pulled out a chair.

'Look, I'm sorry about last night.'

She didn't say anything, refusing to shift her gaze.

'I shouldn't have come over all heavy, but that guy is trouble. He and his sidekick are all over this case I've got going on, and I reckon they're the ones who lifted that corpse from under Giangrande's nose. Whatever they wanted from you, it wasn't the pleasure of your company.'

Aurelia finally turned to face him. Her eyes were red-rimmed, and there were pale-blue bags beneath them. She looked older than her thirty-three years.

'So it's the Ponte Sant'Angelo case they're interested in?' she asked, her tone flat.

'Yes.'

'Well, I figured that. There was the American connection and, of course, I knew that the corpse was missing.' She sighed and took a sip of her coffee, looking him directly in the eye now. 'You don't think much of me, do you?'

'Don't be ridiculous.'

'It's you who is being ridiculous, storming in there like that last night. I'd already made that guy, Scamarcio. I'd made him before I even left here. I thought I'd be doing you a favour going for a drink with him.'

He decided not to say anything; there was too much tension in the room already.

She shook her head and said, 'He claimed he did the same job as me back home and was curious to see how we worked it here — said he was visiting Rome for a conference. He had all these strange questions about our data storage, how the files were ordered, that kind of thing. The whole story smelt off from the start — dead Yank under the bridge, body goes missing, now some weird American comes sniffing around. It doesn't take a genius.'

'So what did you tell him?'

'I just fed him a few false leads. They're clearly after a report — no doubt the one Giangrande filed on the body.'

'He's already written the report?'

'I believe so.'

'But why couldn't they just lift it off the computer when no one else was around? Why go to the trouble of bringing you in?'

'Beause Giangrande is still living in the nineteenth century, and commits everything to paper before he dares go near the word processor. On top of that, he's a pernickety arsehole, and insists on the most illogical filing system known to man. They would never have found that report. They'd probably already tried.'

'Where is the file?'

She sank back in her chair and took a long drink of coffee. He sensed that she was coming down off the anger a bit now. 'Well, that's the funny part. Giangrande told me this morning, just by the by, that he'd taken it home to review, but then his grandson set fire to it. He's got that thing, ADHD — Attention Deficit Hyperactivity Disorder. He's a real little ball-breaker, apparently.'

Scamarcio rubbed his eyes, wondering if he he'd heard right. 'What? That's absurd.'

She shook her head and smiled tiredly. 'Yeah, we were laughing at the irony of it. First the corpse goes missing, then the report is destroyed before he's even had a chance to put it into the computer. He says he's struggling to remember the detail.'

Aurelia leant forward. 'You think his grandson is working for the Americans?'

She suddenly threw back her head and laughed. Scamarcio felt a spike of irritation.

'Look, Aurelia, you can't take it personally when I don't have the time to come and find you. You know what it's like when a case comes your way.'

'Don't patronise me.'

'I'm not. I just get the sense that you expect more from me than I'm able to give right now.'

Aurelia exhaled. The blast of air stirred her fringe and rearranged it across her brow. Scamarcio swallowed and tried to concentrate on the conversation.

'This inquiry has only just come your way, Leo. You've been evading me for quite some time now.'

'That's not true.' As soon as he said it, he knew he was lying.

He had started seeing Aurelia after the harrowing events of the summer, when he'd been involved in a highly disturbing paedophilia inquiry. At the time, he had felt the need for something to ground him in Rome, for somebody to come back to. But as life had calmed and the old routines had returned, that need seemed to have faded. In fact, lately it had been replaced by a new hunger for freedom, a desire to be able to live as he wanted, for space to breathe.

'I don't know why you can't just deal with your feelings. I'm not going to wait around forever,' Aurelia persisted.

'No one's asking you to.'

'You're making this impossible.'

He didn't want to waste working hours on this. 'Thanks for the steer re Giangrande,' he said, pushing back the chair.

10

He sat with the cardinal in his apartments along the corridor from the library. They had been served cappuccino and brioche, and it seemed as if the man was in good spirits.

'Our envoys tell us they need faxes, photocopiers, word processors, transmitters, video cameras, shortwave radios, telex machines, printing presses, and telephones,' said the cardinal, carefully wiping the foam from his upper lip with a silk handkerchief.

'We can bring them in through the channels established by your priests. We will also use our own people — along with representatives from our labour unions.'

'It's not just equipment. Walesa could do with strategic advice. We were hoping that you and your labour movements might lend a hand there also.'

'Of course.'

'We believe that, as the effectiveness of the resistance movement grows, so too will the stream of communications reaching us about activities inside the government and its dialogue with Moscow.'

'On this, your priests will be invaluable. We also have our own people on the inside, of course.'

The cardinal nodded. 'We will always make sure the movement has places where they can hold their meetings and organise their demonstrations.'

Carter turned to the window for a moment. 'We just need to let the natural forces play out. We can't get our fingerprints on this.'

The cardinal smiled at him, rather like a father trying to reassure his son that the impending trip to the dentist would not be too painful.

He returned the smile and surveyed the sunlight etching its way across the diamond panes. For the first time, this felt right; this felt justified. It was indeed a holy alliance — the moral force of the pope and the teachings of the Church, combined with a once-in-a-lifetime opportunity to fight the evils of communism. Finally, this was a mission he could believe in; a mission that wouldn't leave blood on his hands.

WHEN SCAMARCIO ENTERED the squad room, Garramone was waiting for him in his office doorway.

'What was all that about last night?'

Surely the Americans wouldn't have been on to him to complain. It wouldn't make sense.

'What was all *what* about?'

Garramone frowned, seemingly exasperated. 'The triangulation.' He slowed his delivery, talking to him as if he were simple. 'Who were you after?'

Scamarcio felt exhausted and wanted to sit down. 'Oh, that? It turned out to be nothing.' He paused for a beat, trying to change tack. 'Our American vermin have been sniffing around again.' He filled him in about the American's visit to Aurelia, but didn't mention the scene at the bar. 'Have you heard back from the official liaison? Can we hope to shake them off?'

Garramone waved him into his office, and once he was inside he shut the door behind them. The chief walked over to his desk and sank back into his swivel chair. There was a bag of caramels open on his desk and he motioned to Scamarcio to take one, but he declined — he didn't feel like adding to the two spoonfuls of sugar he had already loaded into his espresso. Despite his tiredness, he also didn't feel like sitting down now; he wanted to get out of there quickly.

'I've not heard anything, which in itself is unusual,' said Garramone. 'I was thinking of chasing them up this afternoon. Given that they've moved on to hassling one of the MEs, it now seems like a priority. I might also contact military intel or whatever it is they're now calling themselves, *external intelligence and security*, or some such bullshit.'

Scamarcio sensed that bringing in AISE might not be the best move for the investigation, but he chose to say nothing.

The chief's forehead bunched into a frown. 'Why would the Americans go about things in such a haphazard way? I would have thought they'd have no problem accessing a file or two. It all feels a bit amateurish.'

Scamarcio told him about Giangrande's grandson. When he was finished, Garramone arched an eyebrow and said, 'That sounds like "The dog ate my homework."'

Scamarcio nodded. 'What do you know about our chief ME?'

'In terms of his work, he's always been solid. I've heard that he likes the good life, spends a lot of time on his yacht or at the gun range; that he inherited a load of money a while back, but that he's now going through some tricky times.' He fell silent for a moment before adding, 'Aren't we all?'

Scamarcio figured Garramone must be on a decent salary, perhaps six figures, but he sensed that his wife's tastes were expensive.

'Tricky times. How tricky?'

'He's almost bankrupt?'

'Bankrupt?'

'That's the rumour, but you know rumours ...'

Scamarcio allowed the information to sink in for a moment. He was well aware of the pitfalls of the rumour mill, but he couldn't help feeling that this particular piece of gossip might provide a handle on why his evidence had gone astray.

Back at his desk, Scamarcio's landline rang, and he saw that Forensics was calling.

'Manetti, what've you got for me?'

'To be frank, not much, but there's one curiosity that caught my interest.'

'Go on.'

'That guy on the bridge didn't touch the rubble in his pockets.'

They both fell silent for a moment, considering the implications.

'So somebody might have put it there — might have given him a helping hand?' asked Scamarcio.

'Looks that way. Your comment about God's Banker got me thinking. I did a bit of research, and found that when the Calvi family had that second autopsy done, they discovered that Calvi hadn't touched the rubble in his pockets either. They also found there was no trace of paint or rust from the bridge on his shoes. If he'd climbed up there himself it would have had to have been there.'

'Our guy wasn't wearing shoes.'

'Exactly — I reckon someone took them off so we wouldn't notice the absence of rust.'

Scamarcio sighed and sank back against his chair. 'God, this is a weird one,' he said. 'Why create all those references to Calvi, all those similarities?'

'Search me. That's what they pay you the big bucks for, isn't it? I'll be back in touch if the frogmen come up with anything.'

Scamarcio thanked him and ended the call.

He hadn't yet had the chance to research the original Calvi case thoroughly, so, in light of the new steer from Manetti, Scamarcio thought he should give it some attention. He decided to scan through the key websites for background before pulling those police files that had been computerised. He knew the paper file from London's Scotland Yard would be much more comprehensive, but he didn't want to spend his time negotiating the cumbersome bureaucracy required to release it.

As Scamarcio already knew, Calvi had been a member of financier Licio Gelli's illegal Masonic lodge, P2, who were planning a coup in the event the communists ever came to power. What Scamarcio didn't know was that its members referred to themselves as *frati neri*, or 'black friars'. It was this connection that had led many to believe that Calvi's death on Blackfriars Bridge was a message from his Masonic colleagues.

The day before he was found hanging, the Bank of Italy had stripped Calvi of his job as chairman of Italy's second-largest bank, the Banco Ambrosiano, after it had gone bankrupt following massive debts. Two weeks before the collapse, Calvi had written a letter of warning to Pope John Paul II, stating that such a forthcoming event would 'provoke a catastrophe of unimaginable proportions in which the Church will suffer the gravest damage'.

Light was finally shed on the Calvi case when a mafioso turned informant, Francesco Mannoia, claimed that the banker had been killed because he had lost money owed to the mafia and P2 when Ambrosiano collapsed. The combined order to kill him had come from both mafia boss Giuseppe Calò and the grand master of the P2 lodge, Licio Gelli. In a statement at his trial, Gelli claimed that the killing had been commissioned in Poland.

There was something bothering Scamarcio about what he had just read — something that, besides the manner of death, seemed to chime with what little he knew so far about the mysterious Mr Carter or Bartlett; something that linked him to it, drew him tightly in. But right now he couldn't put his finger on it, couldn't quite pin it down.

11

ON HIS WAY HOME that evening, Scamarcio decided to drop by the morgue. He couldn't understand how a corpse could simply be lifted from under the noses of Giangrande and his staff. The chief pathologist seemed nonchalant, and that troubled Scamarcio.

It was almost 7.00 pm by the time he arrived. Many of the admin offices were already deserted, but he spotted a dim glow spilling out from the autopsy suite. As he entered, he noticed that there was only one light on and that it was coming from the adjoining office to the lab where Giangrande usually worked. He walked into the room and headed towards the office; as he did so, he saw Giangrande's back hunched over a desk, a mobile stuck to his ear. As he stepped closer, he realised that the chief pathologist was speaking English. His command of the language seemed confident, but he was talking in a whisper. Scamarcio took a few more paces and then, on instinct, stepped to the right of the doorway so Giangrande couldn't see him.

'I told you, I no longer have it,' the chief pathologist was saying to whoever was on the line. 'There was no need for you to create a mess.'

He fell silent for a few moments, listening to the response, and then said, 'It doesn't work like that. I hadn't put it into the computer. I do that once I've written a paper copy.'

He fell silent again. 'No, there's nothing left.'

A pause, then, 'I disposed of it.'

It sounded like Giangrande had started drumming his fingers on the desk. 'There's one, yes. I'd sent it for testing early on.'

He sighed. 'Well, of course it will. Obviously, I'll get rid of it.'

Scamarcio was about to turn away, believing that he'd heard enough, when Giangrande asked, 'When will I see it?' He fell silent once more, and then added, 'OK. I'll check tomorrow and let you know.'

Scamarcio sensed that the call was about to end, so he scanned the doorway to make sure Giangrande's back was still turned, and then hurried out of the suite into the night.

Aurelia had cancelled their dinner date, claiming a headache, and Scamarcio had felt too tired and frustrated to object, so he had poured himself a generous measure of Glenfiddich and settled down to think about the one-sided conversation he had overheard in Giangrande's office.

If the rumours were to be believed, the chief pathologist had serious money worries. If the Americans had come around waving a thick wad of dollars in his direction, it was possible that he could have been tempted to hand them what they needed. That's what it had sounded like from the phone call, and would explain the apparent ease with which Carter's body had been removed. Scamarcio considered whether he should share his suspicions with Garramone, but an instinct told him to keep his concerns to himself for now; that either he first needed to establish the truth or that, even if he knew the deception to be real, he should sit on it and think of a way to make Giangrande's duplicity work for him.

He took another sip of the whisky, and pondered the P2 connection to Calvi. He'd read that the secret Masonic lodge had maintained a series of surreptitious international relationships, mainly with Argentina and with people suspected of CIA affiliation. Scamarcio found that interesting. P2 and the CIA must have shared a common goal in keeping the communists out of Italy during the 1980s. To all intents and purposes, the Italian peninsula had been the Americans' landing strip in the Med. If the Reds had come to power, that cosy set-up would have been over.

What troubled Scamarcio, though, was the decision to hang the American beneath the Ponte Sant'Angelo. What was the point of stirring up old grievances by staging such a symbolic suicide — a suicide that raised the ghost of Calvi? Those who had been involved in P2 surely wanted the whole thing dead and buried. And if the CIA had some connection to the lodge, wouldn't they also want to keep that quiet? They wouldn't want to add to the whispers already out there. It made Scamarcio think that whoever had done this was not ex-P2 and was probably not American; that he possibly had a grievance with one or both of them.

So who did that leave? The homegrown mafia was the obvious answer. Was the murder intended as a warning? But, really, what kind of threat could they represent to the biggest, most powerful, intelligence agency in the world? He took another sip of his whisky. The whole thing felt odd and out of sync with the history, as though the timeline was skewed. As the whisky warmed his stomach, he wondered idly whether someone was tossing him a red herring. But if that was their intention, why were the spooks so worried? What was in it for them? He sighed. After the troubles of the summer, the very last thing he wanted was a political case. But the more he looked at it, the more political this inquiry became. *Fuck it*, he thought. Why the hell did he have to be the one to take that early-morning call?

He took in the darkness beyond the window, and poured himself another measure of whisky — slightly more generous this time. After several sips, he reflected that maybe it was the fact that P2 extended its tentacles beyond Italy that should be of interest; that might explain the fresh presence of the Americans. So far, two countries had come up: Poland and Argentina. He flipped them over in his head. Where was it that Blakemore had said Carter/Bartlett was active? *Eastern Europe and Latin America.*

That earlier sense of connection returned — flimsy and elusive, but a connection nevertheless. He picked up the phone and dialled Blakemore.

The reporter sounded harried, if not slightly on edge, when he answered.

'Listen, John, I won't take up much of your time — I just need to know where exactly my dead American was out in the field. Did you get back to your source on that?'

The line went bad, and Blakemore's reply was breaking up with static, but Scamarcio could just about make out the last part of his response: '… will do … Might not … easy.'

He thanked him and hung up.

12

The chief accountant checked the ledger and then checked it once more. The money had come via the Continental Illinois Bank and the Western Pacific Bank in the US to the Vatican Bank here in Rome. From Italy it had been sent to a series of 17 small offshore banks in Nassau, Nicaragua, and Panama. And from there it had been shipped to the cardinals in Poland.

'This is dirty money,' he told the cardinal when he arrived that morning.

'What's dirty about it?'

'It's the proceeds from drugs, prostitution, and gambling. It's mafia money.'

The cardinal smiled and patted him on the shoulder. 'It's not where it comes from that counts; it's where it ends up. You're young — you'll come to understand.'

SCAMARCIO SET THE CAFFETIERA on the hob and switched on the small TV in the kitchen. He'd slept badly the night before, thanks to a nightmare in which Aurelia had been shot in the chest in front of him. His legs had been paralysed, and he hadn't been able to reach her, and in the end he'd just watched her slowly bleed to death. He'd woken in a sweat, and hadn't been able to get back to sleep for several hours. In the end, he'd finally nodded off when the birds had started to sing and the first milky mists of sunlight were seeping through the curtains. It had been a deep, leaden sleep, but just forty minutes later his alarm had prised him awake. Now he felt shaky and discombobulated, as though the rhythm of his body had been interrupted; it was as if everything was out of kilter.

He turned up the sound on the ancient TV so he could watch the morning news. They were all still obsessed with Abbiati. There was another reporter, much younger than the first one, doing a live link from outside the Vatican. Why did they make them stand there if they weren't getting any information from inside? Did they think their viewers were that stupid?

'It seems increasingly likely that Cardinal Abbiati was the victim of a power struggle inside the Church,' said the journalist. 'The same power struggle that some people claim forced the last pope to resign.'

Why does it seem increasingly likely? wondered Scamarcio. Just because some fat old newspaper editor liked it for a theory didn't mean they all had to swallow it. There wasn't any evidence yet. Once again, he cursed Garramone and whatever cretin had allocated him the stiff under the bridge.

'Of course, the previous pope was intent on cleaning up the practices of the Vatican Bank, making it more transparent,' chimed in the plastic blonde anchor back in the studio, feeding the reporter his opportunity.

'That's right, Bianca. The Vatican Bank has come under increasing pressure from the European authorities to clarify its international transactions. The previous pope had really championed that, had brought in a fellow German, a financier whom he trusted, to overhaul it. Many say that there was a faction who could not accept that, who did everything they could to impede his work.'

Bianca nodded knowingly. 'It is indeed intriguing, but I guess at this stage we have to stress that this is just conjecture.'

'That's right. We will need to await the press conference from the Vatican.'

'Yeah, like that's going to reveal all,' Scamarcio muttered. He

pondered Abbiati once more. Where did he fit in? Was he actually connected to the bank? He wondered why the media seemed to be dodging that key question. He guessed it was because they had no idea. Or, worse still, they did, but it would render the whole 'Vatican Bank power struggle' theory redundant, so they chose to ignore it.

His coffee was bubbling over on the hob, so he turned off the heat and carried the filthy caffetiera over to the small table that offered him a view over the rooftops of the banking district. The Bank of Italy was just two blocks away, and a cluster of international banks had their headquarters in the neighbouring streets. There wasn't much residential housing in this area, and flats were expensive, but Scamarcio's father had seen to it that his son wouldn't want when it came to matters financial. How he had seen to it was another story, and Scamarcio tried to block that from his mind; he didn't want it spoiling the taste of the coffee.

He took a sip from the espresso cup an old girlfriend had given him. It was one of those designer ones you could collect, but it was the only one he had left — he'd smashed the others when they'd had a row. *The Vatican Bank*. Those three words were on everyone's lips right now, yet so far the only solid connection was that the murdered cardinal had had his quarters opposite. Scamarcio had been investigating the body under the bridge; however, as Garramone had stressed, he also needed to be looking into Abbiati — he should probably be giving it equal weight. But, apart from the time involved, how was he ever going to get inside that case, and catch even a sniff of what was going on?

He wondered briefly about using Piocosta, but he knew that the Vatican was not the old man's field of expertise. His father's old lieutenant had his fingers in many pies; yet, as far as Scamarcio knew, The 'ndrangheta had never been able to get a cut of church business. Scamarcio considered a second option: he knew that the Carabinieri sometimes consulted for the Vatican police, and he weighed up whether the Flying Squad could manipulate any relationships there to get some sense of what was going on. But he suspected that the Vatican police would shut the Carabinieri right out of this one. This was something to discuss with Garramone.

He pulled out his laptop and ran a search on Cardinal Abbiati. Disregarding the flurry of recent press on his murder, he couldn't find anything interesting — apart from the fact that he hailed from Milan and was unusual in having gained an economics and accountancy degree from the Catholic University before attending Catholic Seminary. But none of the articles contained any mention of whether he worked for the Vatican Bank. Abbiati seemed to have been involved in countless charitable foundations, working with the urban poor in some of Italy's most deprived suburbs. At first glance, he seemed a thoroughly decent man. Strangely, Scamarcio could find no photos of him to accompany the articles.

He googled recent books published on the Vatican, wondering if there were any writers who had dealt with the financial story and the attempts to clean up the bank's practices. He noticed one book that had come out the year before, which seemed the most up to date. It appeared to be a general look at the Vatican; and, according to a brief description, it did include several chapters on the IOR, or the Vatican Bank, as it was better known. Scamarcio ran a search for the author, and was taken to a website that listed an email address but no telephone number. He composed a quick note, asking for help with any background on Abbiati and the activities of the IOR.

He took another sip of coffee, and surveyed the early-morning sunlight etching its way across the rooftops. He sensed that if he didn't find a way inside the Vatican, and find one soon, solving the Ponte Sant'Angelo case would prove difficult, if not impossible. He returned to the stove and refilled his cup. After the night he'd had, it would take more than one coffee to get him through the day.

His mobile started ringing, and his heart sank when he saw it was the boss. He didn't have the energy to speak to him this early.

'I've just had a strange call,' were the chief's first words. 'Did you contact a Giuseppe Felletti this morning about Abbiati?'

'I just sent him an email — no more than a couple of minutes ago.'

'Well, he just rang through to the squad room to check you were who you claim to be.'

'Seems over-cautious …'

'He's on edge about something. He says he's not the right man to help, but has suggested someone who is.'

'OK …'

'He wants the two of you to meet in a café in Prati — Caffè Mulino. It's one of those organic health-food places, all rabbit food and kidney beans.'

'Is he worried about my heart?'

'No, he seems worried about your case.'

'Did he explain who I'm to meet?'

'He said that it would be better if you don't know his name. You have to be there in one hour.'

Great, thought Scamarcio, *I'll barely have time to take a shower.* 'And how do I recognise this mystery source?'

'I told Felletti what you look like, so I'm sure he'll pass it on. Just arrive, and order an espresso or something.'

'They serve coffee in places like that? Isn't it supposed to be carcinogenic?'

Garramone sighed. 'It's Via Pompeo Magno, just a short walk from the Piazza del Popolo.'

Scamarcio had wanted to tell him about Manetti's findings, but Garramone had already hung up.

The café was busy with the breakfast rush. Customers were picking at fruit salad and muesli, sampling the odd yoghurt. Scamarcio reluctantly pulled out a seat and studied the menu.

The place described itself as a 'gourmet café-come-organic osteria', serving seasonal dishes that 'balanced scientific and nutritional values proposed by the Italian Society of Science and Alimentation'. The finest, freshest ingredients were selected from biodynamic and bio-solidarity farms. *What's a bio-solidarity farm?* wondered Scamarcio. He scanned the options, growing increasingly despondent. He noted that the place offered a 'healthy tiramisù'. How could a tiramisù worth eating ever be healthy? He couldn't be bothered to read any more, and tossed down the menu in disgust. He'd stop at one of the greasy bars near the squad room on his way back. Then he sensed someone looking at him, and glanced up. A small man in a long, dark coat and a smart, black hat was standing by the table. He appeared to be in his sixties, and had a thick, checked scarf wound tightly around his neck. He was dressed for winter.

'I'm sorry, Detective. I can see that this place isn't quite to your liking,' said the stranger.

Scamarcio was embarrassed — he didn't want to offend Felletti's contact. He got up quickly and shook hands.

'Not at all, it's fine. Pleased to meet you, Mr ...?'

The man waved a hand away and slowly took a seat. He moved awkwardly, and Scamarcio sensed arthritis or some kind of joint problem. Maybe that explained the unseasonally heavy clothes.

The stranger peeled off a pair of expensive looking leather gloves and laid them neatly next to the place setting. 'Despite appearances, they do good coffee here. That, and they're close to my apartment. I'm afraid I have bit of trouble getting around these days.'

Scamarcio nodded.

The man set down his hat next and carefully smoothed out the short, grey hair at the back of his head. A waitress arrived, and he politely ordered a latte macchiato. Scamarcio decided to choose the same, and then wondered whether the milk would be normal. He hated that soya stuff.

When the waitress was gone, the stranger said, 'Mr Felletti believes I might be of help to you with your current investigation.'

It sounded like a question. As the writer hadn't filled them in on what precisely this man might have to offer, the only reply Scamarcio could come up with was, 'I'd be interested in anything you might be free to tell me.'

The man pulled a puzzled expression. 'Well, it's not like us scholars have huge secrets. Most of it makes it into the book eventually.'

Had Felletti come good and found him an inside man, someone who actually understood the IOR?

The stranger studied him closely for a moment and then said, 'They've got it all topsy-turvy with this Abbiati thing. It makes me cringe, listening to the rubbish they're spouting. It's shameful, really.' The waitress was back with their coffees, and he suddenly fell silent.

When she had left, Scamarcio asked, 'So the power struggle thing is off? It hasn't got anything to do with Abbiati?'

The stranger put down his coffee, dabbing at his mouth with a napkin. 'Not so fast, young man. It's not that simple.'

Scamarcio hoped he wasn't one of those academic types you had to tease it out of while they took hours flexing their knowledge supremacy.

The man shifted in the chair uncomfortably, trying to find a new position that worked for him, and Scamarcio immediately felt guilty. The poor guy had done him a favour making the effort to come out. He tried a smile, and the stranger seemed to warm up a bit.

'What it is you see is that this power struggle between the Opus Dei faction and the rest has been going on for decades; they want to gain ultimate control and throw out the modernisers. Abbiati, though, was never really Opus Dei. They wanted to make him one of theirs; in fact, they tried very hard, but he couldn't be won. He was a decent man, Abbiati — an honest man. He had no truck with their nonsense.'

'Nonsense?'

The man looked off to the side; he seemed to be measuring his response. ' "Nonsense" is the wrong word. "Arrogance" is closer. Probably "evil" would be better. They are all for keeping things secret, maintaining their power base. That has meant covering up some dreadful things, allowing some terrible crimes to go unpunished.'

'Sex abuse?'

'Perhaps.'

Why couldn't he just come out and say it? It wasn't like he worked for the Vatican. But maybe he was just trying to preserve his access, figured Scamarcio. That perhaps also explained why he had chosen to remain anonymous.

'So Opus Dei is on one side, and the reformers on the other?'

'Exactly.'

'Who are they, this Opus Dei? You hear so much about them.'

The old man took another sip of his latte macchiato. 'They're a kind of sect, a secret society — something that is completely forbidden by the Catholic Church, of course. The movement is imbued with fascist ideas turned to religious purposes. The self-flagellation stuff that came out when they made that dreadful American film is just a normal part of the rigid spiritual discipline they impose on their full-time members. Personal identity gets a severe battering — the mindset is totalitarian. They grudgingly accept Roman authority because they still see Rome as orthodox, but also because, as a respected Catholic organisation, it gives them access to a vast pool of high-calibre recruits. Although it has members from many walks of life, Opus Dei primarily seeks to attract those from the upper classes; they prefer young professionals with the potential to rise to positions of power. This strategy allows them to control a great number of banks and financial institutions — it's why they've been dubbed a saintly mafia.'

'So Opus Dei was resisting the move for greater transparency in the dealings of the Vatican Bank?'

'Most definitely. But Abbiati was all for transparency. He'd had enough of Opus Dei and their machinations. He believed their power games were destroying the Church; that they were a cancer eating away at it from the inside.' He paused for a moment before adding, 'That's an opinion shared by many, both inside and outside the Vatican.'

'Why did everyone think Abbiati was Opus Dei?'

The old man laughed, though it came out dry and hoarse. 'They put that rumour out there. It served their purpose to have people believe he was one of theirs.'

Scamarcio shook his head. 'But why?'

'Because people are scared of Opus Dei, of the power they wield. They thought that if he was seen as one of them, it would make him untouchable.'

'Untouchable?'

'That they couldn't get at him.'

'Who?'

'The people doing the forensic accounting on the Vatican Bank — the foreigners who have been brought in.'

'I thought they were just trying to make things clearer. Are they also going back through old books now?'

'But of course. You have to first root out the weeds, don't you?'

'But why would these foreigners be scared? What difference does it make to them if Abbiati is Opus Dei or not?'

'Well, just look at the damage they did to the German chap the last pope tried to bring in. They practically had him committed to an asylum. These people are toxic, Detective. You have to understand that.'

Scamarcio sat back in his seat for a moment and took a sip

of the coffee. It wasn't as bad as he was expecting; in fact, it was almost passable. He extracted a notebook and pen from his jacket pocket, but the stranger suddenly seemed alarmed and almost rose from his chair. 'No notes. I said that to Felletti right from the off.' He quickly scanned the other customers in the café, and then asked, 'You're not taping this, are you?'

Scamarcio opened his jacket, turning the pockets out for him to see. 'No devices, I promise. I don't make a habit of recording casual conversations.'

The old man sighed. 'Sorry, it's just that they have eyes and ears everywhere.'

Scamarcio was impressed by the scale of his paranoia. He doubted that they were dealing with such a cohesive, all-knowing entity, but instead he asked, 'Why would the people trying to clean up the Vatican Bank want to get at Abbiati?'

The old man suddenly looked at his watch and then hurriedly gathered his gloves and hat together. The colour seemed to drain from his cheeks in seconds. 'I'm afraid I really need to go — I'm late for an important meeting.'

'But you've only just got here,' said Scamarcio.

The old man didn't respond.

'How can I reach you?' persisted Scamarcio.

'I'm not sure I can be of much more help.'

'But what you've told me so far has been illuminating.'

'Good, good.' The man was suddenly absent, his mind apparently turning on where he needed to be next.

Why had he shut down on him so suddenly, wondered Scamarcio. Was it the notebook? 'I have so many more questions,' he said.

The stranger didn't seem to be listening. He took a two-euro coin from his pocket and laid it on the table. Scamarcio quickly reached over and slipped a business card into the old man's pocket. He didn't seem to have noticed, and just doffed his hat and shuffled quickly towards the door. Once he'd left, Scamarcio got up from his seat and went to the window, from where he could follow his retreating frame down Via Pompeo Magno. When the stranger was about thirty feet away, Scamarcio realised that he no longer seemed to be shuffling, that he seemed to be moving with much greater fluidity, like a man half his age.

13

'Things are going well,' said the cardinal. 'In almost every town and city, underground newspapers and bulletins are appearing, challenging the state-controlled media. They're tacking them to church notice-boards, police stations, and government buildings. One of my priests told me that they've even seen them outside the TV centre.'

'We couldn't have hoped for a better result. Did you hear that our technicians managed to hack into the government programming — they got a 'Solidarity Lives' banner onscreen at half time during the national soccer championships!'

The cardinal arched an eyebrow. 'You were wise to choose half time. If you'd put it up during the match, you wouldn't have won many friends.'

Carter smiled. 'There's been another positive development: we're finding that our labour union's relationship with the movement is so strong that much of what we need can be financed and obtained through them. The classic covert ops aren't required in this instance.'

'That must make things smoother for you,' said the cardinal.

'It does.'

The cardinal leant back in his chair and adjusted his robes. 'Our priests are requesting more food, clothes, and money to support those leaders who are being hauled before the courts.'

'We will see to that.'

'They're proving an effective source of communication between the different leaders, our priests. They pass their messages back and forth.'

'We need to make more use of them when the shipments come in. Can we call on them for deliveries and pick-ups?'

'I will get the word out.'

'As always, it's been a pleasure doing business with you, cardinal,' said Carter, reaching for his hand.

THERE WAS A BIG, fat white A4 envelope waiting on his desk when Scamarcio returned to the squad room. He tore it open, and immediately noted two stamps at the top of every page. The American eagle featured in both; but when he compared them to the seals of the CIA, FBI, and NSA online, they didn't match. Who was he dealing with, then? He scanned the seal into his computer and ran an images search, but could find no matches. He let out a long sigh, and decided to just read the bloody document. There were ten pages.

They were calling the murdered man Stephen Manning — there was no mention of Simeon Carter or Shaun Bartlett. Scamarcio scanned the basic details on the first page: *Stephen Manning, 62, counterfeiter, wanted by the FBI and the CIA.* That was interesting — why weren't their seals on the document then?

- Guilty of a string of crimes dating back to 1982, most recently establishing a counterfeit lab in Pennsylvania that, in the space of three years, churned out 50 million in fake dollars.
- Head of a cross-country network that pumped dud dollars from Washington to Waco, Chicago to Chattanooga.
- Employed 20 people in his scheme, murdering two of them when things went off track.
- Known aliases: Stephen Mahoney, Daniel Carruso, Myron Timms.
- About to launch an international operation, targeting China and India.
- Conclusion: When tracked to Rome, Italy, he took his own life.

They had enclosed crime-scene photos of the dead man, and recent portrait pictures. Of course, they matched. They also included photos of a birthmark on the right knee that corresponded with the autopsy shots. Where did they get the autopsy stills? Had Giangrande handed them over? Or had they been taken once they'd stolen the body, wondered Scamarcio.

The autopsy concluded that death had been caused by self-strangulation. A pathologist by the name of Dr Symes had signed the report. Who the hell was he? He certainly wasn't anyone Scamarcio had ever heard of, and he didn't seem to be Italian. Under the autopsy report was a note in smaller type: *'Corpse requisitioned under Statute LY6293/ppql 1964 for US suspects arrested on foreign territories.'* So that was it. They'd just taken the body, claiming it was their right under international law. He'd never heard of such a law, and was pretty certain it didn't even exist.

On the final page was a note to the Italian police: *'We are most grateful for your cooperation in this matter. We trust that the enclosed dossier will satisfy your administrative requirements and allow you to bring the case to a satisfying conclusion.'* There was none of the usual *'For any further inquiries, please do not hesitate to contact us …'* There was no telephone number supplied, and no email address.

Scamarcio breathed out, and then took his lighter from his pocket and tossed it on the desk. When he patted his jacket he realised he was out of smokes, and felt newly aggrieved. Sartori was ahead of him at the espresso machine, and seemed to clock his mood. 'What can I get you?'

'Thanks — latte macchiato.'

'You're brave. Last time I tried it, it tasted like baby sick.'

'I've never tasted baby sick.'

'Then you haven't lived,' said Sartori, deadpan, with no hint of a smile. The fat man looked exhausted. His eyes were rat small, and his black crop was greasy.

'Tough time at home?'

'I'm going to get the chop.'

'What? I've heard nothing along those lines. Garramone likes you.'

Sartori sighed dramatically. 'No, Scamarcio you cretin — the chop.' He pointed downwards to his crotch, making an exaggerated sawing motion.

'Seems drastic.'

'Four kids, that's drastic. I can't take it any more.'

'I'll swap you your four kids for two American arseholes.'

'Deal,' said Sartori, downing his espresso in one. 'I hope they're potty-trained.'

'They'll need to be when I've finished with them,' said Garramone, joining the conversation, seemingly out of nowhere. 'Scamarcio, can you give me five minutes?'

He picked up his coffee and followed the boss. Garramone didn't make the turn into his office as usual, but headed instead for one of the larger briefing rooms further down the hall. Something about this set Scamarcio on edge.

When they entered, he saw three men — two in uniform — seated around the conference table. Both of the uniforms were top brass: one was police; the other, military. One of them he recognised as Rome's chief of police, Gianfilippo Mancino, currently flavour of the month after he'd supposedly cracked the child-abduction case that Scamarcio had been involved in back in the summer. The second — no idea. The civilian was Paolo Gatti, chief of media relations. Gatti was never a welcome sight.

'Detective Scamarcio, you know Chief Mancino and Director Gatti, but I don't believe you will have met Colonel Andrea Scalisi — he works with AISE.'

Scamarcio shook hands with each of the three men and, following Garramone's example, took a seat.

'I've called these gentlemen here today to discuss the dossier we have been sent by our American colleagues.'

Garramone's use of the word 'colleague' rang alarm bells. Scamarcio hoped they weren't about to embark on a well-trodden path of dog-like collaboration.

'I feel we need to make a collective decision on our approach from here on in. I will leave it to Colonel Scalisi to explain his agency's take on this matter.'

Why did they need to take a collective decision, wondered Scamarcio. Since when did the police dance to Intel's tune? And the stilted, formal language was unsettling: it made Garramone come across as the weaker party. That should absolutely not be the case as far as AISE were concerned. Those guys needed reining in.

The colonel was broad-shouldered. Scamarcio could not be sure of his height, but guessed he was well over six foot. He had a wide forehead and deep-set blue eyes that reminded him of the actor Anthony Hopkins. His blond hair was cropped short, and he wore a simple silver band on his ring finger. He eased back in his chair slightly and studied Scamarcio. It was not a positive appraisal. No doubt he already knew all about his background.

'Gentlemen, it has been brought to my attention that the Americans are interested in the body under the Ponte Sant'Angelo that your department has been investigating. I believe they supplied you with documents today, explaining their involvement.'

'Whitewash.'

'Excuse me?'

'It was a whitewash — their explanation isn't worth the paper it's written on.' Scamarcio stared at the intelligence chief, and took a sip of his macchiato. Sartori was right. Garramone shifted in his seat beside Scamarcio, looking at him like an embarrassed father at a parent-teacher's evening.

'What makes you so sure, Detective?' asked Scalisi, his tone crisp, giving no hint of irritation yet.

'I have sources in the US intelligence community who have identified the victim differently.'

'Go on.'

'I'd rather keep it to myself for now.'

Scalisi raised an eyebrow at Garramone, as if Scamarcio weren't there.

'I think what Detective Scamarcio is trying to say is that he still needs to verify the legitimacy of this account. He's waiting on all the facts,' said Garramone.

'Is that right, Detective?' asked Scalisi.

'Not entirely. The CSI team has told me that the man under the bridge had not touched the masonry rubble in his pockets. Obviously, that casts further doubt on the Americans' explanation.' Scamarcio paused for a beat. 'Who are they, anyway? It's not clear whether they're FBI, CIA, or some other outfit.'

Scalisi just looked down at his notepad, saying nothing.

Gatti coughed affectedly. It was a hollow little cough, intended to say, 'I'm here. I must be heard. I've waited long enough.' Scamarcio felt like punching the man before he'd even opened his mouth.

'If I might interject ...' Gatti coughed again, sounding even more false this time. 'I think we need to tread very very carefully. We don't want to give any sense of a turf war, any sense that we might have issues with our American colleagues.'

There, that word again. Scamarcio turned in his chair to face the little man. 'Firstly, they're not our colleagues, and secondly we do have issues — fucking serious ones. They made off with the corpse.'

'We don't know that for sure,' said Scalisi.

'They cited a law to justify it in their report. They've as good as admitted it.' Scamarcio tried to keep his tone even, to tamp down his growing anger. He couldn't afford another scene, especially with others present. His mind flashed on the memory of Giangrande hunched over the telephone in his office, but he resolved not to say anything about that for now.

'Detective Scamarcio is frustrated at how they seem to be hampering his inquiry,' said Garramone. 'They've been hassling one of our MEs, too. Their methods do seem quite heavy-handed.'

Scalisi sighed, quickly doodling something on the notebook in front of him. 'The word from up high is that we need to keep them sweet, that we can't afford to upset the apple cart.'

'Why is that?' asked Scamarcio.

'Long story.'

'Try us.'

Scalisi threw down his pen and said to Garramone, 'Can you and I speak alone now?' This time, he did sound irritated.

Out in the corridor, Gatti read Scamarcio the rulebook. 'You see, what with your reputation and everything, we need to make sure it doesn't come over as us pulling a fast one on the Americans.'

'Why would it?'

'Well, you know how it is.'

'No, I fucking don't. You will need to explain, Gatti.'

When he failed to respond, Scamarcio asked, 'Who has the story anyway?'

'No one yet — as far as I know.'

'What are you so worried about, then?'

'If it does get out, it won't look good — it will be Amanda Knox all over again. Will you make sure it doesn't get out, Scamarcio? Could you do that for me this time, for the department?'

'What the hell are you getting at?'

The little man fell silent, but Scamarcio had a good idea of what he was trying to say. Scamarcio had been known, on occasion, to leak stories to a reporter he trusted, but only if he felt it might benefit the final outcome. It was a strategy he believed was justified. 'Why should we care how it looks? We're the police, not the bloody Farnesina. We have a job to do.'

'Yes, but if we put the wrong noses out of joint, we suffer the repercussions. We don't need any adverse publicity.'

'I doubt these guys want it to come out that they've been sniffing around.'

'No, but they could put some other story out there.'

'Like what?'

'Well, I don't know, but they will have all sorts of tricks up their sleeves.'

The man was paranoid. What was it with this town? Everyone seemed more frightened than usual lately. Of quite what, he had no idea. Did Gatti know something he didn't? Did Garramone, for that matter? Was anyone going to tell him who the hell they were actually dealing with? Were they even sure it was the CIA?

His mobile rang. It was a US number — Blakemore, hopefully. He turned his back on Gatti, who was now red-faced, and headed back to the squad room.

'John, that was quick.'

'Yeah, well, don't get too excited.'

'Oh?'

'I think my guy is shutting down on me.'

Scamarcio fell silent for a moment, sensing that maybe he'd compromised something for Blakemore. 'You think they're putting the pressure on?'

'Undoubtedly — that's what they do.'

'Was he able to give you anything?'

'He gave me two words; well, two places really. You wanted to know where your dead guy was active?'

'Right …'

'Poland and Nicaragua — that was all he said before he hung up on me.'

14

'We should talk about Managua,' he said.

'Of course.'

'We need his Holiness to demand that the five priests holding official positions in the government resign immediately.'

The cardinal nodded in agreement.

'And we need to be clear on his upcoming visit. It would be helpful if he could say something along the lines that Marxist-Leninist forces have been using the church as a political weapon against private ownership. They have been infiltrating the religious community with ideas that are more communist than Christian. He must distance himself from the alliances his Catholic clergy have been making with these revolutionary groups.'

'You're talking about the Sandinistas?'

'Of course. He has to step clear away from them — he must condemn that alliance.'

'You're working with our right-wing Catholic groups on the ground, of course?' said the cardinal.

Carter nodded.

'I'm looking forward to the trip. I think it will prove fruitful for us both,' added the cardinal.

He hoped he was right. They needed to up the Contra raids out of Honduras, and the pope's words would be vital in creating the right backdrop.

IT WAS A CRISP AUTUMN AFTERNOON, the sky a deep blue. Scamarcio could still catch the summer-mellowed citrus of the orange trees. Around the piazza, the leaves were deep reds, gold, and bronze; but if it wasn't for that, you might think you were in late September. It was mild today — T-shirt weather, a comfortable 23 degrees.

Piazzale Aldo Moro was bustling. Students were milling about, chatting under the trees, trading jokes as they waited in line by the newspaper stand. It reminded Scamarcio of his university days in Palermo. It should have been a special time, a time of liberty and discovery, of daring and experimentation. But instead he had felt as if he were in a prison, where the same shaky cine-reel kept on playing, the same ugly images flitting by again and again. Sometimes he thought that when he was more settled he would try to study again, try to enjoy it like he was supposed to. But he knew it would never be the same.

The fascist architecture of the main university building loomed over the square. The city council seemed to be waging a running battle with the graffiti artists, who in turn were at war among themselves: blacks versus reds, right versus left, Roma versus Juve.

Scamarcio reflected on the name: Piazzale Aldo Moro. Prime minister Moro had lived through the same dark years as Calvi, had fallen victim to the same dark forces. What had gone through his mind, he wondered, when they had bundled him into their car that morning? What were his final thoughts some fifty days later, when they stuffed him into a linen basket, covered him with a sheet, and pumped two bullets into his chest? All he had wanted was to reach out to the communists, to make Italy a better place. Anyone who tried to do that paid the price eventually, it seemed.

Scamarcio took the steps to the entrance and asked the receptionist for Professor Letta's office. She called up to announce Scamarcio's arrival, and then directed him through the glass doors behind her, leading into a sun-dappled garden: 'Go left out of there and take the second door on the left — his study is up on the third floor.'

He passed through the glass doors and saw more students lounging on the grass, spread out on rugs and sarongs. Once again, he experienced the by-now familiar spike of envy.

It was cool on the staircase, and the smell of cold stone and fresh tobacco hit him as he began the climb. The door to Letta's office was already wide open, and when Scamarcio peered inside he saw a young man sitting in the centre of the room, scribbling furiously on a notepad. Someone was shouting across at him from the other side of the study. Tobacco smoke filled the space, and spilled out through the doorway — it was a rich, heady blend. Scamarcio couldn't quite make out what was being discussed; he didn't want to venture too close and disturb the tutorial.

After a couple of minutes the talking ceased, and the young man finally laid down his pen and shook out his wrist. He laughed at something that was being said, gathered his belongings, and made towards the door. He seemed surprised to see Scamarcio standing there, but nodded politely, bidding him a 'Good morning' before taking the stairs. Scamarcio thought he detected an accent from the Veneto.

He knocked on the open door a couple of times, and a bass voice hollered, 'Enter.'

Professor Letta was sprawled behind his desk, one leg flung across a tsunami of paperwork. He was lighting another roll-up. From where Scamarcio was standing, it appeared to be on the wrong side of legal, although he wasn't sure whether the smell quite supported that.

'Detective Scamarcio, I presume.'

The professor made no attempt to get up, but just extended a huge arm across the desk. His wide palm was warm and sweaty. It was far too hot in the room, and the heat and smoke made Scamarcio want to open a window.

Letta was one of those men about whom everything was big, rather than fat. His limbs were huge, his ears were massive, and even his hair was thick and unruly. The voice, of course, was deep and powerful.

'I can always spot a detective,' said the professor.

'Is that so?'

'It's something about the shirts you chaps wear.'

'Our shirts?'

'Yes, it's that smart-but-casual thing. The collars always seem to be button down.'

Letta was a leading expert in what the Italians termed the 'years of lead': those dark decades of the Cold War that had claimed both Calvi and Moro, when assassination had followed bombing, and the communists actually had a chance at power.

'Thanks for seeing me at such short notice,' said Scamarcio. He wanted to steer the conversation back to the matter in hand.

Letta waved a hand and motioned to a chair. 'Not a problem.'

Scamarcio pulled out the seat recently vacated by the boy from the Veneto, and drew it closer to the desk. When he was comfortable, Letta gave him a quick appraisal, and then took a drag on his suspiciously large cigarette. 'So, Detective, what can I do you for?'

'In a nutshell, I was hoping you could tell me what Poland, Nicaragua, a murdered CIA agent, and the Vatican might have in common.'

Letta guffawed, then took another drag and exhaled quickly. 'Right,' he said. 'Is this for a case?'

'Of course — I'm not here to get my *laurea*.'

'Have you got one?'

'Yes.'

'What in?'

'English Literature.'

'Ah-ha, then no wonder you are bringing me this question.' He paused for a moment, and then asked, 'Have you got any hunches?'

Scamarcio wanted to push things along. He didn't have time for the cat and mouse. 'A few: an American man was found hanging from a bridge in Rome this week. Both the manner of his death and evidence found at the crime scene bore strong similarities to the death of Roberto Calvi back in 1982. I believe this American was working for the CIA. All I know about his past is that he was active in Poland and Nicaragua.'

'Doing what?'

'I'm not sure yet.'

'Why did you mention the Vatican?'

'Well, the Calvi connection. And the body was found near Vatican City.'

'And Cardinal Abbiati was murdered this week?'

'There is that, yes.'

Letta laid down his giant cigarette in a large glass ashtray and then rose from the desk. He walked over to an overburdened bookcase and started running his finger along the spines. After he had selected three or four books, he handed them to Scamarcio and said, 'You can have these on loan — make sure you read them all.' Scamarcio wondered if he was going to ask him to prepare an essay. He didn't even have the chance to scan the titles before the professor said, 'I'll talk you through the basics.' He gestured to the books. 'They should provide you with a bit more colour, once you've got a handle on it all.'

Scamarcio nodded.

'You heard of P2?'

'Yes.'

'Well, not everyone has, so you already have a head start. You heard of Operation Gladio?'

'A little bit.'

'OK. You know what happened to that poor sod they named the square after down there?' He gestured to the window behind where Scamarcio was sitting, the piazza he had crossed on his way into the university.

'Well, just the nuts and bolts, really.'

'That's good. That's better than the millions of your peers who spend their days trying to get onto *Big Brother* or squeeze into a fig leaf so they can spin an oversized roulette wheel and suck Massimo Bidello's cock.' He paused for a moment. 'In all this, you've got to understand one thing: during the 1970s the Americans were shitting themselves, really shitting themselves.' He enunciated the syllables, taking them one at a time. 'Suddenly, thanks to prime minister Moro and his Historic Compromise, they had the terrifying prospect of the communists in government and the loss of all their bases — they were going to be kicked out of the Med. On the day of Moro's kidnapping, the most important members of P2 met in the Hotel Excelsior here in Rome, and, as he came out, their head honcho, Gelli, was heard saying, "The most difficult part is done." You know what he was talking about?'

'The kidnapping of Moro?'

'Chilling, isn't it?' Letta didn't stop to let him answer. 'You know where the Excelsior is?'

'Vaguely.'

'It's just a stone's throw from the US embassy. That tell you anything?' Again, he didn't seem interested in Scamarcio's response. 'The Americans were all over the Moro kidnapping — all over it. We were supposed to think the Red Brigades had taken him, but the Red Brigades had been infiltrated by the CIA. Moro knew this, and had voiced his concerns to colleagues. Moro had also spoken about the existence of Operation Gladio many years before it was officially revealed in 1991.'

'I'm not clear on Gladio.'

'It was what they called a "stay behind" operation, a secret NATO resistance network trained to swing into action in the event of an Eastern Bloc invasion of Italy, or communist subversion at home. The network had been set up immediately after the war in a secret agreement between our military intelligence and the CIA. Gladio members were right wing — very right wing — and a lot of your P2 clowns were well into it. The two groups fitted together hand in glove. So our little Gladio soldiers have fun running around the countryside, reliving their childhood fantasies. They're trained for information gathering, sabotage, communications, and in helping key personnel escape from enemy-controlled territory. They leave weapons dumps all over the place, for use in the event of a Soviet invasion. That ammo then turns up years later in odd places — some of it goes missing.' He paused for breath. 'The whole tea party was in very large part controlled and financed by the CIA.'

'Just inside Italy?'

'No, similar networks had been set up in a lot of Western European countries. At some point, though, the focus shifted more from worrying about a marauding Soviet army to dealing with the communist threat at home. There were a few countries where the left appeared to be gaining ground, and these needed to be dealt with: first and foremost, Italy. So here you saw the kidnapping of Moro, and a wave of bombings killing hundreds that, more often than not, were said to be carried out by leftists. Similar attacks happened in Germany and Belgium. All forms of urban terrorism were used, most often by neo-fascists posing as leftists.'

'What were they trying to achieve?'

'It was simple. They wanted to terrify the public, polarise public opinion, and destroy support for left-wing political movements — the whole thing came to be known as the "strategy of tension".'

'And did it work?'

Letta threw up his hands. 'Of course it worked! Western Europe didn't go Red, did it? The policies followed by NATO countries soon fell into line with the desired Anglo-American trajectory.'

'And where does Poland fit in?'

'It's the same deal. Gladio, the CIA, and your P2 clowns

were funding the Polish shipworkers' union, Solidarity, through the Vatican Bank. Why? Not because they suddenly loved trade unionists, but because they saw that it could spell the end of the Soviet empire. And whose money were they using to keep Solidarity alive? The Americans were digging deep as usual, but you also need to look to the new Polish pope in the Vatican. The Vatican Bank was the main supply line — it provided the secret conduit. They were, of course, vehemently anti-communist. The teachings of Marx threatened their very existence.'

'So you think this is where my dead American might fit in?'

'Possibly.'

'And Abbiati?'

'You tell me. I don't know anything about his role at the Vatican.'

It seemed to be a question, but Scamarcio would not be drawn — he wanted to keep what little he knew to himself for now. 'I can't see any connection with the Vatican Bank as yet,' he lied.

'You mentioned Nicaragua? Your dead American was active there?'

'Yes.'

'That's a slightly different scene. I'm not sure about the role of Gelli and his cronies; I'm not clear on whether the Vatican would have been involved. There are those, however, who claim that once the Vatican went to bed with the CIA over Poland, they'd made a pact with the devil; after that, the Americans could force them to do all sorts of things.'

'So, for you, the connection that is clearest is the Polish one, not Latin America?'

'If you're talking about a link with the Vatican, then yes.'

Letta paused for a moment, stopping to wave a finger at Scamarcio. 'Don't forget, though, that P2 had branches in several Latin American countries: Argentina, Venezuela, and Paraguay, to name a few. But I'd say Poland is your best bet. Maybe something went down there — maybe your dead American was the settling of an old score of some kind?'

'Were P2 ever involved in the Nicaraguan war?'

'There's evidence of *Argentine* involvement, and P2 *were* tight with Peron. There's some other thing niggling at me, too — I think maybe with Banco Ambrosiano in Managua, but I'd need to look into that.'

Scamarcio nodded. Managua was the capital of Nicaragua. If Banco Ambrosiano was there, that brought Calvi back into the circle, and possibly the Vatican, too.

'Who suffered most from what P2 and Gladio were up to? Would there be people around with scores to settle?' he asked.

Letta pushed the air out from his cheeks. 'Well, you know the left were played like puppets; they played them every which way they wanted, and that must have hurt. Then there are the victims of the bombing campaigns waged here: the dead of Turin, Piazza Fontana, Bologna. Those attacks ruined a lot of lives, destroyed a lot of families. There could be people out there with grudges, but going as far as to murder a CIA guy? It seems far-fetched, and we're not even clear on his involvement.'

'The mafia?'

'Well, that was what did for Calvi, wasn't it? How that fits in with your dead American, I don't know. In some ways, the possibilities are infinite.' He paused for a beat. 'I don't envy you.'

Scamarcio felt suddenly tired, overwhelmed by the information he had been given, no longer sure whether it was going to provide him with greater clarity. He handed the professor his card, and left.

As Scamarcio was crossing the square, his mobile rang. He pushed the heavy books under one arm and fumbled for the phone in his pocket. When he finally had it in his grip, he saw Letta's name flash up. Scamarcio turned back towards the university, and thought he could see the professor standing at his window, looking down, but there was too much sunlight to be certain.

'Listen, I just thought of something. Might not mean anything, but maybe you should give it a quick look.'

'OK ...'

'Actually, there is a Vatican connection with Nicaragua, besides the Ambrosiano thing. Nothing cloak and dagger, but, in March 1983, Pope John Paul II paid a visit there.'

'He did?'

'It ended up proving quite significant in the course of the Civil War because of the controversy it caused.'

'How so?'

'In his speech, the pope stressed the importance of church unity as the best way of preventing Nicaragua — and I quote — "from being corrupted by Godless communism". Words like that caused a big rift between the Sandinistas and the many Nicaraguan Catholics who, up until then, had been supporting them. The Contras, of course, used it to lend themselves moral legitimacy.'

Scamarcio remained silent, his mind turning on it all. He wasn't quite sure how it helped him, or if it helped him.

'I'll let you know about the Ambrosiano thing,' said Letta.

Scamarcio thanked him and hung up. He felt like he was digging in a massive field. He needed to narrow the search, make a choice, and see where it took him.

What had Carter been doing in Poland and then Nicaragua? Helping fund the anti-communists, helping bring the money and guns in? And, more importantly, what business had drawn him to Rome? Had he come to look up old friends, or old enemies? And then there was Abbiati. He was probably old enough to have lived through the paranoia of the Cold War, to have shared the fear inside the Vatican of a growing global movement that threatened the very existence of the Church. Had he got caught up in the fight — made a kind of Faustian pact with the Gladio faction, of which Carter was a part, that had now come back to haunt him? As Letta had said, Scamarcio felt that the possible scenarios were infinite, that he was trying to pin down clouds. Yet again, he wished he'd been on a different shift when they'd pulled the American from under the bridge.

There was a decent-looking café at the edge of the square, so Scamarcio decided to stop for a coffee in the hope that it might help focus his mind. The place was empty, and that day's *La Stampa*, along with an empty fag packet, had been discarded on a greasy table. He flicked through the news pages, and as he did so he noticed an item about how the mayor of a major northern town had just donated a sizeable chunk of his wealth to a leading children's charity, much to the distress of his family. The story brought a smile to Scamarcio's lips, as he at once recognised the hand of his father's old lieutenant, Piocosta. The faithful Piocosta had been helping him bring last summer's case to a satisfying conclusion in a way the judges never would.

The barista handed Scamarcio his cappuccino, and he took a sip — the milk was just the right temperature. A thought was beginning to form, tantalising and exciting, but instinctively unwelcome, like the unexpected promise of extra-marital sex or the backstreet aroma of hash when you were trying to quit.

He sighed. He'd been coming at this from the wrong angle. Sure, he didn't have contacts *inside* the Vatican, but if there was one man who could crack this thing wide open from the *outside*, it would be Piocosta. It would bloody well have to be him, with his tentacles in all the hidden corridors and back offices of power, his shifty-eyed friendships with the white-collar murderers and street-gang saints. Scamarcio pulled out his mobile and looked at it, and then put it back in his pocket.

'You got a phone I could use?' he asked the barista. 'I'm out of battery, and I've got a bit of a family crisis to deal with. It's just a local call.'

'No problem.' The man laid down his cloth and led him to a tiny office to the left of the bar. He gestured to a wide, old desk, where Scamarcio spotted a battered white cordless phone amidst some untidy piles of paperwork.

'I'll just be one minute,' he said.

The guy nodded and left him to it. *Far too trusting,* thought Scamarcio.

He quickly glanced behind him to make sure he was alone, and then punched in Piocosta's number. The old man picked up immediately, but said nothing, as Scamarcio knew he would.

'It's me — Leo.'

'Leo, my boy! How are you? Got a case on?'

Piocosta always asked this, as though Scamarcio spent a large part of his time just sitting around, waiting for crime to happen. That might be true in some European squad rooms — but Piocosta, of all people, had to know that the killing in Rome never stopped.

'I just wanted to thank you for putting the fear up a certain northern mayor. I've just seen the story in *La Stampa*.'

Piocosta laughed. 'Oh, I enjoyed that one. How I enjoyed it. I almost think it should be me thanking you.'

Scamarcio fell silent for a moment, trying to work out what he was going to say next. But, as usual, Piocosta was already one step ahead. 'Why do I get the feeling this isn't just a courtesy call?'

Scamarcio smiled, forgetting that the old man couldn't see him. 'Can you meet me in thirty minutes? I've got something to ask you.'

'I look forward to it.'

Scamarcio replaced the receiver, wiping the sweat from his palm. He felt like a recovering addict who'd just scored. Whatever answers Piocosta might be able to provide, he knew they wouldn't come cheap.

15

THE OLD MAN was sitting up at the bar when Scamarcio walked in, giving his oblivious customers the once-over. There was a large glass of orange Crodino before him, along with several small bowls of snacks. A couple of mobile phones were laid out alongside — one silver, one black. As usual, he was wearing his blue beret.

'Leo, my boy!' He jumped down from his bar stool like a man half his age, and embraced Scamarcio in an iron grip. 'Come through, come through.'

He collected the phones from the counter, slipping them into his jacket pocket by sleight of hand, like a pickpocket. Then he led the way through the bar to the huge kitchen out back.

None of his lieutenants seemed to be around, and Scamarcio hoped it would just be the two of them.

'You eaten?'

Scamarcio checked his watch. 'No, not yet.'

'Chiara's made pumpkin ravioli and roast wild boar with rosemary potatoes. Sound good?'

'Definitely.'

Piocosta nodded as if he'd just concluded a deal. 'Leo's here, food for two,' he hollered through the hatch at the wide old woman toiling out back.

'Take a seat — don't stand on ceremony.'

Scamarcio drew out an old wooden chair, and Piocosta parked himself next to him at the head of the table.

'You want me to tell you how it went down?' There was a sparkle in the old man's eyes.

'With the mayor?'

'Yeah, the mayor.'

Scamarcio sighed and then smiled. 'I've got a feeling you're going to tell me, whether I want to hear it or not.'

'It's too good Leo, too good!' Piocosta slapped a palm on the table. 'I used his granddaughters, didn't I? I hit him where it hurt.'

Scamarcio felt a sudden stab of panic. 'Used them how, exactly?'

'I just let it be known that they were in for the same treatment he'd meted out to those foster kids. I've never seen a man open his chequebook so fast.' He shook his head in disgust. 'Obviously, we'd never have touched a hair on their heads, but how was he to know that?' He looked off into the middle distance, reliving the encounter. 'In all my days, I don't think I've ever seen a man so scared. He surprised me, actually. I hadn't expected a monster like that to be so, I don't know, so *human.*'

'Two million euro is quite a donation.'

'Oh yeah, Leo, that it is.'

Chiara arrived with their first course, and placed the food proudly in front of them. She ruffled Scamarcio's hair as if he were a three-year-old. 'Good to see you, boy.'

Piocosta's slightly younger sister had known Scamarcio since he was a toddler, but they hadn't seen each other much in recent years. He had some jumpy memories of playing trains with her in a sun-dappled garden somewhere down south when his mother was still well.

'And you, Chiara. This looks good.'

'So it does,' said Piocosta. 'What a wonder.'

She threw her brother a 'don't mess with me' look, and shuffled back to the kitchen once more.

'Women, you can never pay them a compliment,' Piocosta muttered, tucking into his food. 'So, why did you want to see me? It obviously wasn't just to pat me on the back for a job well done.'

'I wanted to ask you something.'

'Yeah, you said.'

'You know how the Magliana used to do the dirty work for P2?'

'Hmmm ...'

Piocosta's eyes narrowed. They seemed to be telling Scamarcio that they didn't like where this was heading, but he pressed on anyway. 'So who are the hired hands now? For the new cabal, for P3 or P4, or whatever they call themselves these days?'

'The *new cabal*, Leo? You sound like one of those crackpot conspiracy theorists.'

'You know what I'm talking about — the people who count, the people with money. No doubt they've formed themselves into another tidy club.'

Piocosta fell silent for a moment. After a while, he said, 'There's no new lodge, if that's what you mean, not after all that fuss.'

'Really?'

'Really.'

'I don't believe you.'

'Why would I lie?'

'You'd have your reasons, I'm sure.'

After they'd eaten in silence for a while, the old man said, 'Really, Leo, I've got no fucking idea what you're on about. Not everything's a conspiracy. You need to get yourself a wife, have some kids.'

He got up from the table and switched on a huge widescreen TV mounted to the wall. 'I can never find the bastard remote.' He stretched out an arm and turned up the sound manually. It was now very loud — almost too much for Scamarcio to take. They were showing a football match, and the commentators were already shouting anyway.

The old man resumed his place at the table, and took a sip of red wine from a glass jug that Chiara had placed there. Almost as a by-the-by, he muttered bitterly, 'The Cappadona are so busy these days. Those bastards have their fingers in almost every pie in this shithole of a city. Donato's turned them into a veritable corporation.'

Scamarcio had to struggle to make out the words amidst the din, but their significance was not lost on him. He smiled, and took a bite of the ravioli. 'I wonder if they know anything about a dead body strung up under a bridge this week.'

Piocosta raised an eyebrow, and took a long gulp of wine.

Eventually, he said, 'We're going to need to talk about that other thing, Leo — that thing you owe me — and we're going to need to talk soon.'

The food suddenly felt heavy in Scamarcio's stomach, but he forced his mouth into a smile, and said, 'Understood.'

16

SCAMARCIO TOOK A WALK out by the river to clear his head and digest his meeting with Piocosta. A homeless man was going through some bins, hurriedly sorting through plastic and cardboard, his hands burrowing deeper and deeper into the rubbish. There was something furtive and panicked about his movements, and Scamarcio found himself hoping that the stranger was mentally ill rather than famished. Real hunger felt like too much of an obscenity in 21st-century Italy — a G8 country, after all. As he drew closer, he saw that the man was wearing a smart-looking jacket, and when he passed, he noticed the trademark Aspesi label embroidered boastfully into the back panel. Something about this chilled him. Had this man been enjoying a very different kind of life just a few months before? Scamarcio retraced his steps, and handed the poor fellow a ten-euro note. The man took it without looking up, stuffing it into his trouser pocket before resuming his trawl of the dustbins.

Scamarcio walked on, the sand and gravel crunching beneath his feet, the ducks fretting at the water's edge. His mind turned on his mounting debt to Piocosta. Whatever it was he was going to ask of Scamarcio, he hoped he could handle it with minimal consequences, and minimal damage. That was the risk with Piocosta. Yet he felt he had to pay the price. Without Piocosta, it would take weeks, if not months, to come by the information he needed, and that was time he didn't have right now. He needed this case off his slate so he could move onto something simpler.

His phone buzzed in his pocket, and, when he pulled it out, a number came up that he didn't recognise.

'I just wanted to apologise for yesterday,' said a nervous voice.

'Sorry — who is this?'

'We met at the café — I had to leave quickly.'

'Oh, I see,' said Scamarcio, immediately glad of the decision he'd made to leave his card.

'Sometimes the fear gets the better of me.'

'I understand,' said Scamarcio, not really feeling that he did.

'I lead a simple life; I try to keep a low profile, out of sight. Meeting with you felt like going above the parapet.'

Scamarcio fell silent for a moment, hoping to steer the strange scholar back on track. Eventually, he asked, 'How can I help you, sir? Are you in any kind of danger?'

The old man sighed. 'Nothing's happened since we met — although it's probably only a matter of time.'

Was the man paranoid, or was there some basis to these fears? A brief silence followed before the scholar said, 'You were asking me why they'd want to get at Abbiati.'

'That seems like the key question.'

'It is.'

The scholar fell silent again, and Scamarcio hoped he wasn't going to shut down on him once more. 'So?'

'Abbiati was the lynchpin.'

'The lynchpin?'

'The keeper of secrets — he knew it all, going back forty years.'

'You told me yesterday that he was an honest man, all for transparency.'

'That he was.'

'I don't quite follow.'

'If you think of the Vatican Bank as being like any ordinary bank, he was the equivalent of the chief bookkeeper, the finance manager. But unlike a lot of finance managers these days, he could be persuaded to reveal where the bodies were buried; he could show you the grey areas in the profit-and-loss statements. He wasn't interested in kickbacks. He grew up in poverty, and never developed a taste for the high life.'

Scamarcio was struggling to process it all. 'So the anti-reformers, the Opus Dei faction, were worried he'd spill the beans about something?'

'You've got it.'

'What did he have on them?'

'A lot.'

'But why keep this knowledge secret all these years? Why would he respond to questions only now, after so many decades?'

The old man laughed, but it turned into a hacking cough, and he lost control of it for a while. When he'd finally got his breath back, he said, 'Well, there's the rub. Until last month, no one had bothered to ask him. He's a quiet figure, you see; he stays in the shadows. People tend not to notice him. And, until now, not many people had got their heads around the way the IOR is structured, who does what.'

Scamarcio looked out across the water, trying to take it all in. He spotted a few used needles by the water's edge, a child's sock, a discarded tampon. He couldn't see any masonry rubble.

After a few moments, he asked, 'So Abbiati knew some dark secrets?'

'Yes, Detective — dark enough to have him killed.'

17

WHILE HE WAS TAKING the stairs to the squad room, Scamarcio's phone rang once more.

As if to confirm his position as prize asset, Piocosta grunted, 'Your body — Ponte Sant'Angelo, American, right?'

Scamarcio immediately swung back the way he had come, and quickly exited HQ, making for a dingy bar at the end of the street that his colleagues always avoided because the brioche tasted plastic. He didn't want any of them to have any inkling of who he might be talking to.

'Right,' he replied, trying to get his breath back.

'Donato and his dogs,' said the old man.

So Piocosta *was* right — the Cappadona were involved.

'Like you said.'

'Like I said,' said Piocosta with a hint of pride.

'Who were they working for?'

'You're supposed to look to the dead cardinal, apparently.'

'Abbiati?'

'He's the only dead cardinal in town.'

'He sent in the Cappadona?'

Piocosta sighed. 'Leo — that's all I got for you. Like I said, we need to talk about that other thing.'

Scamarcio realised that the old man was going to drip-feed him information from now on, whether he had it or not. It would be like this until their debt was settled.

'OK, let me know when.'

'I'll call you in a couple of days.'

Scamarcio took a breath and said, 'Thanks for the fast work.'

He had expected a 'You bet' or 'Always', but the line just went dead.

It was all too opaque: either Abbiati and Carter had been murdered by the Cappadona at the behest of an unknown entity, or Abbiati had sent the Cappadona to kill Carter, but had then been killed himself. But what business could Abbiati have with the Cappadona? And why would someone like Abbiati want the American dead? Was this strangely symbolic murder somehow a warning to others? This picture of Abbiati as a killer was so very different from the portrait the strange Vatican scholar had painted that Scamarcio decided the first option was more likely — that both Abbiati and Carter had been murdered by the Cappadona, and that someone else was pulling the strings. If only Piocosta had been willing to give him more. The prospect of their next meeting worried Scamarcio, but he needed to push things along; otherwise there would be paralysis in their communications.

He spun through the options in his head: it was clear that his investigation was never going to get properly inside the Vatican; interviews within those walls would be out of the question. On the other hand, access to the Cappadona might not prove quite so impossible. He wondered if there was someone in the Organised Crime Team who could help him. He wanted to keep his use of Piocosta to a minimum if he could.

The squad room was busy when he walked in — a weary group of his colleagues was huddled around the widescreen computer display while Garramone was pointing with a pencil at a street view of somewhere in Parioli, barking orders about a body that was not to be removed. Rather than call someone in Organised Crime with this hubbub going on in the background, Scamarcio took the stairs down to the second floor to see if he could find anyone who might have an in with the Cappadona.

He lit a cigarette on the way down, hoping it wouldn't trigger the smoke detectors, and then figured that, due to the budget tightening, they probably hadn't been checked for months anyway. When he entered the long, open-plan offices of OC, there wasn't a single officer in sight. He wondered what major event could be going down on a Wednesday afternoon to have emptied the place so thoroughly. Then he spotted Pesaro, huddled over his desk in the far corner, scribbling furiously.

'Someone died?' shouted Scamarcio.

Pesaro looked up, blinking a bit. He yawned, and stuffed the pen he had been using behind his ear. Then he leant back in his chair and straightened his spine before folding his arms behind his head.

'Five, to be precise, in the middle of a busy shopping street; there's a bit of a tit for tat going on between the 'ndrangheta and the Sicilians right now.' Scamarcio thought of Piocosta, wondering what he had been up to, whether he'd try to drag him right into it.

'That's where your boys are?'

Pesaro yawned again. 'Not all of them. We've got a drugs bust in Testaccio — it's been in the works for a while.'

Scamarcio slumped into the chair opposite Pesaro's over-burdened desk. 'You got five minutes?'

'Sure. You're the only human being I've seen all day.'

Pesaro's tiredness was infectious. Scamarcio tried to stifle a yawn, but didn't quite manage it.

'Garramone keeping you up late?'

Scamarcio rolled his eyes. 'You know what it's like — he whistles, I run.'

Pesaro yawned for a third time. 'Thank yourself lucky you're not down here. It's a fucking nightmare. Sometimes I think we should stop locking up the old bastards and let the calm return — we could cut ourselves a break.'

They both fell silent for a moment, pondering the new reality.

'Anyway, what can I do you for? I take it you're not angling for a transfer?'

Scamarcio smiled. 'Not just yet.' He paused for a beat. 'Do you have many dealings with the Cappadona? They've been mentioned in connection with a case I'm on, and I need a way of establishing whether they were involved.'

Pesaro removed the pen from behind his ear and used it to scratch at the base of his neck. He was a good-looking guy with determined blue eyes and wavy, almost shoulder-length dark hair. Scamarcio guessed that he was around 35 and that he had his heart set on the top job one day.

'What's your case?' asked Pesaro, locking eye contact.

'Dead American found hanging under the Ponte Sant'Angelo, trussed up to look just like the Calvi suicide.'

'Roberto Calvi?'

'Yep.'

'That's a weird one — that was years ago.'

'Yeah, I'm struggling to work out the connection.'

'And someone claims the Cappadona had a hand in it?'

Scamarcio nodded.

Pesaro started drumming his desk with the pen, his eyes off to one side, thinking something through. Eventually, he said, 'The word is that the Cappadona do the dirty work for some very powerful people — the kind of gentlemen who are excellent at keeping their hands clean.'

Scamarcio got the message: Italy's long history of political corruption and its high-profile attempt to clean up government in the 1990s had been dubbed the 'Clean Hands' affair.

Pesaro locked eye contact once more. 'Unfortunately for you, the Cappadona have been quiet of late, and we're not foreseeing any arrests.'

'None at all?'

'Zero.'

'I need information from them about the Ponte Sant'Angelo death — that, and nothing more.'

Pesaro was shaking his head slowly. He tut-tutted, and glanced down at his paperwork. 'I'd help you if I could, Scamarcio, but I just can't think of a handle — we don't have a grass in there right now.' He fell silent for a moment. 'That could change of course — it's a fluid situation.'

Scamarcio felt a hard knot of frustration in his chest. This wasn't good enough. He needed more.

Pesaro was studying him closely now, and Scamarcio had the sense that he was weighing up the potential usefulness of helping him. Perhaps he had heard the ridiculous gossip that Scamarcio was a supposed favourite of Garramone. Maybe he was thinking that doing a favour for someone like him couldn't hurt.

Scamarcio figured that he had guessed correctly when Pesaro finally laid down his pen and rubbed at his temples, as if a new idea had just come to him.

'There might be someone — but he's a long shot, and not exactly what I'd call a prize asset.'

'Go on.'

'We didn't know it when we took him in yesterday, but we've come to suspect he's one of their errand boys — small time, small fry. Goes by the name of Giacomo Pozzi. He could be leant on to provide information, but I should warn you that the charges facing him aren't steep. He probably won't see the point of a trade-off — if he *is* clan, Pozzi will know better than most that the Cappadona take no prisoners. Whatever you can offer, it probably won't feel like enough.'

'I'll take my chances,' said Scamarcio.

Pesaro nodded. 'Let's take a trip to the cells, then — all this paperwork was doing my head in anyway.'

Scamarcio smiled behind his retreating back. Pesaro would go far.

18

Pozzi was younger than Scamarcio had expected — he wouldn't have put him at much over twenty. He was short and fat, and his dark hair was already thinning on top. His brown eyes were bruised with tiredness, and it looked as if he hadn't had a shave in a long time.

Pesaro made the introductions. When he got to the part about Scamarcio needing help with a case, Pozzi rolled his eyes and leant back in his chair, his arms barred across his chest.

'You fuckers think I was born yesterday?' he said. The accent was pure Roman.

'No,' replied Scamarcio.

'So why do you think I would be so stupid as to turn grass?'

'There's nothing stupid about it.'

'There is from where I'm fucking sitting.'

Scamarcio didn't want Pesaro in the room for what was to follow. So he turned in his chair and said, 'Listen, I can take this from here. I don't want to take up any more of your time.'

Pesaro seemed unsure for a moment, but then he nodded and got up from his seat. 'You know where I am if you need me.'

Scamarcio thanked him. Once Pesaro had left, Scamarcio noticed a sudden stench of sweat in the room, and wondered what was bothering Pozzi so much. At the end of the day, he couldn't force him to turn grass. It would be his choice; it was under his control. But maybe something was preventing Pozzi from seeing it that way. Whatever that something was, Scamarcio needed to identify it — and quickly.

'So, Pozzi, what's your story? How did you end up with the Cappadona?' He decided to play this as if it were a given.

Pozzi looked away, refusing to make eye contact. After a beat, he said, 'Why the fuck do you think I'd tell *you*?' Then, after another pause, 'Anyway, who said I'm with anyone?'

Scamarcio tried not to appear too interested. He yawned, and scratched at an eyebrow. 'My colleagues know who you work for, Pozzi — you can save your breath.'

Pozzi sighed heavily, his arms still barred across his chest. 'You people don't understand shit. You've got no idea.'

'Enlighten me, then.'

'What's the point? There's no point to any of this shit.' He swept a flabby arm across the room.

'For someone so young, you seem to have given up on life, Pozzi.'

Pozzi fixed his gaze on Scamarcio. The boy's eyes were watery and red-rimmed. 'That's where you're wrong. It's life that has given up on *me*.' He dug his fingers into his chest.

Scamarcio laughed. 'When you get to my age, you realise that it doesn't work like that.'

'Oh yeah? Well, that sounds like a crock of shit.'

'Pozzi, if you're going to get anywhere, you need to change your attitude. Life doesn't come to you — you go to it. If you think you're going to build a career inside the Cappadona, you're very much mistaken. What Pesaro won't have told you is that their days are numbered — they're soon to become a page in history, nothing more. If you stay with that bunch of chimps, it won't be long before you wind up back in here, but the next time you'll be looking at decades, not days.'

'Bullshit.'

'I don't care whether you believe me or not, but the fact is that once you get out of here and go back to running errands for those goons, the best outcome you can hope for is jail. The police are going to raid the Cappadona, there's going to be a massacre, and many of your associates will die. If you survive that, then you'll kiss the ground of your 4-by-3 cell. Prison will seem like a golden ticket after that bloodbath.'

'You're just making this up.'

'Why would I bother?'

'You've got your agenda, I'm sure.'

Scamarcio shook his head. 'It's no bullshit, Pozzi. And if I were you, I'd listen.' He paused for a moment and then said, 'But you're right when you say I've got an agenda.'

Pozzi's eyes narrowed.

Scamarcio tried to keep his tone neutral. 'Like I say, there are dark days ahead. There's going to be heavy-duty bloodshed, and I need to make sure that you stay out of the line of fire. You have to believe me on this — it's your life at stake.'

Pozzi remained silent for a while, seemingly thinking it through, and then he turned slightly pale. Eventually, he asked, 'If it is true, then why are you telling me this? Why do you want to protect *me*?'

Scamarcio got up and started pacing the room.

'Two reasons.' He used his fingers to list them: 'One: I badly need your help with a case; two: something about you reminds me of myself when I was your age. I could easily have gone the same way — the same problems were there, the same temptations, but I chose a different path, and I thank God every day that I did. I look at you Pozzi and I see myself and, call me stupid if you will, but if I can make you see the error of your ways, then this day will be one of the few that might actually have been worth something.'

The room fell silent, and all Scamarcio could hear was the minute hand of the plastic wall clock, marking out the void between them. Then, to Scamarcio's surprise, Pozzi's shoulders started to heave and he slumped forward, his head on the table. Scamarcio realised that the young man was sobbing, and it took his breath away for a moment. He had considered his own performance a tad amateurish, but it seemed it was working better than he could have imagined. Something about this made him feel extremely guilty.

Through the sobs, Pozzi said, 'You're that guy, aren't you? The one they wrote about last year — the cop from the 'ndrangheta family?'

Scamarcio was wrong-footed for a few moments, but when he'd pulled his thoughts together he said, 'Yes, that's me. How did you know?'

'I dunno, I just put it together. I remember your photograph from the magazines,' Pozzi mumbled through his tears.

Scamarcio wanted to steer things back on track and get to the bottom of what was upsetting the boy so much.

He tried again, more softly this time. 'So, Pozzi, what's your story? How did you wind up with the clan?'

Pozzi took a few breaths and then wiped his face with a dirty sleeve. 'It started when my mum got ill — she has lung cancer, and I couldn't stand hearing the coughing any more. So I'd go out at night to try and find something to keep me busy. I wasn't a hit with the girls, so that wasn't an option. I applied for a job in McDonalds, but they didn't want me. Then this friend of mine said he knew some people who needed work done on the quiet, and that he could hook me up if I wanted, and that the pay would be good. Me and my mum needed the cash — it'd been tough since my dad left, and I thought if I could bring some extra money in, it would ease the stress, might help her feel better, you know?'

Scamarcio felt ashamed. He hadn't been expecting this.

'So it started out as little jobs — deliver this package here, collect that parcel from there. At the end of my deliveries I'd get 100 euro, cash in hand. I was able to buy my mum flowers, chocolates. I got her room painted. It was good to see her smile after so long. After a while, the small deliveries became a bit bigger

— crates of stuff, longer distances — and they gave me a van. The money got better, too. It's been like that for the last six months. Things were going well until you bastards pulled me in.'

Was he really going to throw this kid to the lions? That was what he'd be doing if he sent him back on the streets as an informant.

Means to an end ... that morality nightmare seemed to come up on every single case these days. It never used to be like that, he reflected. What had changed?

He dragged his focus back to the interview room and the crying boy. He gently drew out a seat in front of the lad, and laid a hand on his arm. Maybe Scamarcio could have a word with Garramone — get the boy and his mother relocated somewhere if it all went to the wall. Get them a new life. He'd started on this strategy, so he had to finish it. It would be the quickest way of breaking this case and, besides, maybe his earlier spiel about helping Pozzi free himself from the clan hadn't been so far from the truth, after all.

'Listen, Pozzi, I'm sorry to have upset you. I'm going to give you some advice now. What I think you need to do is speak to Pesaro once more. You need to let him believe that you're much better integrated into the Cappadona than he realises. Let him think you have a much more important role — that you have information that he needs. That is the only way to save your skin in the days to come when war breaks out between the police and the clan.'

'But I'm just their delivery boy.'

'Tell Pesaro that you know they're building up their heroin operation; that they have gone into business with gangs from Albania; that shipments are coming in off the coast of Puglia, near Bari, and are being brought to Rome. That's the kind of information he'll be looking for.'

'But I don't know if any of that stuff is true.'

Scamarcio shook his head. 'It doesn't matter, Pozzi. People often believe what they want to believe.'

'What'll happen to me once I tell him?'

'My guess is that Pesaro will ask you to inform on the clan. He'll make you his super-grass. And, believe me, if he does that, your prospects are brighter than they ever were.'

Pozzi's hands were shaking slightly. 'But Jesus!' He paused for a moment, processing it all, and then ran a sweaty hand through his hair. 'If they find out, they'll kill me.'

Scamarcio took both his hands and placed them on the desk to steady them. 'Pozzi, look into my eyes. You need to remember two things. One: their days are numbered; they won't have time to kill you, because we'll get to them first. And two: you're not providing actual information, so you're not really hurting them.'

'But what if any of that stuff just happens to be true?'

Scamarcio suddenly wondered if Pozzi really did know more than he was letting on. 'Do you think it might be?'

Pozzi threw up his hands in the air. 'Fuck, I don't know.'

'We'll have your back, Pozzi, and, like I said, there'll be no time for them to act, as we'll raid them first.'

Pozzi hung his head, defeated, exhausted. Eventually, he nodded. 'So what happens now?'

'I'm going to have a word with Pesaro, and then you need to tell him the things we just discussed. But before I do that, I'm going to get you a mobile phone so we can keep in touch when you're out of here. OK?'

Pozzi just nodded.

'I'll wait for you on the corner of Via San Vitale, and hand you that phone. Understand?'

Pozzi nodded again.

'Don't mention the phone to Pesaro, OK? It's very important for your own security.'

Pozzi remained mute.

'Before I go, there's one other thing I need to ask. Do a dead American and the Ponte Sant'Angelo mean anything to you?'

Pozzi looked bewildered and shook his head slowly. 'No. Should it? Should it mean something?' His voice was becoming panicky now, and he reminded Scamarcio of a character in a Kafka novel — the answers forever eluding him, just out of reach.

'No, it's OK. It's not a big deal.' Scamarcio paused for a beat. 'And, Pozzi, you've done a good thing here today. You've put your life back on track; you've been proactive. Your mum will thank you for it. It will mean more to her than a box of chocolates or a bunch of flowers ever could.'

Scamarcio hated himself before the words had even left his mouth. Once again, he told himself that maybe they could swing it for Pozzi. But, on reflection, he hated himself for that, too.

19

SCAMARCIO TOOK THE STAIRS back to Pesaro's floor. He was glad to see that the place was still empty and that there were no senior officers around who might interfere with what he had in mind.

Pesaro looked up from his paperwork.

'Get lucky?'

'Not bad, not bad.'

Scamarcio slumped down in the chair opposite. 'Listen, Pesaro, I'll cut to the chase — that guy's definitely Cappadona, and I think you've underestimated him.'

'What?'

'Well, to me he seems much bigger than a small-time errand boy. Some things came out that makes me believe he's been promoted, and that he knows a lot more than you realised.'

'Like what?' Pesaro's eyes were boring into him like lasers now.

'I think I should leave it to him to tell you. I don't want to get it wrong, as I'm not on top of the drugs scene, but I reckon you might have a gold mine there.'

'A gold mine?' Pesaro started drumming his pen on the desk. Scamarcio saw the ambition spark and flare in those steely eyes.

'Of course, it depends on whether you guys are interested in banging the Cappadona to rights long term, if it's on your agenda. But I think you could end up with some solid steers. You've been good to me today, so I feel it's only fair to share. It could be a career-maker — you need to know that.'

Pesaro scratched at his eyebrow with the pen. 'You sure?'

'My instincts are singing.'

Pesaro fell silent for a few beats. 'I don't understand how we could have missed this' he said. Then, all at once, he was up from the desk, puffing the air out from his cheeks, like a boxer about to go ten rounds in the ring. He reached across his papers to shake Scamarcio's hand. 'But thank you, Leo, I'll look into it.'

Scamarcio shrugged. 'It was you who did me the favour. Let me know how it pans out. I'm curious.'

Pesaro was already heading for the door, but turned to shout behind him, 'You bet. I'll give you a call once I've grilled the fucker.'

Scamarcio smiled and helped himself to a chocolate from a box on Pesaro's desk.

Back in the squad room, Garramone and his murder team had disbanded, and Scamarcio was able to work in peace. He checked a few emails and then headed to the tech-supply room down the hall, where he signed out a mobile phone and sim card he could give Pozzi. He returned to his desk, and entered the number into his BlackBerry.

He reckoned Pesaro's call would come in about half an hour — he wouldn't be able to contain himself. In the meantime, Scamarcio decided to busy himself with one of Professor Letta's tomes. But he hadn't got much beyond page 10 of a very dry book on the Solidarity movement before the phone rang and the Organised Crime number flashed up.

'Pesaro?'

'Shit, you were right Leo. Jesus, were you *right*. He's a fucking treasure trove.'

'I told you.'

'I just don't understand why we didn't see it earlier.'

'Well, sometimes it takes an outsider. Maybe you guys had written him off, and you're all so fucking busy ...'

Pesaro jumped in before he could finish. 'That's it, that's it, there's never the time anymore. Anyway, thanks, man. I'm turning him back out ASAP.'

'When do you think he'll be going?'

'I'm getting the paperwork done now — I'm hoping it should just be an hour or two.'

'Well, good luck, Pesaro. I hope it works out.'

'Thanks, Scamarcio. I'll remember this.' He paused for a moment. 'So *did* they do that Ponte Sant'Angelo stiff?'

'No, I don't think so. But Pozzi was able to point me in another direction, which might or might not prove helpful.'

Scamarcio could tell that Pesaro wasn't really interested, that his mind was already turning on where to take this thing next. 'Glad to hear it. I'd better run. Thanks again.'

He hung up, and Scamarcio was left listening to the empty line. He replaced the receiver and turned in his seat to look down Via San Vitale. He had chosen that street to meet Pozzi because he had a good view of it from his desk and would be able to spot when the young man came out. However, it would mean having to stay put until he did, so he hoped Garramone wouldn't summon him to his office in the meantime.

He returned his attention to the book on the Solidarity movement. Reading it was like trying to sprint through glue, so he decided to flick through the index to see whether the Vatican was mentioned. In the one place it was, the author didn't really tell him any more than he already knew.

His phone rang, and when he saw Aurelia's name appear he was reminded that he hadn't called her since their head-to-head at the morgue. But it wasn't because he was avoiding her — he just simply hadn't had the time. After the visit to Letta, events had overtaken him.

'Aurelia, I was about to phone you.'

'Right,' the delivery was strangely clipped. She sounded tense and on edge.

'It's just been one of those days, you know.'

Aurelia sighed. Scamarcio found it irritating.

'Listen, Leo, I think we need to talk.'

How many times in his life had he heard that?

'Right then — where and when?'

'Bar Girasole. 9.00 pm?'

'Fine.'

'I'll see you there.'

She'd hung up, but he kept the phone to his ear anyway. It was as if his brain couldn't be bothered to react.

He turned slowly in his seat to look down Via San Vitale, and was alarmed to see Pozzi shuffling along, a blue scarf pulled up tightly around his face. Scamarcio grabbed the mobile and sprinted into the corridor, taking the stairs three at a time. This was *extremely* fast work — Pesaro definitely thought he was onto something.

Scamarcio ran out onto the street and caught up with Pozzi just as he was making the turn into Via Genova.

The air was cooler now; the first real bite of winter was on the breeze. He tapped Pozzi gently on the shoulder, but the young man jumped anyway. When he saw who it was, he glanced quickly to his right and left and then once behind him to check that they weren't being observed.

'You gave me a fright.'

'Sorry.' Scamarcio handed over the phone. 'Call me anytime you want. I've entered my number into the memory, but not my name. Don't put my name in. OK?'

'Do I look like an idiot?'

'How did it go with Pesaro?'

'All right, I think. Well, he let me out, didn't he?'

'Did you say what I told you? About the heroin?'

'Yeah, all that, and I added a few other things.'

'Like what?'

'Doesn't matter.'

Again, Scamarcio had the troubling notion that Pozzi knew more than he was letting on, that he was perhaps giving as good as he got. Was the sick mother no more than a twisted sob story?

'So, Pozzi, you remember that dead American I mentioned? The one found hanging under the Ponte Sant'Angelo a few days back?'

'What about him?'

'Well, I want you to find out about that. See if anyone knows why he was murdered.'

'Why would they?'

'Because the Cappadona were paid to kill him, and I want to find out why.'

'I'm not sure I can get that kind of information.'

'Just do your best. It's all points scored with Pesaro and his team. It's one step further to a better life for you and your mum. You understand?'

'Yeah, but why didn't Pesaro ask me about this? Why are you and he not working together? I don't get it.'

Scamarcio shook his head, like he'd heard it all before. 'Neither do I, Pozzi — neither do I. Between you and me, the department is a mess, the bureaucracy is crippling; nothing is co-ordinated. We're forced to do our jobs in this cack-handed way, and it drives us crazy.'

Pozzi nodded, uninterested, clearly desperate to get as far away from Police Headquarters as possible.

'Will you call me as soon as you hear anything?'

'I'll call you,' said the boy. The words were tired and flat. He seemed to have aged ten years since their meeting, and Scamarcio felt another pang of guilt.

Pozzi pulled up his scarf once more, covering his nose and mouth, and shuffled on. Soon he was nothing more than a distant black speck against a blood-red horizon — another lost soul, thought Scamarcio, trying to survive in this godforsaken city.

20

He stood under the shade of some fly-bitten palm trees, watching the pope address the crowd. His words yesterday that the only role of the Church was to oppose the Sandinistas had been very well received by the bosses back in Washington. Their trained exile groups were flooding across the border from Honduras in their thousands now.

The grieving wives and the mothers were now prostrate before his Holiness, a shaking, heaving mass, begging him to pray for the souls of their men who had died at the hands of the Somozistas. But his Holiness's face was a mask of stone. He just stood there, stiff and frozen. It seemed that no amount of crying or pleading would sway him.

Carter took another sip of beer and decided that the pope's refusal was a masterstroke, an act of pure genius. Frankly, they couldn't have written it better themselves.

And indeed, when he'd called Washington later, they'd laughed and said, 'Yeah, we provide the muscle, and he does the PR. It's a marriage made in heaven — literally.'

But something about that troubled him and, for the first time in a long time, he found himself remembering the children on the bridge.

SCAMARCIO WAS IN THE SHOWER when he heard a knock at his front door. He decided to ignore it. He was running late for his meeting with Aurelia, and he didn't want to give her something else to be angry about. But the knocking persisted, growing louder and increasingly impatient. Whoever was outside now seemed to be slamming his bulk against the wood — it sounded like he was prepared to break the door down.

Scamarcio quickly rinsed his hair and turned off the taps, stepping out of the shower and nearly slipping on the wet tiles in his haste to get to the uninvited visitor and wring his neck. He steadied himself and pulled his dressing gown from the hook, shaking it on as he made his way to the front door, not caring that he was dripping water all the way down the hallway.

When he reached the door, the stranger was still throwing himself against the woodwork, back and forth, back and forth. Scamarcio hoped that when he released the latch he'd fall straight into the hallway and he could beat the shit out of him; but instead, when he opened the door, he was surprised to see the two American agents just standing there in their sunglasses, hands in their pockets, as if the commotion had been nothing to do with them.

'You took your time,' said Pitted Skin.

'I was in the shower,' replied Scamarcio, in a tone that implied he was well within his rights to take a shower in his own home at 8.30 in the evening.

'Can we come in?' said the good-looking one. Scamarcio was pleased to note a thick red gash along his upper lip.

'No. You've almost beaten my door down.' He examined the paintwork. There were fresh dents in the wood in several places where the varnish had splintered and come away. 'I'm going to charge you for criminal damage.'

'Oh, come on, enough of the Italian melodrama,' said the better-looking one, practically pushing Scamarcio back inside his own apartment. He lunged forward, but the American was ready and made a deft side step. With his other arm he nudged Scamarcio back a few paces, saying, 'There's no need for a scene. Can't we just go inside and discuss this?'

'You're the ones being melodramatic, trying to break my door down like that. Who the hell do you think you are?'

'None of your business.'

'What the fuck?'

The good-looking one sighed and walked past him into the living room. It seemed as if he already knew the layout of the place.

Scamarcio followed him down the corridor, indignant, suddenly cold in his dressing gown. Pitted Skin trailed behind, easing the door shut behind him, gently this time.

The handsome American made himself at home on the sofa, flicking though some magazines as if he owned the place.

'Why are you here?' asked Scamarcio, towering over him.

'Why don't you sit down?' he replied, not looking up from the magazine. It was last Friday's *Corriere della Sera* supplement. Scamarcio wondered if the arsehole even spoke Italian.

'Don't tell me to sit down in my own fucking home. You've interfered with my investigation — hassled my ME, stolen a corpse. As far as I'm concerned, you are out of here, out of Italy on the next plane, so don't tell me to fucking sit down.'

'That's not your call,' said Terracotta Tan. 'And besides, she's not *your* ME — anything but.' He smiled, as if he knew a juicy secret but would never tell.

Scamarcio's vision was failing, the familiar red mist was descending, and he bit down hard on his lip in the hope of stopping himself from throttling this idiot. He had to keep control. Another violent episode, and they'd take it back to his bosses — if they hadn't done so already. Garramone would tot it up against Scamarcio's other outbursts, and his days would be numbered. He willed himself to keep a hold of his rage, to tamp it down for now.

'Why are you here?' he repeated, breathing out, trying to locate an inner calm that he knew he didn't possess.

Pitted Skin took a seat on the sofa next to his colleague, smoothing out his trousers and flicking away an imaginary piece of lint.

'It's come to our attention that you've been circulating photos of our dead co-patriot around the ex-Intel community back in the States.' The words were neutral and matter-of-fact. 'If you don't let this case drop, it is our obligation to advise you that your friend Blakemore will very soon find himself out of a job. Or worse.' There was no hint of reproach. It was as if they had expected him to do just such a thing, and were now having to take the noisome measures they had been hoping to avoid. It almost sounded like Pitted Skin was reciting his little spiel from a set text.

'Or worse?'

The good-looking one eased back into the sofa and yawned. 'You know how it works, Detective. There are different levels of intimidation.'

Scamarcio was confused by the total absence of emotion in their words. He pulled out a chair from beneath the dining table and sat down slowly. 'So, if I let this thing go, Blakemore is OK?'

'You bet,' said the good-looking one, without conviction.

'Who are you?' he tried again.

'It really doesn't matter,' said Pitted Skin, as if the very thought of it bored him.

Scamarcio decided there was no point in challenging them; there would be nothing to gain. Besides, he was exhausted and just wanted them gone.

'OK,' he said, running a hand through his wet hair. 'I'm tired, I've got other problems to deal with, and this whole charade is starting to piss me off. If I turn a blind eye, will you leave me and my colleagues alone?'

'We will,' said Pitted Skin.

'Right, then.' Scamarcio got up. 'Can I ask you gentlemen to leave, then?'

They both rose from the sofa in unison. The sudden synthesis of their movements reminded him of Agent Smith in the *Matrix* films, and once again he felt uneasy.

Scamarcio led the way down the corridor. 'So I won't be hearing from either of you again?' he shouted behind him, small droplets of water still dappling the floorboards.

Pitted Skin came to a stop on the threshold and turned slowly to face him. There was a cruelty in the set of his mouth that Scamarcio found disquieting. They stood there staring at each other for several moments before the American said, 'That depends on you, Detective. Just try not to change your mind.' With that, he was gone, and Scamarcio was left standing there in his dressing gown, a blast of cold air from the stairwell stirring the hairs on the back of his neck.

21

'We need to talk about Italy,' said the cardinal. 'Our friends fear that too much focus beyond our borders ... and we glance down to find the enemy at our gates —'

'Our friends?'

'The friends I introduced to your predecessor, Van Brulen.'

'Ah, those friends.' Carter paused for a moment, then asked, 'So what is their thinking now?'

'The strategy achieved the objectives they wanted. We now have a suitable government, a safe pair of hands. But they feel that it would be unwise to call an end to the process quite yet — they believe there's a need for a period of consolidation.'

'Consolidation.' He repeated the word, testing it on his tongue. Of course, he'd heard the rumours, but how bad had it been? It had always been left deliberately unclear, the standard policy being that you needed to make it as difficult as possible to get from A to B, to join all the dots. That being as true for agents as it was for the public.

'How many was it in the end?' he asked the cardinal.

'How many what?'

'The attacks, the bombings.'

The cardinal frowned, seemingly confused. He said nothing for several seconds, and then, 'Well, of course, as you know, it started in 1969 with Piazza Fontana, and then we had Brescia ...'

'How many dead?'

The cardinal sighed. 'Don't you know all this for yourselves?'

'I seem to forget the details.'

'I believe it's nearing two thousand.'

Two thousand in fourteen years. And now they were proposing 'consolidation'?

'You've been in Rome a long time now,' said the cardinal, observing him closely.

'It's starting to feel like home.'

'What about family? Don't you miss them?'

'I've met someone — an Italian.'

The cardinal smiled. 'Ah, so you will want to embrace our Italian problem, because soon it could become your problem.' He paused for a moment. 'So what should I tell them?'

'Who?'

'Our friends.'

It was as if something had shifted. He was back in the jungle with Dobbs, back by the bridge.

Quietly, he heard himself say, 'You can tell them that nobody is keener than us for a period of consolidation. We have problems with Iran, problems with Libya. Your value to the US is greater than it's ever been.'

It was as if someone else was talking, as if his soul had fled his body and left a shell behind.

He thought about Dobbs once more, and wondered what had gone through his mind before he plunged his car into the Chesapeake Bay that morning.

SCAMARCIO WAS NURSING his third cappuccino, struggling to pull his brain into focus. He doubted he'd slept more than four hours during the night. When he'd called Blakemore to tell him about the warning, there'd been a humming on the line, and he figured that perhaps they had his apartment wired. That would explain why they seemed to know the layout. Blakemore had seemed strangely calm, as if it all just came with the territory, but he'd suggested that they find a different way to talk. Scamarcio presumed the reporter was going to get a pay as-you-go phone, and that he should do the same. They would need to find a way to exchange numbers.

When he'd explained to Aurelia why he couldn't make it for their drink, she'd seemed concerned and had warned him to tread carefully, asking if there was anything she could do. He'd told her that he didn't want to drag her into this any further and that he'd be in touch so they could meet later. He hadn't had the head space to think about how he wanted their meeting to go; whether it should be the end or not.

From his desk, he watched the morning bustle on Via San Vitale. A moped rider was arguing with a traffic cop who was trying to give him a ticket, while a harried mother was attempting to herd two toddlers into the bakery on the corner; the little boy had torn off his woolly hat and had thrown it on the pavement, and the little girl had removed her right shoe and tossed it into the road. He thought of Pozzi, the tiny speck disappearing into yesterday's horizon. Would he have a wife one day, and a family of his own?

Scamarcio sighed, and made his fourth circuit to the coffee machine. Sartori was ahead of him, loading three sugars into his espresso.

'That stuff will kill you,' said Scamarcio.

'It would be a welcome release,' Sartori replied, downing his coffee in one. He surveyed Scamarcio from beneath his hooded lids. 'I hope you don't mind me saying so, but you look like shit today.'

'Actually, Sartori, I fucking do mind.'

Sartori shrugged, tossed his cup into the overloaded bin, and shuffled back to his desk, where a phone had started ringing.

Scamarcio took his cappuccino and headed out to the corridor for a change of scene. There was a better view of the street from here, and he figured that observing other people's workaday miseries might help him clear his head. He considered his options.

The Americans were a worry, but he couldn't just let this drop — when did the police ever give into threats? But that meant he'd need someone to be covering his back; he'd need to bring Garramone up to speed. And returning to the central question, just who the hell were they, and what were they so worried about? If Carter/Bartlett had been CIA, didn't that mean they had to be, too? There was clearly something major in play; something that connected with the death of Abbiati; something that connected with the Cold War; something that was so important to these people that they'd steal a corpse, doctor an autopsy report, and threaten a flying-squad detective. Yet again, he felt he was only seeing a tiny part of the picture.

His mobile rang, and he was surprised to see Pozzi's name appear. He hadn't been expecting to hear from him so soon.

'Meet me by the Coliseum near where they sell that shit to the tourists,' was all he said, before hanging up.

A trio of pretty Russian girls were buying overpriced ice-cream from one of the street vendors, and a loud-mouthed hot-dog seller was complaining about the tax police to anyone who would listen, but Scamarcio couldn't spot Pozzi in the crowd. He'd give him half an hour. There was a biting cold to the wind this morning, and Scamarcio pulled his scarf up. He noticed a few awkward-looking students decked out as gladiators in breastplates and tunics. They had to be freezing. Was this really what it had come to? That the only way to make money was to beg a few euro from a gormless tourist, who would proudly show off their photos of a 'real Roman warrior' at the next family cookout? Italy was becoming a third world country. It was no better than Mexico; in fact, it was worse. Mexico had prospects.

He kicked a battered Coke can into the gutter, and thought of Aurelia. A platoon of retreating sparrows sliced through the patch of sky above his head, and, as he looked back down again, he saw

Pozzi lumbering towards him.

The squad's latest super-grass barely acknowledged him; there was only the slightest nod of the head. He seemed exhausted, and Scamarcio reckoned he probably hadn't managed more than a few hours' sleep himself. The boy walked straight past him to a newspaper kiosk, where four people were already waiting in line.

'You OK?' asked Scamarcio as he took his place in the queue.

'No. I've had enough.'

His breath stank. Scamarcio thought about getting him something to eat or drink.

'Pozzi, like I told you, you're not dealing in real secrets.'

'Look, I'm going to give you this one thing, then I want you off my back, and I want Pesaro off my back. Understand? I need you to talk to him so he lets me off the hook.' He held up his hands. 'Me and my mum are getting out of Rome for good, leaving all this shit behind.'

Scamarcio took a long breath and nodded, trying to process this new turn of events. 'Good for you, Pozzi,' he said eventually.

'I'm not telling anyone where I'm going, so you can't come after me.'

'We won't.'

Pozzi's features relaxed a bit, and he exhaled slowly. 'So, if I tell you this, will you get Pesaro off my case?'

'I'll try.'

'That's not good enough.'

It was like Pozzi had been on an overnight self-assertiveness course. Maybe Scamarcio *had* stirred something in him after all.

'Deal,' said Scamarcio softly.

Pozzi nodded. 'It was money. Your American had called in a debt with Abbiati. The cardinal didn't want to pay, so he got my guys to off him.'

'How did you hear this?'

'I don't want to go into it; it nearly killed me. I'm getting out.'

Scamarcio wondered if Pozzi was just feeding him a false lead, doing exactly what Scamarcio had advised him to do with Pesaro. 'And you're sure you've got this right?' he asked finally.

'It came from someone in the know,' replied Pozzi. 'Besides, I feel like I owe you. You opened my eyes, started the ball rolling. '

'So who killed the cardinal?'

'No idea.'

'What, you've no idea, or your associate has no idea?'

'I don't know. I'd asked enough. I'd already put my balls on the line.'

Fair enough, thought Scamarcio. 'I'll do what I can with Pesaro.'

Pozzi took out the phone that Scamarcio had given him the day before, and handed it over. 'Take this back,' he said quietly.

'But I might need to talk to you again.'

Pozzi held up a palm. 'I'm out of here — before the shit hits the fan.'

'But …'

'You're no better than them, you know. You all want a piece of me; you all want to own me. But *I* control my destiny, not you.' He stabbed a finger at Scamarcio, turned, and strode off across the piazza, towards the carpark. Scamarcio wondered if Pozzi might be a survivor after all.

22

WHEN SCAMARCIO RETURNED to the squad room, he found Garramone in his office doorway, waving a copy of that morning's *La Repubblica* at him. 'You seen this?'

'No. Is it important?' Stupid question. Garramone wouldn't be mentioning it if it wasn't.

'You got five minutes?' asked the chief.

'Yeah, I wanted to talk to you anyway.'

When they were both seated either side of his desk, Garramone pushed the newspaper across. The front-page headline read 'STRANGE TWIST IN ABBIATI SLAYING: CLAIMS THAT CLOSEST COLLEAGUE WAS A U.S. SPY.'

Scamarcio leant forward in his chair. 'What? That's ridiculous.'

'It feels like we're back in the Eighties,' said Garramone. 'Back with Calvi again.'

Scamarcio was scanning the article, trying to find some clarity. 'But it makes no sense. Why would anyone inside the Vatican be spying for the Americans? What information could they possibly have that the US might want?'

'Beats me,' said Garramone, stroking his chin.

Scamarcio read on, trying to understand who the supposed spy was, but he couldn't find an explanation. 'Who is the colleague? Don't they say?'

'No, it's all kept deliberately vague — protecting their sources, and all that.'

'But how can they make an allegation like this without going into detail?'

Garramone waved a hand away. 'Oh, you know what they're like. They never let the facts get in the way of a good story.'

'But this spy thing, it doesn't make any sense. It feels like we've moved beyond that — the Cold War ended a long time ago.'

'I think that's naïve. It never ended for the Russians — they distrust the Americans more than ever. And there's still a powerful faction in Washington who share that distrust.'

'Yeah, but what secrets could this Vatican spy possibly have for them — next week the pope will be wearing purple underpants? It's ludicrous.'

'The Vatican has a presence in many countries — countries that the Americans might still be interested in understanding better. They may just be using their Vatican mole as an information gatherer, a fact-finder, rather than some James Bond type who jets around in fast cars and seduces blonde bombshells.'

Scamarcio exhaled. 'So we've got an American spy in the Vatican, a dead American under the Ponte Sant'Angelo, and two Americans, unfortunately very much alive, who seem intent on making my life a misery.' He filled in Garramone on the night before's visit and his morning meeting with Pozzi.

'Hmm. So Abbiati had ties with the Cappadona? That's troubling.'

'What are we going to do about the Americans?' asked Scamarcio.

Garramone scratched at an eyebrow. 'Well, we're nobody's puppets, but I'm going to have to run it past AISE, and bring them up to speed. Otherwise there'll be hell to pay.'

Scamarcio couldn't help thinking that running it past AISE was simply going to result in stasis. It seemed clear that they wanted to keep things sweet with their US 'colleagues'; he felt sure that some round-robin policy document existed, stipulating just that.

He thought of the conversation he had heard in Giangrande's office, but, again, decided to keep it to himself until he understood what he was dealing with.

Scamarcio returned his attention to the article. The by-line belonged to a Roberto Rigamonti, a journalist he had never heard of.

'I think I'm going to look up this guy, see if I can get any more out of him.'

'Sure,' said Garramone.

'And what about the Carabinieri — don't they consult for the Vatican police? Would they have a lead into Abbiati?'

Garramone waved the thought away. 'I've already been onto them. They've been frozen right out.'

'I thought that might be the case.'

Garramone seemed perplexed. His mind was turning on something. Scamarcio sensed that he wanted to speak, but was holding back.

'Is that everything, sir?' he asked eventually.

Garramone leant back in his chair and rubbed beneath his nose. 'There's a stupid thing bothering me. It seems like a triviality in all this, I know, but that errand boy for the Cappadona who gave you the steer this morning …?'

Scamarcio smelt danger. 'Yeah — what about him?'

'What did you say his name was?'

'Pozzi.'

'Yeah, I thought that's what you said. You know, I'm sure I saw his name on the arrests list just the day before yesterday.'

Oh God, thought Scamarcio. This, he didn't need. If he told a lie, Garramone would find out straightaway — it was all there up on the file.

'Yes, he was arrested. OC brought him in.'

'So, did they have nothing on him? How did he get back out so fast?'

Scamarcio took a breath, calculating fast. 'Well, it's a funny one. I went to Pesaro, saying that I needed information about a possible link between the Cappadona and the Ponte Sant'Angelo case …'

'What link between the Cappadona and the Ponte Sant'Angelo case?'

Scamarcio couldn't think of a response. It had to be obvious to Garramone that he was floundering. 'The link between Abbiati and the Cappadona, of course.'

'No — you just told me that you got that from Pozzi. When you went to see Pesaro, you couldn't have spoken to Pozzi.'

Fuck it. He did *not* want to tell Garramone about his lunch with Piocosta. 'There was chatter on the underground about the Cappadona perhaps having something to do with the Ponte Sant'Angelo corpse.'

Garramone sighed and shook his head, sinking back into his chair once more. 'Can't you keep them at arm's length, Scamarcio? You give those people an inch, and they take a mile. You're a good detective, one of my best, and I don't want to see it all go up in smoke. I've invested a lot in you; I've had to calm a lot of nerves.'

Scamarcio just nodded, deciding to say nothing. It was the safest policy.

'So you went to Pesaro,' continued Garramone, 'and said you wanted help from Pozzi to find out if this Cappadona link was sound ...'

'Yeah, and Pesaro said, "Funny thing, Scamarcio, because I was going to use him myself. We think he's well placed. So we'll turf him back out and see if we can kill two birds with one stone." '

'Why would Pesaro bring him in if he thought he was well placed? An arrest would make him too conspicuous.'

'Maybe he thought that if he wasn't inside for long, they could keep it from the clan.'

'You can't keep anything from the clan. Pesaro knows that.'

Scamarcio shrugged.

Garramone's eyes were narrowing. He took a pen and tapped it against his teeth. Something about that sound made Scamarcio anxious.

'You know what, Scamarcio — if you're up to your old tricks and causing trouble in my department, I'll haul you in front of a disciplinary tribunal myself. There's a way to do things, a procedure.'

'Sure,' he replied, trying to sound surprised by the implication that he might think otherwise.

'This is a sensitive case, and we don't want to put a foot wrong, especially with AISE and that wanker from media relations breathing down our necks.'

It was the first time he had heard Garramone refer to Gatti like this. He hoped that their shared hatred of the man might mean he was off the hook for the time being.

'Just don't let me hear from Pesaro that you've been fucking things up for him. It shouldn't work like that.'

'Understood,' said Scamarcio. 'I'll get onto *La Repubblica* now, and try and look up that reporter.'

Garramone nodded. He still seemed irked.

23

ROBERTO RIGAMONTI WAS OUT on a story when Scamarcio arrived at the offices of *La Repubblica*. They called him from reception at Scamarcio's insistence, but when he asked to speak to the reporter directly, the receptionist's expression seemed to suggest that Rigamonti had declined. She was left to tell Scamarcio that he should wait and that Rigamonti would be back within the hour.

Scamarcio was irritated by the arrogance of the man; by his assumption that he'd have an entire hour to spare. But when Rigamonti showed up just thirty minutes later, he seemed very different from the quick picture Scamarcio had scratched together; his dark hair was all over the place, his unfashionable glasses were askew, and he apologised profusely for having kept Scamarcio waiting. 'I was with the kind of people where a conversation with a police detective would not have done me any favours. Sorry.'

Scamarcio smiled. 'No problem. Did they give you what you wanted?'

'Not yet. But I'm hopeful that they will.'

Rigamonti led the way across the polished atrium and into a modern-looking elevator. The offices were plusher than Scamarcio would have expected. The crumbling 1950s paintwork on the outside of the building — along with the desiccated piles of dog shit and the overweight hooker he had watched arguing with her pimp just beyond the entry barrier — had suggested a different ambience altogether.

The reporter pressed the button for the fourth floor. 'Do

you mind if we go to the canteen? I haven't eaten anything since breakfast.'

'Suits me,' said Scamarcio. 'I missed lunch myself.'

'You could do worse. The food isn't bad.' There was a moment of silence, and then Rigamonti asked, 'So why did you want to see me?'

'It's about that piece of yours that came out today — on the guy close to Abbiati, supposedly working for US Intelligence.'

'Do you buy it?'

Scamarcio shrugged. 'How can I know?'

The elevator doors opened, and Rigamonti led the way into the canteen. The furnishings were ultra-modern, the glass walls squeaky clean. 'It's on me,' said Rigamonti. 'I can recommend the vitello tonnato.'

'OK,' said Scamarcio. 'Sold.'

When they were seated, with two plates of food in front of them, Rigamonti said, 'I can assure you it's true. My source is solid.'

'Who's your source?'

Rigamonti opened both palms as if to say *Why are you even trying?*

'Sorry,' said Scamarcio. 'Couldn't help myself.'

'It's a guy I've known for some years with extensive contacts inside the Vatican. He's certain that the individual in question has been working for the Americans for a very long time.'

'A very long time?'

'Started in the late Sixties, apparently.'

'Who is he, this spy?'

Rigamonti shook his head and frowned. 'I don't know — the source wouldn't tell me.'

'How can you build a story around *that*?'

The tone was harsher than Scamarcio had intended, but Rigamonti didn't seem to take it amiss. 'Oh, we're forced to build a story around anything these days. Twenty-four-hour news has upped the ante.'

Scamarcio took a bite of his Vitello — it was good. 'So your source thinks that this mysterious man close to Abbiati might have had something to do with his death?'

'He's sure of it.' Rigamonto paused for a beat, rubbing at his temple. 'Detective, I've been missing something. The Flying Squad is investigating the death of Abbiati, isn't it? That's why you're here.' He sounded mildly excited at the prospect of another scoop.

'Well, that would be a first, but I can assure you that, as usual, we've not been allowed anywhere near it. I'm interested because we've had a death in the same week that seems to be connected. How exactly they're linked, I'm still not sure. Your piece on Abbiati stirred my interest, that's all.'

'Is there an American connection?'

'Why would there be?'

'Why would you be interested if there wasn't?'

Rigamonti's round blue eyes blinked back at him. The face of one of the saints came up to Scamarcio's mind, but he couldn't identify which one. He took another mouthful of veal.

'Look, you wouldn't give me your source, and I'm not going to give you the spit and cough on my case — for now. But ...' He paused '... if we can work together on this, there could be something in it for you later. But on my terms and on my schedule.'

Rigamonti nodded quickly. 'Understood.'

'So this shadowy figure close to Abbiati — does your source know what the Americans want from him? The wall came down a long time ago.'

'Depends on your perspective. The way my source tells it, this guy started working for the Americans back when they had ants in their pants about Italy going red. All that business with Moro was making everyone jumpy. The Americans put spies everywhere

— in the Red Brigades, in the neo-fascists, in the government, and in the Vatican, of course. The Vatican allowed them to get about, remember. It was useful to them on a global scale.'

'So this spy of theirs — when the wall comes down in '89, they decide to keep him on the payroll?'

'Yes, because you never know, do you? He could come in handy one day. And indeed, that is exactly what has happened.'

'How so?'

'Look at this country. People are getting really, *really* fed up. One more foreign company fleeing, one more broke father gunning down his kids … It's not going to take much before you see serious civil unrest.'

'Come on, isn't that overstating it?'

'No, it's not. I get out there and talk to people and, believe me, their patience is wearing thin. We've had a succession of disastrous governments, a series of Brussels-imposed coups, and while the politicos gorge themselves at the trough, the people are getting steadily poorer. We're going to see blood on the streets if this economic crisis continues. And continue, it will.'

'You think the Americans see it so bleakly?'

'According to my source, they do. They're worried about Italy and Greece, the domino effect. Apparently, they'd been trying to find out all they could about Grinta and his six-star movement; they wanted to know if he might be bought.'

'Bought?'

'The original idea was to give him a load of money and support so they could use him as a decoy to channel the energies of the indignant masses, perhaps persuade him to enter a coalition with a safe pair of hands. That way, they could stop anything really nasty from happening, prevent an all-out Eurozone disaster.'

'But Grinta has lost support — his star is waning.'

'Yeah, they knew that, and they wanted to put him back firmly in the spotlight. They wanted to make him shine again.'

'But the kind of things he's advocating are way out of line with their agenda.'

'For a while, he was the lesser of two evils. But of course all that's changed since the young lad came along.'

'Curzio?'

Italy had recently sworn in its third prime minister in just two years. Just thirty-nine years old, many were touting Curzio as the big white hope for the country. The way Scamarcio saw it, just because the boy talked the talk and had hastily formed an extremely young, half-female cabinet, it did not make him Tony Blair.

'Of course. They reckon they can mould him like play dough, and so far he seems to be saying all the right things.'

'So where does the Vatican spy come in?'

'My source's belief is that he was the channel between the Americans and Grinta for a while.'

'So why kill Abbiati?'

'Abbiati had concerns; he'd confided to my source that he'd suspected for many years that some of his colleagues kept strange bedfellows. Shortly after, he was dead.'

'But it seems heavy-handed. Did they really need to kill him?'

'If they identify a potential risk — a weak spot — they work to solve the problem, eliminate it. Besides, people are sniffing around the Vatican right now. All that business at the bank is putting them under the spotlight, and God knows how many other skeletons are going to start tumbling out of the closet.'

Scamarcio was getting a headache, the pain making its way up from the troublesome joint in his neck once more. Pozzi had told him it was a financial problem between Carter and Abbiati, but now Rigamonti was presenting an entirely new angle. Had Carter been sent to kill Abbiati, only for Abbiati to get there first? Had Carter's colleagues then dispatched someone else to finish the job? Was Carter the handler of this mysterious spy close to Abbiati? A picture was forming, but it was blurred and lacked definition.

'With all this, you have to look to the past,' offered Rigamonti. 'Whatever their Vatican spy had been doing for the Americans back in the Seventies, it went beyond borders, and possibly still does. We should be careful not to get too hung up on the domestic scene.'

'Did your source advise that?'

Rigamonti sighed. He seemed suddenly exhausted by their conversation. 'Yeah, reading between the lines.'

The reporter's phone rang, and he mumbled a few 'No's and 'Yes's before hanging up. 'Listen, I've got to go. Shall we meet up in a few days, once you're further into this thing? I'm hoping to move the story on a bit, talk some more to my source. You and I might have fresh ideas to trade.' He pulled out a business card from his battered wallet. 'All my numbers are on here.'

Scamarcio took the card and handed him one of his own. 'Let's do that. It's been an interesting conversation.'

Rigamonti got up, hoisting a surprisingly smart-looking satchel over his shoulder. He shook Scamarcio's hand. 'A bit one-sided perhaps?' His smile suggested that he wasn't too worried about that right now. 'I look forward to doing business with you, Detective.'

Scamarcio realised that he'd probably have to honour this particular promise — there was something about the unassuming reporter that he liked.

24

SCAMARCIO WAS HEADING DOWN Via Boncompagni towards his flat when he had the feeling that someone was following him. It was more a sudden sensation of warmth, a stirring of the hairs along the back of his neck, that made him swing around to check who was there. But, aside from a couple of dusty birds bathing in an oily puddle, the street was empty. He walked on, the strange sensation growing; yet when he glanced behind him once more, the birds had gone and the street was silent. He took a breath and turned right into Via Collina. And at the exact moment he did so, his mobile rang. He gave a start, quickly scanning the windows of the apartments facing him, his heart pounding. Had someone watched him make the turn?

But it was only Garramone. When Scamarcio answered, all the boss said was, 'Get back to the office now.'

It had felt like a long day. After his meeting with Rigamonti, Scamarcio had decided to head home, but Garramone had hung up before he could ask any more. Scamarcio made his way towards Via XX Settembre, a busy thoroughfare where he could find some safety in numbers. He hailed a cab for the squad room, and after they'd pulled away from the kerb he leant back and tried to settle his pulse. Someone had definitely been following him. He steadied his breathing and closed his eyes. Had his meeting with the reporter got them worried?

As the cab pulled into Via San Vitale, Scamarcio could see immediately that something was amiss. A large group of officers had gathered on the front steps of Police Headquarters, and seemed to be staring at a large bundle on the ground. Garramone was there, and Chiecci, the head of Organised Crime. Standing immediately to his right was Pesaro, ashen-faced. Scamarcio's stomach flipped. He felt the vitello tonnato move its way back up his throat.

He paid the driver and got out, his legs shaky. He walked towards the huddle, feeling as if everything was in slow motion, as if he might pause and examine each frame of his approach. He started to note irrelevant details: Officer Parodi hadn't shaved; Pesaro was wearing a blue suit that looked new; his boss, Chiecci, had put on weight.

He took a breath and came to a stop next to Garramone. The chief said nothing, just stepped neatly to the left so that Scamarcio could see what they had all been looking at. He leant into the throng and tried to steel himself; he tried to take another breath, to focus.

Sprawled on the ground was a bloodied and battered body: the left eye was missing, most of the teeth had gone, and two fingers on the right hand had lost their tips. Thick, black blood had spread out around the crotch of the jeans, and tied around the neck was a pristine white card with the words 'TAKE BACK YOUR WHORE' handwritten in clear, black capitals. Scamarcio swallowed hard, and tried to take in some air. Strangely, despite all the gore, it was the sight of Pozzi's running shoe that finally broke him. It was one of those ultra-modern ones with silver dashes and complicated stitching. It looked brand new, and there wasn't a spot of blood on it. He could imagine Pozzi choosing those shoes, using his cash to treat himself for once, wearing his purchase proudly when he was out in Trastevere one night, hoping to impress the girls. Scamarcio heard someone sob, then realised with alarm that everyone was looking at him. He rubbed his face with his hand and hurried inside.

The silence in Garramone's office was suffocating. It hung densely all around them like industrial smog or toxic sludge. The only sound came from the ancient wall clock marking the seconds, but even they seemed longer and heavier than usual.

Eventually, Chiecchi said, 'Well, none of us were in any doubt about their capacity for ruthlessness.'

Neither Pesaro nor Scamarcio ventured a reply.

Garramone pinched his nose a couple of times and sighed. 'How far do you think this sets us back with the Cappadona?'

Chiecci pursed his lips. He was a strange-looking man: thin faced, with a sharp chin and drooping brown eyes. His skin was heavily lined, from years of night shifts and nicotine abuse, Scamarcio figured.

'I think getting anyone in there is going to be impossible for a very long time,' replied Chiecci. 'They'll be on their guard. If we were hoping for a slip-up, I doubt we'll get one now.'

'What a mess,' said Garramone.

Scamarcio was about to speak, but Garramone held up a palm to stop him. 'I want to hear Pesaro's version of events. Something tells me it'll be different from the one you gave me yesterday.'

Scamarcio sank back in his chair. If Pesaro was ever going to sell him out, now was the time. Pesaro was immaculately turned out today in a blue designer suit and matching tie, as if he knew what was coming. Scamarcio studied his own dry hands, still shaking slightly, his chipped fingernails, the frayed edging to his shirt, and then he moved on to his scuffed brogues and thinning socks — anything but face down the boss's stare.

'It was a joint decision to turn Pozzi informer,' explained Pesaro, his voice firm and even. 'We'd brought him in after finding contraband in his van. We suspected that he worked for the Cappadona, but we were also aware that he was probably not particularly well placed, that he was relatively low down the pecking order. However, after an initial interview, I began to question this and wondered if, due to a friendship with someone more established in the clan, he did have potential access to important information. After I had finished my interview with him and was writing it up, Detective Scamarcio came to find me, asking if I knew of anyone in the Cappadona who might have information on the Ponte Sant'Angelo death. I was reluctant to mention Pozzi, firstly because I wasn't sure myself whether he was valuable, but secondly because I didn't want one investigation to compromise the other. However, after talking to Detective Scamarcio, I decided that there might be some merit in making a second approach — getting a second opinion, as it were, on Pozzi. So I gave him my permission for an interview. It was after that interview that Detective Scamarcio shared with me his belief that Pozzi was indeed well placed and might prove a useful asset to OC.' Pesaro hadn't paused for breath. His confidence was extraordinary, given the circumstances, thought Scamarcio.

'So I decided to drop the charges, and released him yesterday afternoon. Obviously, we all know what happened next. My assessment remains that he was well placed, otherwise they would not have bothered to send us such a clear message. I also believe that my initial decision was sound. It was a decision taken in good faith, and the fact remains that the outcome could have proved positive for the department.'

Pesaro's measured, reasoned tone was a stroke of pure genius, Scamarcio thought absently. Who hadn't made a bad decision at one time or another in their police career? The important thing was that Pesaro was coming across as decisive, and was following it all through with logic.

'Right,' said Garramone, clearly reshuffling the cards in his head. 'My advice to you, Pesaro is, next time, think harder and think longer. That boy might have been a criminal, but he was a young lad with a life ahead of him, and possibly the chance to turn things around. Your decision has robbed him and his family of that possibility forever. I would also suggest to you, Pesaro, that you should be careful not to be too easily influenced by the opinions of others. Detective Scamarcio is not part of your team; while I value him as a detective, if I were in your position I would have sought a second opinion from your immediate superiors before turning Pozzi loose.'

Pesaro nodded, hanging his head a little.

'I'd like to speak to Chief Chiecci alone now.'

Out in the corridor, Scamarcio was about to offer Pesaro a coffee, but he'd walked off. *Another bridge burned*, thought Scamarcio.

He perched on a windowsill, and leant back against the pane. If he pushed back he might go through the glass and fall onto the street below, landing next to Pozzi. That's what he deserved.

His thoughts were interrupted by Sartori, standing there with two steaming cups of coffee from the bar downstairs, rather than from the crappy machine.

'Figured you might need this,' he said, holding one out. 'I've added a little something to take the edge off.'

Scamarcio smiled and took the paper cup.

'We all have bad days, you know. It can go wrong for any of us, at any time. Don't take it too personally, man.'

'I didn't think they'd get to him so fast — I should have known better.'

Sartori sighed. 'The game is changing all the time. We're all still trying to get our heads around it. Hell, the crims are still trying to get their heads around it. It's like fighting a war where you don't know how many soldiers your enemy has or what kind of arsenal's at their disposal. Don't take it too hard.'

Sartori patted him on the shoulder and then looked left and right before passing him a small bottle of something from his pocket. 'In case you need a top-up. I've got to head off now because it's the wife's night out. If you want a dose of hell to take your mind of your troubles, you're welcome to stop by. But I can well understand if you'd prefer a quiet night at home with a bottle. Anyway, you know my number.'

He waved a hand in the air and walked off.

25

WHEN SCAMARCIO WALKED INTO his flat, Aurelia was waiting for him on the sofa. Somehow, he would have been happier to see the two Americans.

'How are you?' she asked, concern bunching her brow.

'Just great,' he replied, throwing his coat across a chair. The place was a mess; he hadn't cleared up his dinner plates from the night before, and there was a large pile of dirty shirts in the corner that he had forgotten to take to the dry cleaners on his way to work.

She got up from the sofa, reaching for her handbag. 'I know you've got a lot on, but I wondered if you felt like a drink?'

He ran a hand through his hair. 'Would you mind if we took a raincheck?'

She looked down at the floor.

'I'm sorry, Aurelia — it's just that today was a fucker, and my head's fried.'

'You seem to be having a lot of tough days lately.'

He looked at her standing there by the sofa, and wished he'd never given her a key.

'I need to go out. Can I ring you later?'

'You've only just got home.'

'It's a fast-moving case.'

'Leo …'

But he just grabbed his coat and headed for the door. It was the easiest option.

Scamarcio headed to a bar where he liked to go when he wanted to get out of the flat but didn't want to venture far. The place was quieter than usual; there were just a couple of other people at a table in the far corner. He chose a spot close to the bar where *The Inheritance* was showing on a large flat-screen TV. The young contestant looked like a bit of a geek and was doing well. He was rising uninterruptedly past the thirteenth level of a question round on actors or singers. Carlo Conti looked impressed; the showgirls seemed excited. Nobody usually made it this high on their first attempt, and the waiter came up alongside Scamarcio and turned up the sound. When the boy reached the fifteenth level, the studio audience held its breath, and the camera switched back to Carlo and one of his brunette 'professors', who was now pretending to bite her nails in a state of faux anxiety. Then came the sixteenth question: was Loredana Berté an actress or a singer? The boy fell silent, panic in his eyes. He was too young to know. 'Actress', he answered, clearly guessing. Carlo screwed up his face and swept a hand across his brow. 'No, she is a singer.' The geek boy was back at the beginning, right where he had started. The waiter tut-tutted and said, 'I've never seen anyone do it in one.'

'Me neither,' replied Scamarcio.

He asked if he'd mind turning the sound up some more. The waiter said he could have the remote — there were hardly any customers, so it was unlikely that anyone would be bothered by the noise.

Scamarcio switched channels, flicking past a dire German drama series on the motorway police and the *Place in the Sun* soap opera — there was always someone crying on that show. Eventually, he plumped for Sky TG24. They were talking about the disappearance of a church-going housewife and mother of four from a tiny village in Piedmont. The husband claimed to have no idea what had happened to her, and was telling anyone who would listen that she was an excellent mother and always kept the house extremely clean. *God*, thought Scamarcio. *Parts of my country still seem to be living in a different age.*

Then the same plastic blonde who always seemed to be on was talking about the opening of another trial to do with the terrorist attack at Turin station in 1983. Scamarcio took a long sip of his wine and thought of Professor Letta and his quick lesson on the strategy of tension. He studied the bar, and the pits and grooves in the wood, chipping away at one of them with his finger. It was odd that he had just had that conversation with Letta, and now the media were discussing this new trial. He returned his attention to the TV: the reporter had turned to an exhausted-looking elderly man standing to his right, who he introduced as the widower of one of the victims. 'Signor Viola, you have long been campaigning for a full inquiry into the attack, is that right?'

'Yes, we've been pushing for years for a proper investigation. But we've been fobbed off with whitewash after whitewash. We are really hoping that this new trial, more than thirty years on, will finally reveal the truth about whether Italian Intelligence knew about the bombing before it happened. We have long suspected that they have blood on their hands, and now, finally, they will be forced to explain themselves in front of all of us, in front of the world.'

'Are you hopeful about the outcome?'

'It is hard to be hopeful after all these years, but we do feel that we are living in a new, more informed era, and if there is a time when the truth could possibly come out, it is now.'

The reporter handed back to the studio, which switched immediately to an item on local-government corruption in Sardinia. Scamarcio put down his glass. It seemed that the ghosts of the Cold War were hovering everywhere: the dead American hung up to die like Calvi; an American spy inside the Vatican; and now this new trial into one of the worst atrocities of the years of lead. A thought was gradually beginning to form, faint but troubling: could there be a connection to this new trial, a trial about to play out in the high court, a trial that would no doubt captivate the country, and perhaps the wider world? He thought of Pozzi, and his mind flashed on the un-bloodied running shoe and the boy's mangled face. The sadness took hold of him once more, but lurking beneath it was the conviction that the Cappadona were at the heart of this thing. Any long-buried secrets lay with them.

Part II

He saw all the agony He was going to suffer: and the agony was not so much the pain of the crucifixion as the pains of the sins of the world.

From *Mysteries of the Rosary: Agony in the Garden*

26

He watched the coverage on the evening news. The camera work was hesitant. There were so many bodies, so much blood and gore everywhere you turned, it was as if they didn't know where to put their lenses. They were trying to abide by the usual code, but the extent of this particular massacre was making it impossible.

'Ninety-five dead,' said the announcer. 'Most of them had just got off the 9.00 am train from Milan; among them, women and children. We believe a baby as young as one lost his life in the attack. As yet no terrorist group has claimed responsibility, although analysts are suggesting that it is most likely the work of the Red Brigades.'

Women and children. The words circled in his head, and once again he was back in the jungle with Dobbs, struggling to block out the cries, the moans, the blood-choked screams.

Carter tried to recall the words an old friend had said to him the other day. What were they now? Oh, yes — 'It's crazy when you let one thing take over to the extent that you forgive everything else.' He'd been talking about how they were using Nazi war criminals to run their spy networks in South America. But Carter thought it might equally apply to the situation in which he now found himself.

Crazy.

If it went on much longer, he wondered if he would start losing his mind.

AS IT WAS a crisp, sunny morning, Scamarcio decided to get some fresh air and make the walk over to the morgue. He wanted to test his suspicions and establish whether it was true that the chief pathologist had no idea about the poison used on the dead American; from the whispered call he'd overheard, it seemed that it might not be so simple.

He entered the building, scanning the corridor in case Aurelia was coming in or out of somewhere. He vowed to himself that he would talk to her soon, that he'd face up to her understandable anger. However, for now, he needed to push it aside, to allow this case to take priority.

When Scamarcio walked into the autopsy suite, Giangrande was bent over a desk, rubbing at his neck. He looked more tired and less tanned than the last time Scamarcio had seen him.

Giangrande shrugged as if to say, *Why are you here? We no longer have a body.*

Uninvited, Scamarcio drew out a chair to the left of the desk and slumped down. He studied a paper cut on his hand. Without looking up, he said, 'I don't buy your story about the Americans just making off with our stiff; neither do I buy that bullshit about your grandson eating your homework.'

Giangrande sighed. 'Why should I care what you think?'

Scamarcio rubbed at an eye. Yet again, he hadn't slept well. 'I know that you have money worries, and that the Americans paid you to hand over the evidence. When that comes out, you'll lose your job.'

Giangrande remained silent for a few moments. Then he said, 'That's bullshit. What the hell are you talking about?'

'I overheard your conversation with them. There's no point denying it.'

'There's something wrong with your head, Scamarcio.'

'There's nothing wrong with me. I heard every word you said to them on the phone. I was going to take it straight to Garramone, but then I thought I'd better give you the chance to explain yourself.'

Giangrande looked like he was about to protest some more,

but instead he just sighed and pulled out the chair from behind his desk, seeming to forget to sit down. 'What exactly do you think you heard?'

'That they paid you for the body, and to destroy the report and any test results that came back.'

Giangrande said nothing, and just hung his head. Then he asked, 'How did you know I was short of cash?'

'Word on the grapevine.'

Giangrande nodded and finally sat down. After a few moments' silence, he said, 'I made some bad investments. I've got a daughter about to go through university, a wife who doesn't like to work. I suppose I panicked.' He paused for a moment. 'So — what now?'

'It depends on you. You told me that you hadn't had a chance to test that liver sample before the body was lifted. Is that true?'

'Yes and no.'

'Well, which is it?'

'I had taken it, but the results weren't back when I spoke to you.'

'So now they are?'

Giangrande nodded reluctantly.

'And?'

'The deal was that I was to hand them all the files, all the data. I wasn't supposed to divulge it.'

'Giangrande, have you forgotten who you work for?'

The chief pathologist slumped deeper into the chair, and rubbed his cheek with his left hand. Scamarcio noticed that it was dry and cracked.

Eventually, Giangrande said, 'It was radiator fluid — the poison. If you Google it, you'll find it on a list of standard CIA potions.'

Scamarcio nodded, but his mind was sticking on something else. If the Cappadona were to be believed, they had been sent by Abbiati to kill the American. 'That poison, is it the kind of thing any of our home-grown killers might use?'

Giangrande frowned. 'In my thirty years on the job, I've never seen it used in mafia hits. It took them quite a bit of time at the lab to pin it down — it wasn't in their immediate range of reference either.'

That answered it. But if the Cappadona weren't behind the Ponte Sant'Angelo killing, why on earth were they claiming otherwise? It didn't add up.

'So what happens now?' asked Giangrande. 'Are you going to have me dragged before a tribunal?'

Scamarcio shook his head. 'No. I've got something else in mind.'

The chief pathologist looked up, but Scamarcio just shook his head in disappointment and left.

27

'In Poland, you said the situation was such that we would be able to leave no fingerprints,' said the cardinal.

'And?'

'My friends are beginning to feel as if their prints are all over the domestic problem.'

'You're worried about that young man?'

'He's ready to talk.'

'But what can he say after all this time? That someone in the intelligence services helped him plan the attack? He doesn't really understand who he is dealing with and, besides, who will believe him? It will seem the stuff of fantasy.'

'There will always be a handful of reporters desperate to lend his story credibility.'

'But if you're worried about leaving a trace, you need to stay well away — if anything happened to that boy, it would just nurture their suspicions.'

'He's due to take the stand next month. We have no doubt that he'll talk.'

Carter shook his head, and exhaled a deep, long breath. 'But my chiefs would never agree to removing him — they'd see it as messy, ham-fisted.'

'I anticipated that.' The cardinal passed him an envelope. 'Is there anything you can do? We need your expertise — in a personal capacity, of course.'

When Carter opened it, he saw that there was a thick stack of dollars inside.

'That's just the deposit,' said the cardinal.
Carter felt nauseous and had to swallow.

ON HIS WAY BACK to the squad room, Scamarcio ran into a small group of protestors outside the Bank of Italy. 'A DIGNIFIED WAGE', 'A LIFE, NOT AN EXISTENCE', read their placards. Someone thrust a leaflet into his hand, and he noticed the red hammer-and-sickle in the top right-hand corner. 'TIME TO FIGHT,' said the headline. He thought about his meeting with Rigamonti, and the reporter's conviction that serious unrest was not far off.

When he returned to his desk, a bunch of his colleagues were huddled around the big TV screen, the room abuzz with chatter.

'What's going on?' he asked the colleague standing nearest to him.

'Someone's leaked some CCTV footage from the Vatican. It shows a priest from Varese on the staircase to Abbiati's apartment just five minutes before he died.'

Scamarcio didn't get it. 'What's the big deal? Doesn't a priest have the right to be there?'

'Not this priest. He was small-time, from some tiny village near the lakes. No one knows what he was doing there, what business he'd have with Abbiati.'

'Who leaked the footage?'

'Nobody knows. It arrived at the offices of RAI early this morning, addressed to the news room — it was delivered by a courier company who say they were told to collect it from the Vatican post office. There was an anonymous letter with the tape, identifying the priest as a Father Brambani and saying he had no clearance to be there.'

Scamarcio turned his attention to the TV. 'Tell us about Brambani,' the news anchor asked a reporter stationed in St Peter's Square.

'Priest Antonio Brambani was a small-time provincial priest

from the town of Comerio on Lake Varese,' parroted the reporter. 'We understand that he had no reason for being at the Vatican. It is unclear what he was doing on the staircase so close to the time of the cardinal's murder.'

Scamarcio squinted at the screen and then turned away. He wondered how the Vatican police were going about their investigation into Abbiati's murder. Would they have been onto the police in Varese already, requesting them to haul Brambani in for questioning?

He picked up the phone and asked to be put through to Varese.

The desk sergeant who answered did not give the impression that anything major was going down near the lakes. He sounded bored and in need of a cigarette.

'I'll pass you to one of the detectives,' he said, the words slow and tired.

'Nardone,' snapped a new, more alert voice.

Scamarcio introduced himself and then said, 'I just wondered if you guys were acting on that tip about Father Brambani from Comerio, the guy who's been all over the news in connection with this Abbiati thing?'

Nardone sniffed noisily down the line. 'No one has asked us to.'

'Really?'

'We've been waiting for the call, but nothing's come in. You know what that lot are like — all cloak and dagger. They prefer to keep it to themselves. Maybe they're on the way up here to talk to him, but haven't seen any point in alerting us — although they should, of course. They're on foreign territory, after all.'

'You ever come across him, this Brambani character?'

'No, he's never been on our radar.'

Scamarcio rubbed at his temples. He felt a headache starting from the base of his neck again.

'Could you do me a favour, and let me know if anyone *does*

contact you?' He reeled off his number.

'Sure,' said Nardone. 'What's in it for you guys? I take it you've not been tasked to investigate?'

'Fat chance,' replied Scamarcio. 'It's just that there's some crossover with the Abbiati murder and a case that has come my way, so I'm interested in the Brambani angle.'

'Why don't you get onto them yourself?'

'I've been trying,' lied Scamarcio. 'But nobody has been returning my calls.'

'Figures,' said Nardone. 'They'll play it close to their chests, like they always do.'

Scamarcio mumbled in the affirmative, and then thanked him and hung up.

When he was back from the coffee machine, his mobile rang, and he was surprised to see Giangrande's name come up. He wondered if the chief pathologist was in a panic now; whether he would be hassling him from here on in. But instead, all Giangrande said was, 'Aurelia's seriously ill; she's in the Policlinico Gemelli.'

'What's wrong with her?' asked Scamarcio, as he grabbed his coat.

'They don't know. She's been vomiting continuously, her blood pressure is sky high, and she's running a massive fever. She's in the ICU.'

Scamarcio couldn't muster a response — his brain was struggling to take it all in.

'I'll see you at the hospital,' said Giangrande. 'I'm heading there now.'

Scamarcio ran down to the lobby and hailed a cab from outside the squad room. But the traffic was dire, and it took twice the time to reach the Policlinico Gemelli that it should have.

When he arrived at the ICU, they pointed him towards some

windows lining the other side of the corridor.

'You can't go in, but you can see her from out here in the hallway.'

He hurried over to the glass and scanned the faces of the patients in the rooms beyond. He found her almost immediately. Her skin was ashen, her thick, dark hair was pasted to her forehead, and her eyelids looked bruised. She was rigged up to a heart monitor, and there were tubes running from her mouth and nose. He noticed another tube in her arm, connecting with a drip on a stand. A nurse was standing by her bedside, calmly making notes on a clipboard. Scamarcio had been about to try to get her attention when a blonde woman in a white coat bustled past him into the room.

'Excuse me,' he shouted behind her. 'Can you tell me what's wrong with her?'

'Are you the husband?'

'No — the boyfriend.' The words felt strange.

'We're not sure yet; we're still running tests. I'll let you know as soon as it becomes clearer.' She hurried through the doorway and started talking to the nurse.

'OK,' said Scamarcio, knowing that she could no longer hear him.

He slumped onto a seat and closed his eyes. *What the hell is happening here? It doesn't feel real.* Someone placed a gentle hand on his arm, and he jumped. When he looked up, the chief pathologist was standing there, towering over him in his overcoat.

'Are you OK?' asked Giangrande.

'Not really — they don't seem to have a clue.'

'This is a good hospital. They'll set her right.'

Again, Scamarcio couldn't think of anything to say; it was as if his mind was shutting down. Giangrande stepped away and went to look through the windows.

After a few minutes had passed, the female doctor scurried out of Aurelia's room, turning left down the corridor.

Scamarcio jumped up from his chair. 'Can't you tell me anything?' he asked, trying to keep pace with her.

'I've got a theory I'm going to go with,' she said, hurrying on. 'We'll need to irrigate her bowel.'

'What?'

Giangrande ran over to join them. 'Was it an *overdose*?' He looked at Scamarcio as he asked this.

'No. I think she was poisoned. We'll be putting her on dialysis.'

'Dialysis?' repeated Giangrande, stunned.

'I must get on,' said the doctor. 'I'll be back through to talk to you as soon as I know more.'

They both fell silent, tracking her retreating frame.

What the fuck are we dealing with? Scamarcio asked himself. *Or, more to the point, who?*

28

THEY BOTH WAITED on the uncomfortable plastic chairs in silence, neither knowing what to say. Scamarcio studied the battered pea-green paintwork and stained floor tiles, wondering if this hospital had a problem with super bugs. At one point, Giangrande headed for the coffee machine and brought him back an espresso; but, besides saying 'Thank you', Scamarcio couldn't think of anything to add.

'She's a good person, Aurelia,' said Giangrande, out of nowhere.

'I know,' said Scamarcio.

'Well, it doesn't seem like it.'

'I know,' repeated Scamarcio.

The chief pathologist sighed, and fell silent once more. They sat there like that for what seemed like several hours, watching the doctors and nurses come and go. Scamarcio figured that the two of them must have looked like one of those living art installations they staged at modern galleries. He thought about his American visitors, but it didn't quite gel; this seemed too heavy-handed an approach, even for them.

After what seemed like an eternity, the doctor was back. She looked from one to the other of them. 'We've irrigated the bowel and started the dialysis. She's been given a blood transfusion, and is being treated with chelating agents.'

Giangrande leapt up from the chair. 'Arsenic?'

'How did you know?' asked the doctor, eyeing him suspiciously now.

'I'm a pathologist.'

She nodded quickly. 'The blood and urine have just come back positive on that, so my hunch was right. She had all the symptoms — vomiting, abdominal pain, diarrhoea, and her heart rate was all over the place. But it was when I noticed the urine that it first struck me — it was very dark.'

'Is there permanent damage?' asked Scamarcio.

'I don't think so. We got to her just in time. But if we'd left it any longer, I don't think the kidneys would have held out.'

'How long will she be on dialysis?' asked Scamarcio.

'We'll keep running tests, but it shouldn't be more than another twenty-four hours.'

'So she should make a full recovery?'

'I'm hopeful.'

'What about her red blood cells?' asked Giangrande, 'They would have taken a battering.'

'The transfusion should have seen to that, but we'll keep monitoring her blood until we're satisfied.'

The chief pathologist nodded.

Scamarcio leant his head against the wall and breathed.

As he was leaving the hospital, his mobile rang. There was no 'Hello' — just Piocosta's usual growl.

'By the river, half an hour,' was all the old man said.

'Now's not the best time.'

'We need to talk, Leo. We can't put this off any longer.'

Scamarcio sighed. *Could this day get any worse?*

'OK,' he replied eventually, wondering how bad it would be.

When he got to the Tiber, Piocosta was waiting for him under the bridge. He was wearing a new yellow beret — it looked good against his tanned complexion. Scamarcio remembered hearing that it had been 25 degrees in Catanzaro at the weekend. Perhaps the old man had been back at his beachside villa, catching up with family. Piocosta took Scamarcio's hand and grasped it to his heart. 'Thanks for coming,' he said. 'I know you're busy.'

'So what's so urgent?'

'Let's walk,' said Piocosta.

They turned left along the riverbank, pebbles crunching underfoot. The water was clearer than usual, the current mild. Only a few ducks were out on the water, bobbing sedately.

They walked on for a minute or so, and then Piocosta cleared his throat. 'So, as I said last time, I need to call in that debt.'

Scamarcio took a silent breath. 'Hit me with it.'

'I've been running a few new spin-off operations here in the city — money-lending, mainly. It's caught the attention of the wrong people. I was hoping you could get them to look the other way.'

'My people?'

'Of course.'

'What kind of money-lending?'

'Well, you know a lot of small businesses are in real trouble at the moment — they can't get loans from the banks. So they come to us. We're the only people prepared to help them.'

Scamarcio ran a hand across his eyes. 'Shit, Piero — not you as well. Aren't there already enough sharks in the pool?'

The old man shrugged his shoulders. 'We're just adapting to the times, Leo, going with the flow. We're helping folk who have got into difficulty.'

Scamarcio felt his rage and frustration rising. It took all his effort to tamp it down. He wanted to take the old man by the throat and punch his lights out. He counted to ten silently and tried to focus on a patch of ground beyond the river where a shabby cluster of starlings were picking at breadcrumbs. After a moment, he heard himself say, '*Help* them? You call that *helping* them? You lend them money at extortionate rates, and then when they can't pay it back you take over their companies from the inside, forcing them into crooked deal after crooked deal, eating away at them like goddamn parasites. Just last week an old couple, an old couple with children and grandchildren, set fire to themselves in their car because the 'ndrangheta had wrecked their business! You'd destroyed everything they'd spent their entire lives working for.'

Piocosta shook his head. 'The banks did that, not us.'

Scamarcio counted to ten. *That's bullshit,* he thought, *and you know it.* But instead he replied, 'You're not helping the situation. These people are already in trouble — what they don't need is to be bled dry.'

'Oh, come on, Leo, it's the business.'

Scamarcio fell silent once more. He couldn't afford an argument with the old man. He owed him. Was Piocosta cold-blooded enough to harm his best friend's boy? Scamarcio couldn't be certain of the answer.

Piocosta said nothing for several moments, and then asked, 'So, will you help us?'

Scamarcio tried to muster a response that might buy him some thinking space. 'I need a bit of time.'

'Time is a commodity I don't have right now.'

'What squad is it? Do you have any names?'

'No. I need you to find that out, and throw them off the scent.'

Scamarcio nodded, wondering how the hell he could pull that off, and if he was even prepared to try. 'Leave it with me,' he said eventually.

The old man reached up to take him by both shoulders, his small, dark eyes seeking him out. They reminded Scamarcio of tiny black holes, sucking in all the light.

'Can I count on you, boy?'

Scamarcio fought a sudden urge to push him off. 'I'll do my best,' he said.

Piocosta nodded and let go.

The wind was picking up now, and Scamarcio pulled the collar of his jacket tighter against his face. He felt cold, very cold, but he just stood there, watching the retreating frame of his father's old lieutenant melt into the darkness beneath the bridge.

By the time he'd returned to his flat, the tiredness was so strong that he just wanted to head straight to bed, but he knew he wouldn't sleep with the day grinding round in his head. With no idea of what food he had in the house, he reached up to check the kitchen cupboards, but as he did so he noticed an open bottle of wine and a dirty wine glass on the worktop. It was one of his 30-euro bottles of Amarone, but he didn't remember having opened it; in fact, he was quite sure he hadn't. He sniffed the glass, and set it back down on the counter. Who had drunk this, and when? Why had they just left it there like that? He thought back, trying to remember who had been in his flat lately. The Americans, yes, but they'd been in his presence the whole time. Had they let themselves in again and just helped themselves to a drink? Maybe, but it didn't feel right; why would they do that? Besides, it looked as if just one glass had been poured — the bottle was still nearly full. He froze for a moment before slumping into a seat by the kitchen table. Aurelia had been here, just the night before. She had keys to his apartment, and had let herself in. Maybe she'd helped herself to a glass before he got back; maybe she'd been looking for some Dutch courage before she confronted him.

Shit. Was there arsenic in that bottle? Was it intended for me?

He got up from the table and headed for his hold-all, where he kept a stack of evidence bags. He pulled out several, along with some plastic gloves, and hurried back to the kitchen. He put on the gloves, and carefully placed the dirty glass in the bag. He did the same with the bottle, removing the cork from where it had been left on the end of the opener, and replacing it on top of the bottle. He bagged the corkscrew as well, for good measure.

Why hadn't he seen this opened bottle before? He'd eaten at the bar last night, and when he'd gotten home he'd headed straight for bed. This morning, he'd woken late and had decided to grab a cappuccino on his way to see Giangrande — so he hadn't set foot in his kitchen.

He pulled out his mobile, and dialled the chief pathologist. 'Can you meet me at the morgue straightaway?' he asked.

'I've only just got home.'

'Please, Giangrande, it's important.'

The chief pathologist fell silent for a moment, and then said he'd be there within the hour.

'Who do you think did this?' Giangrande asked as he held the wineglass up to the light, surveying it through the bag.

'Your American friends would be my first guess,' Scamarcio replied, returning his attention to the glass.

'They're not my friends, Scamarcio. I made a mistake. For which I am deeply sorry.' Giangrande paused for a moment. 'It doesn't make sense. It seems like an over-reaction — arsenic is old hat.'

Scamarcio shrugged. 'Maybe that's all they could get their hands on.'

'Those people can get their hands on anything.'

'Did they tell you who they were? CIA? FBI?'

'No, they wouldn't be drawn.'

Scamarcio sighed. 'When do you think you can get the results back?'

'I'll put a rush on it. You'll need to clear it for me, though — say it's part of your case.'

'Well, it is now.'

Giangrande smiled. 'So you'll be eating out from now on?'

'You bet,' replied Scamarcio, a tight coil of anxiety in his stomach.

29

WHEN SCAMARCIO STOPPED by the Policlinico Gemelli the next morning, Aurelia was sitting up in bed. There was colour in her cheeks, and the bluey-grey marks around her eyes had faded. However, there was still a drip in her arm, and Scamarcio saw a dense web of different-coloured wires running from her chest to a complicated-looking machine; there seemed to be even more of them than the day before.

He handed her the semi-decent bouquet he had bought at the shop downstairs.

'Did you steal them from a cemetery?' she asked.

'You're definitely on the mend,' he said, smiling.

'The doctor told me it was arsenic.' She shook her head. 'I've got no idea how. I haven't picked up anything unusual; I've not been in touch with hazardous materials.'

Scamarcio pulled out a chair next to her bed. 'No, but you helped yourself to a glass of wine in my flat, didn't you?'

She looked at him, her face a question. 'Yes, I did but ...'

'I think that wine was laced. I've given it to Giangrande for testing.'

'Why would anyone want to poison you?' She arched an eyebrow. 'Actually, stupid question.'

'My bet is on the Americans.'

She scrunched her forehead. 'No — that seems too way out there.'

'They're clearly very worried about something.'

'Yeah, but arsenic, that doesn't seem their style. It's old-fashioned.'

'That's what Giangrande said.'

She sighed and sank back against the pillows.

'How are you feeling?' he asked.

'I'm OK. A bit weak, very tired. But OK, I think.'

He laid his hand on hers. 'I'm so sorry, Aurelia, about everything.'

She turned away from him for a moment, and he thought he saw her shoulders shake slightly. He wondered if she might be crying.

'I've been selfish,' he said. 'I know it's no excuse, but I've been trying to sort my head out, and it's been taking time. I'm sorry you've felt pushed away.' He moved a strand of hair out of her eyes. 'Anyway, I'm going to let you get some rest. I'll be back in later.'

He quickly stroked her cheek, and then left. He wanted to give her some space; he didn't want her to feel embarrassed.

As he was heading for the elevator, he spotted the doctor from the day before. 'How do you think she's doing?' he asked.

'She's making a good recovery. I'm optimistic.'

'When can she go home?'

'It will be a day or two yet. She'll be quite weak for a while — she'll need a hand around the house.'

'We don't live together,' he said quickly.

The doctor eyed him curiously. 'Well, maybe you could just spend some time at her place as she recovers.'

He tried a smile. 'Of course,' he said. 'Thanks again.'

'Not a problem.' She threw him a strange look, and then hurried away.

Back in the squad room, he brought Garramone up to speed on Aurelia. He also told him about the results from Carter's liver-tissue sample.

'This is getting way out of hand,' said the boss, slamming his palm against the desk. 'I'm not having them going around poisoning my fucking detectives.'

'If it *was* them?'

'Who else would it have been?'

'I don't know,' sighed Scamarcio. 'Maybe someone from the summer?'

'I don't think so. There's too much going on with this case — it has to be related.'

The chief eased back against his chair. 'What do you make of this Brambani thing?' he asked, running a tired hand across his face.

'It smells off to me.'

'And me.'

'I called the police up in Varese, and they said nobody had been on to them about Brambani from the Vatican. That seems weird.'

The boss turned his head to the window. 'Why don't you head up north — see what you can find out? We should try to get to Brambani before the Vatican police do.'

Scamarcio nodded, thinking about Aurelia in the hospital, knowing it would look like he was abandoning her. Then he thought about Piocosta, and wondered how the hell he was going to find a way through that quagmire, especially if he was hundreds of kilometres away. But he couldn't let the chief down — not after Pozzi.

'Sure,' he heard himself say. 'When do you want me to leave?'

'No time like the present.'

At Termini station, Scamarcio jumped on the first Red Arrow for Milan Central. He had tried to call Aurelia to explain that he'd had to leave town, but the nurse who answered said she was sleeping and was not to be disturbed. He had hung up, resolving to try again later. He dozed all the way to Milan, and after he'd reached Central Station he took the green line down to Cadorna, where he picked up a train heading north to the lakes.

He tried calling Aurelia once more, but this time the line was engaged. He looked out at the mud-brown flatlands of the Pianura Padana, the soulless housing developments, the derelict factories, the skeletal electricity pylons. Yet again, he wondered about the Americans. *Were* they CIA? If they were in fact from an arcane branch of US Intel, he shared Giangrande's instinct that arsenic probably wouldn't be their style.

His thoughts shifted to Piocosta. What the hell was he going to do about him? Scamarcio couldn't interfere in another police inquiry. He couldn't start granting favours of that magnitude, otherwise it would never end — Piocosta would just keep pushing for more. Besides, Scamarcio found the whole thing morally repugnant. The 'ndrangheta and their loan-sharking operations needed to be shut down, eliminated. He couldn't play any part in adding to the misery they caused. He ran his fingers across his eyelids, and wondered if he could find some titbit to toss the old man, some morsel that might keep him satisfied. But if the police were closing in, that wouldn't be enough — like Piocosta had said, he needed a quick fix. Scamarcio wondered if there was a cleaner way of throwing his colleagues off the scent, whether he could find them some bigger fish to net. He sighed and sank back against the seat. It was hopeless. There *were* no bigger fish: the 'ndrangheta would always be the prize catch.

After an hour or so, they left the plains behind, and Scamarcio caught the first glimpse of dense greens and golds as the foothills came into view. As they drew closer to the lake, the first silver peaks of the Alps rose up above the water, mirroring themselves in its surface, and he noticed a scattering of tiny hamlets, old stone churches at their centre. Far out on the lake was a small wooded island where fragile tendrils of smoke were emerging from the canopy. He wondered what kind of place Comerio would be — whether it was just a few cottages and a shop. He would have to head into Varese if he couldn't find anywhere to stay.

But when the train pulled into the station and he saw the modern-looking semis and factory buildings, he realised that this was a large village, if not a town. He asked the grumpy station attendant for directions, and she reluctantly pointed him up a steep hill beyond the carpark. As he made the climb, he passed large villas with Mercedes and BMWs parked outside; in the extensive garden of one of the houses, a Filipina in full maid's uniform was emptying scraps into a dustbin. It seemed that the economic crisis hadn't yet reached Comerio. Forty-five minutes from Milan, and set in stunning countryside, Scamarcio figured that this was where the managers and CEOs must reside. It was probably a more attractive prospect than a smog-infested flat in one of the graffiti-ridden cul de sacs of the city.

He noticed some steps partly hidden beneath a patch of woodland, and when he crossed the road to take them, he saw a small wooden signpost pointing towards the centre. The climb seemed to grow steadily steeper, but after a few minutes he was rewarded with a breathtaking view of the lake once more, a cluster of palm trees in the foreground providing an interesting contrast with the snowy peaks, dramatic now against the slate-grey sky.

As he took the last few steps to the village, the houses became more modest. Some looked like old barns that had been converted into apartments, and behind several he noticed enclosed courtyards with raggedy lines of washing strung up. Children's bikes lay where they'd been thrown on the ground, and mangy dogs shuffled about, scavenging for scraps.

He was suddenly aware of the familiar warmth along the back of his neck and the tingling of his spine. He slowed his pace, his heart pounding through his ribcage, and his palms growing damp. He didn't want to turn, he didn't want to see who was following him, but he forced himself to do so. Yet when he scanned the road behind him, he saw that the street was empty. There was no sign of life, no hint that anyone else had been there. He couldn't even hear the hum of cars in the distance. He walked on, and tried to steady his breathing. Perhaps he was just on edge after recent events in Rome.

The church soon came into view on his left. It was a simple, white building, its small stained-glass windows almost invisible against the stone. The main entrance was open, and he stepped inside, glad of the sanctuary, of the familiar smells of furniture polish and incense. The place seemed deserted until he spotted an old lady arranging flowers on a small table near the altar. He coughed, and she turned.

'Good evening, Signora. I was looking for Father Brambani.'

'We haven't seen him all day,' she said stiffly, laying down the flowers.

'Do you know how I might find him?'

'Are you a journalist?'

'No, a policeman.'

'You don't look like a policeman. Where's your uniform?'

'I'm a detective with the Flying Squad down in Rome. We're plainclothes.' He stepped forward and showed her his card.

The old woman crossed herself and said, 'I'm sorry, Detective. It's just that quite a few reporters have been around, looking for him. I presumed you were one of them.'

He nodded. 'So you really have no idea where he is?'

She shook her head and fiddled with the glasses hanging around her neck. 'It's a dreadful business — all that nonsense on the news. He's been an excellent priest to us — he's very popular here in the village. There must have been some mistake.'

Scamarcio smiled sympathetically. 'If I could just have a word with him, I'm sure we can clear up any confusion.'

The woman sighed. 'I wish I could help but, like I say, I haven't seen him since yesterday.'

'How did he seem these past days?'

She shrugged. 'Normal, his usual self; there didn't seem anything bothering him, if that's what you mean.'

'Where does he have his lodgings?'

'Right here, behind the church. Do you want me to show you?'

Scamarcio nodded.

The woman quickly tidied away the scissors and string she had been using to arrange the flowers, placing them in a drawer beneath the table. Then she walked towards the main door, motioning for Scamarcio to follow. 'It's this way.'

They exited the church and followed the cobbled lane around to the left, where they soon came across a narrow stone house with four floors. The building seemed to have been recently modernised: some of the external stonework had been replaced with varnished wooden panels, and the small windows were double-glazed.

'His apartments are on the second floor,' said the old lady. 'I do his cleaning, so I have a key.'

Scamarcio nodded, and allowed the woman to step forward so she could undo the lock. When they reached the second floor, she chose a key from a large ring fastened around her handbag and opened the door, crossing herself again.

They stepped into a small room that was warm and very neat. The walls were painted white, and the pine furniture was simple. Scamarcio noticed a small crucifix hanging above a wide desk where different-coloured papers were stacked in several tidy piles. To the left of the desk, in the centre of the room, was a Scandinavian pellet stove, the small flame still bright.

'He must have been here recently,' said Scamarcio.

'Why?' asked the woman.

'Because the fire is still alight.'

'You have one of those things?' she asked.

'No,' replied Scamarcio, wondering where this was going.

'Well, if you did, you'd know that you can fill it with pellets in the early morning before you leave, and it will still be going in the evening by the time you get back.'

'I see,' said Scamarcio. There was something schoolmistressy about this old lady, and he wondered if that had been her former profession.

'The bedroom is over here,' she said.

They passed through a doorway off the living room into a small corridor. There was one door facing them, and two others to the right. She knocked tentatively on the door ahead. 'Father Brambani,' she said softly, 'Father Brambani.'

When there was no response, she turned to Scamarcio, her voice dropping to a whisper. 'This is the second time I've been round today. I came just before lunch to see if he was OK, but there was no sign of him then, either.'

Scamarcio nodded, and she gently pushed the door.

The small bedroom was as tidy as the sitting room. The single bed had been made, a checked throw tucked tightly into the frame, any creases smoothed away. The books on the side table were neatly stacked, and the shoes by the wardrobe carefully arranged in a line. He noticed a pair of sturdy walking boots. This was mountain country, so maybe the priest enjoyed a trek from time to time. The old lady followed his gaze. 'Father Brambani likes to climb Sacro Monte. He does the whole thing, heads right up to the Observatory. He says it helps him communicate with God.'

Scamarcio didn't know the place, but nodded as if he did.

There was something missing in the room, and he wondered where Father Brambani stored his clutter. In most people's homes there was some sign of the overspill of life, even if it was neatly compartmentalised on a bookshelf or piled in a corner; but this apartment just seemed so spare, so sanitised, somehow. He walked over to the bed, and got down on his hands and knees to look underneath. He saw several old shoeboxes arranged in a line, and a stack of magazines. He figured that if the shoes were by the wardrobe, the boxes had to contain something else. He pulled everything out, hoping that the magazines were respectable; he didn't want to embarrass the old woman.

'It doesn't feel right to me that you're going through the Father's things,' she said.

'I'm just looking for a way to find him,' replied Scamarcio, pulling out the boxes. 'There might be something here that helps us.'

He was relieved to see that the magazines were on trekking and adventure holidays. He pushed them to one side, and then lifted the shoeboxes onto the bed and removed the lids. The first one seemed to contain a collection of old letters and postcards. At first glance, they looked as if they'd been sent by relatives — he saw 'Your loving mother' signed beneath several. He moved his attention to the second box, but it didn't seem to hold anything more exciting than a half-used bottle of ink, a stick of glue, some Post-it notes, and a couple of boxes of paper clips. When he took the lid off the third, however, he saw that it was stacked high with newspaper cuttings; on the article at the top of the pile, the date had been written in biro and carefully underlined with a yellow highlighter pen.

He gently pulled out the pile and laid it on his lap. The first cutting had been folded in half, so he spread it out to read the headline: 'TRIAL INTO TURIN BOMBING TO OPEN NEXT WEEK.' The piece was from *Corriera della Serra*, and was dated just three days before. The article beneath it was smaller, and was entitled 'TURIN VICTIMS HOPE NEW TRIAL WILL BRING TRUE PERPETRATORS TO JUSTICE.' It had been published two days before the first. As he worked his way back through the pile, Scamarcio realised that he was going back through the years. The article at the very bottom of the stack was dated 6 September 1983 — the day of the Turin attack. The piece took up the whole of the front page and several pages beyond, the banner screaming: '95 DEAD IN NEW TERROR OUTRAGE'.

Scamarcio laid down the cuttings and took a breath. The old lady was studying him carefully, as if she wanted to make sure he didn't steal anything.

'Do you know why Father Brambani would be interested in the Turin bombing?' he asked.

She frowned. 'He's never mentioned it. Maybe he wanted to talk about it in one of his sermons?'

That's a lot of research for one sermon, thought Scamarcio. He replaced the lids, and stowed the boxes under his arm. 'I need to take these,' he explained. 'I'll return them as soon as possible.'

'Do you think those papers will help you find Father Brambani?'

'Perhaps.'

They left the apartment, the old lady stopping to refill the stove on her way out in case the Father returned. When they were back outside, Scamarcio handed her his card and asked her, or the Father, to call as soon as he showed up.

She nodded silently, seemingly more worried than before at the thought of what might have happened to him. Scamarcio promised her that he would do his best to track him down. Quite how, he wasn't yet sure.

The old lady had advised him to head for Varese to find a room for the night, as there wasn't much on offer in the villages outside. He had settled on a decent place near the historic centre — it had a bit of character, and seemed less depressing than the chain hotels on the outskirts. The receptionist claimed that the lobby was manned twenty-four hours a day, so Scamarcio left strict instructions that no visitors should be allowed up. Nevertheless, once safely installed in his room, he pulled a heavy desk from the wall and pushed it hard against the door.

He took off his jacket and laid the letters out on the double bed, deciding to start with the oldest first. The earliest date he could find was October 1990. He wished he had asked the old lady how old Brambani was. That would help him identify what was going on in the letters, and perhaps shed some light on why he might be interested in Turin.

The 1990 letter was from Brambani's mother. In the second paragraph, she asked her son how he was 'getting on at the seminary'. She went on to tell him that his father would have been 'very proud'. Scamarcio felt that he had been given two clues: If Brambani had been at the seminary in 1990, that would possibly have made him seventeen or eighteen at the time, which would put him at around forty now. The use of the conditional tense suggested that Brambani's father was dead. But when did he die, and how?

The following letters gave no explanation. After he had spent over an hour reading through the entire stack and getting nowhere, Scamarcio pushed the letters away in frustration. It seemed as if he wasn't going to get any real answers until they located Brambani. He wondered if the Vatican element was a wild-goose chase; whether Garramone had been foolish to send him up here. Perhaps he would have made more headway staying down in Rome and working through the Cappadona angle.

He gathered his wallet and keys, having decided to head out for a bite to eat. But just as he was about to put on his jacket, he spied a piece of paper beneath the bed. He picked it up, and saw that it was another letter. It must have come loose from the pile. He went to place it on top of the stack, but as he did so he noticed the date, and felt sure that he hadn't yet read this letter. It was dated September 1998, shortly after Brambani had taken up the priesthood.

The mother wrote:

I must confess to you my son that sometimes I find it very difficult
to comprehend what God had in mind when he sent these men
to destroy our lives. Your father was just a young man with so

much joy ahead of him, so much hope. He never had the chance to watch his children grow, never had the chance to realise his ambitions. Was it God's intention that he was at the station that day? Why did he choose him instead of another? Do you ever ask yourself these questions? I hope you can find the answers that seem to elude me, that you can reach some kind of peace with this.

Scamarcio laid down the letter and studied the ceiling. Was it possible that Brambani had lost his father in the Turin attack? Was that why he'd kept the stack of press cuttings beneath his bed? If so, Scamarcio sensed that he had not found the peace with the case his mother had wished for. He picked up the pile once more and trawled through the remaining letters again, but he could find no further mention of the father's death. It was as if the subject had become taboo between Brambani and his mother.

He reached for his BlackBerry, and ran a search for the Turin Relatives Association. He jotted down the telephone number and email, doubting that anyone would pick up at this time of night. And indeed, when he dialled, it went straight to answerphone. The best thing he could do now was to head out — he was seriously hungry now, and on an empty stomach his mind couldn't quite process the connection between Brambani's involvement with the Turin bombing and the fact that he'd been spotted on Abbiati's staircase just before he died. But Scamarcio felt certain that there was a connection nevertheless.

30

'There's two million dollars missing from the administration account,' said the chief accountant.

'You must be mistaken.'

'I'm not mistaken. It's gone — I can't trace it to any of our other accounts. It must have been drawn out in cash.'

'Are you feeling all right? You look unwell.'

'There's nothing wrong with my health.'

'I think you need to take a holiday, wind down. I didn't really want to discuss this with you yet, but your work hasn't quite been up to par of late.' The cardinal coughed and moved away. 'There's a lot of competition for this job, and people are talking.'

'Talking?'

'About whether you're up to it.'

The chief accountant did feel ill now; he needed air, a glass of water, and he wanted to sit down. He thought of what they'd done to Roberto, and the room started to spin.

SCAMARCIO HAD SLEPT FITFULLY. Despite the country air and the fact that he'd momentarily fled Rome and all the troubles that place brought him, he couldn't get his mind to drift over. On the few occasions he'd felt himself letting go, he'd forced himself awake again, listening for footsteps or hands at the window.

He looked down on the street below. It was an uninspiring morning, bleak and overcast; the good citizens of Varese were hurrying about their business, trying to get their errands done before the rain set in. Scamarcio decided to head for the nearest café so he could grab a cappuccino and call the Turin Relatives Association.

He dressed and headed out, quickly locating a decent-looking place that seemed popular. He found a table away from the breakfast throng, and pulled out his mobile. Thankfully, someone picked up after the second ring.

He introduced himself and explained what he was looking for. The woman who answered said she would hand him over to Director Viola. The name sounded familiar, and Scamarcio had a feeling it would be the same guy he had seen interviewed on TV the other night.

'Viola.'

Scamarcio repeated his introduction.

'How can I help you, Detective?'

'I wonder if you've kept a list of victims of the bombing. I'm looking for one name in particular — a Mr Brambani.'

If Viola had been following the news on the Abbiati slaying, he made no mention of it now.

'Brambani, Brambani … the name does ring a bell, but just give me a second while I consult my files.'

Scamarcio heard him take a slurp of something and then tap a few keys. After a minute or so, he was back. 'Yes, Marco Brambani was one of the victims. Thirty-three years old, father of two.'

Scamarcio exhaled, and entered the details into his notebook. As he was writing, he asked, 'He has a son — Antonio Brambani. I was wondering if he was one of your members?'

'One second.'

Scamarcio heard a few more keys being tapped before Viola was back again. 'No, I don't have anything for an Antonio Brambani. I have a Rita Brambani, though — she must be a relative.'

'Do you have a contact number?'

Viola said he did. Scamarcio made a note, thanked him, and hung up.

He dialled the number, and an old woman's voice answered.

Scamarcio introduced himself once more, and explained that he was looking for her son.

'I'm going out of my mind with worry,' she said. 'I haven't been able to reach him for days, and now his picture is all over the news. The neighbours haven't stopped calling,' she said bitterly.

'Did you know whether he was planning on going away anywhere? Maybe he had a trip in mind?'

'No. He had his church duties. He couldn't just up and leave.'

'Where do you live, Signora Brambani? I was given your telephone number, but no address.'

'In Biella, outside Turin.'

That explained why her husband had been at the station that day.

'I was told you're a member of the Turin Relatives Association.'

'My husband was killed in the bombing.'

'Was your son a member?'

'No, I don't think so.'

'Did you two discuss what had happened much?'

The woman fell silent for a few beats. 'Antonio was ten when his father died. It hit him very hard. But, no, as he got older and his life fell into place, we didn't really mention it.' She paused once more. 'He has an old cinefilm of him and his father that he used to watch in secret when he still lived at home. I caught him crying in front of it once, and it just took my breath away. I'll never forget it.' Her words were slightly slurred, and Scamarcio wondered if she'd been drinking.

'Mrs Brambani, if you hear from your son, will you let me know as soon as possible?'

'Is he in trouble? Do you think he had something to do with the death of that cardinal?'

'At this stage, I don't know. But it's important we find him so he can tell us why he was at the Vatican that night. Do you have any idea what might have brought him to Rome? What business he might have had with Abbiati?'

She sighed, and it came out distorted down the line. 'It's as much a mystery to me as it is to everyone else.'

There was something off about the way she said it, and Scamarcio wondered if she could be hiding something. *Is she hiding her son?* But she'd sounded genuine when she'd claimed she had no idea about his whereabouts.

'I'm not sure it's even him in those pictures. The face is too thin,' she added, quickly.

Somehow, Scamarcio felt sure it *was* Brambani on the CCTV footage, but instead he said, 'Can I give you my number so you can call me if you hear from him?'

'Hang on while I get a pen.'

Scamarcio heard footsteps and the sound of a door being slammed. After what seemed like several minutes, she was back, breathing heavily now. 'OK, I'm ready.'

He gave her his details, and then asked, 'Have any other policemen approached you?'

'No, nobody.'

It's interesting, the complete lack of interest that the Vatican investigators are showing in the Brambani family, thought Scamarcio.

He returned to his hotel room, feeling that he should probably stay put in Varese for at least another night. His confidence was growing that any early answers might be found here rather than down in the capital. He would call Garramone in a while and fill him in.

He pondered the connection between Brambani and Abbiati, thinking back to his meeting with Professor Letta. At some point, it seemed that the Vatican and the P2 lodge had worked together when it came to funding Solidarity. Calvi had been cleaning P2's money through the Vatican Bank. If P2 and Gladio had been involved in stirring up trouble at home, organising terror campaigns that would unsettle the electorate and keep the communists out of power, was it possible that certain figures inside the Vatican were complicit — or that they at least knew? If they were working to defeat the communists in Poland, wouldn't they be equally interested in defeating them at home?

Scamarcio turned his attention to the other boxes he had taken from Brambani's apartment, which he had left lying on the bed when he went out for breakfast. He decided to take another quick look through the one that contained stationery supplies, just to make sure he hadn't missed anything.

He took out the bottle of ink, the stick of glue, and the pile of yellow Post-its, and was about to put them all back when he noticed a black plastic DVD case at the bottom of the box. There was a white label on its rear side, on which someone had scrawled 'Rainbow Club trip' in biro. Inside the case was an unmarked DVD. Scamarcio seemed to remember that the club was a national charity that organised outings for disabled children — he had seen their multi-coloured buses shuttling around Rome.

Scamarcio snapped the case shut and put the DVD back in the the box, assuming it wouldn't take him any further. He replaced the other items and closed the lid, and then just sat and thought. Something wasn't right. After a few moments, he blew the air out from his cheeks and pulled out the stationery items once more, and reached for the DVD again. One of the first things that Garramone had impressed upon him was that no detail, however small it might seem, should be overlooked. He was obliged to at least skim through the film. Anything less would be negligent — and could earn him a dressing-down from the chief.

He loaded the DVD into his laptop and, as he'd expected, the first few minutes showed a group of children with different levels of disability being pushed through Vatican City by exhausted parents wearing fragile smiles. Then the images cut to the children forming a small line in front of St Peter's Square, their wheelchairs side by side. A priest who looked very much like Father Brambani was holding a blond toddler in his arms and waving into the lens. Then the camera panned right, and Scamarcio's breath froze. Shaking hands with some of the parents was a man who closely resembled the image of Cardinal Abbiati that the TV stations had been running. He had the same bald dome, the same penetrating blue eyes. *So he and Brambani had met?* When had this film been shot? There was no date marked on the box, and no timecode.

Scamarcio pressed fast-forward, but Abbiati didn't appear again. Instead, there were images of the little group eating a picnic lunch, tossing bread to pigeons, slowly emerging from what looked like St Peters Basilica, before the screen went black. Scamarcio was about to press stop when the black suddenly turned red — a brilliant, startling red that bled rapidly from the top of the screen to the bottom. The bleed was accompanied by low music in a minor key — a strange and unsettling sound — and then the colour seeped away to form a rudimentary graphic of the crosshairs of a gun. In its sights was the same clip of Cardinal Abbiati shaking hands, but this time the image had been magnified so that his face filled the target.

Just above the music, a voice was whispering. The effect was bizarre and disquieting, and Scamarcio could barely make out the words. After a little while, he thought he could pick up a few phrases: *The very institution I have looked up to all my life, the very institution I've always turned to for comfort and support, has betrayed me*. Then the murmurs became indecipherable once more until, around twenty seconds later, Scamarcio heard the line *How does it feel to have blood on your hands?* The red reappeared at this point, and the disturbing whispering continued for a few more seconds until the screen went black again. Scamarcio tried to spin forward, but the disc just locked. It seemed that it finished there.

His pulse was pounding in his ears now. What the hell was this? Who had made this film, and why? He realised that he needed to get back to Brambani's apartment; he needed to establish whether the priest was behind this, whether any other evidence existed that might explain its existence.

He hailed a cab for Comerio, hoping he would find the old lady in the church, but when he got there the place was empty. He was about to leave, cursing himself for not having taken her number, when he spotted a small, elderly man tending plants by the front entrance.

'Do you work here?' he asked.

'I take care of things from time to time,' said the man, straightening slowly as he rose from the flowerbed.

Scamarcio showed him his card. 'I need access to Father Brambani's apartment. Do you have a key, by any chance?'

'Is this about all that business at the Vatican?'

There was no point in lying, figured Scamarcio. 'Yes, the police are worried about him; we're trying our best to find him.'

The man nodded, and wiped his hands against his apron. 'I don't have a key with me now, but I can fetch one for you.'

Scamarcio thanked him, and said he'd wait.

The man retreated into the church, and was gone so long that Scamarcio was about to follow him inside to check he was OK when he finally returned with a large bunch of keys, whistling softly. The old man pottered so slowly around the church towards the apartment that Scamarcio thought he might give him a shove in frustration, but he told himself to calm down and took a long breath, trying to match his pace.

When they were finally inside once more, Scamarcio cast his eyes around the living room looking for a TV and console, but there was none. He rushed through to the bedroom and headed for the magazines he had left under the bed. He pulled them all out and held them upside down, shaking them violently in the hope that something, anything, might be hidden inside. But no luck.

He turned to the old man. 'Is there a TV in the church, a DVD player, a projector maybe?' The old man shook his head and frowned. 'No, why would there be?' Scamarcio ignored the question and returned to the living room, where he surveyed the desk. He rifled through the neatly stacked papers, but after twenty minutes he couldn't find anything significant — which was precisely the outcome he'd expected on his first visit, and was why he'd headed straight for the bedroom at the time. He was thinking about calling it a day when he turned his attention to the mantelpiece. There didn't appear to be anything noteworthy there — just a few family photos, a conch from a beach, and a large mahogany cross. However, as he looked closer at the cross he noticed something white poking out from behind it. He walked over to pull it out, and saw that it was just a blank envelope. But when he held it to the light he realised that there was something inside. He tore the envelope open and pulled out a single sheet of neatly written notepaper.

He read:

I have dedicated my life to the Church, I have renounced so much. Yet now after over twenty years as a priest, I discover that the very institution I have looked up to all my life, the very institution I've always turned to for comfort and support, has betrayed me. Thousands have suffered at your hands; tens of thousands of lives have been ruined. Now, Cardinal, I ask you: How can you call yourself human? How can you face yourself in the mirror? How does it feel to have blood on your hands? I look at you and I see the Devil. The Devil in the House of God!

We will be coming for you, of that you can be certain. All the sons and the daughters, the mothers and the fathers of the loved ones you stole. We will be coming for you.

The last couple of lines had been underlined many times, as if someone had scored the paper repeatedly.

Scamarcio turned as hard beads of rain hit the window; they started slowly and then quickly became louder, drowning out the murmurs of the village below. Had Father Brambani killed the cardinal as revenge for his father's murder, believing that the Church had some involvement with the Turin attack? But why did he believe that Abbiati was responsible? Who had told him, and who had leaked his picture to the media? Were they one and the same? And where the hell were the Vatican Police in all this?

31

SCAMARCIO HEADED FOR the Varese police station, in the hope that he could speak with Detective Nardone face to face. The desk sergeant led him through to a busy squad room — it was cleaner and neater than the squad room back in Rome, and smelt considerably fresher. The sergeant gestured to a tall man with curly blond hair and a large nose who was drawing coffee from a machine.

When Scamarcio introduced himself, Nardone raised an eyebrow and said, 'For an investigation you're not involved in, you guys seem to be taking this particularly seriously.'

He offered Scamarcio a coffee, but he declined, realising that it would have been his third of the morning.

'So, how can I help you? Did you find out any more about Father Brambani?' asked Nardone once they were seated either side of his immaculately ordered desk.

'I came up here to speak with him, but no one has seen him since the day before yesterday.'

'Hmm.'

'I take it that you still haven't been contacted by the Vatican?'

He shook his head. 'Nada.'

'Don't you find it strange that they have a murder suspect they seem to be doing nothing about?' asked Scamarcio.

Nardone furrowed his brow. 'Well, we don't know that they're doing nothing. They've probably just decided to shut us out of it.'

Scamarcio sighed. 'The whole thing smells off to me. It's weird that that CCTV footage was leaked to the media. It feels convenient — as if they were looking for a scapegoat. If they knew he didn't do it, it would explain why they're not bothering to pursue him.'

Nardone shook his head slowly. 'As I said, we don't know that they're not bothering. We can't just jump to that conclusion.'

Nardone was beginning to irritate him. *Is this man going to give me any help?* Scamarcio talked him through the letters he'd found in Brambani's apartment, and the priest's suspicions that Abbiati was somehow responsible for his father's death. When he was finished, Nardone gave a low whistle and said, 'But that's crazy.'

'Why?'

'The Church would never countenance something like that.'

'Well, I'm not sure we're talking about the Church in general — probably just a few individuals.'

'Even so!'

Scamarcio decided to share with him what he'd learned about P2 and their role in the strategy of tension. After he was finished, Nardone just shook his head and said, 'Where did you get all this?'

'The P2 stuff is starting to filter into the mainstream media. The idea that certain individuals in the Vatican might have had prior knowledge of domestic terror — well, that's a legitimate assumption if they were close to those guys.'

'But nobody ever mentions this Vatican angle.'

'It's not really a *Vatican angle* — as I say, we're probably just talking about certain elements inside the Church.'

Nardone scratched at the back of his head and stared into the middle distance. 'So what do you want *me* to do?' he asked eventually.

'Either you need to be hunting down Brambani for murder, or you need to find him for his own protection.'

Nardone tapped at his chin with his fingers. 'That's a lot of manpower — for a case that happened on foreign soil, which no one has asked us to investigate.'

'I know, Nardone, but at the end of the day he's the priest in a village no more than ten minutes from here. Don't you feel you have some responsibility to find out what's happened to him?'

Hell, it's like pulling teeth.

Nardone fell silent again, thinking it through. After a while, he asked, 'Did any of the people you spoke to give you an idea of his habits, the sort of places Brambani frequented?'

'He likes to walk, apparently — up Sacro Monte, but I don't know where that is. One of his church wardens told me that it helps him communicate with God.'

Nardone gave a slow nod, as if he were on the way to making his mind up. 'Well, in a time of crisis, he'd be needing a good chat with the Lord. Sacro Monte is not far from here.'

And? thought Scamarcio.

After a few more moments, Nardone sighed reluctantly. 'We could send a few men up to do a preliminary search, but I don't want to throw all my resources at this — not until a few things become clearer.'

Scamarcio nodded. *Better than nothing.* 'His walking boots were still in his apartment. If he'd intended to go for a trek, wouldn't he have taken them with him?'

Nardone shook his head. 'In my experience, in times of crisis, people abandon their usual routines. When he left his apartment, he may not have intended to head up there.'

Scamarcio remained silent, turning it all over in his head.

'If he hasn't been seen since the day before yesterday, that's possibly two nights he could have been outside,' added Nardone.

'His pellet stove was on when I went by his place yesterday. My guess is that it's been just one.'

'It was just 4 degrees this morning — if he left without the proper gear, he could be in trouble.'

That Brambani was in serious trouble seemed one of the few certainties so far in this case, thought Scamarcio.

Nardone gave him a desk to work from while he prepared the small search party, and Scamarcio took the opportunity to call Chief Garramone and bring him up to speed. When he was finished, the chief asked, 'But what led Brambani to Cardinal Abbiati? Why would he think he had a hand in his father's death?'

'I don't know,' said Scamarcio. 'I'm still trying to work that out.'

'And we're sure it all connects with our dead American?'

'According to the Cappadona, it was Abbiati who sent them to kill Carter. But Giangrande claims the poison found in Carter's system is not one he's ever seen used by the mafia before. It is, however, CIA stock in trade.' Scamarcio couldn't remember if he'd given the boss this detail yet.

'Fuck,' said Garramone. He sounded as if he was feeling the heat. 'Could this get any more complicated? If AISE tell me to drop it, I might be tempted to listen.'

Scamarcio fell silent, pondering that option.

'When I called the CIA and eventually got put through to someone prepared to listen, they denied all knowledge of the Ponte Sant'Angelo case. They claim they have no idea who the two men are who came to visit you.'

'Well, they would say that, wouldn't they?'

'I guess,' said Garramone, sounding despondent.

'So you're feeling like we should drop it? You want it off our slate?'

'No, don't worry,' sighed the chief. 'Let's keep on it until someone else pulls the cord. I can see that you're like a dog with a bone with this one.'

Was he? Really, how bad would it be if they took this off him, wondered Scamarcio. This inquiry had been nothing but trouble from the start, and if he had to step aside, at least there'd be time to work out what to do with Piocosta. He'd also be able to head back to Rome and get things straight with Aurelia. On the other hand, since his discovery of the letters and the bizarre DVD, his curiosity had been piqued. This case was starting to have a hold on him.

'Just work it through, and get those arseholes off our back,' continued Garramone, 'But I don't want to see any more friction inside the department; the kind of shit you staged with Pozzi must never happen again. And I'd prefer not to have any more of my team poisoned.'

Scamarcio felt the last comment was unjustified. He'd hardly been responsible for the arsenic, but instead he just said, 'Sure.' Some days, he felt like Garramone's pet Pekinese.

'So, Giangrande —was he able to shed any light on how they managed to make off with both the corpse and the autopsy report?'

'He's just as confused as we are,' lied Scamarcio.

'I bet,' said Garramone, sounding unconvinced. There was some sudden chatter in the background, and he said he had to end the call.

Scamarcio set down his phone, and was heading for the coffee machine in the hope that they had something decaffeinated when his mobile rang again. Aurelia's name came up, and he immediately felt guilty. It should have been him calling her. But he'd tried.

'I'll make it quick,' she said by way of a hello.

'You don't need to — I'm not in the middle of anything.'

'Look, I've been offered a job in Munich, and I'm going to accept.'

'What? You're in hospital. What are you talking about?'

'I applied some time back, and the offer has just come through.'

'*When* did you apply?'

'About a month ago now.'

He took a breath and counted to ten. 'Are you going because of me?' he asked eventually, trying to suppress his anger.

'No.'

He decided to step out of the squad room for a few minutes so the call wouldn't be overheard. The change of scenery seemed to do something to his mood, and as he entered the smart, polished hallway, he heard himself say, 'I'm sorry about the past few weeks, Aurelia. I tried to call you at the hospital several times. Garramone sent me up north on this American inquiry, and I couldn't say no.'

She fell silent for a moment and then said, 'You've apologised enough, Leo. I know what it's like when a case takes over; you don't need to explain.' She paused for a beat. 'But this isn't about the hospital, and whether you called or not.'

Scamarcio decided to just go for it; the time would never feel right. 'I guess I've just been scared — scared of investing too much, scared I haven't quite got myself in order.'

Aurelia was silent. He wondered if she was still there, but eventually she said, 'You have to let go of that fear. All relationships are a risk.'

'I don't feel that I have much control over the fear — it's bigger than me.'

'You're thirty-seven, Leo. It's time to come out the other side — you can't be stuck in the past forever.'

'I'm just asking you to be patient. Do you have to go to Munich?'

'It's a good opportunity.'

'I can't give you any guarantees, but if you were here, then obviously we'd have the chance to see if things might work.'

'No guarantees,' she repeated slowly, her tone neutral.

'You're in hospital, for God's sake. You can't just go tearing off to Germany.'

She said nothing for a moment, and then said, 'I'm just letting you know I'm thinking about it.'

32

The images of dead bodies seemed to be a nightly occurrence now.

'It's like there's a war being waged in this country that nobody knows anything about,' said Adele, switching off the TV. 'I thought all that was over; it's 1983, not 1973.' Her words unsettled him, and he felt the need to get out, escape for air.

Carter studied her perfect profile and her thick, dark hair. Her bump was becoming more prominent now. He liked the way it nestled just above her jeans, poking out from beneath her jumper.

'Can you imagine how we'd feel if we lost our child in that way? How do you find peace with something like that? How do you ever move on?' she said.

He felt light-headed. The nausea was rising in his throat, and he forced himself to swallow.

'Are you all right?' she asked. 'You look like you've seen a ghost.'

'The relatives of the station victims are organising a powerful publicity campaign,' he said when he met the cardinal later.

The cardinal sniffed, and turned to the window to take in the pounding rain. 'It's inconvenient. They have the public on their side.'

Of course they had the public on their side. The people had had enough; there was a limit. He felt a sudden urge to throttle this man; to push the evil bastard through the window of his tower, to watch his blood pool and then seep onto the paving stones below. But instead he heard himself ask, 'What are you proposing?'

'On a grand scale, nothing; but on a small scale, there is perhaps something we could do.'

Carter hated his use of the word 'we'. He was done here. He'd farmed it out, but the boy in Mantova had been a bridge too far, and now this? He wanted out while he still knew who he was.

He closed his eyes and then looked across at the cardinal, seeking out the soul within.

'It's what you might call a diversionary tactic,' said the holy man, his narrow green eyes shrinking to small pinpricks in the fading light.

He tried to remember when the cardinal had started taking the initiative. He wondered whether it was their presence that had brought about this change, or whether the capacity for evil had been there all along; whether it had been lying dormant before his predecessor had even set to work.

NARDONE HAD ASSEMBLED a few uniformed officers at the foot of the Sacro Monte near an old stone entranceway. The road was cobbled, and Scamarcio saw a series of little chapels off to the right. They seemed to lead all the way up the mountain.

Nardone followed his gaze. 'You ever climb a Sacred Mountain?' he asked.

'Is there more than one?'

'Nine in Piedmont and Lombardy — all on the UNESCO world-heritage list.'

An officer whispered something in Nardone's ear, and the detective turned swiftly and signalled to the small group behind him. They began the ascent, the officers fanning out across the wide pathway, scanning the banks and ditches beyond. To Scamarcio's left was a dense forest of beech, chestnut, and hazelnut trees. To his right, beyond the pathway, the mountain dropped away to a lush valley, the city of Varese nestling at its base.

'How long does it take to reach the top?' he asked.

'Well under an hour if you're fit,' replied Nardone. 'But in search mode it's going to take us much longer.'

The sky was brightening now, but the cold air stung Scamarcio's cheeks, so he pulled his scarf up tighter, hoping that the exercise would warm him. They walked on in silence, the officers behind them deep in concentration. Scamarcio felt his mobile buzz in his pocket, and when he fished it out he saw Giangrande's name on the caller ID.

The chief pathologist seemed to be hurrying in or out of somewhere, and was short of breath. 'The tests have come back positive — it was arsenic in that wine bottle,' he said.

'God,' said Scamarcio.

'I did you a favour.'

'How?'

'I tried to find out whether the Americans had a hand in it.'

'And did they?'

'They seemed surprised.'

Scamarcio wondered who that left.

'You seem to have a lot of enemies,' observed Giangrande helpfully.

As he passed the little chapels, Scamarcio spotted different configurations of brightly coloured figurines, all of them poised in prayer. Suddenly, just after they had reached what he counted as the sixth chapel, someone gave a shout, and he swung around to see several officers clustered around the stone steps, craning their necks to get a better look at something inside.

'Listen, I've got to go,' said Scamarcio. 'Thanks for the steer.'

'It was the least I could do,' mumbled Giangrande.

Scamarcio pocketed the phone, and headed towards the chapel. The entrance was padlocked and chained, but someone had a key and, after several attempts, the chains fell away. Nardone and a couple of the officers pushed their way inside, but the space was too small for Scamarcio to follow. From his position out on the step, he had a partial view of a large sculpture of Jesus on his knees in prayer, casting his eyes mournfully towards one of the frescoes on the wall. To the right of Jesus's green shawl, where it fanned out across the ground, was a modern running shoe attached to a leg. One of the officers inside shifted to the left, and Scamarcio saw a man in a priest's dog collar stretched out behind the sculpture. He couldn't see any blood, but from where Scamarcio was standing, the man most definitely looked dead.

33

The sun was shining in Washington, baking the pavements and singeing the lawns. It was the first time he'd met the new boss. The one-armed bandit had been shipped off to a retirement home in Florida. Alzheimer's had finally done for him, they said. Or was it all the bad memories?

'It's a pleasure to meet you,' said the new chief. 'I've heard about the great work you've been doing for us out in Europe.'

Carter nodded, feeling tainted. He wanted to get up and wash his hands. Again.

'Do take a seat and make yourself comfortable.' The boss smiled, but when he failed to reciprocate, he fixed him with a curious stare. 'I hear that you have a very strong faith.'

'I'm a practising Catholic, yes.'

'I'm sure that proved invaluable out in Rome.'

He nodded, unsure of how to add to such a trite observation.

'It seems to me that we need to use you wisely. There'll be certain things that are more suited to a man of your character than others.'

'Are you talking about the killing?'

The new director eyed him strangely, concern scoring his brow. 'We don't want to cause you any moral conflict or discomfort. With that in mind and, building on your excellent field work, we believe that you're the ideal candidate to form part of a new team we're building.'

'A new team?'

'Philosophies change, strategies evolve.' He waved a hand away. 'We've come to think that there's a better way to get a country on board.' He seemed personally delighted, as if the world was about to become a much better place. 'Money has always talked, but now we've

found a way to really make it sing.'

'What's the mission?' he asked, cutting him off.

The new guy eyed him with suspicion once more. 'You get the right people to agree to the right deals — the right aid deals, mainly.'

'And how do I do this?'

The new boss shrugged his shoulders. 'You give them an incentive.'

'A financial incentive?'

'Sometimes.'

'And if they don't accept.'

He waved a hand again. 'You don't have to worry about that part. I know you don't like to get your hands dirty.'

NARDONE AND SCAMARCIO had to wait an hour for the police pathologist and the CSI team to arrive, as they'd all been tied up on another case — something that Scamarcio was told was unusual for Varese. Nardone had done his best to secure the scene, taping off the area and erecting a screen in front of the chapel entrance to prevent any passers-by from noticing the dead body inside.

'I don't want to move anything before Forensics get here,' said Nardone. 'Does he look like the guy on the CCTV, you think?'

'Something tells me it's Brambani. I'm assuming you don't see too many dead priests up here?'

Nardone's expression was solemn. 'This is the first.'

Scamarcio heard voices, and turned to see a large, red-faced man manoeuvring his bulk out of a police van. Two other officers wearing 'Polizia Scientifica' jackets emerged from the sliding doors behind him. They lugged their silver cases over to the chapel, fresh packs of overalls beneath their arms. Nardone brought them up to speed.

The police pathologist, who he introduced as Doctor Melodia, bunched up his forehead and said, 'This is *Agony in the Garden*, right?'

Nardone nodded.

Doctor Melodia entered the tiny chapel and knelt down next to the body on the floor. He checked under the eyelids with a torch and then lifted the jumper to examine the chest, carefully pressing it with his fingers before slowly moving his hands behind the man's back. When he was done, he rolled up the sleeves of the priest's jumper, feeling the inside and outsides of the arms, before pulling up the trouser legs and examining the skin on his calves. Then he smoothed down the trousers once more, as if he were worried the body would get cold. The doctor sat back on his haunches, rubbed at his nose, and said nothing.

'Do you think he died from hypothermia?' asked Nardone, breaking the silence.

'It's hard to say until I get him on the table. There's no sign of paradoxical undressing.'

Scamarcio looked blank.

'It's when the blood that the body holds in the core rushes to the extremities and causes a hot flush. The victim suddenly feels too warm, and sheds all his clothing. It's the last stage of hypothermia.'

'How long do you think he's been out here?' asked Nardone.

'Anywhere between twelve to twenty-four hours.'

'How long dead?'

The doctor shook his head. 'I don't know. Again, I'd need to get him on the slab.'

Nardone nodded. 'There seems to be no wounding of any kind.'

'I can't see anything at all,' said Melodia. 'If it's not hypo-thermia, I'm not sure what that leaves. He's a young man; at first glance, he seems healthy.'

Back in his hotel, and waiting for the call to come through with Doctor Melodia's findings from the autopsy, Scamarcio googled the Agony of Jesus in the Garden:

'My heart is sorrowful to the point of death: stay here and pray and keep watch while I go and pray by Myself.' ... He saw all the agony He was going to suffer: and the agony was not so much the pain of the crucifixion as the pains of the sins of the world. Every sin, every injustice, every infidelity He saw and felt at that very moment caused Him to sweat blood. His agony, His sorrow, and so much sinfulness caused the blood to burst from His forehead.

Scamarcio turned away from his laptop and took in the darkening skies beyond the window. Was there any significance in the fact that Father Brambani had been found in that particular chapel? Was there a parallel with Brambani's own agony here? But he sensed that there was reproach in there, too — all the talk of praying continuously, always looking to the Father for consolation — if his letters were to be believed, Brambani had turned his back on the Father. His lifelong faith in the Church had been shattered. Why had he remained a priest, then, Scamarcio wondered. Or had Brambani been about to resign? Was the murder of Abbiati to have been his parting shot?

Scamarcio took stock for a moment. Ever since his early-morning call to the Ponte Sant'Angelo, he had felt as if he had been labouring in the dark on this inquiry. The Vatican was a foreign land where he had no permission to set foot; Carter was an American who had spent much of his life working for the CIA, and yet the real nature of his work remained a mystery. Somehow Scamarcio needed to get inside. He couldn't stay on the outside forever.

He picked up the pay-as-you-go mobile he had recently bought to talk to Blakemore, and dialled the number Blakemore had sent him in a coded email. The code had relied on Scamarcio remembering a particular detail from a drunken night in LA.

'You're still in one piece, then?' asked the reporter.

'Just.' He paused for a beat to change tack. 'You know how you mentioned that Carter might have had troubles at home?'

'Sure.'

'Do you know if he had a wife or a girlfriend?'

'Wife, I think.'

'Could one of your sources put me in touch with her?'

'Hmm,' said Blakemore. 'Might be tricky.'

'Would you give it a go?'

Blakemore fell silent for a moment, and then said, 'Leave it with me.'

Nardone had called to say Doctor Melodia was ready to see them and that they could walk down to his lab together. Scamarcio was putting on his coat to head back to the squad room when his work mobile rang again.

'Scamarcio,' he said, while struggling to hold the mobile in one hand and manoeuvre the other into his jacket sleeve.

'It's Professor Letta — remember me?'

'Of course.'

'You read today's paper?'

Where was this heading? 'Just the sport.'

'So you won't have heard about that Intel guy who's just died?'

'What Intel guy?'

'The one who left a letter claiming that the secret services were involved in Moro's murder.'

He finally got his arm into the jacket. 'That's news to me.'

'It's more grist to the mill. The whole story is going to come tumbling out soon, if you ask me. Anyway, I realised that I'd never told you about Guglielmi.'

'Guglielmi?'

'Colonel Guglielmi was a member of Gladio, and a key figure inside Military Intelligence. He was there at the shoot-out and at the original kidnapping of Moro, but claimed later that he'd been invited to lunch by a colleague who just happened to live nearby.'

Scamarcio wasn't sure how this helped him.

'The other thing is that Banco Ambrosiano did have a branch in Nicaragua — in Managua, as I thought. Make what use of that you will.' Letta paused for a moment before saying, 'And there's one last thing I thought I should mention. Have you heard of the terrorist Vincenzo Guerra?'

'Vaguely.'

'He was with the far right, the NAR, and was found guilty of planting the Santana bomb in 1977 that killed those two Carabinieri. He's spent around 30 years in prison, in Opera outside Milan. I had some dealings with him when I was researching one of my books, and it occurred to me that it might be worth you two having a chat.'

Scamarcio figured that it would probably be unwise to ask for details if there was any chance his normal mobile was being monitored. He thanked Professor Letta for the suggestion, and said that he'd give it some thought.

Detective Nardone was waiting for him outside the Varese police station, huddled under a huge golfing umbrella. The rain hadn't let up all afternoon and, according to the radio, there had been landslides further north.

'Melodia sounded a bit mystified,' said Nardone. 'That's unusual. Most of the the time he's pretty sure of himself. The morgue is just around the corner, so we'll walk if that's OK by you. It will be quicker than trying to find a parking space.'

Scamarcio nodded, surveying the dense traffic inching around the modernist town square up ahead.

'I've been weighing up whether or not to contact the Vatican police,' continued Nardone.

'Don't do that,' said Scamarcio, his tone harsher than he'd intended. 'Not until we understand what we're dealing with.'

'You know, it seems obvious that whoever killed Brambani

left him to be found. There were countless places they could have hidden the body where it would have taken us months to come across it. You saw all that woodland?' asked Nardone.

'Sure.'

'So, why not just leave him there?'

'It's like I was saying,' said Scamarcio. 'If they wanted him to take the blame for Abbiati's death, maybe they also wanted him to be found. It would draw a line under the whole thing.'

'Hmm,' said Nardone. He paused for a moment. 'That means they're probably expecting my call.'

'So, if you don't contact them ...'

'They'll be wondering why. So, do I call them?'

'You call them, but after we've seen Melodia,' Scamarcio said.

Doctor Melodia was pulling a large white sheet over the body when they entered the suite. Above his head was a video monitor, projecting a still of what looked like a heart. Scamarcio wondered if it was Brambani's. The morgue seemed more up to date than the ones Scamarcio was used to in Rome — in fact, both the squad room and the city of Varese in general seemed cleaner and more moneyed than the capital. They said the south started with Rome, and it was true — you could see it and smell it. Up here, so close to Switzerland, there was already a hint of the Nordic affluence beyond, the first tentative suggestions of a fully functioning society.

When Melodia saw them walk in, he pulled the sheet back down again, revealing a pale face and a deep Y-shaped incision now running the length of a muscular, grey body. The pathologist turned to a table to his left and unfolded the black shirt with its clerical collar that the priest had been wearing when they found him. He handed it carefully to Nardone. 'The name Brambani is embroidered on a name tag at the back,' he said by way of explanation.

Nardone nodded. 'The mother is on her way from Turin; she should be here in a couple of hours.'

'OK,' said Melodia. He tapped a few buttons on a keyboard, and the picture of the heart became a close-up, revealing the fine details of the veins and the arteries. Scamarcio wasn't quite sure what exactly he was supposed to be looking at.

'Father Brambani died of a heart attack,' announced Melodia.

Nardone puffed the air out from his cheeks. 'How old was he? He didn't look more than mid-thirties.'

'I think he was around forty,' said Scamarcio. 'Obviously, the mother will tell us for sure.'

'His age is not the problem,' said Melodia solemnly.

Nardone bunched his forehead in confusion. 'Why?'

Melodia tapped at the keyboard again, and another close-up of the heart appeared. 'What does that look like to you?'

'A heart,' said Nardone.

'What kind of heart?' persisted the doctor.

Nardone rolled his eyes, which Melodia saw. Scamarcio felt as if he were back in school.

'I can't really see anything wrong with it,' answered Scamarcio quickly. 'I'm probably missing something. Obviously, I don't have your expertise.'

'No, detective, you're not missing anything at all. That is a perfectly healthy heart, a very healthy heart, the heart of a young man and a keen walker. That is not the heart I would expect to find in a heart-attack victim.'

'But you just said he died from a heart attack?'

'He did.'

'So?'

'So why did a healthy young man die in this way? There's no evidence of blood clots, and no blocked arteries.'

'Can extreme stress bring on a heart attack?' asked Scamarcio. 'He was under a great deal of pressure.'

Melodia shook his head. 'In a case where there was prior heart disease, then perhaps, but it wouldn't make sense in this instance.'

'So you found no other wounds, no hints of any other cause?' asked Scamarcio.

'Well, I found one thing. But it's probably insignificant.'

'Try us,' said Scamarcio.

'Come nearer.'

They did as instructed, and when they were standing so close that Scamarcio felt he might pass out from the smell of formaldehyde, bleach, and body fluids, the doctor pointed to a spot just below the man's left nipple.

'Do you see here?'

Scamarcio craned his neck.

'Here.' The doctor switched on a circular light above his head, and Scamarcio now noticed a tiny red pinprick in the spot where the pathologist was pointing. It looked like the mark of a dart or a needle.

'I don't know what it means,' said Melodia. 'But it might mean something.'

34

DESPITE THE MYRIAD AMBIGUITIES surrounding Brambani's death, Scamarcio slept well that night, rising early so he could make his way back down south. From his pay-as-you-go mobile, he had called Opera prison the evening before, asking if Guerra was prepared to see him, and a few hours later had received a message saying that he could turn up at eleven. He had been granted half an hour with the former terrorist.

As the taxi drew closer to the prison, Scamarcio pondered the likelihood of a visit to the US. If they found Carter's wife, and if she had information, it could lift the lid on this inquiry. But that was probably a case of too many ifs for Garramone.

As they pulled into the carpark, Scamarcio decided that Opera had to be one of the most depressing prisons ever built. The shabby grey blocks rose from the flat Milan hinterland like a discarded Lego set, their high, mud-coloured walls broken only occasionally by mean slits of windows. The complex could have passed for a chemical-processing plant or a factory — there was nothing natural about the place, nothing living. It chimed perfectly with the grim southern suburbs surrounding it, thought Scamarcio. The entire area was a monochrome industrial wasteland, a tableau of some new twenty-first-century hell.

After a quick scan of his card, the sentry directed him through the main doors and into the prison itself, where he handed over his gun. There was a queue of worried relatives waiting in line for visiting time to begin, but he was ushered straight past them, through a scanner and into a long, tiled corridor that smelt of vomit and cleaning fluid. At the end of the passage on the right was a door marked 73. The guard accompanying him knocked, and they entered a small room, painted a sickly mint-green. Scamarcio took a few paces inside, and immediately came face to face with Vincenzo Guerra. The former terrorist was sitting bolt upright behind a battered plastic desk, and was wearing a dark-blue jump suit with red stitching. Guerra cut a compact, muscular figure, and with his razed, dark hair and sharp, black eyes he looked to Scamarcio like a mutant rodent. A small scar ran beneath Guerra's right eyebrow, and he had a strange dent near his right ear.

Guerra nodded at Scamarcio to sit. The guard who had accompanied him said he'd be outside if Scamarcio needed anything. Guerra wasn't even cuffed. Had his behaviour inside been so exemplary? The last time Scamarcio had visited a prisoner, he'd shot himself dead in front of him. He hoped that the officer's relaxed attitude meant he was in for a calmer interview today.

'Thanks for seeing me at such short notice,' Scamarcio said.

'Letta said I should give you a hand with your *investigation*.' Guerra put a strange emphasis on the last word, raising his scarred eyebrow slightly as he said it.

'Did Letta explain what I'm looking for?'

'He said that you were investigating a case that might have links to P2 and Gladio, that you were interested in the *American angle*.' Again, the strange emphasis.

Scamarcio nodded. 'I know a bit about your background, of course; I know why you're in here. I was wondering whether you ever came across this American angle when you were active back in the Seventies?'

Guerra pulled himself even straighter in his chair, and Scamarcio was reminded of a military man, a general. He wondered if that was how the NAR saw themselves back then, as soldiers fighting to save Italy from the Red Peril.

'Yes, I came across it,' said Guerra. 'I was one of the first people to talk about it.' He stretched out an arm and clicked out a joint in his elbow before replacing his hand on the desk. 'The American presence was very real. But it was not like they summoned us all to a meeting and said, "You plant this bomb here; you kidnap that prime minister there."'

'So how *did* it work?'

'Help started coming our way. First, it was somebody who was supposed to be "a friend of a friend", telling us that they knew a good explosives expert, or they knew where to procure certain pieces of kit. Then it was, "Do you need money? If so, how much?" Then, as came out at my trial, we were given access to C4. That was a NATO-issued explosive, and it came from a Gladio arms store. It was the most powerful explosive available at the time. But towards the end, it was more than just money and supplies they were providing. We started to discuss strategy and possible outcomes. Their involvement became more detailed, more intense.'

'Did you know who was helping you?'

'At the beginning, no, we just thought it was people sympathetic to the organisation. But then, when the assistance started becoming more regular and more expensive, we began to ask ourselves questions. We came to think that we might be dealing with a secret faction within the state. Then, over time, we started to realise that we were actually dealing with the state itself. The secret services, the Carabinieri, the Ministry of the Interior, even customs officials — they'd all spring into action to help us pin the blame on the Red Brigades, to help us destroy evidence, to help us flee.'

'And their reasons?'

'To keep the communists out of power, of course.'

'And the Americans?'

'There was this airbase where we used to meet to plan attacks — one of theirs. There were a couple of Yanks who used to hang around when we were preparing for a mission. They'd say things like, "You gotta meet Joe — he knows C4", or "Have you tried this trigger mechanism, it's the most efficient on the market." They always knew what we had in mind, what was coming.'

'And the Church? There was a relationship between Gladio and P2 and, in turn, there was a relationship between P2 and the Vatican ...'

Guerra seemed unmoved by the question. 'P2 and the Vatican were channelling funds to Solidarity in Poland and a few other places in Latin America. You're asking me if the Vatican knew what P2 was up to at home. Most probably. Did they get on the phone to stop them? Of course they didn't. If they knew there was a plot afoot to destabilise the country and stop the communists from taking control, they would have just sat back and let it happen. It fitted perfectly with their agenda.'

'Did you see any evidence on the ground of their involvement.'

Guerra shook his head sharply. 'Detective, I don't think you understand. Why would they need to get *involved*? What would be in it for them? Our homegrown Operation Gladio and their colleagues across the Atlantic already had it sewn up. The Vatican faction didn't need to send money — the Americans had plenty of *that*. And they were hardly in a position to provide expertise. No, the most you can say was that they were *aware*. They knew but they didn't tell because, perhaps more than anyone, they wanted the communists gone.'

'Could the Vatican Bank have laundered money from the US that was intended for Italian terrorists?'

Guerra shrugged. 'Everything is possible. But the role of the Church would have been smaller this time. If they weren't providing the funding supply-lines, the worst you can say is that they were turning a blind eye.'

Scamarcio nodded. *All that is necessary for the triumph of evil is for good men to do nothing.* Is that how Brambani had seen it? Had he come to doubt the good men inside the House of God? Scamarcio still couldn't square away Garramone's mysterious Vatican scholar and his description of Abbiati as a fastidious finance manager, an honest man. That just didn't tally with the kind of man who would turn a blind eye to murder. And, when he thought back to his meeting with the journalist Rigamonti, his claims that Abbiati was concerned about a possible spy inside the Vatican didn't fit either. If Abbiati was complicit in decades of underground activity — murders at home, murders abroad — why the hell would he go around shooting his mouth off about spies working close to him? Scamarcio studied Guerra, with his ramrod posture, his hair cropped so short that it was almost a buzz cut, his fingernails clean and well-filed.

'You mentioned Latin America. Do you have any idea where P2 was sending money there?'

'Nicaragua and Argentina. And the chances are that the Vatican bank was most definitely involved in that.'

'Nicaragua?'

'After the Sandinistas overthrew the Somoza dictatorship, the US and their P2 chums organised the Contras to push them out and rescue the place from communism. The first transfers from the Vatican Bank via Banco Ambrosiano to its Panamanian ghost affiliates occurred the exact time the Contras were organised.'

'How do you know all this?'

Guerra tapped the side of his nose, and the two men stared each other out. Scamarcio was beginning to feel uncomfortable when Guerra said, 'Risky ops like Poland and Nicaragua were never done in the name of the Vatican Bank, but always under the banner of Ambrosiano.'

Scamarcio nodded slowly. The connections to Carter and his work were becoming real now. He paused for a moment. 'This American involvement in our recent history — is it just a thing of the past?'

Guerra pulled a half-shrug. 'Word is that they're sniffing around again.'

'Sniffing around?'

'Things were quieter after the Wall came down, but now we have this economic crisis that's worsening by the day, and our secret services are growing nervous. They fear a powder keg: we have mounting food poverty, small businesses collapsing, banks that won't lend, the mafia moving in ... And when our secret services are growing nervous, you can be sure that their American colleagues are growing nervous with them. Or, more usually, they're the ones who've been putting the pressure on. Just look at what's happening in Greece.'

'How do you mean?'

'There's been a murder, an assassination attempt, blatant illegal political manipulation — all aimed at suppressing the opposition and maintaining, by unconstitutional means, the government that's loyally enforcing Eurozone policy.'

Scamarcio shook his head gently. 'What do you see as the likely outcome?'

'It will end where it always ends — with us toeing the line. Winston Churchill once said, "For a nation to tax itself into prosperity is like a man standing in a bucket and trying to lift himself up by the handle." But neither the European Central Bank nor the US are interested in prosperity for our country — they're here as asset strippers, making off with what they can before it all goes to the wall.' He drew a breath. 'But if you raze a country, if you leave a devastating legacy, you're going to see the communists return. They're not thinking this one through; it will blow up in their faces this time.'

Scamarcio figured Guerra's mindset was still blurred by the fog of the Cold War, but he thanked him for his time, reaching out across the table to shake his hand.

'Good luck with your investigation,' said the former terrorist, rising swiftly. 'It's important that people know the truth about US interference in their democracies. Perhaps during the Cold War it was justified, but now it's just about money. They're the most ruthless criminals on the planet, and they need to be stopped.'

'I doubt I can be the one to do that.'

'Every soldier plays his part.' Guerra saluted him from across the desk, and Scamarcio smiled and headed towards the door. Perhaps believing that your cause was a just one made thirty years behind bars more bearable; it was all part of the mission. How must Guerra have felt, however, when the Berlin Wall came down, when the communist threat was no more? Of course, it didn't mean anything, he realised. The communist threat was still real for him. It had to be. Otherwise, his years in prison would have been for nothing; his mission would have been without purpose.

As Scamarcio was opening the door to leave, the former terrorist said, 'Think about Greece, Detective. If they don't get their way, it could be back to the Seventies for us — we could see the attempts at destabilisation return.'

When he was out in the carpark, Scamarcio turned on his mobile. There'd been four missed calls from Garramone. When Scamarcio rang him back, the chief sounded apoplectic with rage. 'Why did you have your phone switched off?'

'I was in Opera, visiting Vincenzo Guerra.'

'Oh God, Scamarcio, did you fucking have to?'

'We had an interesting chat.'

'Well, whatever he told you is now officially irrelevant. AISE have pulled the plug. We no longer have the case.'

'How can they do that?'

'I got a call from the chief of police this morning. They've obviously put the pressure on, and he's bent over and taken it up the arse, as usual. We don't go anywhere near it. And, Scamarcio, when I receive a call from the chief of police, I have to listen. It's no longer a question of *interpretation*.'

The fact that AISE wanted him gone was interesting: did it mean he was actually getting somewhere? He wasn't going to be pushed around, especially by Scalisi and his fellow poodles. After several moments, he asked, 'Do you have an inquiry for me to move on to?'

'No, not right now — something will come up.'

Scamarcio paused long enough for it to sound convincing. 'In that case, would you mind if I took some leave?'

'Er ... well, of course, if that's what you want.'

'I never took a break after that business in the summer, then there's been the Pozzi thing, plus I've got some personal matters that need straightening out. If now is a good time, I could do with a holiday.'

'Well, I don't see a problem with that. But I'd expected a bit more burning indignation, to be honest.'

Scamarcio sighed. 'If we let every case take over, then where will it end? I've decided it's time to give priority to some other areas of my life.'

Garramone fell silent for a moment and then said, 'I think that's wise.'

But Scamarcio wondered if Garramone sensed he had a very different idea in mind.

Part III

Every sin, every injustice, every infidelity He saw and felt at that very moment, caused Him to sweat blood … It was just another anticipation of when His Precious Blood would be shed on the cross.

From *Mysteries of the Rosary: Agony in the Garden*

35

He pushed the money across the table. De Gasto pushed it back. He pushed the money towards him once more. De Gasto pushed it back again.

Carter sighed. 'De Gasto, I really think this is your best bet. I'm telling you as a friend.'

'I will not be bought.'

'You've got a wife, a young son — just take the money.'

'Material Girl' was playing on a radio in another office down the hall. The whiny, subliminal sound just added to his headache.

De Gasto slammed his fist into the table and made him jump. 'I said I will not be bought! I haven't spent the last thirty years working to free my people from poverty only to sell them out for your filthy dollars. You know what this deal would mean for my country; it would bankrupt us. It would condemn us to a life on the breadline, to a life without education or opportunity, to a life without medical care. You're killing us, slowly castrating us. And you expect me to just take the money and sip cocktails by my pool while this disaster unfolds. We're not all like you, you know. We can't all be bought.'

Carter sighed again, and ran a damp palm across his face. The fan in De Gasto's tiny office wasn't working properly. It didn't seem able to complete its circuits. The air hung dense and heavy.

'De Gasto, if you don't take this money, if you don't accept this offer, I don't know what's going to happen. I can't guarantee your or your family's safety. It's not just about the money any more. They're gunning for this deal, they'll make sure it goes ahead, and that means pushing aside anyone who gets in the way. I'm telling you — just take the easy

option, not for you, but for your kid's sake.' He paused to draw breath, his head pounding now. 'I admire you, I admire your principles, but there's too much at stake. You're running one hell of a risk. You need to know that.'

'Well, I'll take that risk. My mind is made up.'

Carter felt the water collecting in his eyes. Hell, he liked this man; he'd enjoyed beers with him; he'd played soccer with his kid. He couldn't allow this to happen.

'Please, I'm begging you, just take the fucking money.' The rickety fan shook and finally gave up on its circuit.

De Gasto's face was a mask of stone. He collected his papers and rose from the desk, slamming the door shut behind him.

Twenty-four hours later, he was dead.

SCAMARCIO SWUNG THE HIRE CAR into Maple Drive, scanning the piece of paper on which he'd scribbled the address that Blakemore had given him. It was a fine, bright morning, the autumn foliage aflame in the early-morning sunlight. It felt good to be back in the States; just the sight of the huge houses with their perfect lawns, the pristine pavements, and the wide smooth roads stirred something close to happiness in him. He reflected on Guerra's description of the US as the worst criminals in town. Perhaps he was right; perhaps all this verdant perfection was bought from the proceeds of crime, from all the dirty wars. But, hell, at least they had got it right. At least 60 billion euro didn't drain out of their country every year, destined for God knows where. If only the Italian government could tax the mafia, maybe Italy would have a chance of turning itself around, of realising this bold, American dream.

He pulled up outside number 41. It was a large Southern-style house with a pillared porch and green-shuttered windows. There was an extensive lawn out front, and Scamarcio noticed two Mercedes in the driveway: one was a SUV; the other, the latest C-Class.

He killed the engine and stepped out of the car, scanning the street. Aside from a few parked cars, the avenue was empty.

He took off his jacket, folding it over an arm. The birds were in full song, and he smelt honeysuckle and fresh grass-cuttings on the breeze. Before he had made it halfway to the house, the front door swung open and he saw a tall, blonde woman blinking into the sunshine, trying to get a better look at the approaching stranger.

'What do you want?' she shouted, shielding her eyes.

He stopped, only a few metres away now. 'I'm Detective Scamarcio from the Flying Squad in Rome. I was hoping you might give me a few minutes?' He pulled out his badge, and she took a few steps closer to the edge of the porch.

After she had studied the badge, she said, 'I'm sorry, I thought you were one of *them*.'

'Them?'

'Those bastards my husband used to work for. Get inside.' She practically pushed him into the house, and quickly checked the street before slamming shut the front door. Scamarcio wondered if there was anyone else home, whether they had children. That might explain her anxiety.

'Come through to the lounge.' She cut a striking figure in tight jeans and a white, silk shirt. She wasn't skinny, but looked as if she ate well and worked out. She didn't seem much older than forty, and he wondered how long she and Carter had been married.

'Take a seat, Detective,' she gestured to a deep, white sofa. The room was long, with modernist art hung everywhere: some pictures were in frames; others, not. Colourful rugs were strewn across the oak floors, and several pieces of expensive-looking antique furniture lined the walls. From the tall sash windows, Scamarcio caught a view of a large garden at the back of the house with a swimming pool and a tennis court off to the left.

'They told me you'd found him hanging under a bridge,' she

said, placing her hands neatly in her lap. She'd sat on the sofa opposite, and now they were just a few feet apart, separated by an oak coffee table shaped like a teardrop.

'Yes, the Ponte Sant'Angelo. It's very close to Vatican City.' Scamarcio didn't know if this would have any resonance with her, but thought it worth a try.

'Did he kill himself?'

Her directness stole his breath away. 'There was poison in his system; it was a poison that my pathologist had not seen used much in Italy before. But it was a substance often used by the people your husband worked for. Also, there was no sign of his fingerprints on the rubble in his pockets.'

She shrugged. 'He could have worn gloves before handling the rubble. Likewise, he could have got hold of the poison himself. Maybe it was something *he'd* used before.'

Scamarcio thought about the possibility of gloves. The frogmen hadn't found anything; but even if they had, they would have had trouble reading the prints. His mind stuck on the very last thing she'd said, 'Used before?'

'In his work.'

'Sorry, I don't follow.'

'Detective, I'm not one of these Agency wives who have no idea what her husband does for a living. I know he was paid to kill people. We talked about it. Often, in recent months.'

'Who was he paid to kill?'

She sighed, and looked out at the vast garden beyond the windows. The sun was brighter now, the greens more intense. 'Leaders of the opposition, student activists, people who supported the wrong side — women and children, if he had to.'

'Where was this?'

'Wherever he was active.'

'I was told Poland and Nicaragua.'

'That was back in the Eighties. Before that, he did spells in

212

Cuba, Thailand, and Vietnam. Then they sent him to Italy.'

'Do you know why he'd been posted to Rome?'

'He never discussed that with me.'

'Was he in Italy a long time?'

'Most of the decade, I think. Italy was more like his base — from there he'd travel to other places in Europe. Around the middle of the decade, he returned to Latin America, then Washington for a spell, and that was followed by a long stint in the Middle East: Iraq, Iran, a few of the 'stans'; in his later years, he came to be seen as a Middle East expert — that was his speciality.'

'I didn't know that.'

'Well, these things are not that easy to find out.'

'Why are you being so open with me?'

'I've been advised that you are probably one of the few people I can trust.'

Scamarcio nodded, and met her gaze. An unexpected surge of electricity passed between them, and he wondered if Mrs Carter was grieving as much as she should be. But then he reminded himself that raw grief could have all sorts of strange effects on the human psyche — it was often an aphrodisiac.

'So, Detective, you didn't answer my question,' she said, looking away to the garden once more.

'About whether I think he killed himself?'

She nodded, her gaze still fixed on the window.

'I was hoping *you* might be able to help me with that. The evidence points both ways.'

For now, he decided not to mention what he had heard about Cardinal Abbiati having sent the Cappadona to kill her husband. He didn't want to influence her account in any way.

She leant back against the sofa and rubbed the back of her neck, staring up at the ceiling as if hoping to find the answers there. 'He wasn't himself in the months before he died. Something had changed in him — it was as if something had broken. He told me that he no longer believed in the work he did, that he felt as if he had only been a force for evil in this life. He talked about all the people he had killed. He said that, sure, some of them had it coming, but there were too many who didn't deserve to die, who shouldn't have been pushed aside like that. The ends had not justified the means, in his opinion. At the beginning, it had been "My country, right or wrong"; but towards the end, too much of it felt wrong to him. He was approaching retirement, and it was if he was putting his entire career under the microscope. He didn't like what he saw.'

'How old was he?'

'Fifty-five.'

'That seems young to retire.'

'If you've done the fieldwork and put in the hours, they retire you early — if you want it, of course. If not, you're offered deskwork or consultancy — some such thing.'

'So your husband wanted to leave?'

'Yes, he was ready. But I'd also given him an ultimatum. The place was destroying him.'

'Had you been married long?'

'Sixteen years.'

Scamarcio raised an eyebrow.

'Surprised?'

'I didn't think your husband's line of work was conducive to successful marriages.'

'It isn't. It's been hard going, although the Cold War was out of the way by the time I met him. Whether I could have survived that, I'm not sure.'

'How *did* you meet him?'

'At a party.'

'Do you have children?'

She met his eye. 'They never came.'

He nodded; it was his turn to look away for a moment. 'Did

you ever get the feeling that your husband feared retirement — that he was worried about how he was going to fill the hours once he was home?'

'I think he was conflicted. He'd lost faith in the work, the mission. His worldview was not *their* worldview. And it's hard to continue in that environment if you've stopped believing. But, yes, if you ask me now, I think he was worried that all that was awaiting him was a void: years of introspection, years of looking at yourself in the mirror and realising that you've come up short.'

'Did he ever consider turning things around, maybe doing something different — something that would give him a sense of value?'

She shook her head, unwilling to entertain the idea. 'My husband had spent his life in the Agency; it had shaped him, made him who he was. I don't think he was capable of making such a change, taking such a step.'

'So, this ultimatum you'd given him …'

'I wanted him to get out of there before it killed him.'

Scamarcio saw a silent tear roll down her cheek. It dropped off her chin and landed in her lap. 'But he didn't make it in time,' she whispered.

'I'm sorry.'

'The thing is, I ask myself day after day, *Why didn't I act quicker to get him out of there? What was I waiting for?* He could have taken his own life; he clearly wasn't feeling right. That much was obvious. But all the steps the Agency has taken since his death — the phone taps, the surveillance — why would they bother if he had just decided to end it all?'

'They've tapped your phone?'

'Of course — I hear the hum every time I pick up. My husband briefed me, so I know the signs. And I see the same damned surveillance team parked up the street every morning: a white-phone company van and a burgundy sedan. I would have expected them to be more imaginative.'

'So they're probably aware that I'm here?'

She smiled for the first time since they'd met, and said, 'Of that I wouldn't be so sure.'

'Why?'

'You know Simeon's former colleague — the one who was contacted by your reporter friend?'

'Well, I don't know him, I don't even know his name, but I understand who you're referring to.'

'My husband set up a secure channel before he died. That guy contacted me on it to suggest a meeting with you. I doubt they know who you are or why you're here, but if they've seen you walk up, of course they'll be wondering.'

Why did Blakemore's source encourage the meeting, wondered Scamarcio. Was he just trying to be helpful? How confident could Blakemore really be that his so-called sources were sound?

'But what about this house?' Scamarcio asked, glancing around the room.

'I swept it for devices this morning — my husband taught me how to do that, too.'

'Why?'

'He said it might come in useful one day.'

He eyed her closely. 'Didn't he give you any more detail?'

She shook her head firmly. 'Simeon never gave me the detail; that was his way. All through our marriage, he never named names or precise places. He said that was the only way he could be sure I would be OK. As soon as he shared a secret with me, I would be compromised.'

'So you can think of no reason why his employers might want him dead?'

She shook her head again, slowly this time. 'As I said, I don't have the information. These former colleagues of his — the ones who talk to your reporter friend — I sense that they know more but that they'll never tell. For my own protection, no doubt.'

'Before he died, what was your husband working on?'

'Just domestic stuff — domestic crime.'

'I thought the CIA was foreign cases.'

'Yes, but if it's a home-grown operation with international implications, they'll obviously take a look at the domestic angle, too.'

That made sense. 'When two agents who I believe work for your husband's employers visited me, they claimed that he was a counterfeiter responsible for manufacturing millions in fake dollars.'

She shrugged. 'They probably borrowed the cover from one of their cases. Maybe it was the last case Simeon was working on?'

It was an interesting theory, but instead Scamarcio said, 'Can you think of anything that might help me understand who, besides his employers, might have wanted your husband dead?'

She surprised him by nodding sharply. 'In the week before he died, Simeon was very uptight because he said some money had gone missing. It was money he badly needed for something — he didn't say what. He told me the money had long been promised him as payment for a favour, but it hadn't turned up on the date it was due. He felt betrayed, and said that he was going to visit the person who should have paid him, and get to the bottom of what had gone wrong. He seemed shocked. He had been sure that this person would honour his promise — he said he had too much to lose otherwise.'

'This person — did he say who he was, where he was?'

'No, that was the rule, remember. But I had a feeling it was something connected to his work back in the Eighties, because he mentioned Europe. He said he would need to go there for a few days, but expected to be back by the weekend.'

'So when you heard he'd died in Rome …?'

'I thought that either the person he was trying to find had

killed him, or the Agency had. But then I wondered if maybe he'd simply failed to get the money, and whether this fresh disappointment combined with all the soul-searching of recent months had finally taken their toll. Like I said, he needed to get out of that place before it destroyed him.'

He saw the tears collecting in her eyes once more.

'Whether they hung him under that bridge to die, or he climbed up there himself, they still killed him in the end. It was murder, whichever way you look at it.'

36

AS HE WAS LEAVING, Mrs Carter thrust a piece of paper into his hand. When he unfolded it, he saw that the only thing written on it was a long string of numbers.

'What is this?'

'I don't know. My husband gave it to me a few months back. He said I was to open it in the event that something happened to him.'

'So he had a feeling that his life might be at risk?'

'I asked him that, but he said he was just tying up a few loose ends, getting some things straight that had been preying on his mind for a while.'

'And he gave you no idea what these numbers might mean?'

'No. He said he was sure I *would* work it out eventually, when the time was right.'

'But so far you haven't come up with anything?'

'I've tried bank accounts, birthdays, death-days, important dates in history. I even dug out one of his old codebooks. But nothing seems to click.'

'Have you run it past any of his former colleagues — the people who spoke with the reporter?'

'No. He said I wasn't to share it with anyone.'

'But you're sharing it with me now.'

'I trust you, Detective.' Her cheeks flushed slightly, and she broke eye contact, looking down at the floor.

He returned his attention to the scrap of paper, and studied the numbers again. He counted thirty-one of them, but he couldn't identify any immediate relationship, any pattern.

'I'll give it a go,' he said eventually. 'If I get anywhere, I'll let you know.'

She handed him another piece of paper. 'You can reach me on this number. Just this number — don't try any others. And don't email me — they're monitoring that.'

He frowned. 'Why do you stay here if they're watching you all the time? Wouldn't you prefer to get away? Go and stay with friends or something?'

'We don't really have friends — beyond the Agency, that is. My husband's life was not conducive to that. Besides, they'll find me wherever I go, so I might as well stay where I'm comfortable.'

He took her hand to shake it. 'I'll be in touch as soon as I find anything.'

She smiled, and looked him straight in the eye this time. 'Good luck, Detective.'

On his way back to the hire car, Scamarcio scanned the street once more. When he reached the pavement, he spotted a white AT&T truck parked some twenty metres up ahead on the left-hand side. Directly opposite was a burgundy sedan.

He unlocked the hire car, but stopped to check the back seat through the window before he climbed in. He fired up the ignition and made a U-turn, heading in the opposite direction from the surveillance team. But either they hadn't noticed or didn't care, because they made no sign of moving. Maybe they had another vehicle lined up to follow him.

He figured that the wisest thing to do was to stay public. He'd find a coffee shop in the middle of town, and try to get his head around those numbers. He thought back to his conversation with Carter's widow: Carter believed that someone had betrayed him, and Scamarcio felt sure that someone must have been Cardinal Abbiati. He had dispatched the Cappadona to kill Carter, to get him off his back. But why was Abbiati holding this money for Carter, and what was the favour the American was supposed to have done for him? And, perhaps, just as importantly, where was this money from? Creamed off the funding supply-lines they were running to the anti-communists during the Cold War? Once again, he considered the conflicting pictures of Cardinal Abbiati. Was he a ruthless manipulator, prepared to turn a blind eye to mass murder, a man who would kill before he'd repay a debt, a man who frequented one of Rome's most cut-throat criminal gangs? Or an honest man from a poor background, for whom money and the trappings of wealth were not important, a man who was deeply worried that someone working close to him might be a spy? Who was the real Abbiati? Scamarcio's mind fixed on the strange Vatican scholar and his bizarre exit from the restaurant, how his stiff, arthritic movements had suddenly become smooth and loose. Had Scamarcio made a mistake in not thinking more about this man?

He sighed, and turned left towards the centre of the town. When he reached the high street, he pulled into one of the parking bays outside a pharmacy. He had spotted a few coffee shops further up on the right on his drive through that morning. Before stepping out of the car, he felt his pocket to check that the piece of paper from Mrs Carter was still there.

Fairfax, Virginia was exactly what you would have expected from a town so close to the heart of power — it was the essence of America, the steel sparkling and the colours bright. The gleaming shopfronts of the red-brick buildings lining the high street were shaded with bold candyfloss awnings, and lush flower-baskets hung from the doorframes. There wasn't a scrap of litter on the street; Scamarcio wondered whether having so many CIA employees living nearby made for a greater sense of civic decency than usual.

He decided to avoid the two chain coffee shops and to head for the local offering. A blackboard outside said that you could have a stack of pancakes and unlimited coffee for five dollars.

He chose a booth away from the window, and pulled out the piece of paper. He fumbled for a pen in his jacket pocket, and took in the numbers again: 05242241212115122411111123455.

He decided to split them into pairs, hoping it might make the sequence easier to handle. But after a few attempts he gave up on that, as it didn't seem to be bringing him any closer to an answer. What was interesting was the string of 1s after the figure 4. It made him wonder if that section of the sequence should be treated differently from the rest. He drew a line before the first 1, and then examined the numbers either side. But they didn't seem to mean anything.

There were a stack of napkins on the table, and he pulled one towards him and began doodling with his pen. The address of the coffee shop was printed in red italics on the serviette: Browns Coffee, High Street, Fairfax, Virginia, 22033. American ZIP codes had five digits. *Is that important?* he wondered. He searched through the sequence to see if the same ZIP code appeared; maybe it was a local address. But he wasn't convinced that there was much point to this particular approach; it wouldn't have been that easy. Besides, Mrs Carter would have already cracked it if it was. And indeed, as he had thought, he failed to find the numbers in the string. But, for lack of any better ideas, he scanned the first five digits of the sequence, followed by the last, to see if they seemed significant: the final five numbers were 23455. *That could be a local ZIP code — it starts with a 2*, he thought. He googled 'ZIP code 23455' on his phone, and found that it took him to Virginia Beach, all the way down south, but still within the state. He drew a line in front of the ZIP code, and considered the numbers in front of it and the cluster of 1s.

If this was an address, and an address that Carter would want his wife to find, would he use a complex code? It depended on

Marion Carter's experience with such things. Scamarcio doubted that she'd had much; but if her husband had trained her to sweep for bugs, who knew what else he had taught her? He decided to start simple, and remembered the stupid code his father had sometimes insisted on using in his communications. As a teenager, Scamarcio had secretly thought that it was so transparent that the Carabinieri would decipher it in seconds, but he had never dared voice his concerns, as the old man had seemed so proud of this new strategy. At the time he'd been going through a phase of reading Le Carré novels, and had seemed to want to turn his rustic criminal network into something more sophisticated.

Scamarcio tried the code now, starting with the first digit and ending when he reached the cluster of 1s. Each number represented a letter of the alphabet, A being 1, and so on. But when he replaced each number with its appropriate letter, he failed to come up with anything that made sense. He wondered about pushing the code one letter on — 1 being B, 2 being C, etc; but, again, it didn't click. He moved it along one place further, so that 1 became C and, yet again, got nowhere. He slammed his hand against the table and tossed the paper away in frustration. The possibilities were infinite. Then, for lack of any better ideas, he moved 1 to D and, yet again, slowly transformed all the numbers into their corresponding letters. When at last he was done, he took a breath and sat back to study the words in front of him. Finally, it seemed that he'd actually come up with the fragments of something legible: 'FJIEHAYGOOD ROA'. Sure, Haygood Road could be part of an address, but what was FJIE? Was it the same deal as the ZIP? Should those initial four digits stay as they were? 3762 could be a street number, he figured. He googled the address, and discovered that it was a self-storage centre. By the time the waitress was back with his coffee, he knew how he would be spending the rest of the day.

37

THE DRIVE DOWN TO VIRGINIA BEACH was almost like a holiday. He passed forests, then flatlands, and then pretty country towns. He had wondered about calling Carter's widow and asking if her husband had ever handed her a key, but he had rejected the idea — he sensed that she would have mentioned it and would have quickly connected it to the long string of numbers Carter had given her; also, despite her confidence, he felt sure that she was being minutely monitored. He checked in his rear-view mirror for probably the hundredth time, but he still didn't have the impression that he was being followed. They were the experts, though.

His work mobile rang beside him, and Number Unknown flashed up. He leant over to take the phone from the seat, trying to keep his eyes on the road.

'Detective Scamarcio?' asked a fragile voice.

'Speaking.'

'You contacted me some time ago — my name's Roberto Felletti.'

Scamarcio wondered why the author would be calling him now. He'd told Garramone that he wasn't the right man to help with Scamarcio's inquiry.

'Yes, thank you for sending your colleague my way.'

There was a strange pause on the line, and Scamarcio wondered if it was just the long-distance connection.

'That's why I'm calling,' said the writer eventually. 'My friends and I are very worried about him. He seems to have disappeared.'

'Disappeared?'

'He's not answering his phone, and his flat is empty. A couple of us went round there yesterday, and his cats were starving — like they hadn't been fed for days.'

Scamarcio remembered the Vatican scholar's conviction that Opus Dei had eyes and ears everywhere, and that he'd been taking a risk in just talking to him. Maybe Scamarcio had been wrong to dismiss these concerns as paranoia.

'Have you contacted the police?' he asked.

'I thought that's what I was doing.'

'Sure.' He paused for a moment. 'Listen, I'm out of Rome right now, but I'll pass this to my colleagues. What's the best number to reach you on? And I'll need your friend's name and address.' Scamarcio pulled over to the hard shoulder so he could take a note. When Felletti gave him the scholar's name, it sounded familiar. Scamarcio wondered if he'd seen it in one of the books that had come up when he'd first searched for information on the Vatican.

Once Felletti had finished giving him the details, the writer asked, 'Do you think someone in the Church is behind this? There's a lot at stake for them right now.'

'Your friend was very worried about Opus Dei. He seemed to believe they were watching him.'

Felletti sighed down the line. 'It's possible. The spotlight is on the Vatican Bank right now, and there are certainly people there with secrets to hide.'

'He seemed very well informed, your friend.'

'He was close to Cardinal Abbiati; they'd been friends for a great many years.'

'I hadn't realised that. I thought it was a working relationship.'

'No, it was more than that.'

Scamarcio frowned. It seemed an odd turn of phrase.

'Listen, Detective, I've got to go,' said Felletti. 'Will you or one of your colleagues phone me to tell me what's happening?'

'Sure thing. My colleagues will probably want to speak to you all in person. They'll need to know who saw him last, where — that kind of thing.'

'OK. I'll be expecting their call.'

Scamarcio laid down the phone and took a deep breath. What on earth had he got himself into, and why the hell hadn't he listened to Garramone when he'd told him to drop it?

He had been driving for nearly three hours when the bright, blue waters of Chesapeake Bay came into view. He lowered the window and took in the sharp, salty tang of the ocean. He had programmed the address of the self-storage depot into the car's sat-nav, and now a chirpy American woman was telling him to stay on the motorway for another mile, after which he'd pass the toll booths that would take him to the centre. He paid the toll and drove through the outskirts of the beach resort, passing block after block of pale high-rises, with their scrubbed patches of lawn out front. He was reminded of those dreary English seaside resorts where he'd been forced to attend summer language-schools as a teenager. His father had thought it was a 'middle class' thing to do, but Scamarcio had hated the entire experience, from the greasy five o'clock suppers, to the spotty younger sisters, to the hallucinogenic carpets in the bathrooms.

According to the sat-nav, his final destination would be up ahead on the right, and indeed he soon spotted the large neon sign advertising Sammy's Self Storage.

He drew up alongside the kerb, and when he got out the car, he noticed a thin line of blue at the end of the drive, a slash of white in front. The East Coast beaches had never really done it for him. Again, it was probably the English experience: it brought back too many bad memories.

He checked the street for observers before entering the depot.

As he walked into the lobby, he was relieved to see an attractive young blonde on reception. He figured he'd have a better chance with the opposite sex.

He approached the desk, and took out his badge and police card. The young woman squinted at them both, and asked, 'Are you a cop?'

'I'm with the Italian Flying Squad.'

'OK,' she said, stretching out both letters to make it clear she wasn't impressed.

'I'm helping the US authorities with a case, and I need access to one of your cubicles. We believe it's held in the name of Carter.'

'Where's your warrant?' asked the young woman, her eyes scanning his like lasers.

'It's a fast-moving investigation. If you make me come back with a warrant, there's a risk people will die.' It was his turn to hold her with a stare. 'My back-up team is behind me, and will arrive in the next ten minutes. You can help us save valuable time by giving me access to that cubicle.'

She took a breath, seemingly still troubled, but something about his expression seemed to convince her, and she turned to her computer screen and entered the name. After a few moments, she said, 'I have no Carter here.'

Scamarcio wracked his brain to remember the other aliases. 'Can you try Bartlett?'

She clicked the keys a few more times and said, 'No Bartlett, either.'

'Then try Carruso or Squires.'

She tapped some more, but just shook her head. 'I don't have any of them. Where did you say you were from again?' She had her hand on the telephone beneath the counter now, and he noticed a wedding ring.

Of course — Carter would have put the cubicle in his wife's name. What had Blakemore said it was? 'Try Marion Pitt,' he said quickly, wishing that the woman would remove her hand from the telephone.

The young woman tapped the keys once more, and this time nodded, surprised.

'Yes, I have a Marion Pitt. It's cubicle 241. Do you have the key?'

'No. Ms Pitt is currently in hospital after having been wounded by the sniper we're trying to track down.'

'My God,' said the woman, holding a hand to her heart. 'Is there a gunman on the loose?'

'You understand the urgency now?'

She nodded quickly, and reached beneath the counter for a key. 'Do you want me to show you the way?'

'No, I can manage. Be on the look-out for my team when they show.'

She nodded again, saying nothing.

He unlocked the door to the cubicle, wondering what would greet him on the other side. He had the sudden notion that perhaps the place was rigged, that the whole thing was a set-up. But when the door opened he saw that the space was almost empty, save for a small stack of grey envelope files in the far corner. There were only three of them: the one on top was thick, and the unmarked envelope could barely close over the papers inside. There was nothing written in the contents boxes of the other two, either. He figured that this would be the worst place to try to read the documents, so he cradled the files beneath his arm and left the cubicle, pulling the door shut behind him. When he walked back through reception, the young woman was nervously scanning the street beyond the glass doors.

'When the team arrive, they'll give you some paperwork so you can square things with your bosses, explain why the cubicle needed to be opened,' he said.

'OK.' She still looked nervous.

'I have to get on,' he said, gesturing to the files. 'But my squad just called, and said they'd be here in five.'

'All right then.' Her features relaxed slightly.

He hurried through the automatic doors, not wanting to push it any further.

Once outside, he headed for the hire car, trying not to break into a run. He quickly scanned the street and then the back of the car before jumping into the driver's side and placing the files on the seat next to him. He fired up the engine and swung the car around, deciding to head out and away from Virginia Beach as fast as possible. There was a town he had spotted about half an hour away that might be an inconspicuous place to spend the night. He didn't feel like going all the way back to Fairfax.

As he drove away from the resort, the ocean blue shrinking to a small dot in his rear-view window, he fought a growing urge to pull the car over and read the files there and then. Actually, when he thought about it, finding a motel for the night wasn't sensible: in a hotel room he would be alone and exposed, whereas in a motorway café there would be people around, and he could sink into a booth and study the papers in peace.

He joined the freeway and looked for the earliest exit. After a few minutes, the signs told him that a service station was coming up on his left. He made the turn and spotted the ubiquitous Cracker Barrel and Applebee's next to the gas station. The homogeneity of America reminded him of India: the same shops, the same streets, the same lives playing out over and over. He opted for Cracker Barrel, carefully placing the files under his arm again.

Once the smiley, overweight waitress had seated him, he laid the stack of documents on the table and opened the top file. At first glance, it seemed to contain a bundle of what looked like accounting documents. There were around a hundred sheets of paper, all with the same layout. Spanish names had been handwritten in a left-hand column, while figures in dollars had been noted to their right. Some of the names had a long list of figures beside them. There were also some names with no figures, but all of those names had been crossed through. The sums in dollars seemed high: the largest he could find was for $350,000, and beneath that number were many other amounts made out to the same individual.

He shuffled through the papers, looking for anything in this file that looked different from the ledger notes. At the back, he came across a stack of black-and-white photos — all of Latin-looking men, many of them in suits. These photos had the feel of surveillance shots. Scamarcio pulled out a stack of papers that had been resting on top of the photos. Some of the same names he had seen in the ledger documents reappeared, but this time there was a long list of data beneath each of them, noting their ages, addresses, political leanings, family members, and financial situations. The bullet point that interested Scamarcio the most was one that talked about 'amenability.' Beneath one name he read in English: 'After half an hour's discussion, it became clear that Torrijos will not co-operate.'

Scamarcio returned to the ledger documents, and searched for the name on the list. He found it on the fourth page, but it had been crossed through, and there were no dollar sums next to it.

He took a breath and put down the file, increasingly unsure of what he was dealing with. He was startled by the ringing of his phone — the line from headquarters back home was buzzing on the display.

'Scamarcio,' he said, trying to keep his voice low.

'Detective Bracco here. We got your message about that Vatican guy who's gone missing from Prati. The case has been passed to me.'

Bracco wasn't a name that Scamarcio had come across. 'Thanks for getting back to me.' He gave him all the details he had, including the nature of his two conversations with the missing scholar. When he finished, Bracco whistled softly and said, 'Sounds like a hornet's nest.'

'It *was*. AISE pulled the plug, so I'm off it. But obviously we need to look out for the missing guy, whatever.'

'AISE?' repeated Bracco. 'Dark forces at work then.' When Scamarcio didn't respond, he added, 'Anyway, I'll let you know how we get on. Where are you? The dial tone sounded weird.'

Scamarcio did *not* want it getting back to Garramone that he was in the US. He wasn't yet sure whether Garramone would be happy about that; right now, he thought it unlikely.

'I've just popped over to the south of France for some R&R. I'll be back within the week.'

'Right you are,' said Bracco cheerily. 'Enjoy your break. We'll be in touch.'

Scamarcio flipped shut the mobile and took a sip of coffee. It was diabolical — watery and bland. He grimaced, and opened the second file. At first glance, it seemed to contain a large pile of handwritten letters, all in Italian. He scanned the one on top, finding the language cryptic — there were numerous references to 'the mission' and 'the endgame' — but the paragraphs themselves did not quite make sense; he could extract no wider meaning from them. As he flicked through the other letters in the file, he noticed that none contained a date or address, but that they were always written to a 'B' and were signed with the initial 'F'. Towards the back of the stack, he found an airmail envelope addressed to S. Carter, Maple Drive, Fairfax, Virginia 22033 — the house he had visited just that morning. He noticed that the envelope bore a Vatican City postmark, and was penned in the same handwriting as the rest.

He kept scanning through the letters. There were too many to read properly, and he was still struggling to form a clear picture of their real contents when he came across the first reference to 'Solidarity'.

'F' had written:

As you know, all those years back a sum of $5 million was agreed for Solidarity but I made sure we only spent 3. The 2 are waiting for you here, in return for Mantova. They will be set aside, for when the dust has settled.

Was that the money Carter had been expecting? And, if so, what was Mantova? Scamarcio flicked through the remaining letters, but it was another half-hour before he came across a partial explanation.

'He will be in Mantova, visiting his parents,' wrote 'F':

The trial will soon be upon us, and as he has already implicated himself, we feel sure that it is only a matter of time before he begins pointing the finger at others. The media is painting a picture of a mentally unstable, immature extremist, so there is something for you to work with there. We understand the Agency's wish to keep their hands clean, and appreciate your willingness to step in.

Scamarcio put down the letter and took another sip of coffee. Was Carter freelancing on this 'favour' in Mantova? And who was the young extremist he had been sent to kill? He googled 'Mantova, suicide, young terrorist, court case', not really expecting to find anything, but on the very first page the name of Riccardo Paglieri came up, and all at once it came back to him. He hadn't made the link to Paglieri because he hadn't realised the boy was originally from Mantova. Scamarcio must have been about nine or ten years old at the time. He remembered the incessant news coverage of the teenage terrorist who was supposed to have been part of a group of far-right extremists who had placed a bomb under a Carabinieri squad car, killing two officers outside Milan. He scanned the article for more detail: only one terrorist from the Red Brigades had been sent to prison for the atrocity but, shortly after the man was sentenced, Paglieri had penned a letter to several national newspapers claiming that the guy was innocent and that he and three accomplices had been behind the attack. He went on to explain that he and his friends were members of Ordine Nuovo, a far-right organisation, and that they had carried out the bombing with the help of both the US and Italian secret services, with the intention of passing it off as the work of the Red Brigades.

Although his claims were widely dismissed as the ravings of a paranoid schizophrenic, Paglieri was due to stand trial for the bombing. However, that never came to pass, as he killed himself while staying with his parents near Mantova, just days before the court case was to begin. He had been found hanging from an apple tree in their orchard.

Scamarcio's thoughts went from this young man, to the dead American who'd been found hanging beneath the Ponte Sant'Angelo, to Roberto Calvi, suspended below Blackfriars Bridge. There was a definite symmetry there. His next thought was to wonder why 'F' from the Vatican was involved in this cover-up. Yet again, he had the sense that Abbiati had a dual identity; that he was two people, both good and evil.

38

SCAMARCIO TURNED TO the next file. The first of the papers bore the stamp 'Eyes Only' above several paragraphs of text. It appeared to be the continuation of a dossier, but the cover page and index were missing.

The paragraphs seemed to belong to an essay that had begun a few pages back: the author was writing about the 'Applications of the Strategy of Tension in 21st-Century America'. He briefly mentioned the work of a philosopher named Leo Strauss, and claimed that some in American politics favoured Strauss's theory that there was too much focus on individual liberty in American society. This group, who came to be known as the neo-conservatives, envisaged rebuilding America by uniting the people against a common enemy.

Scamarcio skipped a few paragraphs to the conclusion: 'Extrapolating from the work of Strauss, it seemed clear that after the end of the Cold War a new enemy needed to be found: and it would be found in the form of the Islamic extremists emerging from the Arab states.' However, the author noted that before 9/11 the focus for these jihadists had been domestic — they were largely concerned with overturning their own regimes, and were not interested in what was termed 'the American problem'. Indeed, Osama bin Laden had been forced to pay the so-called 'recruits' in his first training videos, so short was he of support. 'Beyond his own small group, Bin Laden had no formal organisation until we invented one for him,' wrote the author.

The next few pages contained an analysis of the historic

application of the strategy of tension throughout various countries during the Cold War. Italy was mentioned, as were Germany and Belgium. The author went on to discuss the 'positive outcome' from the Brabant supermarket massacres in Belgium, arguing that they had helped ensure that crucial NATO missile bases would be accepted by voters. The report then seemed to come to an abrupt end. Over the next few pages, profiles of individuals with Arab names followed. Similar to the profiles in the Latin American file, they listed ages, family relationships, and political affiliations. The profiles also included background on the political situation in the country where the individual was from, and their role in any domestic conflict, but there was no mention of whether they were 'amenable' or not. Scamarcio could find no financial-looking documents and no dollar sums listed. Behind the profile paragraphs were several long lists of more Arabic names, with the words 'protected' or 'deceased' next to them. Behind those was a stack of photographs of individuals and family groups — all Middle Eastern in appearance. Some looked like surveillance pictures; others seemed as if they might have been taken with the subjects' permission.

Scamarcio laid down the file. He had the sudden feeling that whatever Carter had been up to in Europe might account for only a small part of the picture.

39

On the news, they were saying that 50,000 people were facing famine. The government no longer had any money to do anything, so the people would be abandoned to their fate. Some rock stars were trying to raise money again, but he knew it would never reach the starving.

It was the faces of the children that haunted him the most: the hollowed-out eyes, the parched lips, the papery skin. Carter glanced over to his son asleep in his cot, his fat cheeks flushed, his dimpled fists against his chest.

It used to be about principles. After the Second World War, it was about the belief that the communist system was inherently evil, that it denied its people their freedoms. So when did it switch? When did they sell themselves out to the powerful families for a fistfull of dollars? When Eisenhower warned the American public to beware the military-industrial complex, had it already begun? Were they already well on the road to hell back then?

One of the first things they'd taught him at training school was that the best way to kill an enemy was to send the toxin straight to his heart. Use a poison that left no trace, they said, that ate away at him from the inside.

His marriage had been a clever card. It played nicely into the impression that he wanted to settle, that he wanted to build a career back in Washington, back at the heart of the beast. He'd heard that they were running something big, so he had to make sure that he got deep inside it, right to its filthy core.

'You're one of my most experienced guys,' said the boss. 'Given how the strategy has evolved, and given how you've been a crucial part of that *evolution, I think that you're ideal for this. It's a highly select group I'm forming, crème de la crème. Are you up for the challenge?'*

'You bet.'

'When we discussed your involvement, there were some concerns. We know that you're a man of faith; that you prefer not to get your hands dirty.'

Carter shrugged. 'Situations change; people change. Let's just say I've started to view things differently.'

'Why?'

'Because the old rules no longer apply, because we're living in a time that demands intellectual flexibility.'

The boss nodded gravely and rose from his chair, spreading his palms on the desk in front of him. 'It's time to bring the enemy to our gates, Simeon. The people have lost focus, and we need them back on side.' He looked away for a moment, and took a breath. 'Our clients, of course, are always looking for new markets.'

'And where do I come in?'

'You have first-hand experience of the strategy. I know you got to Rome late, but you were there to build on the results, consolidate the gains. You're a master in the art of letting things take their course, but timing that nudge to perfection. We need events to take their course again, but we want you back in the director's chair, enjoying the final rehearsals.'

'Back to the desert?'

'Bin Laden and al-Zawahiri couldn't organise a fuck in a brothel. Their revolutions have bombed; they've got zero support, no network, and nobody to turn to except a few lone wolves. Our problem — and theirs — is that the ragheads are way too busy worrying about what's happening in their own backyards.'

He stepped away from the desk and walked to the window. 'We need them to stop the navel gazing; we need them to cast their eyes our way.' He sighed quietly. 'It's time to create some monsters.'

STANDING IN A PHONE BOX outside the truckstop, Scamarcio dialled Blakemore's number. He hoped the reporter was keeping the pay-as-you-go mobile charged, and hadn't given up on him. When Blakemore had given him the address for Carter's widow, Scamarcio hadn't told him that he was definitely coming to the US. He had used Garramone as an excuse, claiming there were funding problems that first needed to be resolved. Scamarcio had figured that he should wait to see if his trip yielded anything; he didn't want to draw the reporter further into the fray for no reason.

He thought back to his evening visit from the two Americans, and wondered where they were now. Back in Italy, he'd sensed danger; but here, on their home turf, they seemed to have disappeared. What was their thinking in keeping so quiet, he wondered. They appeared to be playing the long game, but he couldn't think why. Or was it the call he had put into Giangrande, telling him that he was taking some leave, that he'd been pulled off the case?

'Are you in the US? I'm seeing a Virginia area code,' asked Blakemore when he picked up.

'Yes. Can you meet me — you and your source?'

'My source won't agree to that.'

'I've come across something that might be significant. It could be good for you, John.'

Blakemore fell silent for a beat. 'Give me until tomorrow.'

'No, I need this now.'

Blakemore whistled softly down the line. 'I'll do my best. Shall I call you on this number?'

'It's a pay phone. I'll find a hotel.'

'OK, Leo, but if this thing *is* significant, maybe you should give your embassy your whereabouts.'

'Sure, John,' he said, thinking that was the last thing he'd do.

He found a Day's Inn off the I-95, and texted Blakemore the number. Then he sat on the grimy cover of the huge bed and waited. The room smelt of stale cigarette smoke and old sex, and there was a large grey stain on the carpet near the bathroom. He wondered who would have his back now he'd gone so deep into this thing. Garramone didn't even know he was here. He thought about phoning Aurelia, but he sensed that his apologies would fall on deaf ears. He still needed to know how she was, though, so he told himself he'd call as soon as he'd heard from Blakemore. Had he known what Carter's dossier would contain, would he still have come? Probably. But did it bring him any closer to understanding who had strung up the American and who had stabbed Abbiati?

He took a long sip of the whisky he had taken from the mini-bar, and lit his third cigarette in as many minutes. He flicked through the hundreds of TV channels all showing the same dire reality shows or 'family values' sitcoms. They made him think of what he'd read about Strauss, about the attempt to mould a way of life and preserve it, to steer America away from the value-free permissiveness of the Sixties. After he'd spent an hour mindlessly channel-hopping, the phone on the night table rang.

'He won't come,' said Blakemore. 'He's scared. He feels as if he's been asking too many questions, and that people are starting to notice. He and his colleagues are nervous.'

'Colleagues?'

'He wouldn't go into it. He's recently retired, but feels as if he's still at risk. That's the game, I guess, if you've worked for those guys.'

Scamarcio fell silent, considering his options.

'So this thing you've come across, do you want to share it with me?' asked Blakemore.

Scamarcio didn't know what he wanted to do. He wondered about taking the first flight out and trying to digest the dossier when he was back in Italy; perhaps finding someone who might help him understand its contents. It seemed like the safer option, although that was irrational — he'd felt more at risk back home than out here.

He tried to assemble his thoughts. 'I need to work out my plans. I'll get back to you.'

'No problem.'

Scamarcio hung up and surveyed the browning paint on the ceiling. Before he took any further steps, he realised he needed to secure the contents of the files somehow. He rang down to reception and asked for directions to the nearest copyshop.

He spent over an hour photocopying the entire contents of the files before scanning the documents onto a USB key. Then he walked next door to a Home Depot and bought a large Swiss Army knife. Although he hadn't had the impression he was being followed, he asked himself again if this was simply because he was dealing with professionals.

When he returned to his hotel room, he tried to call Aurelia, but she didn't pick up. Frustrated, he shoved the knife under his pillow and tried to get some sleep, but his mind was still too full to settle. He turned on the TV again, and spent the early hours of the morning watching C Span and re-runs of *Everybody Loves Raymond*. That show had been on when he had been a student in the States fifteen years before, he realised. He eventually killed the noise, and closed his eyes. What to do about those files? Who could he trust with this?

He sighed, and turned onto his side. He suddenly wanted to get out of the States as soon as possible. It didn't felt right being here, alone and exposed, and directly disobeying orders.

As he punched out the pillow and turned again, he heard the unmistakeable click of the door behind him being opened. He sprang up, but before he could reach for the light a gloved hand was across his mouth, and another was pushing down hard onto his chest, paralysing him. He smelt leather and plastic, and the hint of something sweet like a breath mint. The stitching in the gloves was coarse against his lips.

He heard tape being rolled and snapped, and then felt it being stuck hard over his mouth. The hand on his chest moved away for a moment, but it was back within seconds, and this time the sharp point of something metallic pressed into his skin.

The bedside light snapped on, and he saw a tall man in a caramel cashmere coat standing above him. A blue baseball cap obscured the man's eyes. His right hand was holding a gun against Scamarcio's chest, and with his left he was digging in his coat pocket. He held a small white index card up to Scamarcio's eyes. There were just four words written on it: 'This room is wired.'

The man reached into his pocket and brought out a small stack of identical cards. He held up the next one. It said: 'You have underestimated them.'

And then there was another: 'You need to trust me.'

The man quickly repocketed the cards, and with the gun still hard against Scamarcio's chest, pulled him off the bed so he was in a standing position. The stranger then reached into his other pocket and produced a baseball cap, indicating that Scamarcio should put it on. He nodded at Scamarcio's hold-all, motioning that he should pack up his things. Once Scamarcio had placed the files from Carter's lock-up on the top, the intruder waved him towards the door. Scamarcio placed his palm on the handle, but the man immediately laid his hand on top to stop him. He held a finger up, and tore the tape from Scamarcio's mouth. Then the man nodded, and Scamarcio opened the door. They both stepped out into the cool hallway.

It was silent on the landing, apart from the dull hum of the Coke machine at the end of the corridor. The stranger dug the gun into the left of Scamarcio's spine, and he started walking, careful to keep his pace steady in case the gunman felt tempted to react. The pink-and-blue neon lights from the restaurants across the parking lot were forming spectral patterns on the walls, and Scamarcio felt that he was walking through a long tunnel to some dark destination; that he was on a psychedelic path to a place from which he might never return. The mouth of the gun suddenly dug deeper into his skin, and he realised that he must have slowed his pace for a moment.

He passed through some swing doors and onto a fire escape, the stranger right behind him. When they reached the ground floor, the man nudged him towards a glass door that led to a back carpark. It was not the same entrance that Scamarcio had come in by the day before.

Scamarcio pulled up the large red latch, and they stepped out into the warm night. They were nearly in the southern states — there was a balmy, almost tropical, feel to the breeze. The man pushed him towards a low, metal fence joining the back lot of a fast-food restaurant, and they climbed over it and walked past the fenders of a line of cars. The man slowed his pace a little, as if he were trying to work something out, before Scamarcio realised he was looking for a car to steal.

Suddenly there was a click, and Scamarcio turned to see the stranger holding a computer tablet with a small antenna attached. The tablet's screen displayed a series of green horizontal lines, shifting downwards, which looked like radio waves. The man halted in front of a silver Toyota Corolla, aimed the tablet and its antenna at the window, and immediately the sidelights flashed and the central locking released. The stranger pushed Scamarcio towards the passenger door, opened it, and shoved him inside before relocking the car and running around to the driver's side. As the man climbed in, Scamarcio thought about trying to overpower him, but his captor seemed fast and strong, and Scamarcio doubted he could beat him in a fight. Some instinct held him back.

The man bent low to pull out a kind of panel from beneath the steering column. He was using a torch on an expensive-looking watch to see as he started fiddling with some wires.

After a few more seconds, the engine choked to life, and the stranger sat back and pushed the car into gear. They swung out of the space quickly and sped towards an exit to the right of the lot. After they'd been on the main road for a just a few minutes, they took the turn for the I-95 South and joined the deserted highway, its multi-coloured motels and fast-food joints flashing by. The Toyota was rasping at 120kmph, but its driver seemed unconcerned.

They'd been on the highway for about twenty minutes when Scamarcio's kidnapper finally spoke.

'We're clear,' he said, scanning the rear-view mirror.

'Is that why you stole the car?'

'They know the plates on both of ours.'

Scamarcio briefly wondered how he was going to retrieve his hire car from the hotel carpark. Then he realised how little it mattered, given the circumstances.

'Who are you?' he asked.

'A friend.'

'That doesn't tell me much.'

'It should tell you enough.'

Scamarcio glanced across at him. He had a clearer view of his eyes now, and could see that he was much older than he had first imagined — perhaps in his early sixties. The strength and speed of his movements had suggested someone younger.

'Where are we going?' asked Scamarcio.

'Winston Salem, North Carolina. I have a house there I can use.'

'Use for what?'

Scamarcio's mind flashed on torture, on shadowy interrogation cells, on a whole host of unpleasant scenarios.

'To talk.'

After that he said no more, and Scamarcio wondered if they would complete the rest of the drive in silence. He wasn't sure how long it would take to reach Winston Salem, but he sensed they'd be looking at a couple of hours at least.

After several more minutes had passed, the stranger said, 'If a reporter from the *Washington Post* calls and asks me to meet a Flying Squad detective, I'm not going to say yes. They've got me wired to my balls.'

So this was Blakemore's source.

'I've helped John out a bit over the years,' he went on. 'But this seemed like a bridge too far.'

'So why are you here?'

'Self-preservation.'

'What?'

'You've been stirring up the shit for all of us.'

'I don't see how …'

The man jumped in. 'You can't just go running around the place as if they don't exist. You need to be under the radar, not waving files about in plain daylight.'

'You saw me at the self-storage place?'

'Marion told me she'd given you the string.'

'Did you *tail* me there?'

He didn't respond.

'Or did you already know that the numbers would lead me to Virginia Beach?

'Yes and no.'

'Well, which is it?'

'It's not important.'

Scamarcio sighed, and took in the darkness beyond the window. 'I didn't think I'd been followed,' he said eventually.

'I've been in the business for nearly forty years. I should know what I'm doing.'

Something wasn't adding up. 'Why do you talk to reporters?'

Scamarcio asked after a beat.

The man remained silent for a few moments, and then said, 'A few things have been happening inside the Agency that some of my colleagues and I have found disturbing.' He waved a hand away. 'But again, that's not important.'

Scamarcio wasn't sure he agreed.

'So, Detective, tell me about your investigation. Obviously, I know you found my former colleague hanging under a bridge, and that the Agency has been sniffing around. But, after that, I'm somewhat in the dark.'

'The Agency? So the guys who visited me *were* CIA?'

'Probably.'

'What do you mean, "Probably"?'

'I mean that that's the most likely scenario — for now.'

'I want to call Blakemore,' Scamarcio said. 'I need him to vouch for you.'

'They may have him wired.'

'We've set up a pay-as-you-go.'

The man said nothing, and then eventually nodded slowly, as if he were still trying to make his mind up. After a few moments, he said, 'OK, call him if you must.'

Scamarcio took the phone from his jacket pocket and dialled. Blakemore picked up after a few rings, his voice hoarse from sleep. 'Leo, it's three in the fucking morning.'

'I've got someone here who claims to know you.'

Scamarcio handed the phone across.

'It's Samuel,' said the stranger. He was silent for a few beats, and then said, 'I needed to intercept him.' He fell silent again, and then answered. 'Yeah, I will.'

He handed the mobile back to Scamarcio. 'Have I been kidnapped by the bad guys or your source?' he asked Blakemore.

The reporter sighed. 'Take a breath, Leo — he's sound.'

'So I can trust him?'

245

'Yeah, you can trust him.' After a beat, he said, 'I want this story, Leo — don't forget that.' The phone cut off.

Scamarcio leant back against the headrest for a moment, pondering what he should share with Samuel. He decided not to mention his encounter with Rigamonti and the reporter's conviction that Abbiati believed there was a spy working close to him. Scamarcio didn't quite know why he wanted to hold this particular detail back, but some instinct was urging him to keep it close.

Scamarcio cleared his throat, and then began talking Samuel through the case. When he reached the part about the Cappadona's involvement, Samuel interrupted him for the first time. 'That doesn't sound like the Agency's style — to get a bunch of local thugs involved. They would want to keep things under the radar.'

'Well, according to the Cappadona, it was Abbiati who dispatched them to kill Carter, because he didn't want to settle their debt.'

'That story smells off to me,' said Samuel.

Scamarcio pressed on, telling him about the bizarre DVD, the letters he had retrieved from Father Brambani's apartment, and the discovery of the body in the chapel.

'A heart attack?'

'Yes, but according to the police pathologist, Brambani had a perfectly healthy heart. Then there was this tiny pin prick—'

'Just below the left nipple,' interrupted Samuel.

'How did you know that?'

Samuel smiled faintly. With his right hand he pulled out a packet of Lucky Strikes from his trouser pocket. He tossed them over to Scamarcio. 'Could you do the honours?'

Scamarcio opened the box, and saw that there was a gold lighter inside. He handed over a cigarette, and reached over to light up for him. He took another smoke from the packet. 'Do you mind?'

'Go right ahead.'

Scamarcio lit up, and leant back against the headrest. He drew the smoke down deep.

After a few drags, Samuel said, 'It was a top-secret operation that went by the name of M.K. Naomi, back in the Fifties. We were concerned that the KGB had developed chemical and biological weapons, and we felt we needed to find counter-measures. One of them was the trusty poison dart. It could be fired from a normal-looking pistol, but the dart itself was just the width of a human hair and would completely disintegrate on entering the target. The lethal poison, usually cobra venom or shellfish toxin, would then rapidly enter the bloodstream, causing a heart attack. Once the damage was done, the toxin would denature quickly so that an autopsy would be unlikely to detect that the heart attack had been triggered by anything other than natural causes. That's what did for your Father Brambani. It's old hat, though, a bit Seventies — they've got more advanced methods now, ones that leave no trace.'

'So your former employers may have been involved in his death?'

'Sounds like it to me. But there's something old-school there, something that makes me wonder about limited resources.'

'Limited resources?'

Samuel waved the idea away 'Not important.'

Scamarcio's thoughts returned to the question of motive. 'Do you think Brambani's killers were worried that he'd blab about someone inside the Vatican having prior knowledge of the bombings — that he'd talk about US involvement?'

Samuel shook his head and frowned. 'I don't buy that. They'd be going to a lot of trouble for something that's already out there. There's a young Swiss professor who has written a book on Gladio and the strategy of tension in Italy. He talks quite clearly about US involvement. That guy's done quite a bit of TV in Europe;

the story has already gone public — although the mainstream US media won't touch it.'

'So you don't think the Agency would bother to kill for this?'

'It doesn't seem worth it to me.'

'So who *did* kill Brambani?'

'Oh no, you're not following. *They* killed Brambani. But they didn't kill him to keep him quiet. They killed him for some other reason.'

A police car sped by, its coloured bars flashing. Scamarcio experienced a wave of anxiety. 'Did they want to frame him — to make it look as if he had killed Abbiati and then taken his own life?'

Samuel was nodding slowly now. 'That would seem like a more likely explanation.'

'So that would mean that they killed Abbiati, too?'

'That isn't clear yet. I need you to tell me what happened *after* Brambani — what you've discovered here in the US.'

'You mean the files? Don't you already know what's in them?'

'I'm good, but I'm not *that* good.'

'So you've no idea?'

'I've got my suspicions.'

The sun was coming up, and Scamarcio took in the gently rolling hills beyond the window. In the hazy early light, the colours were sepia yellows and soft greens, and house after house flew the American flag from their porches. Had there been such widespread patriotism before 9/11? He thought back to his days in LA, and couldn't quite remember. Then again, LA had never been the barometer for the wider country. It was the last place you should look to make such a judgement.

Scamarcio returned his gaze to the road ahead. 'The first file contains a series of letters in Italian, sent between Carter and the person I believe to be Cardinal Abbiati. There's nothing of great significance there — they talk about the work they'd both been involved in supporting Solidarity in Poland.' Scamarcio decided to keep back the detail about the Mantova favour, for now. 'However, the second file seems more interesting. It lists a lot of Spanish names, with a series of dollar sums next to them — some of these sums are quite high. The file also includes profiles and pictures of various individuals from what look like Latin American countries. Next to the names are comments on whether they would be "amenable" or not.'

Samuel's eyes remained fixed on the road, and Scamarcio couldn't read any emotion from his features. But after a few seconds he said, 'I'd like to take a look at that file. Perhaps I know what we might be dealing with.'

He fell silent once more. Scamarcio no longer had the energy to make conversation, so he leant back and watched the lush countryside flash by the window.

After a couple of hours in which he thought he might have dozed off, he saw a steely skyline of high rises, water silos, and smoke stacks coming into view.

'Welcome to Winston, Salem — home of big tobacco,' said Samuel.

They were moving off to the right now, away from the skyline. Soon the skyscrapers disappeared, and the rolling hills returned. They drove on for several miles until Samuel took a turn for a place called Yadkinville. He paid the toll booth, and passed through a leafy avenue of large houses before turning right into a country road. He continued for some minutes until he took another right. They were making their way up a dirt track now, with wide cornfields running either side. Eventually they came to a fork in the road, where an old wooden sign pointed left to Toadeye Farm. Samuel followed the track, and yet again Scamarcio asked himself whether he was right to trust this man. Hell, was Blakemore even right to trust him?

They pulled into a gravel drive. The place seemed more like a country retreat than a working farm, but then Scamarcio spotted a flock of chickens clucking fussily by a long red barn at the back of the house.

'This place is secure,' said Samuel.

Scamarcio wondered how he could be so sure. He hadn't noticed anyone behind them for the last ten minutes, but that might not mean anything.

Samuel stepped out of the car and gestured for Scamarcio to follow. He turned a key in a lock, and they passed through glass doors and entered a wide living room. One of the walls was exposed stone, and several animal heads were mounted on plaques above a fireplace. Scamarcio wasn't sure what kind of animals they were — maybe moose. To the left of the fireplace was a long oak table.

Samuel took off his baseball cap and threw it down. Scamarcio could now see that he was tall, with shoulder-length grey hair, tanned skin, and prominent cheekbones. He pulled a pair of horn-rimmed spectacles from his pocket and put them on; combined with his strong chin and high forehead, he reminded Scamarcio of the actor Richard Gere. Scamarcio sensed that Samuel probably wasn't the type to normally don baseball caps; apart from the expensive-looking coat, he was wearing a burgundy wool scarf and tight-fitting brown-leather gloves. His tan brogues were polished to perfection, and his mustard cords were well tailored. Somehow, the smart clothes reminded Scamarcio of Carter hanging from the bridge in his elegant suit, his shoeless feet swinging in the breeze.

'I'm afraid this isn't my place, so I'm not sure if they've got such things as coffee or tea. Maybe we can grab something later,' said Samuel.

He removed his coat and draped it over the back of the chair. He was wearing a smart, green pullover. The collar of a blue-striped shirt was visible at the neck.

'Let's take a look at those files then,' said Blakemore's so-called source.

Scamarcio reached for his hold-all and took them out, before drawing a seat from beneath the table, and taking a position opposite. He placed the stack of files on the table in front of him, and then involuntarily pulled them close. Hesitating, he glanced up at this man who had broken into his room just hours before. But Samuel just nodded at him to continue, and Scamarcio realised he had little choice if he wanted an answer. If Blakemore believed this man to be sound, the chances had to be good that he was.

'This is the Latin file, the one with the Spanish names,' Scamarcio said.

'Let's see it then,' said Samuel, his eyes now fixed on the file. Scamarcio tried to keep his expression neutral, and pushed it across.

Once Samuel had the stack of documents in front of him, he carefully began turning each page as if he were worried that the paper might disintegrate. He read for several minutes, his expression unchanging. Eventually, he replaced the papers in the envelope and closed the cover, his hand still resting on top as if he were unwilling to relinquish it.

'Torrijos was president of Panama. We killed him,' he said. He reached for his Lucky Strikes, and lit up before tossing the packet across to Scamarcio.

'I understand what Carter was doing in his later days now,' said Samuel after a couple of drags.

'You didn't before?'

'I had to ask around to find out about his fieldwork in Poland and Nicaragua. He wasn't an immediate colleague and, anyway, it's all need-to-know. Most of the time we had no idea what the next room was working on.' He took another suck on his cigarette. 'Have you ever come across the term "economic hitman", Detective?'

Scamarcio shook his head.

'Both our National Security Agency and the CIA employed EHMs. Basically, their job was to convince the political and financial leadership of underdeveloped countries to accept massive development loans from institutions such as the World Bank and USAID. Burdened with debts they couldn't hope to repay, these countries were then forced to acquiesce to political pressure from the US on a variety of issues.' He took another drag. 'They were effectively neutralised politically, their wealth gaps driven wider, and their economies crippled. At the end of the day, EHMs like Carter were simply funnelling money from big aid organisations into the coffers of huge corporations and the world's wealthiest families. Over the decades, they conned these countries out of trillions.'

'And this was government policy?' asked Scamarcio.

'Sure,' said Samuel.

'But why would these countries agree to such a shitty deal?'

'The EHMs played on the human frailties of the folk running these places. They used things like bribes, extortion, sex, murder. Sometimes they'd try fraudulent financial reports or rigged elections. Of course, all this is a game as old as empire, but in our era of globalisation it's taken on new, scarier dimensions.'

'But there was all that talk about writing off third world debt. What you're describing doesn't sound like an attempt to cripple these places.'

Samuel laughed — a deep, throaty laugh, but full of bitterness. 'Do you know what the conditions for that debt forgiveness were?' He didn't wait for an answer. 'It required these countries to privatise their health, education, and other public services. They'd have to give up subsidies and trade restrictions that had been supporting their own industries, but swallow trade barriers and subsidisation on rival G8 businesses.'

'Not such a good deal.'

'No.'

'So the dollar sums listed by these names were probably payoffs; they were people Carter had bribed?'

'Of course.'

'And the names that had been crossed through, which had no payments listed next to them?'

'We'd have had to take it to the next stage.'

'The next stage?' Scamarcio guessed the answer as soon as he had asked the question.

'Back to your poison darts,' said Samuel, deadpan.

Scamarcio drew breath for a moment, and then said, 'It seems like quite a big step to go from assisting an anti-communist movement in Poland to trying to corrupt third world governments.'

Samuel furrowed his brow and tapped out another cigarette. 'Does it? To me, it seems like a logical progression. And if they were looking for someone with good experience on the ground, who had spent time nurturing certain interests and crippling others, Carter would have been a sound choice. Anyway, it's not like the one policy led to the other. They were parallel strategies, both in force at the same time.'

'So this is why they killed him? They were worried that he had become disillusioned, that he was about to go public on this?'

'Of course not.' Samuel narrowed his eyes in frustration, and Scamarcio sensed that he considered him a slow study. 'John Perkins, a repentant EHM, wrote a book about his experiences in 2004, and it proved a bestseller. Like the whole strategy-of-tension thing, the EHM concept is in the public consciousness. Maybe they never published the Perkins book in Italy — that's why you haven't heard of it.'

'So why was Carter keeping this file, then?'

'Perhaps he was also thinking of writing his memoirs?'

Scamarcio exhaled, and pushed the Arab file across to Samuel, wondering whether he was going to write this one off, too — whether he would argue that it was all already out there and that his former employers wouldn't have cared one way or the other.

Samuel emptied out the documents and studied them slowly, turning them over carefully as he'd done before. Once again, he didn't look up, and just kept moving through the pages, taking his time with each of them. The seconds turned into minutes, and Scamarcio felt sure that the former agent had forgotten where he was, had forgotten that there was another person in the room with him — had perhaps forgotten what had brought him here in the first place. But eventually Samuel looked up and said, 'This is Dark Star.'

'Dark Star?' asked Scamarcio, leaning forward.

'And there's detail, a lot of it. Al-Zawahiri is in here, and Khalifa,' he said, the colour rising along his cheekbones.

'I don't understand,' said Scamarcio.

Samuel didn't seem to have heard. 'He must have been involved.'

Scamarcio decided to let him follow whatever thread he was on. 'I thought they'd told you Carter had been shoved onto some desk job towards the end.'

'Well, they would say that, wouldn't they? And I guess they'd be running it from somewhere in Washington, so you could probably call it a desk job.' He paused for a moment before adding, 'Somebody must have been really worried about him.'

'Worried?'

'The man was toxic.'

40

'Northwoods was a bold plan,' said the boss, 'too bold for some. But it would have brought us what we needed with less suffering, less expense.'

'But they were proposing acts of terror against US citizens on US streets.'

'Yes, but if we'd been able to pin all that on Castro, we wouldn't have had all that crap to deal with later.'

'But the hijackings, the bombings — those cells would have wreaked real damage.'

'That was the idea, son,' said the boss, his face a scowl.

Carter sensed that he needed to steer the conversation back to safer ground. 'Why didn't Kennedy go for it?' he asked, already knowing the answer.

'He didn't trust Lemnitzer. He didn't trust us, or the joint chiefs. Of course, after all that, he tried to muzzle us — rein us tight in.'

'Wasn't it more like a castration?'

The boss turned away and looked out at the grey sheets of rain. 'We can't let that happen again, you understand. No prints this time.'

'what is Dark Star?' asked Scamarcio.

Samuel appeared distracted now, as if he no longer had time for this plodding detective from Rome. But then he seemed to collect himself. 'Dark Star is no different from the strategy of tension you saw in your country in the 1970s and 1980s. But this time the strategy has been adapted for use against American people, on American soil. To understand its origins, you need to understand the way certain people in the intelligence services have been thinking for the last four decades. The direct predecessor of Operation Dark Star was something called Operation Northwoods. Northwoods was a series of false-flag proposals that called for the CIA, or other operatives, to commit acts of terrorism in US cities and then blame it all on Castro. This would have given the chairman of the joint chiefs, Lemnitzer, and his cabal, the excuse as well as the public backing they needed to launch a war against Cuba.'

Samuel breathed out before taking another suck on his Lucky. 'Sound familiar?' Once again, he didn't wait for an answer. 'Whichever way you look at it, Northwoods was the forerunner to the strategy of tension you saw over there in Italy.' He pointed to the papers in front of him. 'To my mind, this file is an enlightening illustration of how Northwoods has evolved; how the strategy of tension has been adapted for use against the American people in the 21st century.'

'OK,' said Scamarcio, feeling keenly that he should get the hell out — that he needed to be heading straight back to the airport and a flight to Rome.

'What most people don't know is that, since Northwoods, elements inside the US government and her intelligence services have been funding and planning decades of terror against their own people, which they have then gone on to blame on extremists. The modern version of Northwoods has come to be known as Operation Dark Star. But while some information has already leaked out, people are still struggling to believe that it goes on, because it would mean they would have to accept that they have been duped, that their government has been able to herd them like sheep. And, of course, most of the mainstream media won't touch it.'

Scamarcio said nothing; he just wanted to hear the rest.

'So here we are, back with the strategy of tension,' said Samuel. 'You blow up a bomb, and say that your enemy did it. So who *is* the enemy now? Well, not Al-Qaeda. The US shielded a number of Al-Qaeda leaders in the years before 2001, and it's still doing so today — that's what Carter's list is about. From the late 1990s right up until 9/11, there were countless meetings between US representatives and bin Laden's former deputy, Ayman Al-Zawahiri. The FBI even gave the whole thing a codename: Gladio B, alluding to the original Operation Gladio. From 1997 onwards, Al-Zawahiri and other mujahideen were regularly flown by NATO aircraft to Central Asia and the Balkans to participate in Pentagon-backed destabilisation ops there. The idea was to project US power in the former Soviet sphere of influence, in order to access previously untapped strategic energy and mineral reserves. Not only would Russian and Chinese power be pushed back, but lucrative criminal activites, particularly illegal arms and drugs trafficking, would be expanded. Back here in the US, we saw special treatment given to the bin Laden family: all of them were issued with diplomatic passports, no matter who they were or what they did, which meant that when the FBI wanted to investigate them for ties to terrorism, their inquiry was shut right down. Twenty-four of these family members were spirited out of the States on a secret flight shortly after 9/11, without being subjected to *any* form of interrogation.'

Samuel paused, and fixed Scamarcio with a hard stare. 'We were up to our necks in it with these guys, and we still are. Al-Qaeda is nothing but a cat's paw for Western intelligence. It's full of people from Saudi Intel, US Intel, Israeli Intel, and, of course, Egyptian Intel, and it couldn't, and still can't, do anything on its own.'

Scamarcio felt the need to move. He got up from the table and walked to the window. A few more chickens were clucking across the gravel, a couple of them stopping to inspect the tyres on the stolen car.

'So you're trying to tell me that the terror attacks we've been led to believe were planned and carried out by Al-Qaeda were done with American backing?' Scamarcio asked.

Samuel exhaled, sending smoke across the table. 'You sound shocked. But this kind of thing has been going on for decades. I wasn't in the loop, but we all heard the whispers; we all picked up on the vibe. Everyone knew that something was about to go down, and certain people decided to exploit it for all they could. In the week before 9/11, after the cleaning crews had left for the night, vans could be seen driving up to WTC7 and departing a few hours later. Night after night they came. What were they doing there? Wiring the building, of course. For a long time, there's been a faction inside my former agency that has taken the founding principles of our work and distorted them to a point where they are no longer recognisable.'

'But what you're suggesting seems impossible.'

'Yeah, but back in the Eighties you would have said that about your bomb at Turin station. It takes time for the dust to settle, for people to feel comfortable enough to start asking the difficult questions.'

Scamarcio fell silent. Samuel was right — it did take time. *Was that why Carter died when he did?*

41

He remembered how he had watched it all play out on TV. How quick the media had been to come up with 'America under Attack.' That jaunty little tag sounded as if it had leapt straight off a briefing document.

As he watched the buildings fall, he sensed that it was all too neat, too packaged, this time.

Too many people would spot the mistake; too many people would fail to be swayed. He asked himself if he was finally witnessing the defining moment, the moment that he and others like him had spent years waiting for.

Up until now, it had seemed as if no amount of criticism or exposure could weaken the organisation, that no matter how big the scandal, it would always survive. But now he felt a sudden confidence that all this was about to change. Just the thought of it, the sweet anticipation of it, stirred the hairs along the back of his neck and made him sweat.

The boss called him to a café on Q Street later that day.

'The office is a war zone,' he said. 'Everyone's trying to pass the buck.'

Of course it was going to go down like that. Put all those sharks in a tank, and they'd eat each other.

'We've got a problem,' he continued, after a beat.

'I'd say we've got several.'

'Yeah, well, now there's a bunch of geeks who are kicking up a shit storm.'

Carter arched an eyebrow.

'Structural engineers,' said the boss, in the same way he might say 'crack dealers'. 'They're bothered by WTC7. They're asking, if it wasn't hit by a plane, why would it just fold? Apparently, 40,000 tonnes of structural steel can't collapse in free fall without having been blown up first.'

Carter remained silent.

'They're a nuisance.'

'Can't they be contained?'

'Contained? There's hundreds of these fuckers, all respectable, strings of letters after their names. A bunch of these geeks aint the same as a few rednecks foaming at the mouth about alien abduction.' The boss flipped back his coffee. 'We can't discredit them. We need to come up with another version.'

'Another version?'

'Carter, wake up. We need something solid. Go buy us some expert advice.'

He nodded slowly; he felt a soaring lightness in his chest. The moment could not be far off now.

SAMUEL TOOK ANOTHER LONG DRAG on his Lucky Strike.

'The reality today is that most Americans still don't know that a third giant tower on 9/11 wasn't even hit by a plane, yet somehow, suddenly, neatly and symmetrically, just folded like a pancake. The government readily trotted out the version that office fires made all 84 steel columns break at the same time, but that didn't really cut it for the scientists. So the authorities had to come up with other explanations, but many in the engineering community remain unconvinced. It's clear to anyone with *half* a degree in structural engineering that the hijackers who flew those planes did *not* bring down those towers. They were pulled down by people with long-term access to a highly secure site, people who could get their hands on the kind of advanced materials that aren't made in a cave in Afghanistan. So now we've got this remarkably high consensus among experts that the government version can't be right, and we're beginning to see the official story unravel. And, for some very powerful people, that's a serious problem. Despite the fact that the mass media won't touch this story, doubts are starting to filter down. We're at a crossroads moment, where the public are finally beginning to challenge the official line.'

He paused for a moment and took another long pull on his cigarette. He waved his hand through the air, ash cascading onto the oak table below. '*Hundreds* of eye-witnesses that day say they saw explosions. And now, we've got the father of a victim from the North Tower who is asking why the post-mortem on his son found injuries consistent with explosives. He's been sneered at by the mass media — they're even tried to connect him to Al-Qaeda — but he won't give up. This questioning, this tiny seed of doubt, is growing, and there are some who think it won't be long before it starts putting down roots, starts reaching critical mass. The vested interests and their intelligence serfs can run around putting out fires, but lately there are more and more of them to deal with. And what if someone finally finds the smoking gun?

Scamarcio looked over to the file that Samuel now had in front of him. 'You think this is what that file represents?'

He nodded. 'When I asked around, people said that Carter was beginning to be seen as a loose cannon, that he was hitting the bottle. His masters had good cause to be worried. He'd lost the faith, and that made him a liability. A lot of Agency folk have been losing faith — there's definitely what you would call a crisis of morale — but there aren't many among these would-be repenters who were as delicately placed as Carter.'

'But if the American media won't touch this story?'

'There's still a way to get it out there — through the net, through the foreign press.' He closed his eyes for a moment and leant back in his chair. 'You know, the American electorate is as much to blame as the people who are trying to control them. The American public wanted to believe that we are good people; that we're an exceptional country. But this is what governments do; it's what they have always done.'

But something didn't make sense to Scamarcio. 'This endless war on terror … if it's still about having an external enemy, about preserving a state of emergency, it's no longer working. The American people wouldn't back the bombing of Syria; neither would the British. They're sick of seeing their sons come home in coffins. The strategy is no longer delivering the results it was designed for.'

Samuel smiled. 'That's why a rebranding was necessary.' He snapped his fingers. 'The concept had to be simplified, the stakes raised. The words 'Islamic' and 'State' were incorporated into a new threat, and the public were shown a few grisly beheadings. Suddenly, all those people who had been against intervention were now backing an anti-ISIS bombing coalition.' He paused, and shook his head. 'Anyway, the strategy of tension was just the match to light the fire, the spark to ignite the wars. And if you believe Oliver North, they got what they wanted. We've razed seven countries — we've made off with the loot.'

'So this is why they killed Carter?'

'It's the most compelling evidence you've presented me with so far.'

'So where do the Cappadona and Cardinal Abbiati come in?'

'That's your problem.' Samuel sighed and took another smoke. 'What's clear is that for some, Carter and his evidence represented the crucible in which serious trouble might be born.' He cast his eyes to the window, and stretched his long legs beneath the table.

'You said earlier that I was stirring up the shit for you?'

'The faction behind Dark Star knows there's a group of us who have suspicions. They believe we're more cohesive than we really are. I think they came to suspect that Carter was part of our network. Now that you've come around asking your questions, lifting his files, they'll turn the heat up on us.' Scamarcio saw no fear in his face — just weary resignation.

'This group of yours, do you get together? Are you planning something?'

'Like I say, we're not cohesive. And, no, nothing's being planned. We're just a few lonely individuals watching and waiting in the hope that the right moment will come.'

'The right moment?'

Samuel shook his head. 'Right now, you have more important things to worry about. Anyway, you need to look to your own Roman history for how it will all pan out.'

Scamarcio frowned.

'The fear of a phantom enemy is all the politicians have left to maintain their power. But that fear cannot last — these nightmares will soon turn out to be illusions. Rome used to be a democracy, but then, like many empires at their peak, it went broke and had to become a totalitarian state to survive. With the Patriot Act and the surveillance programs run by the Five Eyes, we're already well on our way.'

Samuel fell silent, and surveyed the darkening skies beyond the window. 'We need to head back.'

They agreed that Scamarcio would do some of the driving, and as he swung the car onto the main road, he asked, 'If I give you the photocopies of those files, what will you do with them?'

'There's nothing much I *can* do.'

'Isn't there someone in authority you could show them to?'

'It's political poison — no one would touch it.'

'What about Blakemore?'

'The *Post* isn't what it once was. It no longer has the appetite.'

As they drove along the leafy avenue, Scamarcio wondered whether, like Guerra, Samuel's worldview was somehow twisted — whether, to get to the truth, he needed to take a few steps back. The man's analysis was extraordinary, if not highly improbable, but Scamarcio found himself unable to dismiss it completely

— not just because it came from an ex-Agency employee, but also because it seemed to chime with so much of what was slowly starting to be discussed. In the US, if you challenged the government line, you were branded unpatriotic, like the grieving father Samuel had mentioned. Up until now, being deemed unpatriotic had proved an effective tool for keeping Americans quiet. If, all around you, people were waving flags and setting fire to effigies of Osama bin Laden, what courage would it have taken to speak out? But maybe that courage was now slowly starting to appear. As more people had doubts, it was becoming easier for the difficult questions to surface.

Scamarcio wondered what he would do with this new steer on Carter. Sure, he could hand the files to Garramone, but what would he do with them? Scamarcio was no longer supposed to be on the case, and he doubted that AISE would want to take this up with their American 'colleagues'.

Oh, by the way, we suspect you've been blowing up your own people.

Yeah, and what are you going to do about it?

Besides, perhaps AISE were already up to speed — perhaps they knew exactly why Carter had been killed, and that was why they'd had Scamarcio thrown off the case.

He pondered the Italian connection. If Abbiati had Carter killed after stealing the money he had promised him, what was the CIA's role? Had they simply been trying to tidy up this unexpected mess, draw a line so the true nature of their relationship with the Vatican and Carter's later work never came to light? Maybe they hadn't actually wanted Carter dead, but had been forced into speedy damage-limitation. Yet in the light of the Dark Star file, wasn't his death convenient? Scamarcio remembered Guerra's advice that he should think about Greece. He wondered if Italy's troubled past was as important as the Dark Star file itself; whether the unravelling economic crisis might have had a bearing on Carter's final visit to Rome.

They came to the end of the long line of trees, and Scamarcio figured that he couldn't be too far from the freeway now. He glanced over at the man seated next to him, and wondered at the risk Samuel had taken in meeting him. What had Samuel gained from their encounter? Knowledge, and maybe the reassurance that Scamarcio would keep his head down? There was a tired sadness in Samuel's eyes, and Scamarcio sensed that he already smelt defeat — that perhaps he felt he was living in a society that would always be alien to him.

Scamarcio returned his attention to the road, and in that one, single moment, time froze. To his horror, he realised that a huge red truck was thundering towards them on the wrong side of the road, bearing down on them, doing way more than 90. With no chance of checking his mirror, he swerved to the left, straight into the path of oncoming traffic, his heart ready to crash through his chest, his blood pounding. He couldn't see any cars approaching, so he hit the accelerator, desperately trying to put as much distance as possible between the Toyota and the truck. He glanced in the mirror, and saw the truck gradually growing smaller. A few seconds later, when he checked again, it was just a smear of red fading from view, its horn still blaring. Scamarcio managed to swing the car back into the right lane just before a people-carrier caught up with them in the left. He counted to ten, trying to settle his breathing, but his heart was out of control, and he was struggling to find any kind of equilibrium.

After at least a minute had passed, Samuel broke the silence. 'I would have expected better.'

42

SAMUEL HAD DROPPED HIM at a hotel by the airport, claiming that he'd get someone to collect Scamarcio's hire car and return it. Before they'd parted ways, he'd placed a hand on Scamarcio's shoulder. 'See what you can do with that dossier,' he'd said.

As Samuel had driven off, Scamarcio had experienced a sudden intuition that the man wouldn't make it home. He wondered if Samuel should leave the country. But could he just flee? Or did he have a family waiting for him somewhere? Then he told himself that if Samuel had been in the business forty years, he should be able to look after himself by now.

Scamarcio helped himself to another whisky from the hotel mini-bar, and sank back against the pillows. His flight was due to take off at 7.00 am the next day. He had wanted to catch the evening plane, but he and Samuel hadn't made it to Washington in time. He reached for the remote, and Fox News came on: they were discussing rumours that the president was having an affair with a young pop star.

His work mobile rang, and he saw that Police HQ was calling again.

'It's Bracco. I wanted to give you an update about your Vatican guy.'

'Have you found him?'

'The trail's gone cold. His friends should have contacted us sooner.'

'No leads at all?'

'The last person to see him was the baker on his road. Your

guy went in for brioche at eight on the morning he disappeared, and was picked up on the street CCTV, entering and leaving. After that, we've got nothing — no camera sightings, no witnesses. It's like he just went up in smoke.'

'Shit,' said Scamarcio.

'It smells like a kidnap job — they took him from his flat and bundled him straight into their vehicle.'

'The cameras didn't pick up anything on his street — unusual deliveries, builders who hadn't been booked, that kind of thing?'

Bracco sighed in a 'don't teach your grandmother to suck eggs' kind of way. 'We're going through all the deliveries now, cross-checking them with the residents. So far, there's no evidence of anything strange, but obviously I'll let you know should that change.'

Scamarcio thanked him and hung up. He sank back against the pillows once more, but sat up again when he heard something being pushed under his door. He figured it was probably the bill for the room, and padded over to pick it up, but when he looked down he saw it was a large, brown envelope, and that it was quite bulky. When he tore it open, several black-and-white photographs came tumbling out; they looked like surveillance shots, and reminded him of the pictures he had seen in Carter's files. He held them closer, and realised that the pictures were of him and Piocosta on the banks of the Tiber. They appeared to show him handing money to his father's old lieutenant. There were several wide shots and then a close up that clearly revealed a bundle of 500-euro notes being passed across.

Scamarcio took a breath, and sat back down on the bed. In all his life, he had never handed money to Piocosta. He *had* handed him a Post-it note some months back, when they were out by the river. Was that when these photos had been taken? The season looked about right, and Scamarcio had a feeling those could have been the clothes he had been wearing that sweltering June day.

Who had taken these photos, and who had given them to the Americans to doctor? The phone trilled on his night table, and he jumped. His palms were damp, and the receiver slipped when he tried to take it in his grip.

'We warned you, but you didn't listen,' said a voice with an American accent, but it didn't sound like either of the agents he had met in Rome. 'If you don't walk away, your ties to the Calabrian mafia will be exposed, images of you handing money to your father's friend will be splashed across the Italian media, and you will be stripped of your badge. Your career and reputation will be ruined, and you will wind up in jail on a life term. This is our final warning.' The line went dead.

Scamarcio replaced the receiver, his hand shaking, and lay down slowly on the bed. *Like a corpse preparing for its coffin*, he thought absently. He couldn't ever remember feeling more alone. It was as if he had been involved in a decade-long chess game that he now realised he could never have won. He'd seen plenty of politically inconvenient people end up in Italian prisons for no reason. Hell, some were saying that Grinta would be next. *I mustn't finish up the same way. It isn't worth it. Is it?*

His Italian mobile rang, and 'number unknown' came up. What could they have to add? They'd already made themselves perfectly clear.

'Leo.'

It was Piocosta's growl. Scamarcio had never been unhappier to hear the old man. He'd done nothing about the favour, and they were probably taping the call. *More grist to the mill*, as Letta would say.

'Where are you?' asked Piocosta. 'The dial tone sounds off,'

'The US — long story.'

'What are you doing there? You didn't tell me you were going.'

'I had to follow a last-minute development on a case.'

'Right.' The old man clearly wasn't buying it. 'When do you return?'

'Tomorrow.'

'Leo, I need your guys off my back. Nothing's moving, and the clock is ticking.'

'I've been tied up.'

'You owe me. It can't work this way.'

Scamarcio felt his palms grow damp again. 'Listen, Piero, I'll be in touch once I've landed. We can talk about this then.'

'We'd better. I always call in a debt, Leo. You should know that by now.'

Scamarcio swallowed hard. 'OK,' was all he could muster.

He thought Piocosta had been about to hang up when the old man said, 'I've got something that might help you focus.'

'Focus ...'

'It's about Donato and his goons ...'

'Ah.' Scamarcio felt himself being reeled in even tighter to Piocosta and his poisonous little world.

'Word on the network is that Abbiati was convinced there was a price on his head before he died — but from outside, not inside Italy. He thought that your dead American was out to get him, but he couldn't understand why. He told the clan that he'd kept his promise, that he'd transferred the money as agreed.'

'I'd heard differently.'

'Well, you heard wrong. What did you hear, and who told you?'

'It doesn't matter. Anyway, what made Abbiati believe that Carter wanted him dead, that he wasn't just there to make him settle?'

'Apparently, he didn't go into that. But, according to someone close to Donato, Abbiati was scared, real scared, in the days before he died. That's why he sent them to kill the American. I just got wind of this today, and thought I should send it your way.'

'Right,' said Scamarcio, knowing that his debt with Piocosta had just doubled.

Scamarcio ended the call and closed his eyes. How the fuck was he going to sort this thing with Piocosta?

He reflected on the new information the old man had given him. Had Pozzi got it wrong, or had Piocosta? Instinct told him that Piocosta was the one more likely to come by accurate information. If Piocosta's steer was solid, what — or, more to the point, *who* — had made Abbiati so scared? Had Carter threatened him? Stranger still: Abbiati was convinced he had deposited the money, but Carter believed it gone.

He opened the mini-bar for another whisky, and realised that the tentative beginnings of any resolve to leave well-enough alone seemed to have evaporated.

43

SCAMARCIO HAD BEEN CONVINCED they would find some reason to stop him on his way through Dulles, but everything proceeded normally. By 6.30 am he had cleared customs and passport control, and had ordered his first coffee of the day. As he spooned away the inedible plastic froth, he studied the businessmen hurrying past, the students browsing the bookshops, the tourists in duty-free — looking for anyone who seemed out of place, who seemed less than convincing. But everyone appeared to fit into the scene; everyone had their role. His pay-as-you-go mobile rang, and he laid down the spoon and took a sip of the watery coffee before checking that there was no one sitting too close who might overhear. The nearest customer was about ten places away, so he decided to stay where he was.

'John, you've caught me just as I was leaving.'

'I figured you might be on the first flight out.'

There was something about Blakemore's tone that troubled him. 'Is everything OK?' he asked.

'Samuel is dead.'

'Dead?'

'He was found in the early hours, hanging from the Potomac Bridge.'

Scamarcio couldn't muster a response; the circuits in his brain were struggling to process the news. Was everyone he dealt with on this case doomed to suffer?

'He didn't kill himself — obviously,' continued Blakemore.

'I figured that,' said Scamarcio eventually.

'You were probably the last one to see him alive. Watch yourself. Whatever you've got, it's toxic.'

That word again. Scamarcio decided not to fill him in on the details of his meeting with Samuel. Given what had just happened to him, he didn't know who was listening to the call, or how Blakemore might react.

The reporter eventually broke the silence. 'Samuel called me after he'd seen you. It must just have been a few hours before he died. He said he had forgotten to tell you something, that he wanted me to pass on a message.'

Scamarcio's mind still wasn't turning over properly; he couldn't get the connections to fire.

'He said to remind you that, and I quote, *These people are very good at getting other people to do their dirty work for them.*'

'Was that it?'

'Yeah.'

'Poor bastard.'

'He'd done some bad things in his time.'

'What kind of bad things?'

'Let's not go there.' Blakemore sniffed, and it came out too loud down the line. 'You get on the wrong side of some of those guys, and you're finished. You've come around asking questions, now two ex-agents are dead. It feels like something's going down, something big.'

'When you say "some of those guys," who do you mean?'

'Whoever is behind this thing — perhaps they're Agency, but perhaps they're not mainstream.'

'Did Samuel tell you that?'

'No, just putting two and two together. Anyway, Leo, I'm going to let you get on with it. Like I said, patience is my middle name. If you want to give me a call when the dust has settled, I'd appreciate it.'

Scamarcio's mind was still turning on Samuel and his final

words of advice when the line suddenly went dead. He felt a wave of disquiet. Blakemore would have waited for him to sign off, wouldn't he? Or had the call just dropped out? He thought about phoning him back, but something told him this would be a bad idea.

After a couple of glasses of acidic red wine on the flight home, a thought slowly began to form. What if Carter's former employers wanted him out of the picture, but subtly, so they manipulated Abbiati into killing him? They diverted the money, made it look as if Abbiati hadn't kept his side of the bargain, thereby luring Carter to Rome to track him down. Meanwhile they pulled Abbiati's strings, convincing him that Carter was out to get him. They then did a whitewash with the whole suicidal-tendencies story. But what a lot of effort to go to. Why didn't they just kill Carter themselves? It would have been cleaner and simpler. Abbiati had no doubt complicated things by bringing in the Cappadona, and the strange Calvi symbolism had got the Rome police interested. Scamarcio doubted that the Americans would have wanted either of those two elements. Some important parts of the picture were still missing.

After having slept for the remainder of the flight, he joined the enormous queue waiting to get through passport control. There seemed to be hundreds of travellers arriving, and just two officials to deal with them all. It was always the same: everywhere you looked, Italy was grinding to a halt. He clenched his jaw and looked away. He just wanted to hand over the files, maybe hand over the responsibility, and discuss his next steps with Garramone.

When he eventually cleared customs, he hailed a cab, deciding to head straight for Garramone's office. They pulled out of the airport loop and onto the autostrada, but instead of making the usual turn-off for the city limits, the driver kept on going.

'Hey,' said Scamarcio, 'we've missed the exit.'

The driver said nothing, and just kept his eyes fixed on the road ahead. Scamarcio felt heat snake along his spine.

'What are you doing?' he persisted. 'Why didn't we turn?'

Again, the driver didn't respond. Scamarcio threw himself back against the seat. 'Fuck it,' he said. 'Fuck it.' He pulled out his mobile, but didn't have a signal. He couldn't make sense of it. He should have been able to get a signal out here — it was a clear run.

After a few more moments, the driver swung off the autostrada, but he was taking them into an area of the city that was unfamiliar to Scamarcio. He saw what looked like warehouses and industrial parks, and then they passed a scrapyard and a car-demolition site.

'Where are we going?' he asked, no longer expecting an answer.

He was thinking that when the car slowed he would try to throw himself out — but when he pulled the handle, the door remained locked.

After they'd driven past what looked like a food-processing plant, the driver pulled the car into a yard with two long prefab buildings to its right. Three men were waiting for them, and as they entered, the trio bolted the gate shut behind them. One of the men was small and muscled with short, dark hair, a pug nose, and mean eyes. He was wearing a long brown-leather jacket, jeans, and Timberlands. The other two were taller, thinner, and younger — in their early twenties. With their greasy, blond hair, spotty complexions, and baggy, blue eyes, they looked quite similar, and Scamarcio wondered whether they were brothers. Both were wearing black puffa jackets, jeans, and sturdy-looking walking boots. He couldn't decide which one was uglier.

As the car came to a halt, the guy with the pug nose reached for Scamarcio's door and grabbed him, manhandling him out of the back seat. The brothers came up alongside their colleague to help, and Scamarcio knew he hadn't a hope. One of them took a swing at Scamarcio's jaw, and the next thing he knew he was on the ground, trying not to choke on his own blood.

'Bring him inside,' said a voice. Looking up from his position on the ground, Scamarcio saw a tall, dark-haired man in a black suit and tie standing by the prefab. He looked like he'd just come back from a funeral.

One of the brothers hauled Scamarcio up off the tarmac and shoved him towards the building. Scamarcio's jaw was pounding, and something felt very wrong with his left leg. The guy shoved him again, and he stumbled forward and fell over. The other brother towered over him now, and released a large blob of spittle that landed next to Scamarcio's mouth. He wanted to vomit.

'Quit fucking around and get him inside,' hollered the man in the funeral suit.

The thin smile disappeared from the lips of the blond youth, and he pulled Scamarcio up once more and frog-marched him towards the building.

As they passed the man in the suit, Scamarcio saw that he was dark skinned, with small, ratty eyes and a thin mouth that was little more than a gash. Although their skin tones were completely different, there was something about him that reminded Scamarcio of the two blond boys.

The man surveyed him dispassionately as he passed, and the total absence of light in the stranger's eyes took Scamarcio's breath away for a moment.

He was pushed inside the prefab, and the first thing he noticed was the smell. It was an unmistakeable odour he had encountered at numerous crime scenes: decomposition mixed with the salty, iron tang of fresh blood. Someone had died inside here, and died recently.

They marched Scamarcio deeper inside the building, and a light was switched on. Once the bars had spluttered to life, his gaze froze on a pair of manacles attached to the wall, and a wide, red stain beneath them. Then his eyes moved reluctantly to a workbench on which a lathe was positioned. Next to it was another table, where a series of knives and hammers were laid out. While he was taking in the knives spread out like a surgeon's kit, he had the sudden conviction that this was where Pozzi had died, and that the man in the funeral suit was Donato Cappadona.

44

THE BROTHERS GRIM pushed him up against the wall, and attached one of the manacles to his wrist. The iron was sharp and cold, and it pressed tightly into his skin. Then, for good measure, the one who Scamarcio decided was the slightly uglier of the two punched him in the stomach. He collapsed to the ground, hard waves of pain forcing him up into a foetal position. He wanted to vomit again.

'We've got a surprise for you,' said the uglier boy. His voice was strangely high and effeminate.

One of the boys — he didn't know which one — spat on him again. He closed his eyes, and before he opened them he heard them walk away. After several moments had passed, the space fell silent.

He didn't know if he'd blacked out or fallen asleep, but some time later he heard the sound of footsteps approaching again.

'He's well buffed. What I wouldn't give ...'

'Shut up, Mauro,' said a slightly deeper voice. 'You can save that shit for later.'

Scamarcio pulled himself up against the wall, willing himself not to panic. What the fuck was going on here?

He only registered that the lights had been off when a switch was flicked and he could dimly make out the area around him once more. Much of the place was in shadow, but some instinct told him that it was nighttime now. The blond boys were walking towards him, smiles on their faces.

'Ready for your surprise?' asked the one with the high voice, kicking him hard in the leg.

'Go fuck yourself,' said Scamarcio.

The boy smiled lasciviously. 'I'd rather fuck you.'

Scamarcio closed his eyes and swallowed. When he opened them, he saw someone approaching behind the boys. The stranger seemed to be dragging a large bundle alongside him, but it kept flopping over to the side.

As the figure and its strange cargo drew ever nearer, Scamarcio felt himself turn extremely cold, and then hot, and then cold again. He started to shake, and his breath wouldn't come. He wanted to close his eyes, but he forced himself to keep them open.

'Aurelia,' he whispered.

But she wasn't responding. Her eyes were open, but there was no sign of life behind them — it was as if her soul had already fled. Her blouse was ripped, and there were bruises on her arms and shoulders. 'Oh God,' he murmured. 'Oh God, what have you done?' He couldn't help himself, and did close his eyes this time.

When he looked again, he saw that the man in the funeral suit was positioning her at the carpentry table. She had slumped down like a rag doll, and he lifted her hand and placed it near the lathe. To Scamarcio, she seemed like a living corpse; it was as if the fight had long since left her. How many days had she been here? Was she being held prisoner all the time he was in the States?

The man in the suit left her by the lathe, and pulled up a chair so he could stare down at Scamarcio sprawled on the floor.

'So, Leone Scamarcio, Lucio's boy. How funny that our paths should cross. From what I hear, your dad was a conniving little shit who deserved everything he got.'

Scamarcio said nothing.

'The thing is, *Leo* ... Can I call you *Leo*? I feel like I know you already.'

Again, Scamarcio said nothing.

'Anyway, the thing is, Leo, I've had enough of you sticking

your nose into my business. My associates have had enough.'

He gestured to where Aurelia was sitting near the lathe. 'Me and your lady friend here have had a lot of fun together, but now it's time to get serious. It seems that my colleagues have not been working hard enough to get the message through to you, so it's been left to me to come up with something clearer.'

Scamarcio felt sick again.

'In case you're wondering, you're about to watch me grind off each of her lovely fingers, one by one. And if that little show doesn't focus your mind, I'm going to try out my knives on her. Unfortunately, they're not the best knives; nothing like those high-end ceramic things my wife likes. Sure, they do the job, but it takes twice as long, and it's messy — it's never a clean cut.'

Scamarcio coughed. His throat was dry, and he needed water to talk, but somehow he managed to get the words out. 'Please — you don't need to do any of that. I'll drop this thing; I'll drop it right now. Please just leave her alone.'

The man in the funeral suit smiled. 'Funny — I told them that's what you'd say.' After a moment, he asked, 'Do you know who I am?'

'Donato Cappadona?'

'Got it in one.' Cappadona got up from the chair and walked towards the lathe.

'So the message is getting through now?'

'Yes.'

Cappadona took Aurelia's hand and placed it next to the blade. Again, she made no sign of moving and just sat slumped there, oblivious. Cappadona was reaching beneath the table to switch something on when Scamarcio screamed, 'I told you. I'll do it, I'll back off. It's over — you've won.'

Cappadona smiled, and laid down Aurelia's hand before returning to his seat. After he had flicked something from his suit trousers, he said, 'Another thing you can do for me is tell that old cunt Piero Pierocosta to keep his filthy hands out of my till. Testaccio is ours.'

Scamarcio nodded. His tongue was like sandpaper, and he felt it catch on the roof of his mouth.

'Now,' said Cappadona, leaning forward in the chair. 'My friends have another request. You've been busy in the States. They want to know whether it was a fruitful trip.' As he asked this, he turned to look at Aurelia and licked his lips. If he hadn't been manacled to the wall, Scamarcio would have torn out his eyes with his bare hands.

Cappadona swung back around and suddenly clicked his fingers at the blond boys. 'Where's his bag?' he barked.

One of them reached behind him and picked something up from the floor. He brought Scamarcio's hold-all over to Cappadona, who placed it on his lap and unzipped it.

'What are these files here?' he asked, waving one of them at Scamarcio.

'I don't know — I'm still trying to work that out.'

'Don't you fucking bullshit me,' Cappadona hissed, turning back to Aurelia for a moment before fixing his eyes on Scamarcio once more. He felt as if that stare might kill him. The evil was tangible; there was no humanity there.

Scamarcio took a breath, and tried to steady his nerves. When he had found some semblance of balance, he asked himself if Cappadona spoke English. Then he wondered if he had already seen the Italian file. From his questions, it would appear not. He was about to attempt an explanation when, out of the corner of his eye, he noticed a movement. Aurelia was slowly pushing her hand across the table towards the knives, but she wasn't looking at them; she was still staring into the middle distance, her eyes glazed over. He panicked. Was she going to stab herself? Had whatever happened with Cappadona broken her? But something told him that she was tougher than that; that the rebel in her would be trying to fight back now. Perhaps the lifeless pose had been nothing more than an act, designed to put them off their guard. He quickly returned his attention to Cappadona, not wanting any of them to follow his gaze.

'The one file that makes any sense is the Italian one,' Scamarcio said, trying to keep his voice steady. 'It talks about the Solidarity movement and some money that was sent from the Vatican.'

Cappadona raised an eyebrow. 'I'm sure my friends will be very interested to hear *that*,' he said, looking to the ugly brothers for confirmation.

'What else?'

'I haven't had a chance to read it properly.'

Cappadona jumped up from his chair. In less than a second, he was holding a blade against Scamarcio's throat. He could feel the icy steel digging into his flesh. How long before it broke the skin? How long before the blood came?

'Quit bullshitting me.' Cappadona drove the blade down harder.

'It's true when I say I haven't read it all. But the letters talk about a favour — in connection with that young terrorist Paglieri who was found hanging. But it's vague. Whoever wrote it doesn't go into detail.'

Cappadona exhaled sharply and nodded at the two boys. They dutifully shuffled over and he handed the blond one the knife. Then he returned to the chair and pulled something from his jacket pocket. Scamarcio saw that it was a packet of Marlboros. Cappadona drew out a gold lighter from the same pocket, and lit up slowly and carefully as if this were a delicate act that had to be performed with precision. Scamarcio thought about the table of knives, and swallowed.

The orange eye of Cappadona's cigarette blinked back at him in the semi darkness.

'Paglieri,' he grunted. 'That cowardly little shit.' Then he fell silent and just stared into the middle distance. The man's face was impassive. Scamarcio had no idea what would come next.

Suddenly, without warning, Cappadona rose from the chair, strode over to where Aurelia was slumped across the table, grabbed her by the hair, and jerked her head back sharply. He pulled out his cigarette and ground it into her right cheek, holding the butt tight against the skin. Aurelia was howling now, a primal, animal scream that made Scamarcio sweat. Had Cappadona noticed that she had been trying to reach for the knives? How was that possible? He was pulling her head back so hard now that it looked like he might break her neck. Scamarcio felt his bowels loosen.

After what seemed like an eternity, Aurelia's screams became shuddering sobs, and Scamarcio felt that he was about to lose his sanity. Something in his soul was going to rupture. But then Cappadona finally let go and Aurelia slumped forward, her head smashing against the table. Scamarcio wondered if she had passed out from the pain. The thought of it was a relief.

Cappadona was panting now. Scamarcio wasn't sure whether it was because he was out of shape or because he was aroused by the violence. He was walking towards Scamarcio, his eyes never wavering from his for an instant.

'You're going to give me every last detail you've discovered in the course of your investigation. Every single fact. If you hold anything back, any tiny thing, I will know. And next time we're going to take your girlfriend's pain to a whole new level. She'll discover nerve endings she never thought she had.'

Scamarcio glanced over to Aurelia, but, rather than remaining slumped where Cappadona had just thrown her, he realised that she was slowly rising from her chair. *No,* he thought. *No, No. This is madness.* If any of Cappadona's mutts spotted her, it would be over in seconds. The brothers weird were standing to Donato's left, and might or might not have an angle on her approach. The short, dark guy seemed to be towards the back of the space, organising something into boxes, but he could turn around at any moment, and if Cappadona himself were to look back to the table again …

Scamarcio's heart was hammering in his chest now. There were too many unknowns. He felt they had just seconds left to live. He wanted to close his eyes again — shut it all out — but he used all his inner strength to keep going.

As Aurelia continued her approach, Scamarcio looked to the left of the two brothers. He glanced up at a spot above their heads, and then looked away quickly as if he didn't want them to notice. Both the brothers and Donato automatically followed his gaze, and, as they did so, Aurelia struck. She sank the knife into the base of Cappadona's spine, again and again, in a rage so intense that Scamarcio felt sure she had lost her mind. Cappadona howled in agony, writhing around on the floor like a tortured crow. His cries brought the squat, dark-haired guy running in from the back of the room, shouting and waving a gun, but Aurelia spun around like a dervish and stabbed him in the stomach before he could let off a single bullet. He fell screaming to the ground, where she stabbed him again.

To Scamarcio's astonishment, Aurelia retrieved the guy's rifle from the floor and kicked back against the two brothers, who were now on top of her. She caught the uglier one in the groin and he fell to the concrete, but the other one was still on his feet, reaching for his Beretta. She let out a scream so intense that it made the hairs on the back of Scamarcio's neck stand on end, and then she smashed the guy across the face with the butt of the rifle, bringing him to his knees. She smashed him again, harder this time, and he slumped to the floor next to his brother, who was now trying to get up. Her eyes dead, Aurelia trained the gun on the boy and fired twice. One of the bullets went wide, but the other hit a kneecap, and he collapsed on the ground.

She walked over to Scamarcio, her expression neutral. 'Hold your hands up.' He closed his eyes, knowing what she was about to do. She fired, and the chain on the manacle fell away.

Scamarcio grabbed his holdall, and they ran outside. The car that had brought him here was still in the yard, and Scamarcio spotted the driver seated at the wheel, listening to the radio. Scamarcio swung the door open, punched him in the face, and slammed his head against the dash several times before dragging him out and throwing him onto the concrete. The keys were still in the ignition, and Scamarcio jumped into the driver's seat while Aurelia leaped onto the seat behind him. He pushed the car into reverse, taking it at speed, pumping the accelerator. Then he swung it into first, and made for the metal gate. He rammed it hard and the gate gave, but not enough, so he reversed and tried it again. Some pieces broke away, but the gate still wasn't open. Two men who he hadn't seen before came running into the yard, and he reversed once more, nearly knocking them over, the tyres burning, the engine screaming. It had to work this time. He closed his eyes. There was a groaning and a crashing, and he realised that the metal was finally about to come away.

As they made it onto the road, he glanced back to look at Aurelia. She was slumped against the seat, and her eyes were glazed over again. There was no sign of the woman he used to know.

45

AFTER WHAT HAD SEEMED like several hours of silence, Scamarcio had left Aurelia at the hospital. She'd told him that she needed to be alone for a while, and when he'd protested, she'd just laid a hand on his wrist and gently asked him to go. Something about the way she'd looked at him told him he should do as she wished.

Everything seemed to have sped up now, permanently. No sooner was he back in the squad room than he received a call from Detective Nardone, up in Varese.

'Scamarcio, I'm glad I caught you. I've been trying a few times, but never seem able to get through.'

'Things have been hectic.'

'I just wanted to let you know that Brambani's mother said something that might be significant. She claims she didn't think of it before, but is now asking herself if it's relevant.'

'Right …' Nothing felt relevant anymore.

'She says that a while ago Antonio came to her, claiming that someone very high up in the Church had told him a terrible secret; that it had made him question his calling. He was extremely anxious about it — was thinking of leaving the priesthood.'

Scamarcio sighed and sat down. 'Did he explain what this secret was?'

'No, she claims not.'

'And the person who dropped this bombshell?'

'Brambani just said that it was somebody very senior — someone who commanded a great deal of respect.'

'What about afterwards? Did Brambani talk any more about leaving the priesthood?'

'She says he never mentioned it again, so she decided not to raise it — she was worried about him losing his way, going off track, so she didn't want to stir up any doubts he might still have.'

'I see.'

'I thought I should let you know.'

'Thanks, Nardone. I appreciate that.'

'It might tie into your idea that Brambani believed someone in the Church was responsible for his father's death.'

'Perhaps.' He needed to wind up the call. 'Listen, I'm just on my way to see my boss, but I'll give you a ring later and fill you in on where I'm at. Have you heard anything from the Vatican police?'

'I tried to call them, but was told the person I needed to speak with was out and would ring me back. That was two days ago now.'

'Figures,' said Scamarcio.

'Indeed.'

The chief was hunched over his desk in a threadbare woollen jumper when Scamarcio limped in. Garramone seemed to be studying several columns of figures, making a note in biro against certain numbers. It reminded Scamarcio of the documents he'd seen in Carter's files.

The boss looked up from the paperwork and raised his eyebrows when he saw Scamarcio standing there. 'What the hell happened to your face? I thought you were supposed to be on holiday.'

'I was.'

'Must have been a shitty vacation.' He glanced at the files under Scamarcio's arm. 'What are those?'

'The product of my vacation.'

Garramone inclined his head to the side. 'Why do I have the feeling that I'm not going to like what I'm about to hear?'

'No idea.'

Scamarcio took a seat uninvited. He winced when he sat down.

'What the hell happened?'

'Donato Cappadona decided to teach me a lesson.'

'Cappadona?'

'Yeah. Payback for Pozzi. Plus his friends wanted to find out what I knew.'

'His friends in the Church?'

'That would be my guess.'

The chief groaned, and ran a hand through his hair. Scamarcio saw dandruff sprinkle onto the table. 'Jesus, Scamarcio, you're in trouble,' he said, as if it had nothing to do with him. Well, technically, it didn't. He'd ordered Scamarcio off the case.

'They took Aurelia D'Amato,' Scamarcio said quietly, almost hoping the boss wouldn't hear.

'*Took her?*'

'She was at their place when they dragged me in.'

Garramone turned pale.

'Look, you should probably know — we've been having a relationship. They took her to get at me.'

'Shit,' said Garramone, running a hand across his closed eyelids. 'Is she OK?'

'I don't know,' said Scamarcio. 'She's at the hospital. Physically she seems all right, but there could be other damage.'

Garramone looked confused for a moment and then seemed to get it. 'Jesus,' he hissed. 'What the hell did they *do* to her?'

Scamarcio didn't answer. He still didn't really know, but he didn't feel like sharing his suspicions with Garramone.

'How did you both get out of there?'

'Aurelia — she stabbed Cappadona, and then shot three of his goons.'

'What?'

'I don't know if they're dead, but they're definitely not OK.'

Garramone just stared at him, wide-eyed.

They sat in silence for a while, neither of them moving, before Scamarcio pushed across the files he had found in Carter's lock-up. 'Take a look at the one on top — if you've got the time.'

Garramone looked down at the envelope absently, then moved his columns of figures off to one side and pulled the new file towards him. He flicked through the first few pages before asking, 'What the fuck is this'?

'It's why they killed the American, why they strung him up under the bridge.'

When Scamarcio was done talking him through his trip, Garramone said, 'This just sounds like all that conspiracy crap you find on the internet.'

'Samuel was found hanging from the Potomac Bridge just a few hours after he spoke with me.'

Garramone paled again. 'This is bullshit.'

'What if it's not bullshit?' said Scamarcio. 'What if there's something to it? Carter was involved, he lost the faith, and they didn't want him talking, so they got Abbiati to kill him.'

'So who killed Abbiati? Father Brambani, like we're meant to believe?

'I don't think it's that simple. I think Brambani was set up. You know that Vatican scholar has gone missing — the guy the author Felletti sent our way?'

Garramone was shaking his head again, quicker now. 'No, I didn't know that. Why the hell didn't I know that?'

'I was busy in the States. I thought you'd have been filled in.'

'Who the fuck was going to fill me in if you didn't? It was your fucking case!'

'It had been taken off me.'

'That's irrelevant.' The chief slammed his hand onto the desk.

'I think it's possible that Donato Cappadona took him; I need to find that out. If I can get to the scholar, I think we can close this thing, put a lid on it. He feels like the final element.'

'How are you going to get to him if he's gone missing?'

'There's a Detective Bracco already on it. I'll work with him to track the guy down.'

'Do you even know where he lives?'

'Felletti gave me an address.'

Scamarcio wondered if he should just head down to Prati and ask around. He knew that Bracco had already done this, but he felt that he needed to be doing something, that he needed to be out on the ground, rather than cooped up in the hospital, failing to get Aurelia to talk to him.

Garramone pinched his hands into a tight steeple. 'We're no longer supposed to be on this case. What's the point in you trying to track him down?'

'So we're just going to sit on the most explosive dossier that's ever crossed our desks, and pretend we didn't see it? God, how do you live with yourself?'

He was out of his seat now, pacing the room.

Garramone turned white for a moment, and Scamarcio thought he was going to jump up and deck him. But the boss just closed his eyes and eased his neck back against his chair. The sponge was still protruding from beneath the plastic. When the words came, they were measured and neutral: 'I can find someone to send it up to, but after that I don't know what will happen. It seems too sensitive for us to handle. I don't want to compromise the department.'

'But you'll pass it up?'

Garramone sighed. 'I'll pass it up, but first I want to establish how the Abbiati thing feeds into this.' He paused. 'We need to get rid of this case, Scamarcio. It's poison — for you and everyone around you.'

'Let me find this guy, and wind this thing up.'

The chief rubbed at an eye. 'The Cappadona have you in their sights now, and fuck knows what the Americans want. I'm going to arrange protection for D'Amato, and I think you should keep a uniformed officer with you for the time being.'

'Fine for D'Amato, but don't worry about me.'

'Don't be an idiot. You can't win this one.'

Scamarcio said nothing.

Garramone shook his head again and sighed.

46

SCAMARCIO WALKED BRISKLY through Prati, scanning the cafés and shopfronts. The pavements were bustling, and the size of the crowds troubled him; he figured that with so many people out, a gunshot might pass unnoticed. The warm feeling at the back of his neck returned several times, and he kept glancing behind him, certain he was being followed. But he couldn't spot anyone in the immediate throng who didn't seem convincingly occupied with pedestrian concerns: he took in a tired father with his troublesome young son, a group of tartily dressed schoolgirls, a fat boy delivering tomatoes ... But, yet again, he reminded himself that the Americans were experts, and if the Cappadona came looking, they wouldn't waste their time on pavement shootouts, but would resort to the trusty drive-by. He wondered if he should have accepted Garramone's offer of the uniform.

He turned his attention to the street up ahead, and yet again felt the familiar warmth on the back of his neck, the tightening of his spine. He swung around to check behind him, but saw nothing.

He walked on, and still the sensation wouldn't go away; he couldn't shake it. He stopped and glanced behind him once more. However, this time his brain wouldn't accept what his eyes were telling him, and he wondered if it was just tiredness playing tricks: the Vatican scholar was loitering at the window of a bookshop, trying not to look as if he knew that Scamarcio was there. Scamarcio closed his eyes, and opened them again. The scene remained unchanged: the old man was still there.

'What the hell ...' he shouted, hurrying over and grabbing the scholar by both shoulders, rougher than he'd intended. 'We've been looking for you for days. Your friends told us you'd gone missing.'

'I had.'

'So? Don't tell me you managed to pull a fast one on Donato Cappadona?' Donato was losing his touch if all his prisoners managed to escape, especially one as elderly and frail as this.

'Cappadona? I have no idea what you're talking about.' Scamarcio noticed that the old man's hands were trembling.

'So where have you been?'

The old fellow wouldn't look him in the eye, and just stared at the ground. 'I decided to get out of town for a few days. Like I told you, I felt like I'd gone above the parapet. I needed to disappear.'

'But why didn't you *tell* anyone? Your friends were very worried.'

'I didn't want them to know. I'm not sure who I can trust.' The man's voice cracked, and his shoulders sank a little. After his own recent brush with the Cappadona, Scamarcio could no longer dismiss these fears as paranoia — the old man had good reason to be scared.

'So you intended to come back?'

'I would have stayed away longer, but my Filipino helper let me down. I couldn't just let my babies starve.'

'Your babies?' *Jesus*, realised Scamarcio. The man had come back for a few mangy cats. His mind flashed on his earlier glimpse of him, loitering by the window.

'What were you doing, lurking in the shadows? It looked like you were following me.'

The old man seemed flustered, and his cheeks reddened. 'No, I wasn't, not really. Well, I mean, not today. I saw you pass and ...'

'What do you mean, *not today*?'

The scholar took a handkerchief from his pocket and wiped the sweat from his brow. He tried to use the same handkerchief to clean his glasses, but the lenses were becoming smeary, so he wiped them against the hem of his sports coat instead.

'What do you mean, *not today*?' repeated Scamarcio.

The old man took a breath and said, 'I *might* have been following you in the past.'

'You *might* have been following me?'

'I was worried — worried about where the police were going with this.'

'Why should you be worried?'

'I knew you'd talked to Rigamonti.'

Scamarcio felt utterly confused. The old man seemed to read this, and said, 'Look, my apartment's not far. Come up, and I'll explain.'

The scholar seemed so small and frail, so nervous standing there in front of him, that Scamarcio heard himself agreeing.

The old man turned and said, 'It's this way.' He took a right, and led Scamarcio down a smart street full of expensive hairdressers and perfumeries. After a minute had passed, he stopped outside an attractive Liberty building, ivy shrouding most of its pink façade. They entered the marble lobby and then rode the wide elevator to the third floor in silence. The scholar turned left out of the lift, and came to a halt outside a broad oak-panelled door. He pulled out a set of keys, and Scamarcio heard the latch release.

'After you,' said the old man. Scamarcio felt another wave of disquiet, and wondered whether he'd been set up again, whether there was a kill squad waiting for him inside.

But as he stepped into the apartment, all he saw were a couple of fat, grey cats dozing lazily in an armchair beside a gas fire. The walls of the large living room were lined with books, and yet more volumes formed tottering piles on the floor. Scamarcio noticed a flurry of papers strewn across a wide oak desk positioned to provide a good view onto the street. Beyond the window, it looked as if the rain was turning to sleet, and the sudden change in the weather seemed to be causing a shift in the mood of the drivers below: several horns blared, and someone screamed at someone else that their mother was a fluffer. The Vatican scholar sighed and said, 'I wanted to get double-glazing, but it's so ridiculously expensive.' He gestured to an armchair on the other side of the fire from the cats. 'Do sit down.'

Scamarcio was immediately glad of the warmth and the comfortable upholstery. He was burned out.

The old man took a seat on the leather sofa opposite, and Scamarcio noticed that his movements seemed stiff and arthritic once more. Out on the street he had seemed more nimble, and Scamarcio wondered if he had one of those conditions that came and went — whether that might also explain the strange change in his gait outside the café on Via Magno.

'So why were you following me?' Scamarcio asked.

The old man folded his hands in his lap. 'I was worried — worried that you'd get to Rigamonti and that my cover would be blown.'

'Are you the spy?'

He snorted. 'Don't be ridiculous.'

Scamarcio just stared at him, seeking an explanation.

'I'm the one who told Rigamonti about the spy,' he said eventually.

'Who told *you*?'

'Like I said, Abbiati had seen some ugly things in his time. It wasn't that he *suspected* that one of his colleagues kept strange bedfellows — he *knew* that he did. And he understood perfectly who these bedfellows were.'

'Why didn't you tell me this the first time?'

'I've been very afraid.'

'Of the Opus Dei faction?'

'Of course.'

'So that's why you were worried that I'd talked to Rigamonti?'

'Yes.'

'So why *did* you talk to him? Wasn't it a risky move?' asked Scamarcio.

'Something has to be done — there needs to be movement now.'

Scamarcio decided to leave this particular point for later. 'How well did you know Cardinal Abbiati?'

The man looked away for a moment, seemingly embarrassed, and Scamarcio suddenly wondered if there'd been some sort of relationship between them. He could see no pictures of any family in the apartment — no wife or children.

'We were extremely close,' said the old man eventually.

Scamarcio nodded. 'Could you tell more about him? I'm interested in the man himself, what kind of person he was. I've been presented with this picture of him as a cold-blooded killer, and it's not squaring with the accounts I've been getting from people like you. I want to know who this man is, who he *was*, whether he was good or not.'

'Good?'

'Whether he would be capable of murder.'

The scholar removed his reading glasses and rubbed his eyes. Scamarcio thought he saw moisture there.

'Well, I can set you straight on that,' said the old man. 'As I told you, he was a thoroughly good man, a deeply honest man, a man who would be prepared to tell the truth at any price. He had no interest in personal wealth or advancement, and he would never in a million years have been capable of killing another human being.'

'Would he have been capable of paying someone else to commit murder on his behalf?'

The scholar frowned, seemingly disgusted. 'No, absolutely not.' He paused for a moment and then asked, 'Who is he supposed to have killed?'

'It doesn't matter,' said Scamarcio. 'This thing with Father Brambani on the staircase to Abbiati's apartment, how does it seem to you?'

'Like a fabrication, like the usual rubbish they peddle. What business could that young man have had with the cardinal? That poor lad was set up. Abbiati was killed by the usual suspects — they wanted him out of the picture.'

'Father Brambani seemed to believe that Abbiati had prior knowledge of the Turin bombing, that he was somehow complicit.'

'What?'

'Brambani lost his father in the attack — someone high up in the Church had told him that Abbiati was involved.'

'But that's ridiculous. Abbiati was a finance manager at the bank. What the hell would he know about Turin?'

'You're aware of the rumours of P2 involvement in domestic terror? If the Vatican was laundering money for them ...'

'I've heard the rumours, and I wouldn't be surprised if someone knew all about what was going on during the years of lead, but that person would most definitely *not* have been Abbiati.'

'How can you be so sure? If he was the one handling the books ... if he saw the money coming in and going out ...'

The scholar sighed and threw open his palms. 'You just know someone, Detective. I knew Abbiati for many many years, and I can assure you that he'd never have been involved. He would have run and told the first person he found. He would have seen the whole thing as morally repugnant.'

'But he didn't tell them about the false accounting.'

'That's slightly different. Lives weren't at stake.'

'Well, they would have been if that money had ended up in the wrong hands, as it sometimes seems to have done.'

The scholar remained silent, shaking his head now. Scamarcio decided not to push it; he needed this man to help him, and right now there weren't many people around in a position to do that.

The old man sighed and cast his gaze to the window. 'Someone clearly let that poor parish priest think that Abbiati had been involved in Turin, knowing that he would seek him out. As to Brambani's mental health, to consider such a move — well, God knows what they did to him to get him to that point.'

Both men fell silent for a moment, and Scamarcio wondered yet again where the Americans fitted in. He considered all these people who appeared to be getting other people to kill for them — all these distorted identities.

'There's one other thing,' said the scholar after a while. 'Abbiati might have been scared in the past; perhaps that's why he didn't speak out earlier. In the days before he died, he was certainly very worried about the spy.'

'Worried in what way?'

'He believed that this man had been working for the Americans for many years, that they shared some uncomfortable secrets. With all the forensic accounting going on, he reckoned that the spy had a new reason for wanting him gone.'

'This spy was with Opus Dei?'

'That was Abbiati's belief.'

Scamarcio stopped for a moment. 'You know, you're playing a dangerous game chatting to reporters. In your position, I would have approached the police first.'

'But you have no jurisdiction inside the Vatican.'

'No, but out here in Prati we do. We could have offered you protection.'

'Could you? I suspect it wouldn't have been that easy.'

Scamarcio said nothing. Perhaps the old man had a point.

The scholar shook his head sadly, and looked out as the rain started to drum against the window. 'Anyway, it's no game, Detective. I just wanted to do right by my friend. There are some dark forces at work, and I want to see these criminals brought to justice. I was scared before, but that fear is turning to anger now. These people can't be allowed to get away with murder, otherwise where will it end? We're talking about the Church, after all — if you can't root out the evil from there, what hope is there for the rest of us?'

47

ON HIS WAY TO VISIT AURELIA, the idea of distorted identities kept circling in his mind. Once more, Scamarcio's thoughts returned to Calvi, to the untouched masonry rubble in Carters' pockets, and to the proximity of both to the Vatican.

He stopped for an espresso in the hope that it would help him shake the exhaustion he felt. He walked into a bar near the Quirinale, and took a copy of the *Gazzetta dello Sport* from the counter. Sky TG24 was on in the background, discussing the disappearance of a young girl from her parent's garden in Bergamo. Scamarcio wondered briefly if the same sick minds from last summer's case were back at work.

He studied the paper for a while and then, when the news anchors started talking about the Turin trial, he looked up. They were giving a rundown of upcoming proceedings now — the victims who were likely to take the stand, the expert witnesses who would be called. Scamarcio put down the paper. He thought back to the favour that Carter had carried out for the mysterious 'Mr F', remembering the young boy who had been strung up to die in his parents' orchard just before he could take the stand. Was it possible that Abbiati had spotted a way to kill two birds with one stone? He wanted Carter dead, but was his cryptic murder also intended as a message to others to keep quiet — others who, thirty years on, might have felt tempted to speak out, who could attest to the fact that key figures in the state and the church knew that home-grown bombings were imminent, and that some of them had even gone so far as to facilitate them? Abbiati had staged a dramatic death for the American — a death that would ensure that this supposed suicide wouldn't stay under the radar, a death that would cause his Agency colleagues considerable alarm. And, returning to the core dilemma, who was 'F'? Why 'F' and not 'A'? Was 'F' the spy Abbiati had been so worried about? And, if so, where was 'F' now, and what was his role? Scamarcio sensed that 'F' was pulling the strings; that Abbiati and the others were dancing to *his* tune. If 'F' had had a decades-long relationship with Carter, it would have made more sense for 'F' to order his killing, rather than Abbiati, the honest bean-counter. Besides Brambani's strange conviction that he was involved in Turin, Abbiati didn't seem to have anything to do with this.

And then it came to him: he had been so very slow. How could he have missed it? He picked up his mobile to call Piocosta. He knew it would cost him dearly.

'I've got a strange question,' said Scamarcio by way of hello.

'You always do.'

'Could you could find out if the Cappadona ever met Cardinal Abbiati in the flesh?'

Piocosta exhaled, and it came out as a shriek down the line. 'It's a bit specific, that one. That kind of detail can only come from someone high up who was involved in setting up the deal. The people who talk on the network, they're lower down the food chain. I can't just go and pick up the phone to Donato and say, *'Oh, by the way, I hear you and that dead cardinal were fast friends — tell me all about it.'*

Yes, the last thing Scamarcio wanted was for Piocosta to pick up the phone to Donato. He had no idea what condition the mob boss was in — whether he was even conscious.

Piocosta paused for a beat. 'Anyway, Donato hates my guts at the moment. He's out for blood.'

'Why?' asked Scamarcio, sensing that he already knew the answer.

'I don't want to go into it.'

Scamarcio sighed. 'So there's nothing you can do?'

Piocosta fell silent, and Scamarcio knew what he was thinking. 'You said we'd talk when you were back. Well, you're back now. I need to know things are moving, Leo,' said the old man eventually.

Scamarcio felt his palms grow warm. 'Of course.'

'So?'

Scamarcio took a breath. 'Let me know when.'

'It will be in the next few days. I'm glad we're on the same wavelength, Leo.'

Scamarcio said nothing and just hung up.

When he got to Aurelia's place, she was huddled under a duvet watching daytime TV. It was one of those voyeuristic afternoon shows where left-wing psychologists who looked like Marx, and botoxed criminal lawyers who dressed like whores, spent hours poring over the morbid minutiae of recent murders. The programmes were always fronted by ex-showgirls, and the lawyers never seemed able to pull their puffa lips into a smile.

'How are you feeling?' he asked.

'How do you think?' she replied.

He took a seat on the sofa next to her, placing her feet on his lap. He still hadn't dared ask her what had happened with Cappadona.

'Why don't you move into my place for a while?' he said. He surprised himself with the question. The surprising thing wasn't the fact he had asked it, but that the idea of Aurelia living with him felt like a good thing — like something he wanted.

She turned to face him. She looked better now that she'd left the hospital. There was colour in her cheeks, and some light had returned to her eyes. 'I don't think that's a good idea,' she said.

'Why not?'

'I need some time to get my head straight.'

'But you'd get plenty of space at my place.'

'No.'

'But you can't stay here on your own. You need to rest, be looked after. Besides, we don't know if the Cappadona are going to retaliate. You could be at risk.'

'Garramone has arranged protection.'

Scamarcio had already spoken with the uniform outside her door.

'That's not the same. I'd feel much more comfortable if you were with me.'

'*You'd* feel more comfortable, but I wouldn't.'

'Please, Aurelia.'

'No, Leo. Can you please go now?' she said, turning up the sound on the TV.

Even though he was still supposed to be on leave, Scamarcio headed to the squad room, hoping to find something, anything, to distract him from the pain and guilt he was feeling. He knocked on Garramone's office window. The blinds were down, and when there was no response from inside, he knocked once more and poked his head around the door. Garramone was seated at his desk, red in the face. Opposite him were the three amigos: Andrea Scalisi from AISE, the little rat Gatti from media relations, and Rome's chief of police, Gianfilippo Mancino.

They all turned to look at Scamarcio standing there in the doorway, and he had the unequivocal sense that his time was up, that he was about to attend his own funeral.

'Leone, why don't you join us,' said Garramone, sounding exhausted. In the muted light, the hollows under his eyes were deep gouges, and there was a thin sheen of perspiration across his forehead and upper lip.

Scamarcio pulled out a seat and took a place next to the chief of police. He felt sure that they could all hear his heart pounding.

Garramone turned to face him. 'As you know, we were asked to drop this case, but you decided to fly to the US anyway and to continue with your investigation.'

'It was more a matter of combining business with pleasure. I had an old friend I wanted to look up.'

Garramone scratched at an eyebrow and glanced down at the notepad in front of him.

'But it wasn't your business, Scamarcio. We had told you to drop the case,' said Scalisi, not even bothering to look at him.

Scamarcio focussed on keeping his tone even, and his nerve steady. He glanced to the left to the chief of police seated next to him, and asked, 'Sir, could you explain to me how this works? I'm confused. I don't understand how AISE has the power to tell the Flying Squad to drop a case.'

He had expected the chief to turn puce, to start shouting something about respecting his superiors, but his reaction was quite the opposite. He shifted in his seat and barred his arms across his chest, the right edges of his mouth forming a tight smile that Scamarcio guessed Scalisi couldn't see from this angle.

'Yes, Detective,' he replied after a few moments. 'I've been asking myself the same question.'

'There are forces at work here that are far bigger than the Police Department can understand,' said Scalisi, a fat vein pulsing in his neck. 'We are dealing with extremely sensitive diplomatic issues that could threaten half a century of excellent relations with our American colleagues. The consequences of this could prove disastrous for our country.'

Scamarcio wondered how much Garramone had told them. Had he mentioned the Dark Star dossier? He couldn't see it anywhere on the desk. Scamarcio sensed that maybe Garramone had kept this information for himself and perhaps the chief of police.

'They have asked us repeatedly to back off, and we have to

listen,' continued Scalisi. 'And besides, Scamarcio, as I was just explaining to your superiors, your position in the force is now extremely fragile.' He pulled something from his pocket and slammed it on the desk in front of Garramone. Scamarcio leant in closer, and saw that it was a stack of photographs — no doubt, the same photos that had been slipped under his hotel door in Washington. He exhaled, trying to count to ten slowly in his head.

Garramone flipped them over and studied each one carefully before passing them to Mancino. The chief of police bunched his brow and, after a quick glance, set them back on the desk in front of Garramone.

'Who is that in the pictures with you?' Garramone asked, his tone even, but his eyes on fire.

'Piero Piocosta — my father's old lieutenant.'

'Why are you handing him money?'

'I swear to you, sir, as God is my witness, I've never handed money to Piocosta.'

'So how do you explain these?'

'I think someone doctored the picture to make it look like money.'

Scalisi snorted, as if such a thing were impossible.

'So what were you doing with Piocosta?' Garramone persisted.

'We were just having a conversation.'

'About what?'

'This and that. He likes to check up on me now and again — it makes him feel like he's looking out for me, like the old man would have wanted. I never talk about my work, of course.'

'So what *were* you giving him in this picture?'

If Scalisi and the rodent Gatti weren't in the room, Scamarcio would have told the truth. He would have explained to Garramone and the chief of police that a Post-it note had been handed across, listing the names of some hugely powerful figures in politics and big business who had committed terrible crimes against children. The note had been given to Piocosta because Scamarcio knew that, thanks to a corrupt and fatally inefficient legal system, Piocosta was the only one who would be able to exact any form of justice, who would be able to make these men pay in some small way for their crimes. Scamarcio knew that if he came clean about this to Garramone and Mancino, they wouldn't be happy — but, at the end of the day, they would probably understand. Scalisi, though, traversed a darker world. Instinctively, Scamarcio didn't trust him; he sensed he was the go-to guy for rich men with squalid secrets, and he asked himself, yet again, who had taken those photos and why. The fact that they were now in the hands of AISE proved that they had a strong interest in keeping Scamarcio quiet, in protecting their powerful friends.

Scamarcio's mind turned quickly, desperately seeking out an alternative story to present to the room. After a few seconds, he said, 'It was just a locket — my mother's locket.'

'Why were you giving Piocosta your mother's locket?' asked Garramone, his forehead etched with confusion.

'It's a long story,' sighed Scamarcio, 'but basically there was some bad blood between me and Piocosta. Shortly after my father was murdered, I discovered that Piocosta and my mother had been having an affair. She kept a photo of the two of them in that locket. I decided to give it to him as a way of saying that I'd forgiven him after all these years.' He shrugged his shoulders, trying to seem embarrassed at having to reveal such an intimate family secret.

Garramone was eyeing him closely now, and Mancino shifted once more in the seat beside him, but said nothing. Scalisi broke the silence by shouting, 'I can't believe you expect us to swallow this bullshit!'

Scamarcio kept staring directly ahead at a small patch of wall above Garramone's head. 'I don't care if you swallow it or not, it's the truth — and there's nothing I can do about that, one way or the other.'

The little rat made his irritating 'I must be heard' cough, and they all turned reluctantly to look at him. He bore a faux look of apology, and his beady little eyes seemed to be dancing with excitement. He coughed once more and then announced, 'I had a call this morning from Fabiana Morello of *La Repubblica*.'

Scamarcio felt something die inside him. If that old whore was sniffing around, it could only spell more misery.

'She's seen the photos,' said Gatti, almost triumphantly.

'How is that possible?' asked Garramone, looking Scalisi directly in the eye as he posed the question.

'I have no idea,' said Gatti. 'But she's planning on running a story on how Scamarcio was the Police Department's big bright hope, was Italy's big bright hope, but now it's come out that he's corrupt, and it's as if all hope for the country has died. It's allegorical — quite clever, really.'

Is this guy for real? thought Scamarcio.

'Anyway, as a courtesy, she wanted to let me know and ask us if we had any comment.'

'My only comment,' said Garramone, 'is how the hell did that bitch get those photos?' Once more, he fixed Scalisi squarely in the eye. The boss's neck was growing red, and Scamarcio didn't think he'd ever seen him so angry.

Chief of Police Mancino surprised them all by rising from his chair at this point, and turning to Colonel Scalisi and Gatti. 'I'd like you both to leave now. I want to speak to my colleagues alone.' He had a deep voice and towered over Gatti, sitting hunched in his chair like a piece of fresh roadkill.

The two of them reluctantly gathered their things, but when Gatti was out of his chair and about to make for the door through which Scalisi had already stormed, Mancino grabbed him by the arm and leant right into his mean little face.

'If you don't kill that story and kill it now, you'll be out of a job. You kill that story, and you tell that cunt that if she dares run with it we will make her life a living hell — unpaid taxes, unpaid speeding fines, unpaid parking tickets — we'll find something to beat her with, and we won't stop until she's ruined. You hear me? If I see that story in the paper, Gatti, I will personally make sure that you are never employed again by any police department or any business or corporation along the length and breadth of this godforsaken peninsula.'

The rat now looked more like a mouse, and nodded mutely. Mancino released his grip on his arm, and the head of press relations scuttled away. Scalisi was loitering outside, and kicked the door shut hard.

When they had both finally gone, Chief Mancino remained standing and turned to Scamarcio. 'You need to sever your ties with Piero Piocosta,' he said, his tone flat.

Scamarcio nodded; it was what he had been expecting. How he was going to pull it off was another matter, but, right now, it seemed like the only option if he wanted to keep his job. Did he, though? He wasn't sure about that anymore. He wasn't sure about anything.

'Chief Garramone has talked me through the contents of the files you found in the US. We have come up with a strategy. He'll explain it.'

Scamarcio nodded. 'OK,' was all he could manage.

'Chief Garramone speaks highly of you, and I trust his judgement. But I can't let one individual compromise the entire force.'

'Yes, sir, I understand. I'm sorry that those photos came out. I have no idea who took them or why.'

'If you're as good a detective as Chief Garramone believes, I'm sure you have *some* idea. There are people who want you gone, Scamarcio, and there's only so much we can do to help you. There are only so many warnings we can give. You need to start helping yourself; the impetus has to come from you. This will be the last time I discuss this with either of you. One more hint of trouble, and you're out. Is that clear?'

'Very, sir.' Scamarcio hung his head.

The chief of police nodded at Garramone and left.

Garramone sank back in his chair and exhaled slowly; after a few seconds of silent contemplation, he leant over to pull something from beneath his desk. When he placed it in front of him, Scamarcio saw that it was a bottle of good brandy. The boss bent down once more, and retrieved two dirty-looking tumblers from another drawer.

'Let's have a drink, Scamarcio,' he said. 'God knows, we both need it.'

Back in his flat, Scamarcio reflected on the events of the previous forty-eight hours. Mancino was right; he needed to sever his ties with Piocosta, but how? He owed him badly, and he wasn't sure what the old man might do should that debt not be settled. Maybe Scamarcio should clear the debt and then end their contact. But how the hell was he going to persuade the force to turn a blind eye to a loan-sharking operation? Garramone was on his case after Pozzi. Scamarcio wouldn't be able to get away with pulling another stunt like that.

He poured himself another large measure of Glenfiddich, and took in the deepening darkness outside. In his mind's eye, he saw Blakemore's dead source, spinning above the Potomac, and then his thoughts turned to Aurelia. He didn't know how bad it had been, so he couldn't know what strength it would take for her to put it behind her. However, the one thing he did know was that their encounter with Donato Cappadona had finally clarified matters. He knew that he didn't want to let Aurelia go. He wanted her to stay in Rome, and he wanted to keep seeing her. But something told him that he'd taken way too long to make up his mind this time. He picked up his mobile and dialled her number, but it just went straight to answerphone once again. He tossed the phone aside, sank back against the sofa, and closed his eyes. With all the stress of the encounter with Colonel Scalisi, Scamarcio now realised he had forgotten to tell Garramone about his idea that the Turin trial might have played a role in shaping Carter's murder.

He felt profoundly grateful to Chief Garramone and even Mancino in all of this. Mancino had surprised him. He had written him off as a yes man, a political player, but today he had seemed quite different from that early picture; he'd almost come across as a man of principle. Or was it just a question of the usual muscle-flexing? Did he simply want to prove that Scalisi and his goons couldn't push him around? No, that wasn't it, decided Scamarcio. Once they'd left the room, he could have fired him on the spot, but he'd chosen not to. And that probably took courage. He was fortunate to have such support from his superiors, and Scamarcio realised that maybe, after everything that had happened, he did want to be in the force; that this was where he needed to be. He couldn't be intimidated by the likes of Cappadona and Piocosta, otherwise what hope was there? For him or for anyone? He resolved not to let Garramone down, and to try to get things straight with Piocosta. It was pointless trying to have a foot in both worlds — worlds that could never be reconciled. If he clarified this, if he laid those old ghosts to rest, he wondered whether the other pieces might also start falling into place. He tried calling Aurelia once more, but again she failed to pick up.

He walked to the window and cast his thoughts out into the darkness. He could lay the old ghosts to rest, but the shame would still be there — the need to prove himself. And if he wanted quick results, would he be able to get them legitimately, without running to Piocosta every time? That was the question. He'd have to put himself to the test, to see if he could make it on his own. It was a frightening proposition.

He scanned left and right along the street, but there didn't seem to be anyone around. He pulled down the blinds, resolving to make regular checks from now on.

As he sank back into the sofa, he reached for the file of Italian letters he had collected from the lock-up in Virginia Beach. He wanted to take a proper look now. He'd only skimmed them before, and he felt it would be careless to dismiss them completely just because the focus seemed to have shifted to the US. He started going through them slowly, reading each one carefully, but it was still proving difficult to decipher a wider meaning, to build a clearer picture.

An hour later, he hadn't even reached the middle of the pile, and he pushed the letters aside in frustration. They weren't bringing him any closer to an answer. He was about to go into the kitchen for something to eat when his mobile rang. 'Number Unknown' appeared, and he knew that it couldn't be Aurelia.

'It gets weirder and weirder,' said Piocosta.

Scamarcio felt nervous just hearing his voice now. He fought a sudden impulse to hang up. 'What does?' he asked, after taking a moment to order his thoughts.

'Donato and that cardinal. Sounds to me like the left hand doesn't know what the right hand is doing in that outfit.'

'Which outfit?'

Piocosta tut-tutted and then sighed. 'The Cappadona, of course. What's wrong with you, Leo? It's like talking to a simpleton.'

'Oh, right.'

'Are you OK? You sound ill.'

'No, it's just jetlag — I need some sleep.'

'Well, get some. You're no good to anyone like this.' He paused for a beat. 'Anyway, so I put my feelers out, and, like I told you, it's tricky, because it's all stuff dealt with up high, plus they're really jumpy right now — I think something major has gone down. Word is that your goons made a cack-handed attempt at reeling in one of their small fry, and then tried to turn him into a grass. You heard about that?'

'I did hear something, yes.'

'Well, apparently the clan showed your chimps exactly where to stick it.' Piocosta laughed quietly, and Scamarcio felt nauseous for a moment.

'What's made its way to me is that Donato and his crew were a tad confused when Abbiati was murdered and it was splashed all over the news,' continued Piocosta. 'The photo that the news channels have looks nothing like the guy who Donato knew as Abbiati. The Cappadona think that the guy who died was someone else, and that the journalists have got it all arse-about-tit. I guess if the Vatican stays schtum, mistakes will happen. But why someone from the Church hasn't corrected them by now is anyone's guess.'

'Hmm,' was all Scamarcio could add. It wasn't the journalists who had got it wrong, he knew now — it was Donato. The man who had sent him to kill Carter was not Abbiati, but the elusive 'F'. He'd just been using the cardinal's identity as a cover, as a twisted means to an end.

'And, if you ask me, there's something weird about this whole thing,' continued Piocosta.

'It already sounds pretty weird.'

'The rumour I'm hearing is that the Cappadona cleaned up big time — 1.5 million, to be precise — but they never even had to get their paws dirty.'

'What do you mean?'

'When they got to the bridge, they discovered that the job had already been done for them, but they decided not to mention that to the cardinal, because they'd only had 10 per cent up front. So Donato kept quiet, and just pocketed the cash.'

'What do you mean, the job had already been done for them?'

'That Yank was already hanging when they showed — nodding like a sunflower in the wind. Weird, eh?'

48

Scamarcio had been about to call Pinnetta. He knew that his dealer's 'special blend' wasn't going to provide him with any greater clarity, but after Piocosta's news he felt the need to lose himself for a few hours, to clear his mind and allow the dust to settle where it might. But before he could make the call, his mobile rang once more. 'Detective Scamarcio?' asked a voice that sounded familiar, but which he couldn't quite place.

'Speaking.'

'It's Roberto Rigamonti from *La Repubblica*.'

Scamarcio thought of the Vatican scholar's recent revelations, and wondered if he'd contacted the reporter. 'Mr Rigamonti — what can I do for you?' he asked.

'I think it might be a case of the other way around. Could you meet me in Testaccio in an hour?'

Scamarcio glanced at his watch. 'Is it urgent?'

'It might be.'

Scamarcio took a breath. 'OK. I'll be there.'

'There's a wine bar on the hill — Caffè degli Specchi. I'll be waiting there.'

Scamarcio approached the shadowy hulk of the pot-shard hill from which Testaccio derived its name. The mound had been formed from Roman amphora fragments discarded from ships on the nearby Tiber. The old stockyards lay rotting nearby, and Scamarcio caught the salty taint of rust and dead seaweed on the breeze. As he drew nearer, beads of red, yellow, and green from the fairy lights danced out at him, and he thought he could detect the first slices of jazz above the traffic noise. In the twentieth century, the pot-shard hill had been claimed by Rome's car repairmen, who had dug out caves for their garages. These had since been transformed into trendy nightclubs and wine bars.

Scamarcio found the bar that Rigamonti had suggested, and immediately spotted the reporter at a table beside the jagged wall to the left. He appeared to be busy responding to emails on his BlackBerry. Scamarcio drew out a seat, and Rigamonti looked up, throwing him an anxious smile.

'I'm glad you came,' he said.

'Your call sounded important.'

'Well, it's a strange one — I'm not sure if it is or isn't. I need to run something past you to find out.'

A pretty young waitress appeared, and Rigamonte ordered a large glass of Amarone. Scamarcio opted for Nero d'Avola.

'Go on,' he said, keen to head back to a call from Aurelia, and Pinnetta's special blend.

After a few beats, the reporter said, 'I've been looking deeper into this Abbiati thing — the Opus Dei angle, and all that.'

Scamarcio scratched at an eyebrow. 'Yes, them again.'

"The people in the know are very jumpy.'

'I'd formed the same impression.' He thought of the Vatican scholar and his revelation that he was Rigamonti's source. He decided not to mention it for now — he'd wait to see if the reporter brought it up.

'Understandably, if you ask me,' continued Rigamonti.

Scamarcio just raised an eyebrow, not wanting to be drawn.

'There's a faction inside the Church who are extremely dangerous, actually far more dangerous than I'd first realised,' said the reporter in a hushed tone.

Scamarcio rubbed a hand across his mouth.

'It seems that they employ one of Rome's most brutal criminal gangs to do their dirty work.' Rigamonti delivered the line as if he expected it to stir a dramatic reaction.

'Are you talking about the Cappadona?'

'How do you know that?' Rigamonti looked disappointed.

Scamarcio smoothed a hand across his eyebrow and closed his eyes for a moment, trying to blot out the scene in the prefab. 'It came my way a while back — we have an underworld source who told us they did Church business.'

The reporter nodded, still disappointed. 'I met with them,' he said, after a few moments.

'Who, the Cappadona?'

Rigamonti nodded.

'How did you get in *there*?'

'Long story.'

'OK.' Scamarcio decided not to press him any further, remembering what had happened last time he'd tried to get him to reveal his source.

'Anyway, the reason I called you is that I heard rather a disturbing story when I was talking to one of them. They told me that they'd recently poisoned a police detective who had tried to turn one of their men. This detective had been looking for leads on the Abbiati slaying.'

Scamarcio exhaled slowly and then took a long drag on the Nero d'Avola. So it had been the Cappadona and not the Americans who had put the arsenic in his wine. *Figures*, he thought absently. His mind flashed once more on Pozzi and his unbloodied running shoe, but he tried to stay focussed on whatever else the reporter was about to tell him.

'I thought that detective might have been you — I just wanted to let you know.'

It appeared to be a question, but all Scamarcio said was, 'Thank you, I appreciate that.' He knew it wasn't just goodwill in play here.

Rigamonti fell silent for a few moments. '*Did* they kill Cardinal

Abbiati?' he asked. 'Obviously, they would only go so far with me. There were hints, but it wasn't made clear.'

Scamarcio took another long sip of his wine and leant back against the chair. He surveyed the trendy media types at the next table. They looked as if they all belonged to a mysterious sect which dictated that you had to wear black, that your jeans should cling to your bird legs like paint, and that your glasses should have huge TV-sized frames.

Scamarcio returned his gaze to the hungry reporter. 'Listen, Rigamonti, how it went down seems to be complicating itself by the hour. But I promise you, once I've got a grip on it — if I get a grip on it — I'll send it your way. I think you'll find the story is far more interesting than you imagine.'

'The drinks are on me,' said the reporter.

49

WHEN PINNETTA SHOWED UP later that night, it looked like he'd lost at least ten kilos since Scamarcio had last seen him.

'Are you ill?' he asked his trusty dealer, suspecting AIDS or some terrible drug-borne disease, although he had never formed the impression that Pinnetta dabbled in the hard stuff.

Pinnetta snorted, and pushed the package across to Scamarcio. 'No, you cretin. I've been going to the gym.'

'The gym?'

'I'm trying to clean up my act. I've met this really good girl, and I want to get things straight. I've been exercising three times a week, eating healthy, haven't been touching that stuff,' he said, pointing at the small package Scamarcio now held in his hand as if it were contaminated. 'I really want to make a go of it. I'd ditch the dealing if there were any sodding jobs out there, but it's a bloody desert. But as soon as I find something legit, it's *au revoir* to this crap.' He stopped for a moment. 'Actually, you know of anything going where you work?'

'You know I'm with the police, right, Pinnetta?' Scamarcio asked.

His trusty dealer waved a hand away. 'Yeah, I know I wouldn't be right for all that detecting stuff, but maybe there's something lower down the ladder you could think of. I'd really appreciate it.'

This was all Scamarcio needed. He still hadn't got Piocosta off his back, and now his drug dealer was asking him to find him a position in his department.

'I'll see what I can do,' was all he said.

Pinnetta grasped his hand, gratitude flooding across his face. 'That's really good of you. I've got to go straight; I've got to get my life in order. We've been talking about having kids. It's time to get serious.'

Scamarcio nodded and handed him a 50-euro note before escorting him back down the hallway. As he was heading towards the elevator, Pinnetta turned and waved, a spring in his step. *Shit,* thought Scamarcio, *if my dealer can get his life straight, why the hell can't I?*

He padded back into the living room and opened the packet, reaching for his roll-ups on the sidetable. When he was satisfied with his handiwork, he pulled out the blind and surveyed the back and forth of life on the street below: a smart young couple were walking along hand in hand, laughing, their heads thrown back, their smiles wide. He experienced the familiar spike of resentment; he'd formed the impression that people were only exuberantly happy like this in commercials. He felt ripped off, as if everyone else knew where the party was, but hadn't invited him. He had always felt as if he were on the sidelines, he reflected. When it came down to it, there were very few human beings whom he genuinely liked, whom he felt he could trust. From an early age, he'd decided that everyone had their agenda. But it was different with Aurelia, and maybe it was different with Garramone. He didn't want to lose her, and he didn't want to disappoint the boss; the man was investing too much in him.

He let out a long tendril of smoke, and studied the Fattori on the wall opposite and the Malesci positioned beneath it. His father had seen to it that he'd inherited a vast wealth in paintings; it had been the easiest way to make sure he saw the money. The Fattoris held the real value, because Malesci had just been his apprentice, but Scamarcio had always preferred the work of this little-known Tuscan artist. He loved the sun-soaked corns, the piercing skies, the robust warmth, and ripe vitality of these uncomplicated summer scenes. They had hinted at a simple, happy life that, as a boy, he had wanted for himself. He'd wished he could inhabit them, that he could press down into the lush grass, safe and out of sight.

He got up to check the street once more, but couldn't see anything unusual. He took a long drag on the joint and thought about the Cappadona. He didn't need any new enemies right now; it was getting to be a long list. He reflected on the strange news from Piocosta. That Carter was already strung up when the Cappadona arrived seemed to point to two simple alternatives: either Carter had hung himself, or his employers had killed him. But the initial questions remained: why the Calvi symbolism, and why the heavy-handed approach if the Americans were behind his murder? A quiet death would have been so much easier for them to handle.

He tried Aurelia once more and, yet again, she failed to pick up. He decided that he'd head over to her place once he'd finished the joint.

The pile of Italian letters was still where he had left them. He turned them over listlessly, not really feeling like studying them properly, and then he surveyed his own mail stacked messily by the door. He'd take a look at that first; there could be bills that needed paying.

He picked up the letters, and behind two bills from Enel and Enercom he noticed an airmail envelope with a US postmark.

He tore it open, and when he saw the name 'Samuel' signed at the bottom of the first page, he caught his breath. When had he sent this? And how did he have his address? The first page seemed to have been written in biro; the second, in fountain pen. They were two completely different handwriting styles, and the fountain-pen page looked like the handwriting he'd seen in the Italian file.

On the page in biro, Samuel had scrawled:

I hope this comes in useful.

Good Luck!

Scamarcio pulled out the page behind. Scanning through the first paragraphs, he came across a reference to Greece. He turned the sheet over, and saw that it had been signed by 'F'; as usual, there was no date:

Given events in Greece, some are saying that we may need to revisit the strategies of the past. Perhaps we should all meet for coffee and brioche and refresh our memories. My friends would very much welcome your expertise. Besides, it is a beautiful autumn in Rome and I would recommend a trip.

Why hadn't this letter been in the file? How come Samuel had it?

Scamarcio thought of Guerra's words once more, and wondered if it was more than money that had brought Carter to Rome. Had this been sent recently? Had it been this letter that had enticed Carter to Italy?

He got up from the sofa, stepping over to the window to raise the blind. He thought of Samuel and Donato Cappadona, and the old anxiety took hold of him. Pinnetta's blend was not the right drug for this case. Scamarcio pulled out the blind and looked down at the street; but this time, as if validating his fears, he saw Pitted Skin and his good-looking colleague crossing the road towards his apartment. They were checking the street now to make sure they weren't being watched, and Scamarcio felt the hairs on the back of his neck bristle. Was this an independent visit, or were they in consort with the Cappadona? After Donato had failed to convince him to back off, were they the cavalry?

He thought for a moment. He didn't want to call Garramone. And he couldn't call Piocosta; he couldn't afford another huge debt with him just at the time he was hoping to walk away. So who did that leave? Nobody … He thought, *What the hell, I'll have to call Garramone*, when an idea came to him: Giangrande. He'd told the chief pathologist he had another plan in mind, but would not, for now, expose his deception to the bosses. Whichever way you looked at it, the doctor still owed him. He dialled his number, his hands trembling slightly.

'Leo, how can I help you?' His tone was cordial — no doubt he was still wondering if Scamarcio was planning to reveal his secret.

'Can you get down to my flat, 26 Via Flavia, Flat 4b, ASAP? Your two Americans friends are heading up here, and I think it's going to turn nasty. I can't call Garramone — you're the only one who can help. Please, Giangrande. And bring a gun.' He ended the call before Giangrande could protest.

He ran to his bedroom for the FS Inox his father had given him on his 16th birthday, retrieved the bullets from his side table, and loaded the chamber before stowing the Beretta in the back of his jeans and returning to his spot by the window.

He reflected on what he'd just done. It was madness. He and Giangrande could never cut it against two possible CIA agents, and God knows what back-up they had behind them.

Fuck it, he said to himself. *Fuck it, fuck it.*

He reached for his mobile once more and dialled Piocosta, his hands shaking heavily now. He tried not to let the words run into one another: 'It's Leo. I need your help. Two CIA agents are heading up to my flat, and I'm in too deep this time.'

'We'll be there in ten. Stay calm.'

There was a hammering on the front door, and he knew that the Americans had already arrived; they'd been faster than he expected. He took a breath and tried to steady his climbing pulse. The walk down the hallway felt like a marathon, his right leg was shaking, and the back of his shirt was sticky with sweat. When he finally reached the door, his fingers kept slipping on the latch, and it took several attempts before he could open it.

Pitted Skin and his colleague were smiling at him.

'You don't look well, Detective', said Pitted Skin as he pushed past him. His colleague followed behind, acknowledging Scamarcio with the briefest of nods.

'It was something I ate in the States,' replied Scamarcio, trying to keep his voice level. 'Our Italian stomachs tend to rebel when presented with all that grease.'

Pitted Skin took a seat on the sofa and removed his sunglasses, placing them in his pocket. The gesture disturbed Scamarcio, and he couldn't help thinking that he wouldn't have removed his glasses unless he was about to kill him. He could see now that the man seated before him had deep-blue eyes and dense, long lashes; they made for a strange effect against his battered complexion.

'So, Detective,' he said, holding a finger up to the light and examining a nail. 'You were in the US. And you were busy, too.' His colleague had taken a seat next to him and had also pushed his sunglasses up onto his head.

Scamarcio pulled out a seat from the dining table, swung it around, and sat astride it; he didn't want his gun rubbing up against the chair back.

'I'm sure you already know where I went and who I saw. I'm not going to talk you through it.'

Pitted Skin yawned. 'Yeah, you're quite right, Detective, we already know. You can save your breath.' He sounded resigned, if not a little defeated.

'What do you want, then?'

Pitted Skin yawned again. 'Not much anymore. We did our bit, we tried to warn you, and we thought you'd listen — but you didn't. And now we've all got a problem.' As with their previous meeting, he sounded as if he wasn't particularly pleased that this problem had come his way, as if it were an extra chore he could have done without. 'But before we go on, could you settle a bet for us? What's your theory?'

'My theory?'

'Your theory about this case — what do you think really went down?'

'You've made a bet on it?'

'Yeah. Knowles here' — he gestured to his colleague sitting beside him — 'has formed the impression that you're actually a quick study and that you're highly capable of cracking this thing wide open.' He placed a hand on his chest. 'For my part, I have to say that I'm a little less convinced.' He rolled his tongue around the inside of his cheek, and pointed a finger. 'I reckon you've been a bit slow on some things. I've noticed that you sometimes miss a few clues. So will you settle this bet — tell us how you think it really went down?'

Scamarcio needed to buy time until Piocosta showed. Sure, he'd pretend to settle their bet if it bought him another ten minutes.

'I'll settle it, but first I need to know who you are. CIA? NSA? FBI? You have to be working for one of them.'

Pitted Skin waved a hand away. 'No, Detective, you're not following. *We* ask the questions.'

Scamarcio sighed. It was pointless. 'How much have you got riding on this bet?'

Pitted Skin arched his eyebrows and shook his head ruefully. 'A cool ten thou, would you believe?'

'That seems like a lot.'

Pitted Skin sighed. 'You know how it is when you're away on a job. Us agents get so fucking bored out in the field, we have to invent ways to pass the time — that, or we go crazy.'

Scamarcio had the feeling that they were already well on their way. Maybe a few too many fake suicides had damaged their minds.

'Come on then, Detective — don't keep us on tenterhooks. Knowles wants to take his wife to Maui. As soon as he's won, he can pick up the phone and give her the good news. It'll keep the divorce papers at bay for another year.'

Scamarcio took a long breath, and tried to order the cards in his mind. What should he tell them: the truth, a lie, or a mixture of the two?

'My theory,' he said, stopping, losing his thread already. His head was starting to ache. 'My theory,' he continued, stumbling again. He had to get a grip; he had to make this situation work for him. Why not run a partial theory past them, test it for its validity? He fell silent for a few moments, trying to reach a decision.

Eventually, he said, 'My theory is that your agency, whoever they are, set up both Abbiati and Carter. You made Abbiati think that Carter was out to get him, and you made Carter think that Abbiati had not paid up for the favour.' He decided not to mention that he knew that 'F' had borrowed Abbiati's identity — that the finance manager at the Vatican Bank had nothing to do with any of this. 'In this way, you made sure that Abbiati had Carter killed.'

'Why did we want Carter dead?' asked Knowles, rather like a parent grilling his child before a spelling bee.

They *were* crazy. 'Because Carter had worked on Dark Star, and was about to go public with what he knew.'

Knowles gave a loud 'Ha!', triumphant now. He swung around to his colleague and held up a palm for him to reluctantly high-five with.

Scamarcio felt like he was in a scene from a twisted film. How would they kill him? Would there be torture? He swallowed hard, remembering the lathe in Donato Cappadona's lock-up, trying to steady his climbing pulse.

'But you're missing an element,' said Pitted Skin, his eyes narrowing.

Scamarcio thought quickly. 'The Carter killing was a mess. You hadn't expected all the Calvi symbolism; you hadn't expected Abbiati to bring in the Cappadona.'

Pitted Skin was nodding slowly now. 'Yeah, it was way more than a mess. There was a shitload of damage limitation to be done.'

'Is this what's happening now? Damage limitation?'

'Don't get ahead of yourself. I'm still not convinced my colleague has won this wager.'

Knowles rolled his eyes in faux frustration. *What a charming double act*, thought Scamarcio. How often did they put on this little show? How many people died after watching it?

'Go on, Detective. You were telling us that it was a mess.'

'Yes, you had a problem. But couldn't you have foreseen that Abbiati would have needed someone else to kill Carter for him? He was a frail, elderly cardinal — he would have had to call in help.'

He thought he saw something strange pass between them.

'That's for sure, Detective, but we were expecting something subtle — a quick hit in a dark alleyway, not the song-and-dance Abbiati gave us,' explained Knowles, all matter-of-fact again.

'Why do you think he did that?' asked Scamarcio.

Pitted Skin waved a finger at him. 'No. You tell *us* why you think he did it.'

Scamarcio sighed and looked up to the ceiling for a moment. 'I believe it was because of the Turin trial about to be heard in the High Court here. I think Abbiati, yourselves, P2, and the Gladio faction all had prior knowledge of Turin and the other terror attacks. In the light of recent scandals to hit the Church, Abbiati and others were extremely concerned that if it were to come out that they had *any* inkling of planned bombing campaigns, the Vatican and its global reputation would be shaken to its core. So Abbiati saw a way to kill two birds with one stone. He wanted Carter off his back — he was scared he was out to get him because you'd fed him that fear, you'd been nurturing that paranoia — but he also saw a chance to use Carter's death as a warning to others to keep quiet. The reference to Calvi with the masonry rubble was a reminder of what could happen to you if you went against the Vatican and its powerful friends. I don't know this, I have no evidence, but the Vatican Bank's involvement in channelling funds to anti-communist movements like Solidarity and the Contras makes me wonder if they ever helped fund anti-communist movements at home. And if, in so doing, they helped fund terrorism — terrorism that killed thousands. If that came out, it would make the sex-abuse scandal look like a petty crime.'

Pitted Skin was nodding, impressed now. He made a soft clicking noise, as if he were contemplating something for the first time. 'Yeah,' he said, looking troubled for a moment. 'You're good — I'll grant you that.' He turned and gave Knowles a nod, but the jovial mood from before seemed to have shifted. There was a darker atmosphere in the room now. *Where the hell is Piocosta?* wondered Scamarcio.

'What was the favour Carter had done for Abbiati?' asked Knowles, seemingly slightly less bothered about whether Scamarcio got it right this time.

'It was for killing that terrorist, Paglieri, before he could take the stand.'

'Ten out of ten,' said Pitted Skin, but Scamarcio suddenly had the strange sensation that this was actually news to him, that maybe he didn't already know this. He at once found himself wondering if some of the rest of it might have been news to him, too. Had he been bringing *them* up to speed? He wondered whether they were in fact using him to help them, whether their superiors had kept certain information from them.

'So who killed Abbiati?' asked Knowles.

'You set up Father Brambani to make him think that Abbiati was involved in Turin. How you did it, I don't know. You sent him to dispose of Abbiati, and then you killed him and made it look like suicide.'

'Why would we want Abbiati dead?' pressed Knowles.

'He was becoming an inconvenience — for you and your friends inside the Vatican.'

Scamarcio had to buy more time, so he made a quick decision: he'd have to play his penultimate card.

'Abbiati knew where the bodies were buried — he could show the forensic accountants where the money had gone and exactly whom it had been helping during the years of lead. That was a big worry for some people, both inside and outside the Church. But, more to the point, Abbiati knew there was a spy inside the Vatican: the mysterious 'Mr F' who had been the conduit between Carter and the unsavoury elements you guys did business with here in Italy. He could have told the world about the dark plans you hatched together. So your Mr F borrowed his identity, used it to kill Carter, and then used it to remove Abbiati himself — ingenious, really. I'm guessing that your Mr F is still very much alive and well, that he's still pulling the strings somewhere from his ivory tower over there' — he gestured behind him in the direction of Vatican City — 'that he's still on the payroll, playing the middle man in yet another disgusting scheme that you, and the big corporations that fund you, have cooked up to defraud us. What will it be this time? Another bombing campaign so we elect a nice, safe government that'll then sell off all our assets abroad? Or aren't you even going to bother with elections? Are you just going to ship in your stooge, as and when required? Or rig the ballot? After all, we're no longer a democracy here.' Scamarcio was ranting, desperately playing for time now.

Pitted Skin snorted. 'Detective, you still think we live in a democracy over *there*? If you know about Dark Star, you will understand that things have moved on a bit.'

'Dark Star seems far-fetched,' said Scamarcio.

'It has divided opinion.'

'Is it possible?'

He shrugged. 'Everything's possible.' He moved to get up, and said, 'Anyway, it's been real nice chatting, but we need to wind this up. Knowles gets his ten thou — I concede defeat on that.'

He nodded to his colleague, and they both stood up from the sofa in one smooth, fluid movement. Again, Scamarcio was reminded of Agent Smith in *The Matrix*.

Knowles leant over and picked up a black backpack from the floor by his feet. Scamarcio didn't remember having seen him bring it in. The American placed it on the sofa and unzipped it, and Scamarcio spotted a cord of thick white rope inside. Knowles took out the cord and wound it around his left arm several times before going over to the dining table and pulling out a chair. Scamarcio noticed that there was something automatic about his actions, as if this was a task he'd performed often. Knowles pushed the chair into the centre of the living room, positioning it directly beneath the light hanging from the ceiling above. He then climbed onto the chair and removed the shade from the lamp before pulling the fitting several times to test its strength. He attached the rope to the light fitting, creating a perfectly shaped noose. Scamarcio had been so busy watching him that he hadn't realised that Pitted Skin now had a gun pointed at his chest.

'You need to climb up here, Detective. I need to test the length,' Knowles said, as if he were a handyman carrying out repairs.

'Why the fuck would I want to do that?' replied Scamarcio.

'Come on, Detective,' said Pitted Skin flatly. 'You knew it was always going to end like this. We did our best to warn you.' He took something from his pocket and passed it to Scamarcio. He saw that it was a blister pack of Valium.

'I need you to take all of those,' said Pitted Skin, like a conscientious doctor.

'No,' said Scamarcio.

Pitted Skin just eyed him coldly. 'It will be so much easier if you just play along,' he said tiredly.

'I'm not going to allow you to make my death look like a suicide.'

'So we'll just shoot you.'

Scamarcio eyed the gun that Pitted Skin was holding. It looked like a Beretta, similar to his, and what little effort would it take for them to lift his own gun from the back of his jeans? Who would know that Scamarcio hadn't pulled the trigger?

'You've been depressed, you've just been exposed as corrupt, your job has gone up in smoke, your woman has left you ...' Pitted Skin droned on, as if he were reciting a shopping list.

This was it. In one swift movement, Scamarcio swung around and kicked the chair out from under Knowles, leaving him hanging onto the piece of rope. Then he sprinted towards the front door, skidding on the parquet, with Pitted Skin just inches behind. Scamarcio launched himself at the latch, tearing the door open, and as he did so he saw Giangrande running down the corridor, a gun in his right hand.

'Shoot him in the leg,' he shouted at the chief pathologist. 'Quick.'

Giangrande fired, but the bullet was wide, and ricocheted off the walls. Pitted Skin was ready for him and let off two shots, just missing him. Giangrande tried and failed again, and this time the American was able to find a decent angle, and caught him in the upper arm. Giangrande stumbled to the floor, grasping his bicep and moaning in agony. Scamarcio saw their last chance of escape spiralling away from them. He moved to duck a new bullet, and landed hard against the wall. But from his new position on the ground, he was offered an early glimpse of Piocosta and four of his huge assistants pounding down the hallway. towards them. They were all wielding Franchi SPASs, and seemed to assess the situation in an instant. Piocosta let off a long round, several shots hitting Pitted Skin in the right leg. He fell to the floor, swearing, and clasping his thigh.

Scamarcio realised that Knowles now had him in his sights, but Piocosta's mutts were ready, and immediately took aim. 'Don't kill him,' yelled Scamarcio. 'Don't kill him.'

Knowles fell to the carpet, clutching his left leg, his teeth gritted in agony. He fired off two bullets on his way down, but both of them lodged in the wall.

Scamarcio ran over to the prone Americans, and wrestled the guns from their hands. 'Let's get them inside,' he said. 'Quick, before they leave blood everywhere. And round up the bullets and shells.'

One of Piocosta's heavies was manhandling Giangrande, and when he started swearing, Piocosta asked, 'Who is that guy?'

Scamarcio just waved a hand and said, 'I'll explain later. Come on — let's get them into the flat.'

They took a man between them, dragging them by their arms along the hallway and into the living room. Pitted Skin was heavy, so Scamarcio had to slow down, seemingly to the frustration of one of Piocosta's men who had the agent's other arm. Scamarcio looked behind him, and saw a long trail of blood snaking its way along his parquet floor. He wondered if it would ever come out.

'Shit,' panted Giangrande, as he stumbled along next to Piocosta. 'What have you got me into, Scamarcio?'

'You wanted to keep your job, didn't you?'

Giangrande said nothing, and just clutched at his arm.

'Let's just put them by the sofa for the time being,' said Scamarcio.

They dragged the men into the living room and left them on the floor. Piocosta took a few paces, seemingly thinking about his next move. Giangrande sank into the sofa and closed his eyes.

'How do you want to play this?' asked Piocosta eventually. 'You sure you want them alive?'

Scamarcio sighed. 'They could be CIA. We can't kill them — the game's a bit different here.'

Piocosta raised an eyebrow. 'If you say so.'

Scamarcio rubbed his hands across his face and thought. After a few seconds, he turned to the stricken agents. 'It's finished now, you understand? I want you to leave me alone and fuck off back to the States. You can't win — it's too late. The information is already out there. I've passed on what I know to my chief, and he's already passed it up the hierarchy. There's nothing you can do to make this situation right.'

Piocosta's lieutenants had their guns trained on the agents' chests. Knowles was still rolling around on the floor, but Pitted Skin was looking up at Scamarcio, hatred in his eyes.

Scamarcio just stared him out, trying to find his nerve. 'It must be clear by now that I have powerful friends. You kill me, and they will kill you. And they couldn't give a fuck who you work for.'

Pitted Skin just grunted, his teeth still gritted in pain.

Scamarcio noticed that Giangrande seemed to be trying to fish something from his pocket, and he wondered for a crazy second if the man was about to produce his gun. But the chief pathologist just pulled out a mobile and said, 'Perhaps you should listen to this?' He saw that he was holding up an iPhone. He went over to the sofa and took it from him.

'Press *Play*,' said Giangrande, between breaths.

Scamarcio did so, and an American voice came on. '*We need your report to disappear,*' someone was saying. It sounded like Knowles. '*We know you have money troubles, so we'll make it worth your while.*'

'*Why?*' It was Giangrande speaking now.

'*We've got a little bit of a problem we need to tidy up. You make that report vanish, and there'll be a quarter of a million euro in your account by tomorrow.*'

Giangrande appeared to have gone silent.

'*Give it some thought. Personally, I think it's a good deal — especially with the Italian economy the way it is right now.*'

Scamarcio pressed *Stop*, and handed the phone back to Giangrande.

'I recorded the whole thing,' said the chief pathologist. 'Perhaps it could be of use.'

'Did they pay up?' asked Scamarcio.

'No,' replied Giangrande.

Scamarcio looked down at the two prone agents. 'I'm going to give that recording to a reporter I know. It looks like, instead of quarantining your mess, you've just made it a whole lot worse.' He noticed Giangrande blanch, and reminded himself to tell him that he would do no such thing.

'What I don't get,' continued Scamarcio, 'is why you didn't just leave it be? If you hadn't started sniffing around, we might just have bought this whole thing as the suicide it really was.'

'The suicide it really was?' spat Knowles. 'That's horseshit.'

'When Abbiati's thugs showed up, Carter was already dead. He was already hanging.'

He saw the two agents exchange confused glances.

'I have it on good authority that the Cappadona were paid handsomely for a job they never had to do.'

Pitted Skin just looked up at the ceiling, sighed, and closed his eyes.

'What's going to happen now,' said Scamarcio, 'is that you two are going to do a bit more damage limitation   but this time on your own careers. There's going to be some serious diplomatic fallout when this shit hits the fan. If I were you, I'd get your sorry arses back to Washington so you can start explaining yourselves. My friends and I will dump you at the nearest hospital, and then I never want to see either of you again. If you or one of your colleagues fuck with me again, you'll be dead.'

Scamarcio motioned to the two lieutenants guarding Pitted Skin, and they grabbed him and hoisted him up. 'You're going to lean on these guys as we go downstairs as if you're old friends who have had a bit too much to drink,' said Scamarcio to the two Americans.

He turned to one of the other heavies guarding Knowles. 'My bedroom is through there,' he said, pointing out back. 'Go to the closet — you'll find two long winter coats. At the bottom of the wardrobe is a first-aid box with bandages. We can do a quick patch-up before we leave so they don't bleed on the way down.'

The man nodded and hurried off. When he was back with the bandages, he got to work on each agent, his associates holding a gun to their heads so they wouldn't try anything stupid. They draped one of the coats around Pitted Skin, and the other around Knowles. Fortunately, Piocosta's men were almost as tall as Scamarcio, so manoeuvring the two Americans was difficult but not impossible.

Once they had made it out into the corridor, Scamarcio called the lift, and was relieved to see that it was empty. As they stepped out into the marble lobby, the old lady from downstairs came in with her Chihuahua. She eyed them all suspiciously — Scamarcio had always had the impression that she didn't trust him.

By the time they made it out onto the street, a police squad car was pulling into the road, its bars flashing — of course, someone would have heard the gunshots. Piocosta calmly pointed to the right and said, 'That's our van, parked up in front of the goods entrance.'

They headed over to the black Mercedes, pushing the two agents into the last row of passenger seats before Piocosta's men and Giangrande got into the first. Scamarcio and Piocosta jumped up front. Piocosta fired up the engine, his hand steady as a rock — unlike Scamarcio's, which was trembling now against his thigh. In the rear-view mirror, he watched one of the two uniforms descend from the Panther and scan the street before entering his building. The other one stayed in the car, undoubtedly on the radio to base the whole time. How long before the computer told them that it was his address?

'What's the nearest hospital?' asked Scamarcio.

'Policlinico,' said Piocosta

'Let's drop them there.'

The traffic wasn't bad for once, and it took them just a few minutes to reach the street entrance to Accident and Emergency.

'There'll be a surveillance camera on the doors to A and E,' said Piocosta. 'We should dump them here and let them walk the rest of the way. If they fall, someone will find them.'

'OK,' said Scamarcio, sensing that this wasn't the first time Piocosta had done this.

Scamarcio jumped from the passenger seat and ran around to the pavement. Piocosta's men checked that the road was clear of potential witnesses, then released the sliding door and started to haul Knowles out onto the concrete. Once they'd got him out, they propped him up against the wall and went back for Pitted Skin. Suddenly, as one of the men was lifting him from the car, the agent tried to head-butt him, but Piocosta's heavy was too quick for him, and punched him in the jaw. Scamarcio thought he heard something crack. They pushed Pitted Skin onto the pavement next to Knowles, not caring if he toppled over, and then they all piled back into the van, Piocosta shouting at them to get a move on.

When they were a few minutes away and nobody had said a word, Giangrande asked, 'Do you really think they'll stay away? Won't they send in others now?'

Scamarcio glanced out at the skein of shadowy streets flitting by. 'I get the feeling that it's all got a bit out of control for them — that they might see the wisdom in letting things be.'

'I always thought it was a fight to the death for those guys,' said Piocosta.

'I don't know, but if I were them, I'd be aiming for containment right now.'

The old man tut-tutted and said, 'I hope you're right, Leo.'

50

SCAMARCIO HAD SLEPT the sleep of the dead that night. As he was still supposed to be on leave, he didn't wake until 11.00 am, a good twelve hours after he had first laid his head on the pillow. He surveyed the dusty webs of sunlight filtering through the window, and thought about what he'd done the night before. He'd been told by the chief of police to drop all ties to Piocosta, but at no time in his life had he been more indebted to the old man. Why hadn't he just called Garramone and have done with it? Was it because he wanted to preserve his career? Now he had compromised himself, irrevocably.

His thoughts turned to the dossier, and he wondered about the 'strategy' that the chief of police had claimed they'd come up with. It seemed clear that it wouldn't involve the intelligence services; Mancino and Garramone had other ideas. Scamarcio manoeuvred himself out of bed slowly, his arms stiff and sore. Pinnetta's special blend was in a tin on the windowsill, and he shuffled towards it, stopping on the way back to search for a lighter among the debris coating the chest of drawers. When he'd found it, he quickly located some Rizlas in his dressing-gown pocket and sat back down on the bed to roll up, his eyes heavy. It took him several attempts; but once the joint was to his liking, he lit up and climbed back into bed, reaching for his mobile on the side table. He tried Aurelia once more, and yet again there was no answer. He threw down the phone in frustration, and it dropped off the table and onto the floor.

Scamarcio sank back against the pillows, and took several long drags. He wondered how Giangrande was feeling this morning. They'd dropped him at the Pertini hospital so he could be patched up, briefing him on a cover story about a mugging gone wrong. He wondered if the chief pathologist was relieved that Scamarcio wasn't going to sell him down the Swannee, or perhaps petrified that he was now a marked man whose only allies were the 'ndrangheta . It couldn't have been an easy call. If Piocosta hadn't offered to place two men outside his building and one on his corridor, Scamarcio doubted that he would have slept at all the night before. He would have probably lain there for hours, one ear listening out for intruders. No doubt that's what Giangrande had done.

Scamarcio was about to take another drag when there was a knock at the front door. He stared up at the ceiling and didn't move, thinking it through. It couldn't be Pitted Skin and Knowles back so soon — they wouldn't be able to walk yet, and they wouldn't have been able to get past Piocosta's guys. If the Americans had sent a team around, Scamarcio would have expected an unannounced entry followed by a quick kill, rather than such a genteel knock. He wondered if the knock was simply Piocosta's guy coming to check that he was OK, or the police from last night, curious as to why the wall outside his apartment was riddled with bullet holes.

He sighed and pulled himself out of bed, heading for the door. The joint was trailing ash on the floorboards, but, unable to spy an ashtray, he cupped a hand beneath it and deposited it on a saucer beneath a dying plant.

He padded down the hallway and reluctantly pulled back the latch, opening the door just a fraction so he could see who was standing there before deciding to go any further. He closed his eyes for a moment and then opened them again, just to check that his eyes weren't deceiving him. Carter's widow was in the corridor, a couple of expensive-looking suitcases at her feet.

He pulled the door wider and tried to think of something to say. But the words wouldn't come. She ran a hand through her hair, embarrassed. 'I'm so sorry to disturb you like this. I got your address from that reporter you know — the guy who's in contact with some of Simeon's ex-colleagues.'

'Sure,' said Scamarcio, entirely confused.

'I guess you're wondering why I'm here.'

Scamarcio realised that he was being rude, keeping her standing in the hallway. 'Why don't you come in?' he said. 'We can talk inside.'

'Thanks.' She smiled, and went to pick up her bags, but Scamarcio got there first and carried them into the flat.

He gestured her to the sofa in the living room, and said, 'Can I make you a coffee?'

'No. I'm fine, thanks.'

He felt like an idiot, standing there in his dressing gown. 'Do you mind if I get changed?' he asked.

'No problem.' She smiled again, and he felt a different kind of confusion.

He went into his bedroom, threw on some jeans and a T-shirt, and then headed straight back out.

There was another knock at the door, and he figured it might be Piocosta's guys coming to see who the visitor was. He was right: one of them was standing out in the hallway, his hand resting on his trouser pocket, gun ready.

'It's OK,' said Scamarcio. 'She's just a friend from the US.'

The huge mutt nodded and turned back down the corridor towards the elevator.

Scamarcio padded back into the flat and pulled a chair out from beneath the dining table, only to realise it was the same chair that Knowles had stood on to fix the noose from the night before. There were still shoeprints on the cushion. He took a seat quickly.

Mrs Carter appeared to be reaching in her jacket pocket for

something. She handed over a piece of paper, and Scamarcio saw that it was a print-out of an email addressed to 'The widow of Simeon Carter'.

'I received that the day after I saw you,' she explained. 'Please feel free to read it. I think you'll understand why I decided to come straight here.'

Scamarcio opened it. The email was dated the 26th of October.

Dear Mrs Carter,

We have never met but I have heard so much about you over the years that I feel as if I know you. I have thought long and hard about whether to contact you. Often I came to the conclusion that what you didn't know couldn't hurt you, but then I placed myself in your position and decided that, after everything, I would prefer to learn the truth.

I understand that you are grieving now, as am I. But maybe in this time of grief we could help one another. I think Simeon would have wanted that.

There is no delicate way to phrase this so I will just try to keep it simple. My name is Adele Clerici, I am fifty, and for the last thirty-one years of my life I have been your husband's mistress. We met when he was posted to Rome. We would see each other six or seven times a year and we have a son together, Danilo, who is now thirty-two. I know these will probably be the hardest words you have ever had to read, and for that I am sorry. But I hope you can appreciate how painful it was for me when I discovered that Simeon had married. You can understand perhaps that I always felt as if you were the mistress and I the rightful wife.

Over the years, I formed the impression that Simeon loved us both but was incapable of choosing. Obviously having a son together complicated things in his mind. Simeon was an incredible, loving, warm-spirited man and I consider myself extremely lucky to have known him, as I'm sure, do you.

I am writing to you now because I am worried. Simeon seemed very depressed lately and disappeared from my flat several days before he was due to leave. Recently I came across a newspaper item about an American found hanging under the Ponte Sant'Angelo and I just knew it was him — call it a sixth sense. As yet, I have not had the courage to go to the police. I was concerned I might run into you there or perhaps I just didn't want to learn the truth; perhaps I preferred to keep the hope alive for a little while longer.

Do you think you could find it in your heart to let me know what happened to him? I haven't slept for a long time and I am so concerned for my son. If you were prepared to come to Rome to meet me, I would be most glad to welcome you. It seems strange I know but I feel as if I need to see you in order to be able to start to draw a line under these years.

I am so sorry for the pain and extra suffering this letter will be causing you.
— Adele Clerici

Below the name was a Rome telephone number and address.

Scamarcio laid down the email and looked up. Mrs Carter was dry-eyed, her expression blank. He sensed that she'd already done all her crying. She returned his gaze, blowing the air out through her mouth.

'I'm sorry,' was all Scamarcio could think of to say.

'Don't be. It happens.'

'Are you going to see her?'

'I was wondering if you'd come with me.'

Scamarcio was taken aback. 'Sure, if that's what you want.'

'She seems to be suggesting that Simeon killed himself. I figured you'd want to know about that.'

'Of course,' said Scamarcio. He looked at the letter once more. 'Do you want me to call her, fix up the meeting?'

Mrs Carter closed her eyes and nodded, as if she were fighting her better judgement.

'Shall I do it now?'

She nodded again.

'The phone's in the next room. I'll just be a second.'

He padded through to the kitchen and picked up the landline. He punched in the number, strangely nervous now, as if all this concerned him personally. After a few rings, a woman answered. It was a soft voice, well spoken.

'I was hoping to speak to Adele Clerici,' he said.

'Speaking.'

'My name's Detective Scamarcio from the Rome Flying Squad. I have the wife of Simeon Carter here.'

He heard a sharp intake of breath. 'Oh God,' she whispered. 'It's true, isn't it? It was Simeon under that bridge?'

'We were hoping to come and meet you,' said Scamarcio. 'We can be there in half an hour. Would that be OK?'

The woman was sobbing now. When she got her breath back, she said, 'Yes, do come.'

51

ADELE CLERICI LIVED IN a handsome apartment block near the Spanish steps. Along her street were gold-mirrored coffee shops and oak-panelled bakeries. Scamarcio and Mrs Carter took the old elevator to the sixth floor, and, when they stepped out, Carter's former mistress was waiting for them in the hallway. She looked good for her age, and was immaculately dressed in a blue-striped shirt and charcoal-grey pencil skirt with matching pumps. Around her neck was a collar of pearls, and her dark, shoulder-length hair hung glossy and full. She had large brown eyes with strong eyebrows, and, as they drew nearer, Scamarcio could see that there were only a few wrinkles across her brow. If anything, she looked as if she might be Mrs Carter's slightly older, slightly more sensible, sister.

Scamarcio took a breath, wondering whether there would be fireworks, but the two women just walked towards each other slowly and then embraced. Mrs Carter surprised him by laying a motherly hand on Ms Clerici's shoulder and suggesting that they should perhaps all go inside.

Once they were seated in the large living room and Ms Clerici had composed herself, Scamarcio decided to get the worst part over with.

'I think you've worked out why we're here, Ms Clerici,' he said softly.

She nodded slowly, not quite able to meet his eye.

'I'm extremely sorry for your loss.'

She returned his gaze for a moment and nodded again.

'From your letter, it seems you speak excellent English. Do you mind if we switch out of Italian? I'd like Mrs Carter to be able to understand what is being discussed.'

She nodded once more.

'In your letter, you wrote that Simeon had been depressed. Was he perhaps disillusioned with his work? Mrs Carter had formed a similar impression.'

To his surprise, Carter's former mistress shook her head. 'If only,' she said. 'If only it was that simple.'

She got up from her chair and walked over to a mahogany cabinet by the window — there were several photographs in small silver frames on top, and she picked one up and brought it over to Scamarcio. A laughing, brown-eyed boy was staring back at him. He had curly, blond hair and a cheeky, dimpled smile. Scamarcio passed the photo over to Mrs Carter, and she immediately put a hand over her mouth. Maybe the resemblance was too close. Her eyes were welling with tears now, and he remembered that she and Carter had never been able to have children. This extraordinary-looking child must have come as the most painful of blows.

'That's Danilo when he was a baby,' explained Carter's mistress, as if any explanation were needed. 'He's why Simeon killed himself.'

'I don't understand,' said Scamarcio.

'My son is ill, Detective. He has cancer, and has just a few months left to live. Simeon couldn't take it. I saw it break him. All that guilt at never having spent enough time with his boy, all those years of lost opportunity. I watched his eyes when we got the news, and something went out in them at that moment. I had the feeling he'd do something stupid — and he did.'

She looked down at the floor, thinking something through for a moment. 'It's always the women who have to stay and fight; it's always the women who hang in there until the end. The men always bow out early, don't you find?' she asked, looking up at Mrs Carter.

52

It is cold up on the bridge, and he's afraid. He thinks of Calvi. Is this how he had felt when they strung him up to die?

Now, more than thirty years later, this is it, the end. Either it's the work of the Lord or the work of the faction. They now have the means to poison people slowly, to let them rot away over time, so is that what they've done to his son?

Whatever the truth of it, it doesn't really matter. Not where he's going. His only wish is that he might be around to see them sweat, to watch as the whole system spins out of control, to see the panic cross their faces. He thinks of Adele and how she'll cope. She's the strongest person he knows — she'll find a way.

Carter checks the noose one last time and then pats both his pockets before tossing the plastic gloves into the Tiber. He remembers the cubicle in Virginia Beach, and smiles.

He snaps off the lid of the vial, and swallows. Let the madness begin.

ON HIS WAY TO VISIT AURELIA, Scamarcio decided that, like her, Adele Clerici was tough. She'd just learnt that her lover had died, but she'd got up, put on her make-up, faced his wife — all with such grace and composure, all while her son lay dying.

He knocked on Aurelia's door, but there was no response. He tried again, but was met with silence. He was about to turn away when the uniformed officer who had been watching her place came down the hallway.

'She's gone to the shops,' he said.

'Is there anyone with her?'

'Her parents.'

Scamarcio smiled faintly, feeling both relief and disappointment. She was shutting him out; that much was clear. 'Tell her I dropped round,' he said. 'I'll try again later — name's Scamarcio.'

The officer nodded.

Scamarcio retraced his steps down the corridor and headed back into the rainy afternoon. What could he do to reach Aurelia? He was running out of ideas.

On his walk to the squad room he thought about Carter. He wondered if he was finally getting to know him; whether he now understood what had been going through his mind when he strung himself up to die. He was a broken man, long disillusioned by a life of sacrifice for a cause he no longer believed in, a man so deeply angry that he was ready to give up his secrets to the world. Then, on top of all that, came the final blow: the news that his son was dying.

He had to find some satisfaction in his own death, some fleeting sense that it hadn't all been a wasted effort. And how could he achieve that? By transforming his suicide into a murder, and making his death as inconvenient as possible for the figures he had come to despise. By putting masonry rubble in his pockets, by administering himself a poison, and by choosing a location close to the Vatican, he could make sure that the right officials started asking the wrong questions. It was his last up-yours to the people he hated, to the dark entities who had pulled his strings for decades. He must have been aware that the Turin trial was fast approaching, so he knew his timing was sound. And who wasn't to say that some new atrocity wasn't being planned in the event that Italy didn't play ball with Brussels? Perhaps his death was a warning about that as well.

Scamarcio felt that he owed this tragic figure something: all the material Carter had been collecting, all the effort he'd gone to, had to yield a result — it couldn't just be swept away.

Scamarcio pulled out his normal mobile and called Blakemore. The Cappadona had seized the pay-as-you-go, but had left his other phone, for some reason. He hoped it was an oversight. 'Leone,' he said. The reporter didn't sound that happy to hear from him.

'I just wondered if you were ready for that story.'

Blakemore sighed. 'Leo, some weird shit's been happening. Our Intel sources have been shutting down on us, and then, just a few days ago, management called us to a meeting and warned us to beware of high-octane stories emerging from the spy world. There's a prankster on the loose, apparently.'

'A prankster? That's bullshit.'

'Of course it's bullshit,' hissed Blakemore, his voice dropping to a whisper. 'But it's clear that there's no appetite for this thing, whatever it is. And whatever it is seems to be connected to you. And Samuel.' He paused for a beat. 'I can't stick my neck out, Leo. My girlfriend has just told me she's pregnant.'

'Shit,' said Scamarcio, then corrected himself. 'Congratulations, I mean.'

'I've never known all the usual channels to just shut down. It's crazy,' said Blakemore.

Scamarcio couldn't think of a reply. His mind was too busy turning on where this left him. He'd just had two American agents shot. He was right at the heart of this thing. There was no way they'd let him carry this secret around. But he wasn't the only one with the information now: Garramone had seen the dossier, and Mancino, too. They couldn't take them all out. The thought consoled him, and made him think that he should still try to do his best by Carter. He pulled his thoughts back to the conversation. 'Right, I get it. We should probably wind this up, then.'

Blakemore sounded relieved. 'You take care of yourself, Leo. I want to hear from you when all this is over.'

He hung up, and the empty line echoed back at Scamarcio. He moved over to the side of the street and pulled out his wallet, looking for the business card that Rigamonti had given him. He finally found it wedged behind a five-euro note — one of those new ones that looked like fake money. Wasn't it all fake anyway, he thought. The cash in circulation no longer bore any relationship to the assets the banks actually held.

The reporter picked up after a few rings. 'It's Detective Scamarcio. Is now a good time?'

'Sure. Just finishing something — now's good.'

'I've got that story for you, if you want it.'

'You bet,' said Rigamonti.

'Meet me tonight for a drink in Trastevere, and I'll talk you through it. Bar Solari, Via Giano, 9.00 pm.'

'Looking forward to it, Detective.'

Scamarcio realised that he'd arrived at Flying Squad headquarters without quite registering the rest of the walk. He noticed that there was still a reddish smudge on the concrete where Pozzi had landed after being thrown from the car. What a mess it was, the way the world turned, he thought. Once again, the feelings of guilt returned.

He took a breath and climbed the steps, nodding to the desk officers as he went in. Garramone was running down the stairs, so Scamarcio asked, 'Have you got five minutes?'

'I missed lunch and was just heading out. Want to join me?'

'Sure.'

When they were seated at a table in the semi-decent café opposite, Scamarcio said, 'It's clear to me now.'

'What is — the meaning of life? A life as far away from your father's old cronies as possible, I hope.'

Scamarcio felt the anxiety creeping out along his nerve endings. If the chief caught even a hint of what had gone down the night before, Scamarcio's career would be over. But he hadn't mentioned it, so perhaps he was safe, for now. He tried to steady himself, and said, 'That, yes. But I was talking about the American.'

He carefully set out his theory, finishing with his belief that Carter had taken his own life, making sure his death would cause as many problems as possible for the people he had come to loathe.

When he was done, the chief said, 'That poor soul.'

'He probably killed people.'

'I've killed people.'

'In the line of duty — it's not quite the same thing.'

'He thought he was serving his country, too,' shrugged Garramone.

'The people he killed were innocent civilians.'

'According to the dossier, many of them were politicians, already corrupt.'

'No, it was the incorruptibles that ended up with a bullet in their chest, but that wasn't Carter's doing. I think he was just the bagman, the guy who tried to buy them. He'd had enough of the killing by then.'

Garramone nodded slowly, saying nothing. Eventually, he asked, 'I've been thinking about the Calvi symbolism. Do you think Carter might have been involved in his death?'

Scamarcio shrugged. 'The consensus is that Gelli and the mafia were behind that. But it's interesting that Calvi died in June 1982, shortly after the Americans started working with the Vatican to fund Solidarity. Gelli did later go on to claim that Calvi's death had been commissioned in Poland, and that it was ordered by the people connected with his work in financing Solidarity on behalf of the Church.'

Garramone nodded. 'So all that could lead us straight back to Carter?'

'Yeah. But the death of Calvi is not mentioned in any of the papers I found.'

'That means nothing.'

Scamarcio shrugged. 'Anyway, what's the plan now — where's the dossier?'

Garramone stretched his legs beneath the table and took a sip of the mineral water the waitress had set down. 'Obviously, relations with AISE are rather strained.'

'I got the impression that Chief Mancino and Scalisi don't exactly see eye to eye.'

'You could put it like that,' said Garramone.

'Does Scalisi know about the dossier?'

'No.'

'So?'

'So, we're going to try and keep it that way.'

'What? You're just going to sit on it?'

'No. We're sending it to the Foreign Office, to Emma Badaglio.'

Badaglio was the foreign secretary, and one of the few figures in Italian politics to command international respect. She had negotiated some extremely delicate diplomatic deals, freeing Italian hostages from trouble spots around the world, and was always one of the first to insist on a hard line against some of the world's most brutal regimes.

'She's one of the few people we can trust to do the right thing with this,' said Garramone. 'And of course we'll alert her to our suspicions that a new strategy of tension might be being planned for this country.'

'And Chief Mancino is in agreement?'

'Actually, it was his idea.'

'What do you think she'll do with the information?' asked Scamarcio.

'My sense is that she will try to use it to our advantage. Italy badly needs some bargaining chips right now, and it might prove a powerful asset.'

'Do you believe what that file seems to be suggesting?'

Garramone sighed, and shrugged his shoulders. 'How can any of us know? It's intriguing, that's for sure. I looked up some of the names in there — one of them was Bin Laden's number-two, for Christ's sake. And if you read some of the stuff on the internet, the possibility that there was secret-service involvement is most definitely out there. But how can any of us be sure? We still don't really understand who killed Kennedy after all these years. And if you think about our own country — the fact that evidence is now starting to emerge that the intelligence services were involved in the years of lead, that the police and the Carabinieri might have had a role — all that doesn't seem to have made a huge difference to the way people lead their lives. It's as if everyone just wants to forget and move on.'

Scamarcio nodded. After they'd taken a few moments to eat, Garramone said, 'How do you feel about your situation?'

'In what way?'

'Well, I presume the Americans know you had the dossier, and if this mysterious figure 'F' is still around, there's the possibility that could cause problems for you. I don't know how far we could step in to protect you long term. If you're going to be out on the streets working, you'll be exposed. Hell, you'll be exposed at home in your flat now. You've caught their attention.'

'But you've seen the files, too. Aren't we all at risk?'

'The Americans won't see it like that. They're not going to go around taking out the chief of police and the head of the flying squad. You're more vulnerable — they'll see you as a softer target.'

'But what would getting rid of me achieve at this stage?'

'It would be a warning shot across our bow.'

Scamarcio thought back to last night, and swallowed. 'But once Badaglio gets moving on that dossier, won't they back off?'

Garramone laid down his sandwich for a moment. 'I don't know. I would hope so, but I can't read their minds. However, in the event of trouble from either quarter, what I don't want to see happen is for you to turn to your father's old network for help. I know you might feel at risk, but Chief Mancino was right when he said there must be no more communication between you and Piero Piocosta. That has to end. Because, if there is a next time, if someone takes more photos that make their way to that bitch Morello, or someone records the wrong conversation, we'd have no choice but to let you go.'

Scamarcio wondered if someone had told him about what had happened the night before, after all. He felt nauseous; the stress had properly got a hold of him now. He took a long breath and said, 'Yes, sir. I understand.'

'I hope so. I don't want to see you fail, Leo.'

Scamarcio looked away for a second. He couldn't meet the boss's stare. After a few moments, he said, 'I've got somewhere I need to be.'

Garramone eyed him with concern. 'You haven't finished your sandwich.'

'You can have it.' Scamarcio tried to place a ten-euro note on the table, but the chief pushed it away.

53

HE KNOCKED ON AURELIA'S DOOR once more, but, yet again, he was met with silence. He waited a few more minutes, but no response came.

Back at his flat, Scamarcio took a long drag on a joint, and ran through the conversation he would soon have with Piocosta. Whichever way he cut it, it still didn't sound good. He'd asked too much of the old man lately to simply call it a draw and walk away.

His thoughts were interrupted by the doorbell. When he pulled back the latch, Simeon Carter's widow was standing in the corridor, looking drained. He had forgotten that her suitcases were still in his living room.

'How did it go with Ms Clerici?' he asked as he led her back into the apartment.

'It was OK,' she sighed. 'She's an extraordinary woman. I can see what he saw in her. What I can't understand, however, is why he didn't just marry her. What was he doing with me?'

Scamarcio returned to his place on the sofa and gestured her to a chair. 'Men find it difficult to make a decision sometimes. You came along, and he was probably bowled over. But he couldn't face losing *her*. So he just kept on with these two separate lives, and the months became years. In my experience, women are more black and white than men. When they need to cut something off and move on, they do. They prefer clarity.' His chest felt hollow. He thought of Aurelia, and wanted to head straight back to her flat, to see if she had returned.

Mrs Carter took a seat and looked down at the parquetry, her expression solemn. After a few moments, she asked, 'Did you ever get anything from those numbers that Simeon left?'

The question didn't make sense to him. 'Weren't you in contact with Samuel?'

'Samuel?'

Again, the question confused him. 'He's somebody who used to work for the same people as your husband. He's the guy who talked to my reporter friend. Actually, he claimed he knew you — he told me that you'd tipped him to the fact that you'd given me the string.'

'Ah,' she said, after a few moments. 'So *that's* Samuel.'

'So you didn't know him well, then?'

'He was just someone my husband said would be in touch should anything ever happen to him.'

He frowned. He didn't believe her.

She seemed to read this and said, 'Simeon left me that guy's contact details, and told me I should call him if I ever had problems. After Simeon died, that guy rang a few times, just to check how I was, that I wasn't being harassed — that kind of thing. I told him that you'd visited me, that I'd given you the numbers.'

'Samuel gave me the impression that he didn't know your husband. That he'd had to ask around to get information about his work ...'

She shrugged, and shook her head. 'I can't help you. All I know is that Simeon left me his details. From that, I'd presume that they must have known one another.'

'Indeed,' said Scamarcio, as a thought occurred to him.

'Anyway, what about those numbers?' she persisted. 'Did they give you anything?'

Scamarcio decided that, at this stage, he had little left to lose by telling her. 'It was a simple numeric code. Each number corresponded to a letter in the alphabet. When I converted the numbers, I got the address of a self-storage place in Virginia

Beach. I found some files in your husband's locker.'

'What was in them?' she asked, locking eyes with him.

He talked her through the contents, finishing with a description of the Arab file.

'So that dossier seemed to be suggesting that certain elements in the Agency were sponsoring a terror campaign against Americans? That they had been protecting key figures in Al-Qaeda for years?'

He nodded.

She suddenly threw back her head and laughed. Her whole body heaved, and she seemed unable to get a grip on herself. He wondered if the laughter would soon turn to sobs, whether she'd finally lost her mind after all the recent stress. But, after what seemed like a long time, she pulled herself together and took a breath. 'I'm sorry,' she said. 'I'm sorry. It's just that it's so funny.'

'Funny?'

'Yes,' she said, wiping away a tear. 'It's inspired. Simeon was always such a prankster.' She laughed again, and Scamarcio began to feel irritated.

She seemed to sense this, and tried to compose herself. 'You see, I told you a small lie. What I didn't mention is that when he gave me those numbers, he told me not to bother with them, but just to hand them to anyone non-Agency who came around asking. That code was probably so simple that anyone could crack it. He wanted those dossiers to be found — it was his last "fuck you", wasn't it?'

'Well, yes, I guess it was, along with the masonry rubble and everything else, but I don't see what's so funny about it.' Again, he wondered if the shock of her husband's death, followed by the discovery that he had a mistress and a terminally ill son, had thrown Mrs Carter off balance.

'Don't you get it?' she said, throwing a palm open. 'That file was a work of fiction. He made the whole thing up to be found by someone like you! He wanted to make as much trouble for them as possible. He wanted to create a *scene!*'

'But how can you be so sure that file isn't for real?'

'Don't you know anything about Intelligence, Detective? They'd never keep shit like that in a file — written down on paper! It's ludicrous. The risky stuff is a whisper in a dark corridor between two people, quickly forgotten. It's not set out like some goddamn financial report.' She lent her head back against the chair and laughed once more, but this time it was a light little laugh, uncomplicated and free.

'Surely they'd need to commit some things to record,' said Scamarcio.

She shook her head. 'No, not that stuff; they'd keep it close.' She sighed, but was still smiling. 'Simeon told me he was planning something big. He said it would blow peoples' minds, that it was all about the presentation. It would be the presentation that did the work and reaped the results.'

'So you think this dossier was his parting shot?'

'Oh, I know it, Detective, I just know it. Maybe that guy Samuel was in on it. Simeon always gave me the feeling that he wasn't the only one with doubts — that there was a group of them who were troubled.'

Scamarcio thought about Samuel's response when he'd asked him if he already knew what was in the files. *Yes and no* was what he'd said. Then he remembered the letter that Samuel had forwarded him from 'F'. Why hadn't he just left it in the file? Was it because he wanted it to stand out — because he wanted to present it as an important postscript, an indication of events to come? Once more, his thoughts returned to the possibility of a new strategy of tension. He felt a chill against his skin, and walked to the window to check the street below. But apart from a couple of road sweepers, there was no one.

54

IN THE SLEEPLESS DAYS that followed, Mrs Carter's words circled in Scamarcio's head. In some ways, he sensed that she could be right. Why make that numeric code so easy? But, as she herself had said, if he'd wanted those documents to be found, Carter would have needed to make it simple. Was there a chance that he'd indeed created those files, but created them as a representation of a truth that he knew had never been committed to paper — a truth that he felt it was finally time to push out into the open? Scamarcio felt sure that the reality lay somewhere in-between; that it wasn't as simple as Mrs Carter seemed to be suggesting.

He went into the living room and opened the blinds. It was a glorious November day, and in the distance the hills rose up resplendent in the early-morning light. A slight breeze was stirring the trees below, and he watched the last of the autumn leaves fall gently to the ground. He checked the street for anything unusual, but, aside from a tight, black knot of businessmen hurrying to work, the pavement was deserted. Piocosta had offered him a continued presence at his apartment, but he had declined, saying he believed the threat had now passed. The old man had snorted as if he were a simpleton.

Scamarcio walked into the kitchen and turned on the small TV before opening the fridge to find the coffee for the cafetière.

'Data out today shows that Italy has finally returned to growth,' said the newsreader on Rai Uno's morning show.

Scamarcio set down the bag of coffee on the worktop and turned towards the television, not quite believing what he was hearing — it did not chime with the general misery in evidence.

'In the last quarter, there's been a rise in GDP of 0.01 per cent,' continued the news anchor, straight faced.

0.01% per cent? thought Scamarcio. *And they call that growth? What's the real difference between 0.01 per cent and 0 per cent, or -0.01 per cent, for that matter? A couple of Armani suits sold to some fatcat in Shanghai?*

He sighed. The whole thing felt obscene, when people were still gassing themselves in their cars, or culling their kids because they couldn't eke out their severance pay one day longer. He felt as if they were all being taken for a ride, as if he could no longer trust anything he heard on TV or read in the papers. Since Carter's Dark Star dossier, that sensation had been building. He was about to turn back to the coffee pot when the anchor continued:

And there's some other positive economic data out today. At a time when international companies are pulling out of Italy in their droves, it has been announced that the American car giant Chrysler is to build two major production plants in Lombardy, creating 5,000 jobs.

What? thought Scamarcio. Then: *Why?* He didn't get it. Why were the Americans investing in Italy when the rats were fleeing the sinking ship in their masses? Hell, even Fiat had just shifted the bulk of its production abroad. Didn't the Americans prefer to create jobs on their own turf? Wasn't it going to cause huge ill feeling back home? It seemed crazy. He couldn't follow the logic.

In other news, Marco Crozza, the 24-year-old hacker from Bologna who was awaiting extradition to America after he broke into NASA's top-secret computer system, has had all charges against him dropped, in a move which has come as a surprise to his legal team. His lawyers claim they have no idea what prompted the sudden change of heart and, as yet, US prosecutors have not offered an explanation. Crozza is expected home in Bologna tonight, where the town is preparing a welcome party after his five-year stay in Rebibbia prison.

Scamarcio looked away from the television to the intensifying sunshine beyond the window. So this was what they called a 'good-news day'? He had a strange feeling. He poured the coffee into the caffetiera, screwed the top into place, and then just stood there watching the flame get to work. As the pot slowly started to tremble and hiss, the odd feeling just grew.

'A major triumph for Emma Badaglio today,' read the announcer:

Andrea Bevilacqua, accused of selling arms to Iran, who for the last three years has been awaiting trial in a San Diego prison, is to be released this week. Foreign Secretary Badaglio has long been negotiating for his freedom, and claims that the case against him was riddled with inconsistencies from the start. Bevilacqua's release is being hailed as a major victory for Italian diplomacy.

The caffetiera was shrieking now, and Scamarcio turned off the heat. He poured his coffee, and took a seat at the rickety kitchen table. The decision to send the dossier to Badaglio was proving a sound move.

His mobile rang, and 'Number Unknown' appeared.

'Seems like a nice day for a walk by the river,' said Piocosta.

Scamarcio took a few moments to craft his response. He'd have to see him one last time; there was no way around it. 'Two pm suit you — usual place?'

'I'll be there.'

Scamarcio hung up, and returned his gaze to the window. The naked branches in the trees were completely still now — the breeze seemed to have disappeared.

Within seconds, his phone rang again, but this time it was a number he didn't recognise.

'I'm just calling to ask you to stop phoning,' said Aurelia. Her voice was quiet but steady. She sounded calm.

'Where are you? I've been trying to reach you for days.'

'Munich. I took the job.'

He felt his chest tighten. 'I thought you said that you were going to wait, that we were going to try to work things through?'

'Things changed, Leo. I needed to get out of Rome.'

The pain in his chest was growing, and his lungs felt heavy. 'Please, Aurelia, don't do this. I'm sorry I dicked around for so long, but I really want to make things work. I know what I want now.'

'No, Leo. I don't think you do. I think your feelings are being muddled by pity, by a sense of responsibility. I can't be in a relationship with someone just because they feel sorry for me.'

'No, that's not it. You don't understand.'

They both fell silent. Scamarcio could hear the sound of brakes screeching on the street below. Someone was swearing now. The smell of hot tarmac wafted through the window.

After a moment, Aurelia said, 'This situation isn't right — it hasn't been right for a long time. It's time to call it quits and walk away.'

'But ... I don't get it. Why are you just giving up? I want to be with you. I miss you.'

The tightness in his chest was almost like a burning now, and he sensed her drifting away from him, to a place he could never reach. 'I need you,' he said, hoping this might pull her back.

But there was no response, and after a few moments the line went dead.

55

ON HIS WAY DOWN to the Tiber, he stopped at a kiosk to buy that day's *La Repubblica*; but, after a quick flick-through, he couldn't find anything by Rigamonti. What was he waiting for? Scamarcio had been checking the paper for five days now, but the reporter hadn't penned a single article since they'd met in Trastevere. He was infuriated by the absence of the story, and then wondered if he was just furious with himself — furious about the total mess he seemed to be making of everything. He sighed, and reminded himself that maybe Rigamonti was simply busy preparing his big piece.

Scamarcio called up the reporter's number from his contacts, trying to keep his tone light. 'I just wondered how it was going?' he asked.

'Hang on a minute.'

He heard heavy breathing and the muted sound of the phone being held against against Rigamonti's shuffling frame. It sounded as if he were walking out of the newsroom to take the call elsewhere.

The static on the line eventually cleared, and he said, 'My career has gone up in smoke.'

'What?'

'I took your story to the news editor, and he seemed really fired up, like he wanted to do a big number on it. But then, suddenly, everything goes quiet — I hear nothing more, and he starts behaving weirdly, doing his best to avoid me. Then, just a few days ago, he's moved off to Sport, and I'm made Crap Correspondent

— celebrity break-ups, presidential visits. You get the picture — I've been sidelined.'

Shit, thought Scamarcio.

'I'm sorry, Rigamonti,' he said after a few beats. 'I reckoned this thing would have had a real impact.'

'Then I guess we both over-estimated the freedom of our press.'

Scamarcio heard some movement in the background, and the line went quiet for a moment. The reporter came back on a few seconds later. 'Listen, I've got to go. I'll give you a bell in the coming days, and we'll catch up.'

'Sure,' said Scamarcio, convinced now that Carter's revelations would never see the light of day.

Piocosta was waiting for him under the bridge. He was wearing his usual blue beret, and his skin had lost some of its tan. His father's old lieutenant looked tired, and Scamarcio sensed that the net was fast closing in on his loan-sharking operation.

'How's it going?' the old man asked. 'You don't look too good, for someone who's supposed to be on leave.'

'I've got a lot weighing on my mind.'

'Well, it's clearly been a fucker, this American thing.'

Scamarcio said nothing.

'Let's walk,' said Piocosta.

They turned towards the river. The weather had changed; the water was a muddy brown now, and the current was picking up. The ducks all seemed to have disappeared, but then Scamarcio noticed them clustered anxiously beneath some bushes by a mouldy pontoon. He wondered if they sensed there was a storm coming.

'Thanks for the other night,' he said.

Piocosta waved a hand away. 'Don't mention it. That's what I'm here for.'

If only it were so simple, thought Scamarcio.

They walked on for a minute, and then Piocosta cleared his throat. 'It's time, Leo. I've waited long enough.'

Scamarcio took a silent breath, and then said, 'I can't do it.'

'You can't do it, or you won't do it?'

'Both.'

Piero Piocosta didn't speak, and Scamarcio wondered whether the old man would feel *any* moral obligation towards his father.

After a few moments, Piocosta said, 'So that's it?'

'That's it.'

The old man tut-tutted and shook his head. 'You know, Leo, if you think we cleaned up that little mess for you the other night, you're very much mistaken. Word is that there's a hefty price on your head. Someone inside the Church wants you gone.'

'I'm aware of that.'

'Yeah, but are you aware that the Cappadona are out for blood? Donato's a vegetable; from what I hear, he'll be shitting in a bag and sucking pap through a straw for the rest of his days. His headcase sons are gunning for you, and they won't stop until they get what they want.'

Scamarcio suddenly felt cold, but all he said was, 'That information doesn't come as a complete surprise.'

'Why didn't you tell me about what happened with Donato? I should have known.'

'I can't give you every detail of a police inquiry.'

'It's not every detail — it's just one big fucking important detail.'

Scamarcio chose not to respond.

'You're Lucio's boy. I've got to look out for you, I promised him that much. But I'm worried about you, Leo — real worried. This is one huge fucking mess you've got yourself into, and who the fuck is going to protect you now? Don't look to your pig friends for help. They wouldn't piss on you if you were on fire.'

'Yeah, but you want favours in return, and they're favours I can't deliver.'

Piocosta sighed. 'You need to think about that one. You gotta understand which side your bread is buttered. Don't get confused — there's too much at stake.'

Scamarcio took a breath, and closed his eyes for a moment. 'Piero, if I start working for you, if I start cleaning up your shit, my career is over — everything I've worked so hard for, all the time I've invested, it would all be for nothing.'

'Nothing is wasted — it's all life experience.'

Fuck it, I'm not going to start taking life lessons from Piero Piocosta.

'The way I see it is that you don't have many options left, Leo. You've got enemies inside the Church, enemies in organised crime, and God knows what those Yankee sons of fluffers have in mind. You're a marked man, and you need all the help you can get.'

'I can manage fine on my own.'

Piocosta threw up his arms in despair. 'You're not getting this, are you? You walk away from here today, and you won't live to see next year. I know the game. I *play* the fucking game every day of my shitty little life, and if someone wants you dead, dead you'll fucking be — unless you go get yourself some serious help, and get it now.'

'And you're the help, are you?' Scamarcio turned away from him, shaking his head. 'It's you who's not getting it, Piero. If I start trying to take the heat off you, if I try to get an inquiry shut down, eventually someone will start asking questions. "No smoke without fire" is what they'll say, and it won't be long before all their initial suspicions of me are confirmed. I'll be out of there in a second, and no good to you any more.' He took a breath. 'It can never work. You need to understand that.'

'Leo, let me make it real easy. You've got a choice: either you save your career, or you save your hide. You can't do both.'

Scamarcio said nothing.

'It's time to get real. You're living in cloud-cuckoo land if you think life's just going to return to normal.'

The wind was picking up, and Scamarcio felt the first hard droplets of rain against his face.

Piocosta sighed and turned away from him, raising his hand in a sad salute. 'Anyway, I'm done here. You know my number,' he said before walking away.

Scamarcio stood there, watching his retreating frame. He took a breath and inhaled the charged air. The rain was falling heavily now, and he let it soak him, hoping that it might rinse it all clean away, cancel everything. He closed his eyes and tried to clear his mind, tried to identify a way out. But the harder he tried, the more difficult it became. All he saw was darkness.

He opened his eyes and took in the pounding river, the swollen skies, the first rumbles of thunder, and in that moment he knew the old man was right. He couldn't win both battles. He'd gone too far this time to come out of this unscathed. And things were different now; he had Aurelia to consider. She'd been the one who'd taken her revenge on the Cappadona, so they'd also be coming for her. It wasn't just about saving his own skin any more — it was about protecting the woman he loved. Although she was hundreds of miles away, he couldn't just give up on her; he needed to know she was safe.

He bunched his fingers into a fist, and released them before turning up his collar and starting to run.

'Hey, Piero', he shouted, 'wait up.'